Praise for the Mycroft Holmes Novels

"Authorized by the Conan Doyle estate—and great fun to boot."
—*Seattle Times/Post Intelligencer* on *Embassy Row*

"Fawcett creates, in Mycroft, a Holmes that is much more sympathetic and personable than the famous Sherlock. Unlike Sherlock Holmes's detection and deduction, Mycroft relies more on action, negotiation, and manipulation—rather like John Le Carré's Smiley. The book is appealing, with a nice dash of actual Victorian political characters and events. It's fun to read."
—*San Jose Mercury News* on *Embassy Row*

"Fawcett combines his always evocative Victorian atmosphere with lively prose and brisk storytelling. The story's assassin is hidden in a large school of red herrings; Holmes, Guthrie, and the supporting characters are all nicely developed; and Fawcett deftly captures the feel of luxury passenger trains in the Victorian era."
—*Booklist* on *The Flying Scotsman*

"*The Flying Scotsman* will appeal to a broad band of fans. Quinn Fawcett keeps his story line within the wonderful world described by Doyle. The pompous Mycroft handles the weight of the British Empire on his shoulders with an aplomb that makes him a fantastic character and his novels very entertaining."
—*Midwest Book Review*

"A perfectly viable, rich premise for a nostalgic historical retreat, and Quinn Fawcett actually writes rather well, capturing the period and the rhythms of period dialogue."
—*Indianapolis Star* on *Embassy Row*

"The star is Holmes, and the narrator is his sidekick. But the Holmes is Mycroft, Sherlock's older, smarter brother; and the narrator of this promising series opener is Paterson Erskine Guthrie, not Dr. Watson. There are some nice touches displayed here, and Fawcett's fluent prose captures a wealth of detail without slowing down the proceedings."
—*Publishers Weekly* on *Against the Brotherhood*

"Maintains the integrity of the Sherlock Holmes canon. Fawcett seems to have captured the flavor of Doyle's work. I would pick up another Mycroft Holmes/Guthrie adventure. My interest is piqued."
—*The Mystery News* on *Against the Brotherhood*

Quinn Fawcett

The Flying Scotsman

A MYCROFT HOLMES NOVEL

A TOM DOHERTY ASSOCIATES BOOK

NEW YORK

This is a work of fiction. All the characters and events portrayed in this novel are either fictitious or are used fictitiously.

THE FLYING SCOTSMAN

A Forge Book
Published by Tom Doherty Associates, LLC
175 Fifth Avenue
New York, NY 10010

www.tor.com

Forge® is a registered trademark of Tom Doherty Associates, LLC.

LIBRARY OF CONGRESS CATALOGING-IN-PUBLICATION DATA

Fawcett, Quinn.
    The Flying Scotsman : a Mycroft Holmes novel / Quinn Fawcett.
        p. cm.
    "A Tom Doherty Associates book."
    ISBN 0-312-86364-0 (hc)
    ISBN 0-312-87689-0 (pbk)
    I. Title.
    PS3556.A992F39 1999
    813'.54—dc21   99-22251
                                                              CIP

First Hardcover Edition: October 1999
First Trade Paperback Edition: October 2000

Printed in the United States of America

0 9 8 7 6 5 4 3 2 1

Author's Note

The character of Mycroft Holmes is used with the kind permission of Dame Jean Doyle.

The *Flying Scotsman* of the North Eastern line had a long and illustrious career. Although I have been at pains not to deviate too significantly from its history, even though the story is set in 1896, just after the Railway Race to the North that occurred in 1895, I have used the route taken by the train since 1892, although changes in the route were made before and since then. Changes in the configuration of the train were rare except during the actual speed runs, but the Directors did consent to them more than ten times by 1890, and so I have extended their gracious allowance to the fictional events of this story.

For JODY

The Flying Scotsman

Chapter One

"I WISH WE had not agreed to attend this infernal wedding," my employer, Mycroft Holmes, said as the carriage drew up in front of St. Paul's Cathedral at ten minutes before eleven o'clock on a shining April morning. It was one of those days that poets write about, sweet and lovely, perfect for the wedding we were there to attend. We had come directly from his flat in Pall Mall and planned to go to the embassy of Sweden-and-Norway as soon as the wedding was finished, where we were scheduled to put the finishing touches on an agreement to supply

Sweden-and-Norway with help in improving their rail system in exchange for access to Scandinavian ports. It was an important step in assuring that Germany would not control the North Sea, and one toward which Mycroft Holmes had been working for some months. This wedding had provided Prince Oscar a plausible reason to be in England without making his other purpose apparent, as so many of his fellow royals were doing; it was a diplomatic triumph for the Queen, and was recognized as such in every embassy in London.

"You might not feel so beleaguered if the Prime Minister had not insisted that you be responsible for the welfare of the Prince," I remarked to him as we went toward St. Paul's in an ever-slower procession of carriages.

"But he did. Like it or not, the whole of this occasion is in my hands. So be it. And frankly, Guthrie, since he has given me the responsibility, I am relieved that he was willing to give me the authority to deal with the situation." He gave an exasperated sigh. "There is nothing worse than responsibility without authority to enforce it, which was the case until now. What else would I want to have to do?"

This was a less acrimonious remark than some he had made earlier; I realized he was more resigned to these impositions than he claimed. I considered my response, and said, "Does this mean you have received the official authorization you requested?"

"It was delivered shortly before you arrived. I would not be here without it." Mycroft Holmes had been muttering all the way to the Cathedral, his annoyance becoming muted as we neared our destination; now that we had arrived, his complaints were a low, rumbling growl. "I dislike making these appearances. It draws too much attention to what we are doing. We succeed best working discreetly, without bringing ourselves to public notice. Let the royals glitter and wave; let me do my work in private. A state wedding is far too visible, no matter how useful it may be to our purposes." He swung around to look at me, his fine morning coat perfectly tailored to his tall, portly form; in the nine years I had worked for him, he had maintained the same physique consistently and, I suspected, would do so far into old age. He sighed as I climbed down behind him. "Oh, Guthrie, what we agree to do in the name of duty."

"True enough," I said with a touch of amusement. "To attend a ducal wedding is imposition indeed." In the years since I entered Mister Holmes' employ as his confidential secretary, I had come to know many of the secret workings of the diplomatic world in which Mycroft

Holmes played so signal a role that I sometimes believed that nothing in the world was as simple as it seemed. It was now obvious to me that most of the apparent swift triumphs of statesmanship were the result of long, delicate maneuvers, some of which I had been part of as a function of my work for Mycroft Holmes; I had traveled through Europe and Asia Minor, Egypt and India, been shot at more than once, had faced assassins and conspirators and the desperate men who inhabit the shadow world of espionage. There were a few events in my past that I could not recall without blushing, and even the suggestion of recalling them made me realize that there were aspects to this work that no gentleman would want to undertake. To be here, in morning dress, for a happy and glorious occasion was a new experience. From my point of view, this wedding was more of a treat than an ordeal.

"It is, it is; but there's no help for it," said Holmes, as he motioned me to follow him up the steps into the cathedral. "It is a pity that Sir Cameron should have been one of the Prince's hosts here in London: he may put two and two together about my presence here."

"How could he think anything but that you are serving the Queen?" I asked, thinking it was unlikely that Sir Cameron was capable of making such an association, given his bibulous predilections. "In such a gathering, who will notice the likes of us? Knowing Sir Cameron, he will be seeking bigger fish than we are," I remarked, as we made our way through the illustrious throng. "You are not going to be singled out amid so many foreign luminaries."

St. Paul's was filled with the highest-ranking men and women in England, as well as nobles, diplomats, distinguished men of business and their wives and daughters, all rigged out for the wedding of George Albert Oliver, Duke of Marlborough, and Queen Victoria's great-grand niece, Sophia Augustina of Hannover, the youngest daughter of Otto of Hannover. There had been a week of diplomatic festivities in antic-ipation of this event, with the Prime Minister taking center stage and leaving the diplomacy to Mycroft Holmes. It had given us a superior opportunity to conduct the kinds of negotiations with the Prince that required circumspection in order to be successful. Most of Prince Os-car's evenings had been taken up with balls and receptions, occasions that Mycroft Holmes viewed as a necessary irritation. The wedding was the most brilliant occasion in the social calendar, a spring celebration to end the season with a magnificent display of British importance, for it commanded the attendance of half the royal and noble houses of Europe.

"You cannot think that we are the only ones watching." Mycroft Holmes said as he removed his silk hat and stepped away from the central aisle, moving into the shadows and away from the illustrious swarm of glittering high-born men and women. "In a place like this, there are so many lovely targets for so many groups of rebels, I can only imagine what the men guarding this event must be going through."

I recalled the problems we had had some time ago with the Japanese embassy, and I could not keep from cringing. "I had not thought of it that way," I admitted as I looked about trying to determine where the Swedish-and-Norwegian party would be seated along with the other component of the Scandinavian country, Denmark.

"Prince Oscar has been very cooperative, and I could not be more grateful to him for being as forthcoming as he has been, his evenings with Sir Cameron and his cronies aside," Holmes said as if reminding himself as well as me why our attendance was so crucial. "It is a minor thing to do this to please him, I suppose, and an excellent cover for our greater purpose. I know I should not complain at this request. He has done a great deal for us, after all." His hooded grey eyes under heavy brows were deceptively lazy; I had discovered in the last two years that this apparent abstraction concealed the most constant activity of his mind.

The Cathedral was more than half full, and the ambassadors of most of the countries of Europe were already in their seats, all adorned with Orders, medals, and honors; the women shone with fine fabrics and jewels, only the hour keeping them from trains and tiaras—in the evening at the ball, at the completion of the reception, their full finery would be displayed.

I saw the Prince of Wales' state coach draw up at the front of the Cathedral and be immediately flanked by men in dress uniforms of Coldstream Guards. The Prince was greeted with excitement, for it meant the wedding party was not far behind.

"Where is Prince Oscar?" Holmes fretted aloud, watching the entrance to St. Paul's. "I am not easy in my mind about him coming here."

"You have told him so," I reminded him, speaking loudly enough for him to hear.

"And I wish he would be convinced," said Holmes, looking annoyed.

"Because of Sir Cameron or because of the Prince's brother?" I asked, for in the last week of private negotiations we had come to understand that his younger brother, Grand Duke Karl, was sympathetic to German ambitions and looked askance at Prince Oscar's continuing support of Britain.

"Among others. A gathering of this sort is a veritable magnet for malcontents of every stripe, and for worse than malcontents. Self-styled rebels and anarchists must take occasions such as this as the greatest opportunity to make themselves known to the world. Think what a single small bomb would do if it were to go off within a block of this place, with the traffic moving at a crawl. Nothing is going to begin on time, not if this turgid pace continues." He made an impatient gesture with his silk hat. "If it should turn out that any mishap occurs, Her Majesty's government will have to endure it at a time when it is essential that we show the extent of our security," Mycroft Holmes went on, motioning me to his side again as the Prince of Wales entered the Cathedral, his escort making a path for him to the front of St. Paul's and his place of honor, as all the company bowed to Edward. His appearance signaled that the wedding party was not too far behind. Music welled from the organ as half of the choir filed into their stalls; the rest of the choristers would come in with the wedding procession.

"There is his coach," I said as I glanced out the door and spied Prince Oscar's coach among the others lined at the steps of St. Paul's. "He is with some of the Danes. They are all riding together. Thank goodness Sir Cameron is not among them."

Mycroft Holmes' tone was dry. "I should be grateful to him, I know, and I am, Guthrie, I am; but it does not change my disquiet—" He came toward the open door. "I suppose that I am borrowing trouble: I certainly hope I am, but given what we know about Prince Karl—"

"You mean the Brotherhood and the alliance they wish to have with Prince Karl," I said, recalling what had been revealed two days ago. I had had enough experience of that pernicious organization to share my employer's apprehension. "If only we had some confirmation of that anonymous note you received last week. It might convince Prince Oscar about his brother."

"Indeed," said Holmes, "I cannot be sanguine about that association. Whether Prince Karl has any intention of harming his brother, I fear the Brotherhood must have." He straightened up as the Scandinavians got out of their carriage. "I hope we have convinced Prince Oscar that the possibility of acts against him is real. He may have listened to us, but he is not persuaded."

"Are you certain of his indifference?" I asked, watching the Prince and the Danish delegation make their way toward the entrance. "He listened most attentatively, I thought."

"So he did, but he was more interested in our railways than in anything we said about the Brotherhood." Holmes prepared to bow to the newly arrived dignitaries. The place was so filled with music and the roar of conversation that it was becoming difficult to hear him clearly. I stood beside him as he had instructed me to, watching the Prince make his way into St. Paul's.

Prince Oscar was in his very best form, his morning coat crossed by a sash and Order of St. Olav, as well as the Collar of Stockholm, which, as heir to the Swedish-and-Norwegian throne, he was not only entitled but expected to wear on such state occasions. Among all the Danes he stood out by the respect he was accorded by them. A man of thirty-two, he was a bit taller than average, with dark-blond hair and candid blue eyes in a long head, his nose straight and narrow. His features were not remarkable beyond the usual. He had a pleasant, open demeanor and comported himself in an unassuming manner that was engaging; it covered a keen mind and a capable intellect. I had enjoyed his wit while we met for our private meetings. Without his finery and the deference he was shown by others, he might well be mistaken for a European businessman or journalist visiting London; of late we had seen a great many of them in England.

"Your Highness," said Mycroft Holmes as Prince Oscar caught sight of him. He bowed to the Prince, saying, "I am delighted to see you." He indicated the rear pews. "Our place is here to the back; we will meet you on the steps afterward."

"Thank you, Mister Holmes; I am aware you would rather not be here, and I take this as a favor to me. One which I shall not forget." The Prince bowed slightly; his accent made his English clearly foreign, but good enough to make the country of his origin not immediately obvious.

"Your Highness is gracious," Holmes said, with more sincerity than the occasion demanded.

"Not particularly, but I thank you for telling me so," said Prince Oscar with a whimsical smile, then continued on his way down the central aisle.

"I wish I knew why he insisted on our attending," said Mycroft Holmes as he watched the Prince. "He said it was nothing important, but I am not so certain. That causes me trepidation, I must confess."

"Hardly insisted," I remarked. "He only said he would appreciate our coming."

"Oh, he insisted, Guthrie—he insisted. He phrased it very diplomatically, but had we refused, we would not have had his agreement about naval facilities. That is what troubles me, for I cannot satisfy myself that his only reason was a gesture of bonhomie. Say what you will about what we have agreed to in regard to trains, the access to Sweden-and-Norway is far more important than a few locomotives." He glanced out the door and turned away with an expression of distaste. "Another reason I would rather not be here," he said, indicating the carriage that had just arrived. "He is also here at Prince Oscar's request, to thank him for helping him to kick up his heels a little without bringing embarrassment to his embassy."

Sir Cameron MacMillian was descending from this carriage, his brindled mutton-chop whiskers brushed out like the ruff on a tomcat. His face was ruddy, which was probably the result of drink, for he was known to favor a dram to start the day. Unlike Mycroft Holmes, age had taken a toll on Sir Cameron; he was paunchy, his hair was thinning, and he walked unsteadily, as if in need of a cane. He was in the company of several Scottish peers, basking in the privilege of his title, Prince Oscar's courtesy, and his ill-deserved reputation for heroism. Turning to nod to the crowd that had gathered to view the arrival of guests at the Cathedral, he beamed at the acclaim waiting behind the line of uniformed police. He sauntered along with his fellow-Scots, acknowledging the calls of journalists who lined the entrance to St. Paul's with a salute that made me bristle.

"If we step back he will not see us," I said to Mycroft Holmes.

"He will not notice us in any case. We are not the ones Sir Cameron is here to see. Indeed, he is here to *be* seen." Mycroft Holmes was as caustic as I had ever heard him. "He is not worth our concern. But he could be a distraction."

"True enough," I said, thinking of all we had endured in Germany as a result of Cameron MacMillian's ineptitude and the times since when encounters with him had led to trouble.

"Sadly, the Brotherhood knows him, not just you and I, and they are not so reasonable as we are; after the dèbâcle in Germany, they have wanted to see him disgraced at the least, although they may be wasting their time," said Mycroft Holmes. He looked at MacMillian's retreating back, scowling. "If he were not here, we would have less to bother about." His next few words were lost in the swell of the organ. ". . . since the Brotherhood knows him, and he has got free of them, I cannot want him to show himself anywhere. His very presence alerts the Brotherhood, and they will use any means to silence him."

"Do you mean they will try to harm MacMillian?" I asked, thinking that this was impossible. "Surely not here, and not now."

"What better time?" Holmes asked me, pulling me back toward the rear of the Cathedral. "A single act on this occasion would do more to create dissension than any less public act they might perform. Think what an incident here would do toward upsetting the prestige of the British Crown abroad. What is an exploded bridge compared to an assassination in Saint Paul's?" He looked directly at me, his eyes grave. "And you wonder why I am apprehensive about this occasion?"

"How . . . Have you heard something?" I had been with Holmes for most of the last week, and I could recall no occasion that might have served to alert him to any danger. The music was changing, indicating that the wedding was about to begin; the last of the carriages were setting down their passengers; the wedding party was the final one in line.

"It is not so much what I have heard, but something my brother's scamps have heard in the last few days. The warning we had was familiar to them. One of them sent me word late the night before last. I had hoped that we would not have to be—" He saw the last of the guests take their seats and motioned me to join him in the rear pew. "At least we are permitted to be among the lesser personages. We are not so likely to be singled out. And thank God I have been given full authority and responsibility in regard to the Prince. On an occasion such as this, he might be dragged into any number of predicaments. I have the full support of the government in this, which is the only way it is feasible for me to assume the obligation." He slid along the pew toward a man in an Italian uniform.

"Here?" I asked, but the question was destined to remain unanswered.

A fanfare brought the entire gathering to its feet; the wedding party had reached St. Paul's. The choir began a joyous anthem and the celebration began.

The wedding went on for more than an hour; the Archbishop of Canterbury, officiating in vestments that rivaled the state gown of the bride, intoned the long service, punctuated by glorious song, choruses from *Jephtha* and *Susannah* as well as more traditional wedding hymns.

The choirs vied with one another and with the distinguished soloists to shine on this grand occasion. Being so far to the rear of the Cathedral, I paid more attention to the music than the actual service, which I was unable to see, though the service itself was enlarged to include all the pomp the occasion could command.

As the bride and groom turned to leave the church, another peal of brass and organ announced their union. Again the congregation rose, this time with happy relief; there was a counterpoint of conversation as the couple went out to the steps to the state carriage that was waiting to carry them back to Buckingham Palace, where a state reception would fill the afternoon.

"We will have a chance to talk with the Prince now, as he waits for his carriage," said Mycroft Holmes, scanning the crowd. "I will be glad to have this behind us. I can hardly blame Police Commander Winslowe and Superintendent Spencer for washing their hands of this occasion; they are conspicuous in their absence, but no one in their position can feel entirely sanguine about the police in this situation. Were I serving in their capacity, I, too, would want to wash my hands of Prince Oscar's safety—hence my own perplexity in that regard."

I moved to the far aisle with him and joined the throng coming out to see the newly married couple get into the carriage to begin their ride to Buckingham Palace with an escort of the Coldstream Guard. Mycroft Holmes was not far behind me, taking a moment to look over his shoulder to watch the progress of Prince Oscar up the central aisle with his company of Danes.

At the front of St. Paul's the illustrious guests milled, waiting to get into their carriages and trying to exchange a word or two or make arrangements for the later events. Toward the bottom of the shallow steps, uniformed policemen stood to make the departure from the Cathedral as orderly an occasion as possible. Between us and the main door there were three companies of ambassadors with members of their royal families. I doubted we would be able to reach the central door before Prince Oscar got into his carriage. Sliding through the crowd, I reached Mycroft Holmes and went jostling with him toward Prince Oscar; Holmes' imposing frame made it possible for him to get through the people without hindrance; I went along in his wake, glad for once that I had learned to follow his lead. Only the Grand Duke of Cracow stared, affronted, at Holmes and me as we went behind the Polish delegation. "You must excuse me, Excellency," Holmes said as he continued on his way.

"I must ask you to let me by, Excellency," I said, as I attempted to follow my employer. I was not so fortunate as Holmes had been.

"You, sir, are a dreadful—" the Duke started to declare.

I did not hear the rest of it; Holmes summoned me in a forceful voice. "Do not get separated from me; I don't want to have to wait much longer."

I knew Holmes was eager to be away from this gathering and back in his flat again; I shared some of his impatience, but I could not help but be impressed by the company around us. I put my hand out the better to wedge myself through the crowd and was very nearly able to keep pace with Mycroft Holmes. I also began to share some of his exasperation with the festivities for they interfered with our purpose. I knew from experience that this general confusion accorded opportunity to those seeking to do ill. My experiences of six months ago had demonstrated this to me in such a way that I was not likely to forget their lesson anytime soon. I continued to shoulder along in Holmes' wake.

I saw the Prime Minister move away from the gathering and climb into a nondescript carriage waiting on the side of St. Paul's. I was startled at this apparent lapse in protocol and I faltered, tugging at Holmes' sleeve to point out this unorthodox behavior.

Holmes displayed none of the dismay I might have expected at such news. "I know, Guthrie; I know. He has declined his responsibility on Prince Oscar's account and wishes to put himself at a distance from this occasion. I must hope others are not so astute as you are."

"Yes, but Mister Holmes," I protested, "who is here as the representative of the government? Not that there are insufficient royals, but you know"—I saw something in his face that silenced me.

"I know only too well, Guthrie," he said in a low voice. "Beyond the responsibility for Prince Oscar, I fear the Prime Minister has deputized me to stand wholly in his stead once the wedding ceremony itself is over." He must have seen astonishment in my face, for he laughed, a trifle less humorlessly than usual, which served to warn me that this arrangement was not entirely to his liking. "There have been rumors that there might be trouble, and the PM is determined it will not stick to him."

"I know about the rumors," I reminded him without apology. "But these have been discounted. You said so yourself."

Holmes rubbed his chin with his big, long-fingered hand. "You must forgive me, my dear Guthrie. I was sworn to keep the arrangement silent and have done so until now." He sighed as we reached the edge of the crowd and found a place between the Londoners gathered to watch the occasion at an imposed distance. He stood, doing his best to be inconspicuous, which for a tall man of corpulent build and dignified mien, was not as readily accomplished as he might hope. He seemed to follow my thoughts and said, "This is one time I could wish for more of Edmund Sutton's gifts."

At the mention of his actor-double, I said, "I should have thought you have learned much from him. Your disguises have fooled even me."

"Ah, Guthrie, that is the problem in a nutshell. It is one thing to vanish with the aid of a disguise, and quite another to do it without disguise. If Sutton were here, he could make himself invisible."

"An actor—invisible." I laughed, as I did my best to watch the crowd without drawing undue attention to my surveillance.

"Oh, yes. I have seen him do it just as surely as if a magician had waved a wand. It is a talent in him I envy. I certainly could have used such a talent that one time I trod the boards." He stared at the line of carriages drawing up to receive their glittering passengers. "This is what troubles me the most, this confusion."

"But the police are everywhere," I observed, for I had not often seen so many Bobbies at a public occasion.

"And they claim they can handle anything," Holmes agreed. "In ordinary circumstances I might agree. But what if a malcontent should leap from the crowd? Do you think the police would be able to do anything in the chaos that would ensue? Or if a kidnapper should be driving a carriage, he might easily make away with those inside before anyone knew what he had done. There could be a demonstration that could cause embarrassment to the government or a similar outcry from the Scandinavians here in London. The Prime Minister has said he does not anticipate any incident, but you see he is gone and I am here."

"As a scapegoat!" I exclaimed.

"Nothing so sinister," Mycroft assured me. "Only as a lieutenant. If the Prime Minister supposed anything untoward would happen, he would not have given me the blanket authority he has. He would have divided it among three or four men so that he could claim he did not know their ineptness. With only me, he must assume the whole responsibility for his judgment and bring my work more into the open, which would serve no one's purpose." He rocked back on his heels. "I hope Tyers has attended to the task I left him."

"Securing Prince Oscar's passage home," I said, "without exposing him to some of the very elements you fear here."

Prince Oscar's carriage was now third from the lead of carriages; the Prince began to make his way down the steps, his delegation around him.

"Just so," Holmes said. "He cannot go with the official party because Grand Duke Karl has a number of supporters in the Sweden-and-Norway contingent who may be planning some mischief. I can't tell you how grateful I am to you for uncovering that unpleasant intelligence."

"But you told me the Prime Minister had decided it would be a bad show of faith not to send Prince Oscar back with the delegation." I was surprised at this news; I began to wonder what else Mycroft Holmes had not told me.

"He was persuaded to change his mind," Holmes said. "In return for my clandestinely taking on the position of his deputy, he agreed to make other arrangements for the Prince."

One or two of the lesser Hapsburgs objected to the attention being paid by the police, which slowed the loading of their carriage. This resulted in a backup of wedding guests that began to spill out of the area set aside by the barriers. After some soothing of Austrian nerves, the carriage moved off and the Swiss got into their state carriage without fuss; it was now time for the Swedes and Norwegians to be away. The crowd began to mill as the delay to get into their vehicles became more intrusive.

"It will not be much longer," Mycroft Holmes said to me; I could hear the relief in his voice, which told me he had been more apprehensive than he had been willing to confide.

"And it went well enough," I said, just as a rifle shot cracked.

FROM THE PERSONAL JOURNAL OF PHILIP TYERS

I have secured the passage required for HRHO, which will take him from Plymouth to Amsterdam and from there to Sweden; our government will protect him in his travels, as per our arrangement. MH has said the wedding delegation is to be avoided at all costs. . . . The ship departs tomorrow night from Plymouth. . . .

Chapter Two

MYCROFT HOLMES WAS jolted as if he himself had been the target of the shot. He stood very still as shrieks and exclamation erupted from the splendid gathering; the footman holding the carriage door collapsed as if he were a marionette with cut strings, and a moment later blood welled from a gaping wound in his side. I felt something on my face that was warm and wet; I reached for my handkerchief to wipe it away, not daring to look at the stain on the linen. There were shrieks and confusion that began to spread. One of the leaders of the coach's team tried to rear up and was controlled with difficulty by the postilion mounted on the other leader. It was as if this were a signal. The Prince swung into the coach and Mycroft Holmes slammed its door shut, shouting to the coachman to make haste. A moment later the matched team of six Cleveland bays sprang away from the front of St. Paul's, the coach careening indecorously as it swung into the street. "Get a doctor!" Mycroft Holmes cried, though he and I both knew the man was beyond all mortal help. I was about to kneel beside the footman when the crowd began to surge and my employer motioned me to stand where I was.

For a moment the world was suspended, only the clatter of hoof-beats punctuating the terrible thing that had just happened. Then a small band of uniformed policemen surged forward, attempting to surround the remaining high-ranking guests, while several mounted units of the Coldstream Guards rushed into the square and joined those in full kit who had been escorting the various members of the royal Houses. Some twenty or thirty dismounted. The greater number of them surrounded the Queen's carriage, though she herself was still inside the Cathedral. The rest began politely, but firmly, herding the members of the royal family who had already been gathered by the police to shelter inside the Cathedral. Those Guards who remained mounted drew carbines that I hadn't even noticed among the complicated trappings of their saddlery, changing in the blink of an eye from being part of the pageantry to seasoned soldiers. These new riders took up their traditional defensive positions at the edge of the crowd in a kind of disciplined scramble that was intended to hold the illustrious guests in and keep any further assailants out. This tactic had the added and unwanted impact of creating a clear division between those who were potential targets and those who were not.

The people who had come to stare and heckle now became fearful and unruly; toward the middle of the crush a woman screamed and then panic set in. Nothing could be done to stop the turmoil that had taken hold of everyone on the steps and below. As the wedding guests strove to get away from the dying footman, the crowd swayed, bulged, swayed again, and people tore away from it, bolting into the side streets. The press was changing into a melee.

As the chaos spread, Mister Holmes said to me, his tone sharp, "Guthrie, did you happen to notice where the shot came from?"

I shook my head, I had not noticed what the shot had done, if anything, beyond inciting panic. I folded my handkerchief and thrust it into my pocket.

"I noticed that the footman of Prince Oscar's coach was struck; he has not risen that I can see," said Holmes, his voice eerily calm in the increasing turmoil. "I think that it came from the south side of Saint Paul's, probably that eyesore." He pointed to the Georgian building that gave offices to several foreign trading companies. "That's just the sort of place that would afford a good view of the steps and is likely to be empty for an event of this sort. It is slated to come down next year." His expressions said that he would have preferred to have had the building demolished before now. "Try the upper windows or the roof. Anything lower would not give any angle from which to fire."

A Guards Major was coming toward Mycroft Holmes, his manner purposeful and his demeanor disapproving. "I understand I am to put my men in your hands, sir," he barked.

Holmes tapped my shoulder. "Go, my boy," he told me as he turned to face the Major.

I hastened to obey, making my way across the street through the tangles of carriages, policemen, spectators, and a number of running members of the press, who were bound toward the confusion instead of away from it. I adroitly avoided the most predatory of these men, knowing my employer would not be pleased if I should be caught and dragged into a confrontation with them.

As I reached the Georgian building, I took stock of its five stories and wondered how long it would take me to reach the roof. Before I could enter, a dozen men, most speaking languages that were not English, came spilling out, as if afraid they might miss the entertainment. I stood aside and then slipped inside. I found myself in a wood-paneled rotunda with three hallways leading to various parts of the building. I took the one directly ahead of me. I supposed it would lead me to stairs, being more central to the building than the other two, for I could see this structure had to have had a lift installed. My guess was rewarded: a narrow staircase wound down to a rear hall.

I sprang up the stairs, wishing I had my pistol in my pocket. I reached the first landing and glanced along the doorway; nothing attracted my attention, so I continued upward. I was halfway up the next flight when a door above opened and a man in Eastern European clothes shouted to me, "Higher. It is higher." He blanched at the sight of my face, and I did not suppose it was because one of my eyes is blue and the other green.

"I'll do it," I told him. "Get away from here."

"There is another stair," he called as I continued upward.

That stopped me a moment. "Where?" I yelled back.

"East corner. For tradesmen. The gate in the delivery yard is closed, but I don't think it's locked." He ducked back into his door and I went on, listening closely to the rumble of trouble from the street. The police did not seem to be containing the reaction of the crowd. I could feel my heart beginning to pound, and not simply for the upward climb; I did not know what I would be encountering when I reached the roof or the top floor. I decided on impulse to start with the top floor, so that the culprit could not escape below me while I searched the roof. I worried briefly that the man might already be gone or in a different building altogether.

As I reached the top floor, I heard a loud noise above me; the roof door had slammed closed. This ended any hope I might have had of surprising the blaggard, although I knew the chance of doing so was slim. I also abandoned my intention to search the top floor first; haste was needed and I was determined to make the most of my opportunity before it vanished entirely. I took three long, deep breaths and kept running upward only to find the door locked. I kicked at it several times and it splintered open ferociously, banging against the wall at the back of the stairwell.

The roof was empty. The second stairwell tower was on the east corner of the building; its door was closed, but that was not necessarily indicative of flight. Perhaps I should have searched the floor below. But since I was on the roof, I decided to make a cursory search of the side overlooking the front of St. Paul's in case the shot had come from here.

I did not actually think I would find anything; I supposed the full search would be made by the police, but I knew Mycroft Holmes would expect this of me. I could hear the sound of police whistles mixed with shouts and the general noise of a burgeoning riot. I forced myself not to look over the edge but to concentrate on the waist-high rim of the roof.

To my astonishment, I was rewarded for my inspection: a chink in the masonry, obviously newly made, showed a metallic scrape and below it a single shell casing glistened in the narrow gutter. It was as great a treasure as gold would have been, a wonderful bit of metal that might reveal more than anything else on the roof. I knew it would be unwise to move the shell until the place could be examined. I had no doubt that I had come upon the place where the assassin had waited to fire. I did not yet know what Mycroft Holmes would make of it, but I was certain he would glean much from it. I thought it was an unaccountable oversight to leave the shell casing behind, unless he intended it be found. So I made a point of finding a way to stand that would draw as little attention to the casing as possible.

Which made me wonder if it were the actual shell casing; might this not be deliberately left behind to mislead us. I knew I should raise some kind of signal and pondered what it should be. I finally looked over the roof and searched in the milling crowd for some glimpse of my employer. I was fairly certain that I would not see him.

The first I could discern anyone in the crowd, I noticed a small knot of military officers with a tall, portly man in their midst. No doubt this was Mycroft Holmes. I had no notion how to attract his attention without adding to the roiling confusion below.

Then, to my relief, Mycroft Holmes glanced toward the building, looking toward the upper floors and the roof. I knew he was looking for me. I leaned forward as far as I dared and waved my hat over my head to signal I had found something. Or so I hoped he would realize was my intent. I saw him shade his eyes the better to see me against the brilliant sky. I pointed toward the shell, nodding to indicate its importance. I was not surprised to see him give me a broad wave and point toward the building.

Half a dozen soldiers turned toward the Georgian building where I stood; I motioned them to hurry. I did not bother to shout—no one would hear me.

The door at the far side of the roof opened and then a young subaltern of the Guard burst out onto the uneven surface, a service revolver drawn and one arm windmilling to steady him. He gathered his dignity and came toward me, his face set in firm lines. "Good God, man. Are you hurt?" He clearly did not require an answer. "What have you found? Is the poltroon about?"

"If he were, I would not be standing here by myself, exposed to his shots, would I? And I am unhurt." My tone was not as respectful as Mycroft Holmes would like, but the man's officiousness put me off. I would offer him an apology when and if he caught the fellow. "I have found this," I went on, showing him the brass casing.

"I should take this," said the officer.

I held up my hand to stop him. "I think we should wait until Mycroft Holmes comes. The Prime Minister will expect him to handle this. I'm certain you have provisions for abiding by Mister Holmes' authority." I could see the resistance in the man's eyes and I did all that I could to distract him. "I think the man might have gone down the other stairs. I haven't had a chance to look there."

"Why didn't you say so?" The man hurried away, signaling his soldiers to follow him.

As I watched him go, I sighed a little, knowing this was only the beginning of the fuss that would result from this attempted assassination; my employer would be held accountable for anything that transpired as a result of this distressing development. It would cause no end of difficulties for Mycroft Holmes, who preferred to work away from the glare of the political arena. I leaned over the edge of the rail, hoping I might find someone in the crowd who was clearly trying to escape. Not that I thought any accomplished marksman would do anything so reckless, but I had known others to make just such a mistake; I had the scars to prove it.

I noticed that the soldiers were debating what to do, their officer exclaiming that the assassin was no doubt well away from this place and so it was useless to send his men pelting after the criminal. A few of his men were protesting, saying they ought to give chase, to maintain public confidence if not to catch the would-be assassin, which made me want to laugh at their confusion. Then I heard my name called and saw Chief Inspector Calvin Somerford coming toward me, and I was relieved.

"Guthrie," said the Chief Inspector, his words slurring around the stem of his pipe. He was not the stiff sort of policeman that was most often found around such grand occasions as this one. He was in a dark suit, not quite formal morning wear, but several notches above his usual garb; he stood a bit taller than I, was about forty years of age, with clever, sardonic features. This man had been assigned to the Prince when Oscar arrived in England and had been shadowing him ever since. This event in St. Paul's was the one place he had been excluded, the presence of the Coldstream Guards being thought to be sufficient deterrent to any assassin: This was now patently inadequate. "Mister Holmes coming up, I suppose, to have a look around?" Most of his phrases ended with an upward inflection, making him sound constantly inquisitive. I thought this was indicative of the man himself.

"Yes. He will be up shortly," I said, glad to have another man to help me maintain the scene to Mycroft Holmes' standards. I went to shake his hand as much to show solidarity as to be cordial, for in such a setting, form came after substance.

"Well, they can't say Mister Holmes didn't warn them of the risks." He nodded toward the lip of the roof. "Looks like you were standing a mite too close?" Without waiting for a reply, he looked about, his eyes narrowed critically. "I'm surprised we didn't have anyone up here? You'd think they would see the potential, wouldn't you?"

That had been bothering me since the shot rang out, but I had not pinpointed it until Calvin Somerford voiced it so well. "Yes," I said, as I looked about. There most certainly *should* have been someone on this roof—other than the assassin—and the lack of someone was becoming more glaring in my observations.

"One man, I should say?" Chief Inspector Somerford observed, his manner seeming so laconic that one of the soldiers scoffed at this remark.

"It seems likely," I said, unwilling to impart more while so many could overhear us. "You cannot want to speak—"

Chief Inspector Somerford coughed to show he understood. "I'll just have a look around? And to think it's only Wednesday. What will we have on our plates by Friday?" He nodded once to the soldiers. "Mind you let my men up when they arrive. I'll need their help." His diffidence was rewarded with a shrug of assent. I knew that Chief Inspector Somerford was a very canny fellow, able to do a great deal without appearing to, which Mycroft Holmes had realized was a major skill in diplomatic circles.

I went back to the place where it seemed that the assassin had waited; I wanted to bring little attention to myself. I succeeded so well that when a shot rang out, I staggered back and had to steady myself against falling.

Chief Inspector Somerford was the first to move. He ran to the rear of the roof, from the direction that the shot had come, and he pointed, "You! There!" he shouted, his quiet voice an authoritative bellow that shocked two of the soldiers into coming to attention.

Unsure if I should leave my position, I faltered, just long enough to see Mycroft Holmes step out onto the roof, showing no signs of effort from the long, quick climb up the stairs in spite of his portly build. I had often been aware of the man's remarkable strength and endurance, and that made me respect him increasingly, for great as his intellect was, it was not his only attribute worthy of high regard: his appearance of indolence was nothing more than a ruse, and one I had come to know as a deliberate ploy used to encourage his enemies to underestimate him, much as his carefully maintained impression of a sedentary life made possible by his redoubtable double, Edmund Sutton. He strolled up to me. "Found anything, dear boy?"

"Nothing much," I said. "But I think we should—"

"—discuss it later. Yes. Of course." He looked to the opposite side of the roof. "What *is* Somerford carrying on about? I don't suppose they have caught anyone but a cutpurse or a mudlark." He sighed. "The Prince is safe and we will join him when our work here is finished. We will need to tend to matters here, and then I will be able to review what you have found." He leaned down to look at the marks I had discovered. "Heavy weapon, by the looks of it. Very good rifle, probably with a big-game telescope attached to give him a more accurate shot. From the sound of the weapon, it was of a heavy caliber. My first thought was one of those American Sharps rifles that they use to so unsportingly kill their buffalo. But from the high crack that followed it may well have been one of the German weapons created for hunting big game in Africa. With their long, 30-caliber bullet and faster rate of firing, they are increasingly popular among those who trade in assassination. Such a weapon would be ideal for our criminal; he had to kill with one round."

I shuddered as I again glanced over the wall at where the footman still lay. Staring at the corpse and pool of blood that was barely visible five stories up, I was reminded of the Brotherhood. "So it did—but not the intended target," I said.

Mycroft Holmes nodded. "Also the new Weiss scopes are very powerful, but present only a narrow field of vision. That might explain how a professional could have missed his kill. And this was most certainly an attempt to kill the Prince. He was close enough to have been intending the worst; in such a crowd, if his purpose was only to frighten, he would have sprayed the coaches or something of the sort. In fact," he went on thoughtfully as he picked up the shell casing and turned it over, end on end, in his long fingers, smiling grimly as he saw his suspicions about the caliber were correct, "it is a bit perplexing that nothing more was done. He was after Prince Oscar, and failing to accomplish his mission, he fled, since he knew he would not have a second chance here today." He began to twiddle with his watch-fob, a sure sign of his growing apprehension. "This fellow hasn't finished with the Prince, you may be sure of that."

Inspector Somerford approached slowly shaking his head. "There you are, Mister Holmes. A most perplexing business?"

"Perplexing is the least of it, Inspector. I am not at all perplexed. We can have no doubt as to the culprit's intentions," Mycroft Holmes declared. "He was going to kill Prince Oscar; and we must assume that since he failed to do so, he will try again."

"What, Mister Holmes? No one would be so foolish," exclaimed Inspector Somerford. "He was foiled, and he put us on the alert. If the intention is to cause embarrassment to the government, this has been done. If it is a domestic matter, then why come to England to kill the Prince? Much better to make a point about your own country in it, if you follow me. That is why I am taking this as a sign that England's foes are at work."

"You may pursue your theories, Chief Inspector; Guthrie and I will pursue mine." Mycroft Holmes made a gesture indicating he meant no criticism of the Chief Inspector's goals. "Together we will be able to uncover the reason behind this lamentable event. Will you arrange for me to have access to this roof tomorrow? I may want to see how he hoped to accomplish his ends, and with all that confusion below, it would be useless now. Our combined efforts must lead us to the truth."

"Of course," said Somerford, making a kind of salute with his palm down, as the Americans do.

"Those years in Canada were . . ." Mycroft Holmes said, his thoughts fraying as he put his concentration on the roof once more.

But I was not satisfied. "Years in Canada?"

"Um?" My employer turned a deceptively mild gaze upon me. "Oh, yes. Somerford was in Canada as a young man; he came back to England when he was twenty-three. It explains his accent, and his manner of saluting." He then clearly put the whole of the matter out of his mind as he crouched down to study the groove that had supported the rifle barrel. "Most interesting," he murmured, as he studied the angle of the thing.

In spite of my intention to ask him nothing until he volunteered, I could not help but say, "Why interesting?" just as he wanted me to do.

"Well, my boy, this groove was cut in place with a chisel, one that made a single impression, which suggests that the shooter brought it along for such a purpose, which in turn implies that he has done this kind of thing before and knew to come prepared." He did not quite smile, but he did rock back onto his heels and nod to show his satisfaction. "If the man knew to do this, he is no amateur; and there will be a record of him somewhere." He put his large, well-shaped hands together as if in prayer, which I now knew meant he was searching his astonishing memory for any similarity to other cases of which he had knowledge; his deepening frown indicated he was not identifying anyone to his satisfaction. "Well, I shall devote some time to it later." He rose, dusting his fingers off against one another. "If the man is experienced—as we must suppose he is—he will have melted into the crowd, milled with them, and made his escape without attracting any attention; so whomever the soldiers have caught, we will discover that the poor creature is not our assassin." He pointed to Chief Inspector Somerford. "I want you to call around at my flat this evening, Chief Inspector. Your men will have completed their first search of the area around Saint Paul's. You and I will have much to discuss."

Calvin Somerford made another of his American salutes. "Eight o'clock, then?"

"I'll tell Tyers to have a supper laid for nine, if that will suit," said my employer, ignoring the incredulous stares of the soldiers who watched their discussion. "Guthrie will be with us, of course, and you may bring your assistant, if you like."

"I'll think about it," said Chief Inspector Somerford. He raised his head and peered up at the sky. "No rain for a while. That's something in our favor?"

"Tomorrow. The weather will change by evening," I said; the small fragment of a bullet that was lodged in my hip had provided me accurate weather predictions since I acquired it in the streets of Constantinople, almost four years since. "You'll want a tarpaulin after that."

"He's very reliable," said Mycroft Holmes, motioning to me to follow him. "I think we can leave the police to their work," he said as he pocketed the shell casing. "Until this evening, Chief Inspector. And do try to keep the soldiers from falling over each other; it is bad for morale." His single crack of laughter brought indignant stares from the soldiers and sly smiles from the two policemen accompanying Chief Inspector Somerford.

"I would like to think," I said as we stepped through the door onto the top of the stairs, "that there will be a straightforward solution to all this."

"My dear Guthrie, no more do I, no more do I," said Mycroft Holmes wearily as he began his descent.

FROM THE PERSONAL JOURNAL OF PHILIP TYERS

MH returned shortly before G from the aftermath of the wedding in separate conveyances, G having returned to his rooms in Curzon Street to change his clothes before reporting for his assignments from MH. It is apparent that there is a deal of confusion surrounding the events at StP this morning, and the confusion is mounting. By morning, it will be bruited about that mounted Cossacks charged the Scandinavian delegation singing "God Protect the Tsar," and there will be many who will swear to have seen it, or something as preposterous. I share MH's apprehension that by nightfall tomorrow there will be so many rumors about that we will be unable to discover a means to sift the wheat from the chaff, as the saying has it. By Friday, no fact will be untainted. To forestall the worst of this, MH is preparing a number of memoranda and other dispatches that I must presently deliver, most with the hope of discovering the truth of today's events before they are forgot or distorted. The list is a long one and I will not complete my rounds in less than ninety minutes. I have agreed to carry my pistol, little though it pleases me to do so.

Word has just come from Sutton that he will arrive soon after midnight, when his performance concludes, which will relieve MH greatly. He has offered to purchase papers so that MH can read about the events as they are being reported to the British people, which MH believes may point to issues we have not yet considered.

A police constable has been provided to MH to carry messages between him and Chief Inspector Somerford, so that confidentiality can be preserved and so that there need be no delay when messages must be carried. MH is not as pleased with this arrangement as he might be. He does not like exposing Sutton, his double, to anyone who has no need to know of his arrangement with MH, but I suspect that his reasons are more complex than that.

The Prince is safe, and no one is aware of his hiding place, which is just as well.

Chapter Three

WHEN I RETURNED to my employer's flat in Pall Mall, it was midafternoon and clouds had blown in, blotting out the glorious blue of heaven's canopy, and my hip was underscoring this change with a dull, muffled ache that told me it would rain before the next morning. I found the sitting room closed off and the flat ringing with an uneven rendition of the duet "Suoni la tromba" from Bellini's *I Puritani,* executed—if that is not too strong a word—by solo bass: Mycroft Holmes often sang in the bath when he had solved a problem to his satisfaction, and today, eventful though it was, was no exception. I smiled with relief as I hung up my overcoat on the rack just inside the door.

Tyers, who was preparing to leave, rolled his eyes upward and whispered, "At least he has a plan. Better him singing than brooding. He's got the front of the flat empty, in case we're being watched. He's fairly certain we are. I'll confirm it for him."

I chuckled softly; five years ago I would not have been so bold, or so unconcerned, but after the hectic life Mycroft Holmes had thrown me into I had begun to revere him less and respect him more and to understand his enjoyment in the game. "I have my pistol. Shall I need it?"

"Probably not, at least not here," said Tyers. "I should return in less than two hours; if I am gone more than three, alert the police. There's tea ready on the cooker." With that he pulled his muffler around his head and ducked out the front door. I closed the door behind him and shot the lock-bolt home.

"That you, Guthrie?" Mycroft Holmes called out, interrupting his assault on Bellini.

"Yes, sir," I replied at once. "At your service."

There was a vigorous sloshing while my employer climbed out of his tub. "I'll be with you directly. There's port in the study. Pour for yourself and fill a glass for me. We have work to do." The energy in his tone warned me that it would be a demanding evening.

"Yes, sir," I said, and went along to the study, sliding back the doors and going to turn up the gaslight. The bright, warm glow suffused the room, and I looked about with the pleasure of being in a familiar place. The port was in a decanter on a Spanish silver tray, with four thistles beside it. I chose two and poured the dark wine into them, relishing the strong, nutty aroma that rose from the thistles. I set one on the occasional table next to Mycroft Holmes' preferred chair and sat down in the one opposite it. I put my glass aside while I waited for my employer to join me.

Ten minutes later Mycroft Holmes strolled into the study; he was properly attired for a convivial evening, and I supposed he would shortly leave to visit his club across the street. He nodded his approval at my more practical attire—I was dressed in a dark tweed hacking jacket over a rolltop jumper and driving trousers, as Mister Holmes had requested. "Very good. That is exactly what I requested. You could blend into almost any public place in London but the opera or a Whitechapel stew." He sat down and picked up his thistle of port. "Thank you, Guthrie. Today has been a trifle taxing."

"That it has," I agreed, holding my glass untouched. He sipped to taste his own. I waited to learn what his afternoon's reveries had revealed to him.

"That poor footman. The body will be at the morgue by now. I should go along and have a look at it in the morning." He shook his head. "Sad thing, to have such a death occur."

"That it is," I said with feeling. The image of the man crumpling had haunted my eyes like a photographic exposure since I'd come down from the roof. "Four seconds sooner and Prince Oscar would have been hit."

"We must be glad of the warning and the reprieve it has given us." The expression on Mycroft Holmes' face was hard to read. "Be very certain we must not lapse into unfounded optimism or security. That shell casing should tell us that, if nothing else."

"How do you mean?" I knew the question was expected of me, and I waited for the answer with the conviction of one sure in his purpose.

"It is a most unusual shell, that came from the casing. I can think of only half a dozen men in Europe who would have cause to have such a shell." He coughed. "I will explain later." He scowled.

I decided I did not want to pursue this just now. "Any word yet from Chief Inspector Somerford? Or his superiors?"

"No, nothing from any of them. Not Somerford, not Winslowe, and not Spencer. We'll learn more when Somerford comes to dine." He dawdled over his next sip. "We have made arrangements to send the Prince home under heavy escort," he went on after a moment.

I had come to know that tone of voice. "Oh?" I said politely, wondering what we would actually do.

"Or something of the sort, in any case," said Mycroft Holmes, with a nod of his big head. "I will need you to work out the details while I am across the street. We must not be too obvious, but we must use all means possible to ensure Prince Oscar will reach his country without being in danger again. You will have to arrange discreet protection for the Prince and contrive, if you can, to be sure he is kept under guard—"

"Like a prisoner?" I dared to interject.

Instead of dismissing my remark, Mycroft Holmes directed his profound gray eyes at me. "There are times, my boy, when royalty looks very like a prison. Oh, to be sure the accommodations are better than Brixton Gaol, but they are equally as confining, and the sentences are for all lifelong." He coughed once. "Never mind. Our duty now is plain and we do not have a great deal of time to fulfill our obligations. So. Given the presence of so many of Her Majesty's relatives in London, we must be trebly careful, for another incident could bring about precisely the kind of doubts we would most want to keep from the minds of such high-ranking persons." He slapped his knee. "I am going to give you some travel schedules, and you will work out what we have to do in order to guard Prince Oscar and how we may best escort him from our shores to his. We are fortunate indeed that he is inclined to favor Britain, for if he did not, an event such as the one we witnessed today would set the seal upon Scandinavian support for Germany." He shook his head. "You and I know, Guthrie, how much influence the Brotherhood has in German affairs. It behooves us to proceed with care. We cannot play into their hands now, when we have come so far toward limiting their ambitions. You know where in Europe the Brotherhood is strongest. You would do well to make every effort to keep Prince Oscar away from such locales."

"Certainly," I said at once, setting my thistle aside, the port no more than tasted. I could see restlessness building in him, and I knew he would want me to work immediately. "Do you want me to work here?"

"Yes, if you would not mind terribly," he said with uncharacteristic diffidence. "I think it would be wiser if you would not put papers about in any case."

"No, sir; I would not," I assured him, mildly annoyed that he would think I would so forget myself as to do such a thing.

Mycroft Holmes cocked his head, his expression mildly inquisitive. "Guthrie, what do you make of this? The attempt on the Prince's life?"

I was so startled by his question that I hesitated to give an answer. "I suppose it must mean he has enemies, as we have realized. What royal does not? But whether it is an enemy of Britain, an enemy of Sweden-and-Norway, or an enemy of Oscar himself, we do not yet know. It may be a direct action of the Brotherhood, in which case it is all three; but the Brotherhood rarely works so openly, so it would be foolish to assume only one of the possibilities is operating here."

A solemn smile was my reward. "Very good, Guthrie. Unlike the police, you have not yet chosen a theory to serve your purposes. Our years together have honed your thinking. Excellent. There are a few permutations of the possibilities you have outlined, but generally you have hit upon the salient points."

Praise from Mycroft Holmes still delighted me, and I smiled to show my appreciation; I would have tried to turn the compliment; but in the past when I had attempted such a gesture, my employer had not encouraged such courtesy. "Thank you, Mister Holmes."

"Not that there are not other factors to consider." Holmes sipped his wine. "There are numerous possible motives for this attempt. It could very well be the act of those who oppose Britain and seek to embarrass or discredit her. There are many on our streets who fail to appreciate the benefits of our associations with their homelands. Nor can we rule out those few remaining Anarchists. While they prefer bombs, I have had experience with those of that ilk using rifles as well, though rarely as professionally." He pulled at his lower lip. "What do you think, Guthrie?"

"I think that such an eventuality is unlikely," I replied, knowing that most of my employer's discourses were his way of thinking aloud and making sure he had considered all the possibilities by hearing them aloud.

Mycroft Holmes nodded slowly. "We should not overlook that this was an attack against a royal. There are those few who still see the Directorates of the French Revolution as being right. That the only way for the masses to gain power is to destroy all those with privileged blood. This might not be the first shot fired simply in jealousy by that type of fool. Nor can we assume the assassin is, or was hired by, someone only from this country or the Brotherhood. After all, Sweden-and-Norway sits over Germany, shares a sea with Russia, and has extensive dealings with all of Europe. I suspect there are men in several nations who would benefit from the Prince's death, directly or indirectly. And speaking of those benefitting, his brother may have arranged the attempt on his own, without the help or approval of the Brotherhood. He certainly has the most to gain and the resources to enable him to commit such an act. Finally, you have to take into account the fact that a footman, not the Prince, was killed. Although I think it remote, I cannot dismiss out of hand that the assassin was actually in Prince Oscar's pay, under instructions to make the event appear to be an attempt on the Prince's life. While I deem it highly unlikely, this may be part of a convoluted plot to eliminate his brother from the succession entirely—in self-defense."

I regarded Holmes dubiously. "Highly unlikely," I seconded.

"Oh, no doubt, my boy, no doubt. Some of these possibilities are indubitably more likely than others, but without hard evidence of the assassin's employer it behooves us not to dismiss any possible source for the threat." He had another sip of port, rolling the wine on his tongue appreciatively. "There is, finally, the most obscure possibility of all— that the footman was not only the target, but an integral part of a conspiracy to frighten Prince Oscar into capitulation or submission to those whom the footman supported with his life."

"I will endeavor to keep this all in mind, sir," I said with feeling; the complexity of the diplomatic world never failed to astonish me; that Mycroft Holmes had it all in his thoughts, at the ready, every hour of the day and night commanded my highest admiration.

"Yes. Well, see you put your observations to good use. I will be leaving in a short while; I expect to see progress upon my return." He clapped once as if to conjure results from the air like a magician. "You know where the maps are kept."

"Indeed yes," I said, hoping to show a good level of dedication.

Mycroft Holmes chuckled. "This isn't Alexandria or Constantinople, my dear boy. You may be at ease." He made his way to the door, his steps ponderous, as if visiting the Diogenes Club weighed him down with obligation and responsibility by virtue of his membership.

"Yes, sir," I said, rising out of respect as was my habit.

I watched him leave from the front landing, going into the long spring sunset to cross the road, walking as if oblivious to the traffic around him. I wondered again at the mercurial nature of this most steadfast of men, that these two extremes should exist within him in successful juxtaposition. As I went back into the flat, I paused for a moment, listening. Then I made my way back to the study and began to puzzle out an itinerary that would take Prince Oscar back to Stockholm without exposing him to any more incidents. Beyond all doubt, the British government could not sustain the embarrassment that the assassination of a foreign royal while in British protection would lead to; that was obvious to the meanest intelligence. I had been about the world enough now to know that prestige was as valuable as the coin of the realm—sometimes more valuable.

For the next hour I worked with the various schedules Mycroft

Holmes had provided, covering a sheet of foolscap with my notes and growing increasingly dissatisfied with the possibilities. I had almost come to the conclusion that it might be better to invite the Scandinavian navy to come to escort their Prince home, if such a request would not have dreadful implications for British-Scandinavian relations in the immediate future, which would render the work of the last two weeks useless. With a sigh I put my pencil aside and rubbed my eyes, then rose to my feet and stretched. I told myself that more than my shoulders and hip were growing stiff, and that I needed a turn around the room to limber up my brain as much as my muscles. I noticed a new addition to the framed drawings on the wall—a charcoal study of a ruined Cornish castle, vacant and forlorn on a spit of rock over the clawing breakers. I stopped to study it and noticed the ES signature in the lower right-hand corner of the work. Another one of Edmund Sutton's sketches, I thought, recalling the portfolio of stage designs he had brought here several months ago. He had reminded me then that actors must know how to draw, not only to paint scenery and props, but to put on makeup. In the time I had been in Mycroft Holmes' employ, my opinion of Sutton's profession had improved so that I now began to expect that in his own way Edmund Sutton was as remarkable a fellow as the man who employed us both, an observation Sutton found ludicrous when I suggested it to him some three months since. I thought he underestimated his talent, but he would not agree: he told me that had he a greater gift, he would have continued to pursue leading roles he had once attempted instead of the character parts he now essayed. I turned my attention to a handsome watercolor of the Lake District in high summer. I supposed the lake in the watercolor must be Windermere, but that was probably because I thought all the lakes were Windermere.

I had just resumed my work when Mycroft Holmes returned from his club. Dusk had turned the flat gloomy, long purple shadows engulfing the rooms. He turned up the lights in the hallway, remarking how eager he was for tea. "Not that the port and brandy are not superb at the Diogenes Club, for they are, but I fear I have to keep a clear head this evening and tea is just what's wanted."

I recalled that Tyers said the kettle was ready in the kitchen. "I'll attend to it." When I was young, I often helped my mother prepare tea. No one in the family thought it odd that a son should help with such work for, as my mother said often, "You must not rely on women and servants to look to your comfort, my lad; they may not always be available to you." Our family had one servant, and as she grew older, it fell to me, as the son of the household, to help with things Hatley could no longer do. I went to the kitchen and moved the kettle onto the hottest part of the cooker, as I had been taught to do while still a schoolboy. The sugar caddy and milk jug were set out on the preparations table, and these I set on the brass-fitted butler's tray while I warmed the good stoneware pot Mister Holmes insisted upon.

"Guthrie," Holmes called from the study, "are these your notes?"

"On the foolscap—yes, sir." I measured out tea from the tin, choosing the Assam that Mister Holmes favored when he was faced with long hours of study.

"Not much worthwhile, is there?" His voice was louder and his step in the hall warned me of his approach.

"It has . . . difficulties, sir," I said, choosing my words carefully.

"So it would appear." He was standing in the door, my pad of paper in his hand; he scowled down at my notes. "Dear me, I had no notion we had allowed such disorder to arise."

"Such disorder?" I asked, my attention more on preparing tea than on his observations. The smell of roasting lamb was very strong, honing my appetite. There were cups on their racks, with saucers behind them. I took two down and placed them on the tray.

"There is almost no coordination with British schedules. Oh, the trains are not too inconvenient, but other posted sailing times—Good Lord, man. Have you ever seen such stuff? You would think the world still ran by sails and tides to look at these." He tapped the page with an accusing finger.

"For some, they still do," I reminded him, for steam had not wholly taken over the sea-lanes yet.

"But not enough to justify some of these schedules. They have accommodated their old schedules when they no longer have to." He snorted with impatience. "The Prince would be as obvious as a boil on a nostril if we had to guard him at one of the ports between here and Stockholm." He peered into the kitchen as I continued to set out lemon curd and preserves to accompany scones and Scotch petticoats. "We must find another way, Guthrie. This will not do."

"No, sir," I said, mildly distracted. For a couple of ticks, I could not remember where Tyers kept the clotted cream, and then I opened the cooler and brought it out; on the lowest rack a large jug of oxtail soup waited to be heated for our supper. Next I set out spoons and serviettes while the kettle began to thrill. I recalled I should have prepared three baked eggs for Mycroft Holmes, but it had slipped my mind; and even after all these years I was not that familiar with the cooker. I turned to my employer and prepared to apologize.

"My dear Guthrie," Mycroft Holmes exclaimed, "I could not manage half so well were I in your shoes. When Tyers returns, if he has time between tea and supper, he can bake eggs if we require them. I doubt I'll want them." He looked at the tray. "Quite masterful, upon my word."

"Thank you, sir," I said as I went to pour the water, just on the boil, onto the leaves in the teapot. The sharp scent of black tea rose with the steam as I put the kettle down once again, this time on the cool part of the range. I checked the butler's tray to be certain everything we required was in place, then I picked it up and started for the hallway.

"Let me open the door wider, Guthrie," Mycroft Holmes volunteered. "You will want to be able to move easily."

"I'd appreciate that, sir," I said, surprised at how heavy the butler's tray was thus laden. Holding it, I made my way down the hall crab-fashion; the brass handles of the tray were polished and a bit slippery, making the grip hard to maintain. All in all, delivering the tea was trickier than I thought it would be.

"I'll clear a place on the tea table," Mycroft Holmes offered, gathering up the schedules in a single gesture. "There you are."

I set the tray down with relief. "Thank you, sir."

"Nothing, I assure you," he replied in as good form as he would show an ambassador. "I'll pour, if it's all the same to you."

"Thank you," I repeated, wiping my hands on the nearest serviette. "We should have our supper ready an hour after Tyers returns."

Mycroft Holmes sat down, his long head angled forward as he prepared to pour the tea. "Do you think we will be able to find a safe route for the Prince?"

"It will be difficult," I admitted as I sat down. "The Prince has said he does not want to travel on a Royal Navy ship, for fear of offending Germany." It had been a matter of contention from Prince Oscar's arrival in Britain, and one upon which he had remained firm. "He must not be given a military escort. Since the PM agrees with him, there is no more to be said."

"Yet finding appropriate civilian transportation is proving difficult. Have you considered the royal yacht?" Mycroft Holmes held out a cup-and-saucer to me; I accepted it awkwardly, for it seemed strange to have him serve.

"I thought it was not available for this service. Too many of Her Majesty's relatives would take offense at so singular a display of favor." I had taken notes at two meetings when this had been considered, and I recalled how vehemently the Swedish Ambassador had insisted that such a distinction was unwelcome to Prince Oscar, for it could lead to the kind of upset that could color diplomatic dealings. "I don't think the Prince will change his mind simply because the transportation is—"

"Confusing," Mister Holmes finished for me. "I think you have read the situation aright. Sadly, wiring for the Prince's yacht at this point would be a concession that the government would not like, an admission that we cannot vouch for his safety." He paused as he added sugar to his tea. "There is also now the necessity of a decoy."

"A decoy?" I repeated, feeling rather foolish.

"For the assassin to follow. Surely you see the need of it, Guthrie; you comprehend the importance of Sutton so well," Mycroft Holmes said, so confidently that I could only nod. "We must assume the assassin will not stop with a single attempt, and that when he continues his efforts he will be more determined. Therefore we must contrive a decoy to keep the Prince safe."

"Was that why you were singing in the bath, sir?" I ventured to ask, as Mycroft Holmes took his first long sip of tea.

"One of the reasons, Guthrie, yes." He smiled at me, his expression so benign that I was almost afraid to move. "While the Chief Inspector is here, I want you to follow my lead."

"Of course," I said, wondering why he should take such pains to remind me to do the very thing I had done from the first hours of my employment.

"Good. Very good, my boy," he approved as he drank more tea. "You have become most astute in the last few years."

Surprised at this unexpected praise, I tasted my tea as well, noticing only that it was a trifle too hot. I sat a bit straighter in my chair. "It's what you've been watching for since Prince Oscar arrived. You have expected something of the sort from the outset. There is more to this than the assassination attempt, isn't there? It is not so simple as you have implied; more is at stake."

"I believe so," said Mycroft Holmes, taking a scone and smearing lemon curd on it. "And I rely upon Tyers to bring me the confirmation of my suspicions in the next hour." He bit down firmly and chewed.

"The Brotherhood, no doubt," I said feeling a combination of fatigue and exhilaration at the realization that I would once again be in the fray.

"No doubt," Mycroft Holmes agreed through a bit of scone. "They want Prince Karl Gustav on the throne one day, allied with Germany and aiding their cause of European collapse. No doubt you have noticed how often the Brotherhood works most injuriously in the nations around Germany, undermining their integrity and binding them to German purposes."

"That is the aspect I cannot understand: why would a man of Prince Karl's stature and position want to belong to an organization dedicated to the destruction of the very institution to which Karl himself has been born?" I was not hungry—nerves were robbing me of my appetite, a development I found disturbing for it was not one I often encountered.

"He has most certainly been promised a favored position with the Brotherhood when they triumph. Karl Gustav is a younger son, and in the usual course of things, he will live his entire life in the shadow of Prince Oscar, who, barring mishap, will one day be King of Sweden-and-Norway. How ignominious for Karl Gustav, perpetually condemned to the conscripted life of royalty, with responsibilities and obligations that would make the average man shudder, with little or no chance to achieve the position that all the demands support. No, Karl Gustav had no reason to eschew the privileges the Brotherhood has promised and no reason to refuse to aid Germany, for their policies could provide him the advancement that he, like Hamlet, so conspicuously lacks." He had another decisive bite of the scone.

"But isn't he making, well,"—I felt myself redden at this lurid comparison—"'a deal with the devil?'" I could see that my choice of image amused my employer.

"In more ways than one," said Mycroft Holmes, after he took a long sip of tea. "For whether or not Karl Gustav ever achieves his desire to supplant Prince Oscar, he will always be at the beck and call of the Brotherhood. It is their damnable practice to aid you so you will be beholden to them, and then to compel you to do their bidding in all matters that suit their purpose." He poured more tea, using the strainer to keep the dark leaves from getting into his cup; it was a fastidious gesture, reminding me of the narrow, restricted life he was believed to live and how far that carefully maintained façade was from the truth.

"Do you think Prince Oscar is aware of the problem?" I had heard many of the discussions that passed between my employer and the Scandinavian Prince and I could not recall any remark His Highness might have made directly on the subject.

"He has been told, of course. Whether or not he is convinced is another matter." He stirred his tea as he dropped in sugar. "I have tried to alert him, and I know he is aware of the actions of the Brotherhood; but I am less certain he understands the role his brother is playing in the Brotherhood's activities. I very much doubt he would entertain the notion that Karl Gustav could have had any role in the event today." He lifted his cup. "More's the pity."

The door to the kitchen opened and Tyers called out, "I am returned," his voice sounding a trifle breathless, suggesting he had rushed up the backstairs. "I have two replies. Others will be carried 'round by nine in the morning."

Mycroft Holmes nodded in satisfaction. "Were you followed?"

Tyers appeared in the doorway, still unwrapping his muffler. "Yes, sir, I was. And I was most particularly careful to observe my followers." He pulled a small portfolio from inside his coat and handed it to Mister Holmes. "The information you requested. The two replies are with it." He bowed a bit.

Holmes took the portfolio and put it on the arm of his chair, a gesture so negligent that I knew it had to be deliberate. "Thank you, Tyers. Now, about the man following you?"

"When I left—by the front, as you ordered—I was observed by a young man, no more than twenty-five, fair, with a moustache and a French necktie. He was well turned out and probably fancied himself a cut above most of those around him, a bit of self-delusion in Pall Mall. His suit was a good copy of Bond Street tailoring, probably done by one of the Chinese tailors offering such suits. He had what appeared to be a tattoo on his wrist, but aside from catching a glimpse of its color—which was bluish as so many tattoos are—I cannot tell you anything more about it. He followed me for my first two calls, but I lost him near Saint Martins-in-the-Field, as you instructed I should. I was able to satisfy myself I had got clear of him before I continued on my errands." His expression changed slightly, showing his appreciation for his skill in eluding his pursuer. "After my third call, a man looking like a West Country squire gone to seed followed me."

"Is that Vickers' man?" I asked sharply, remembering my first work for Mycroft Holmes that had taken me to the men of the Brotherhood in England.

"I would think so," said Mycroft Holmes, frowning.

I could not entirely suppress a shudder. "If that's the fellow I think it is, he has a whiff of corruption about him." My own dealings with him had been brief but their impact remained, like the smell of a dead rat under the floorboards.

"That is the man and most certainly the whiff," said Mycroft Holmes, his tone as dry as his features were unreadable. "The man is known to whip the bottoms of the boys attending his school for the most minor trespasses." He took a deep breath. "He will undoubtedly report your calls to Vickers, wherever he has gone to ground."

Foolish though it was, I could not keep from a moment of rec-ollection, and the image of Vickers' face before my mind's eye was enough to chill me to the bone. "Is he still in England, I wonder?" I asked. "He was gone long enough that he might have decided to return to the Continent."

"Or Ireland," said Mycroft Holmes. "I shouldn't wonder if he hasn't decided to go there and stir the pot." His face had hardened, seeming now to be hewn from granite. "I will find him."

I did not doubt for an instant that he would.

FROM THE PERSONAL JOURNAL OF PHILIP TYERS

Having returned from the errands MH sent me to do, I had supper to make for the arrival of Chief Inspector Somerford, who, fortunately, was ten minutes late and was willing to have a second pony of sherry before sitting down to eat. The soup is almost ready, an oxtail with barley, and I will have it in the tureen shortly and then put my concentration on the main course—in this instance I am grateful MH likes his lamb served rare. I seasoned it with garlic, olives, and cumin, as they prepare it in Egypt, one of the dishes I learned to make there. There is new bread and fresh-churned butter. I have to finish the buttered turnips and green peas in creamed cheddar in order to put all on the table in twenty minutes. . . .

When supper is on the table, I will prepare a full report of my errands and the two men who followed me. MH will want it in his hands before he retires.

Chapter Four

CHIEF INSPECTOR CALVIN Somerford set down his sherry, the pony still half-full. "If I drink any more of that, I won't be able to think during dinner." He offered a small deprecatory nod. "I don't have a head for wine?" His habitual upward inflection made it seem he had doubts about it.

"No matter, Chief Inspector," said Mycroft Holmes, as if remarking on a minor blemish. "Not all coppers have to be hard drinkers."

"If you ask me," said Somerford, "too many of them are? You can't do your work when you're foxed."

The old-fashioned expression took my attention. "That's what my old grandmother would call it," I told him, glancing at my employer as I spoke.

"So did mine," said the Chief Inspector. "I think it describes the state of slight intoxication very well, don't you?"

"It does create an impression," I said, noticing out of the corner of my eye that Mycroft Holmes was encouraging these observations.

"Yes. So many of the old expressions are so vivid? Foxed. Disguised. Bosky. Swallowed a spider?" He shook his head. "No. That means got into debt, as I recall."

"Like being in the River Tick," said Mycroft Holmes, unctuous as a cat.

"I believe so," I agreed, curious why Mister Holmes would want us to have such a discussion, for plainly he did, encouraging it in his oblique way and signaling me covertly to continue. "I'd reckon those phrases change quickly to keep in the mode." It was a safe observation and one that would open more doors to language, if that was what my employer was seeking. "Those phrases serve as a kind of code, to give information to those who have need to know it."

"Yes, the cant will do that, and occasionally they use it to obfuscate," said the Chief Inspector. "So many of the terms used by the criminal classes are intended to mislead anyone overhearing them?" He pursed his lips. "That is one of the reason our spies are so useful—they understand what they hear?"

"So you do use spies," said Mycroft Holmes, as if this revelation were astonishing.

"Of course. We sometimes use other words for it, but that's what it comes down to? They are men—and very occasionally women—of the criminal class, who are willing to help us in order to preserve themselves; Commander Winslowe has said that we must make the most of any aid we can, and that includes the use of spies. What else would you call them?" He rocked back on his heels, looking more than ever like a lecturer in a good school. "Anyone in my position must find dependable men who can ferret out answers for me where I cannot go?"

For an instant the porcelain prettiness of Penelope Gatspy crossed my mind, and I remembered how well she did her work. I owed her my life, a debt that I began to think I would never repay. Indeed, after that one shameful lapse of three years ago, I doubted she would ever be willing to give me the opportunity to do so, for she lived in that dangerous twilight world of spies and assassins, embracing a life most women did not know existed. My tongue felt like flannel in my mouth, and I could not speak the words that jangled in my thoughts.

"A prudent approach, I would think," said Mycroft Holmes in remote approval. "And have your . . . ah . . . ferrets told you anything about the killing today?" His bluntness brought Chief Inspector Somerford up short. "I would think you would have every spy you have ever used on the hunt for this man."

"I haven't had time to speak to them all yet, but the word is out, the word is out," said Chief Inspector Somerford.

"What word is that?" Mister Holmes asked, his attitude courteous without showing inappropriate interest.

"Oh, that we want this criminal, who is not your usual killer. This isn't some outraged husband, or vengeful rival, or a depraved maniac, or someone seeking to advance his political cause, or an ambitious and greedy fellow, or even a desperate brigand. We have let it be known that this man is the agent of a foreign and hostile power, whose aims are to create trouble for Britain all over the world? That's a fairly strong argument to use with most of the practiced organizations for crime in London. Most of our criminals are patriots, in their way, and will not help such a man to escape." A smile slipped over his face. "It is true. Many criminals are very proud to be British? They look down on criminals in other countries."

"I have heard something of the sort. It strikes me as odd," said Mycroft Holmes with an hauteur that would have been more appropriate to a Royal Duke.

"Oh, yes," Chief Inspector Somerford declared, "criminals have pride, just as any man with a trade does?" He put a finger to his lips. "Too much sherry."

"Would you like something else?" Mycroft Holmes asked, as solicitous as if he entertained royalty. I was growing more and more puzzled. "A glass of porter? A cup of tea?"

Chief Inspector Somerford shook his head. "No. Thank you, what I want, Mister Holmes, is a spot of food. That will do the trick?" He smiled a bit, though it took concentration.

"I will see if Tyers will put the soup on now," said Mycroft Holmes, and to my amazement left the room to speak with Tyers. What on earth was he playing at? I did my best to mask my confusion as I studied Chief Inspector Somerford, continuing our conversation as best

I could. "About your spies? Can you tell me anything about them?" I was beginning to sound like him, every statement an implied question.

"I can't. Not very much? They are engaged in dangerous work, don't you know? Not at all like what you and Mister Holmes do." He made a sloppy wink. "I told Superintendent Spencer himself that we are too trusting of our informants, but when one works on the streets, one sees things others do not."

"I would think it must be dangerous," I said, hoping he would vouchsafe more information.

"Well, it is," said Chief Inspector Somerford. "We lost one of our . . . spies earlier today, in fact?" His face was drawn and he was white around the mouth.

"Oh, dear. On top of the trouble at Saint Paul's. How dreadful for you." I realized that he was very upset, and for the first time I suspected that his distress was as much a part of his sudden drunkenness as the sherry was. "I would imagine this has been difficult, dealing with so much."

"That it has," said Chief Inspector Somerford flatly. "We could not afford to lose this one. Well, we can't afford to lose any of them, but this one . . ." He shook his head repeatedly.

"I am sorry to hear it," I told him with feeling. "If you depended upon him, it must be doubly hard to have him go."

"It was." He steadied himself. "He was found drifting? in the Thames not far from Blackfriar's Bridge. His . . . his fingers were burned to blackened sticks and . . . and they'd blinded him? The eyes were gone?" He turned away, his hand covering his face. "I'm sorry," he said after a long moment.

"No need," I assured him. "When something like that happens, anyone might be knocked off his pins." Without intending to, I touched my face where the footman's blood had spattered. I would have offered him the rest of his sherry, but I supposed he would refuse it; as it was, I tossed down the last of my own, mentally drinking to Penelope Gatspy, wherever the Golden Lodge had sent her.

"I'll be myself again in a moment?" he said, his voice muffled. Then, abruptly, he raised his head and looked at me; his face was a mask of pain. "There. You see? I'm over my funk."

"Whatever you say, dear fellow," I said at once, hoping that my employer would appear again quickly, for I knew I was floundering in my dealings with this man, what with the resurgence of the blood spatters this morning making me feel a trifle ill. Right then I would have rather been rushing down that alley in Constantinople with the four Turks after me than sitting here with this distraught policeman.

He made a visible effort to steady himself. "You're supposed to grow accustomed to these things, being a copper? But I never have."

I noticed a spot of blood on his cuff—not unlike the ones on my own clothes from the morning—and I suppressed a shudder. "The attempt on the Prince and the discovery of that body all in one day. I don't see how anyone would get used to it." My voice shook a bit, too, and I made no apology for it.

Whatever Chief Inspector Somerford might have said was stopped when Mycroft Holmes came to the door and announced that supper was served in the parlor. His manner was so obsequious he would have done the most important butler proud. "The soup is hot and Tyers is bringing it just now. We may have to wait a bit for the lamb, but I am certain none of us will mind." He led the way grandly, and we tagged along behind him like schoolboys trying to be as grown-up as the master.

The parlor was set up for dining, the drop-leaves of the table having been raised and a cut-work linen tablecloth I did not know Mycroft Holmes possessed laid upon it. The service was bone china and the glasses were cut crystal, the napery fine linen. The lay-out was worthy of a diplomatic retreat; and though Mycroft Holmes could be a stickler for form when required, he rarely demanded such punctiliousness in his ordinary conduct. Why was my employer trying to overwhelm this Chief Inspector of police? As we took our seats, Tyers came in and put the tureen in the center of the table, between the two silver candelabra. He proceeded to ladle out the soup in silence while we settled ourselves in place.

"Isn't the aroma wonderful?" Mycroft Holmes asked no one in particular, as he inhaled the fragrant steam rising from his bowl.

Chief Inspector Somerford allowed that it smelled delicious and did not wait for Mister Holmes to take a first spoonful. He reached for a French crescent roll, broke it in half, and thrust the larger piece into the soup, then, when some of the savory liquid was sopped up by the roll, bit it gratefully. "Excellent," he said as he chewed.

If Mycroft Holmes thought this gauche, he said nothing of it. He used his spoon very correctly, sat as if he were in attendance at Windsor, and punctuated his performance by making wry comments on the change in the weather.

"They say we can expect another storm in a day or two, but who can tell?" Mycroft Holmes said as if this were significant information. "I have always thought the spring to be a most changeable time of year."

Trying to behave as he wished, I did my best to pick up this conversational ball. "So it is," I agreed. "It can make planning difficult." I was given a quick smile of encouragement, so I went on. "They say the signs are for a wet spring."

"Ah," said Mister Holmes, "that would account for it."

Somerford had finished his crescent roll and was almost finished with his soup. "Sorry. I'm not much good at small-talk at the best of times, and today I can't manage it at all?"

Again Mycroft Holmes nodded sagely. What was he playing at? I continued to wonder. He was as bad as the most hidebound bureaucrat in Whitehall. "Not in the police requirements, I suppose."

"Small-talk? Not usually, no," said the Chief Inspector. "It's not what we're about." He saw that Tyers was about to pour claret into his wine-glass, and he put his hand over it. "No, thanks. I'm half-sprung as it is." Another one of the phrases from seventy years ago. "Water will do me."

"Would you like some more soup?" my employer inquired. "There is a bit more in the tureen, and our supper isn't lavish."

Chief Inspector Somerford shook his head as if recalling himself from unwelcome thoughts. "No. It would be wasted on me? I have had a most taxing day and the night isn't yet over, is it?" He allowed Tyers to fill his goblet with water. "I have a meeting later tonight? I should be alert for it." He took another crescent roll from the covered bread basket. "These are very good?"

"Thank you. They come from that little French bakery three streets away. Tyers fetches them fresh in the morning." Mycroft Holmes spoke so smoothly that had I not known it to be a lie, I would have believed him utterly.

"I know the one you mean," said Chief Inspector Somerford. "If this is any sample of their wares, they must be very good?" He broke the roll into two parts and buttered the stub of one end. "Strange, how danger can increase and decrease hunger at the same instant."

"I suppose that is true of many things," Mycroft Holmes agreed, his hand moving slightly to signal me to speak.

"Yes, indeed," I said, hoping I would find the words I needed. "Exhaustion can be like that—it sharpens hunger as quickly as it takes hunger away."

"True enough," said Chief Inspector Somerset. He moved so that Tyers could remove the soup bowls and chargers, leaving our dinner plates unencumbered. "I miss the simple pleasure of dining with one's family."

"You are unmarried, are you not, Chief Inspector?" Mycroft Holmes observed.

"I am a widower," he answered, "and my work has become as demanding as a mistress?" He chuckled at what I supposed was an old joke with him. His face became more somber. "I don't envy you your present task, speaking of demands. You must be working through the night, looking for safe passage home for Prince Oscar."

"The coordination of various steamship lines is a headache," Mycroft Holmes confessed, saying much more than I would have thought prudent, even to a Chief Inspector of police.

Tyers put the platter of lamb on the table, the standing rack looking like temptation itself, the smell reminiscent of Constantinople. A relish of apples and onions had been put in the center of the roast and was turning pink from the juices of the meat. "Mister Holmes," he said, presenting the carving knife and fork to his employer. "I'll bring the rest."

"Very good," said Mycroft Holmes. "Oh, and Tyers—will you be good enough to find out if the Prince finds the club to his liking when you're finished serving?"

I had to work not to appear stunned. How could Mycroft Holmes be so lax? It was feasible that he was laying a trap, of course, but why should he want to trap the Chief Inspector? Was there someone among his men who might be dealing with the Brotherhood or one of the more obstreperous Irish groups? Much as I was inclined to doubt it, I could not wholly rule out the possibility.

Tyers offered no change of expression. "Of course, sir," he said, continuing to look after our wants, his demeanor correct to a fault. Only when he was done did he bow slightly. "I will take a few minutes to cross the street, if that is suitable?"

"Fine, fine," said Mycroft Holmes, waving Tyers away as if dismissing a dairyman or some other menial; I had to resist the urge to bristle on Tyers' behalf.

As Tyers withdrew, Chief Inspector Somerford looked aslant at Mycroft Holmes, his expression bordering on smug. "Been with you a long time, has he?"

"Oh, years and years and years," said Holmes making this truth sound as if he were used to enjoying Tyers' excellent service without question. "Fine sort of fellow, in his way."

This time my effort to keep silent was nearly impossible. I could feel heat mount in my face as I remarked, as coolly as I could, "He's proven his loyalty on more than one occasion."

"As well he should," said the Chief Inspector, unimpressed. "It is his duty."

Mycroft Holmes was busy slicing the rack and putting our portions onto our plates, so he did not say anything at first. When all the meat was distributed, he said, "But so many are lacking in duty in these days, Chief Inspector. Think of how many men of Tyers' position have run off to America rather than fulfill their obligations. They do not go to India or Australia or even Canada, for fear they might have to answer the call of duty if they remain within the embrace of the Empire. So they go to where the raff-and-scaff go. Not that for Tyers. Nor for Guthrie."

I had to struggle not to stare. "At least in America a man may make his way on ability and industry, not by rank or privilege." I spoke in response to a slight, subtle pressure on my toe from Mister Holmes' shoe.

At that Mister Holmes chuckled. "You must forgive Guthrie, Chief Inspector. He has a tendency to leap to the defense of any he thinks may be downtrodden, and he has a high opinion of American principles. A very strong, egalitarian spirit wells in his bosom." He smirked, looking from me to Chief Inspector Somerford. "We have debated this issue time out of mind but he will not relinquish his commitment. You, having been there, may be able to show him his folly. I may doubt his basis for support of such sentiments, but I do admire his tenacity."

Chief Inspector Somerford took a long draught of water before he spoke. "You are a most tolerant man, Mister Holmes. Few men of your position would be willing to employ anyone whose opinions were so different from his own."

"Yes. Well, he is very good at languages. His German is excellent and his French is impeccable. I will put up with a deal of disagreement for such skills as Guthrie has." He poured wine for himself and absentmindedly filled the Chief Inspector's glass as well.

"And Swedish? Has he learned Swedish?" Chief Inspector Somerford drank in the same mildly distracted manner that Mycroft Holmes had poured.

"A little," was Holmes' reply as he made a small gesture to me to keep quiet. "In time, if we have more negotiations with the Swedes and Norwegians, it may be necessary for him to increase his vocabulary. For now, he knows enough to know when the translators are not being accurate, which is useful."

I hated being spoken of as if I were not in the room, so it was an effort for me not to protest; I knew my employer was up to something, though I could not guess why he wanted to create a trap for Chief Inspector Somerford. I had seen Mycroft Holmes pose successfully as a Turk, as a Frenchman, and as a Hungarian, but never in Turkey, France, or Hungary, and, I thought with a certain furious delight, I had seen him attempt to play Shakespeare. I managed to curb my rising indignation and attempted to suit my responses to the subtle clues I was receiving from Holmes as part of this outlandish portrayal. This current impersonation seemed more difficult since he and Chief Inspector Somerford were English and in the heart of London; as irritating as I found his behavior, I knew better than to question it. I began to cut my lamb, although I had no appetite now, nor any likelihood of having mine restored at any time soon.

Chief Inspector Somerford laughed aloud. "I've thought for some time that would be a problem for diplomats. Having someone like Guthrie there would be an edge?" He sipped his wine again; Mycroft Holmes topped off the glass before he put the decanter aside and went to work on his meat.

I recalled there were side-dishes still to be served; had we been dining alone, I would have gone to the kitchen to fetch them myself. Given Mycroft Holmes' performance tonight, I thought better of it. "Mister Holmes," I said a bit stiffly, "when Tyers returns, let us hope that he will finish providing our food."

"Not so equal when you want your dinner, are you?" Chief Inspector Somerford said, smiling a bit.

The laughter with which Mycroft Holmes greeted his witticism was far more than the remark deserved. I stared down at my plate, hoping to control my temper, for much as I knew that my employer was egging Somerford on, I was unable to keep from feeling much stung by the ungenerous remarks made. "I shall do the work myself," I announced and rose to go to the kitchen just as Tyers came back into the flat.

"Beg pardon, sir," he said in an undervoice to me, then, more loudly, "I'm sorry to have taken so long."

"It's all one to me," I answered, and returned to my seat at the table.

"So you're back," said Mycroft Holmes as Tyers came into the parlor. "How is everything over the way?"

"It's all in place," said Tyers. He bowed again and went to get the side-dishes.

"So you've put Prince Oscar in your club," said the Chief Inspector, lifting his glass in a mocking toast. "Under guard?"

"He is protected," said Mycroft Holmes. "Today's incident is one too many for us to face the possibility of another." He shook his head and caught a morsel of lamb on his fork. "It would be worse than an embarrassment to have him harmed now, in any way."

"What do your fellow members think of having him there?" Somerford asked.

"Each has his opinion, no doubt," Mycroft Holmes replied with strong indifference. "I do not suppose that a single night can be intolerable."

"So they were not all for it?" The Chief Inspector managed a lopsided smile; I realized he had told the truth—he had no head for wine.

"Who would expect them to be? Few of the members like to have attention—any attention—drawn to them, even to the extent of having special guards posted to protect His Highness." Mycroft Holmes sighed. "But these men, like London's criminals, are patriots and are willing to act to aid the country in this time of need."

"Commendable," said Chief Inspector Somerford. "Loyalty of that sort is rare." He finished the wine Mister Holmes had poured for him; his remark was directed at me. "You don't see much of it in America."

"With such diversity, how could you have it?" Holmes asked with a derisive turn of his lip. "They are energetic and hardworking, but their lack of tradition is a stumbling block that may yet prove insurmountable." Of all the remarks I had heard him make about America over the years, he had never before expressed himself in so pretentious a manner in regard to that country. He looked up as Tyers returned with our side-dishes. "Very good. We'll have our port and cheese in the study."

"As you wish, sir," said Tyers, more like a mannequin than I would have thought possible. He bowed and left us alone.

I looked over at Mycroft Holmes as he helped himself to the buttered turnips while he nodded to the green peas in cheddar sauce, saying, "Have some, Chief Inspector."

"Glad to," muttered Somerford as he struggled to spoon out some of the green-and-gold onto his plate. He fumbled and dropped a couple of the cheese-slathered peas. "Sorry. Shouldn't have done that?"

"No trouble. The cloth is going to the laundry tomorrow in any case." Mister Holmes took the peas away from him and added some to his plate. "Guthrie, have the turnips and pass them on, there's a good lad."

I did as I was told, though I knew I would not eat half of what I served myself. If I had been more at ease, I might have enjoyed the peas, but I could not make myself like turnips and never had done so.

"Odd eyes you have, Guthrie?" said Chief Inspector Somerford.

"So I have been told," I said in my most neutral tone.

"One blue and one green? Don't see that often." He used his fork to push the peas up against a piece of roll. "A hundred years ago they might have thought you a witch for having such eyes."

"Some parts of the world still do," I said. "And woe betide those who have strange eyes, or scars, or birthmarks."

"True enough, true enough," said Mycroft Holmes, indicating he wanted to get away from this digression as quickly as possible. "Tell me, Chief Inspector, are you hopeful that we will identify the shooter any time soon?"

"I would like to do so, certainly?" he replied, doing his best to become serious once more. "But in matters of this sort, one must assume something more than simple aggravation is at work." He shook his head. "I would not doubt that we will have clues aplenty by tomorrow, but which among them will be worth pursuing, who can tell?" He sighed. "These are dangerous times we are living in, Mister Holmes, make no doubt about it."

"That's true, and the danger is many-faceted," Mycroft Holmes opined.

"I must agree with you," said the Chief Inspector. "One has to do so many difficult things?"

I recalled what he had told me about the police spy, and I very nearly forgave him his snobbery. I could not imagine what a shock such a discovery would be, let alone the obligation he must now feel to his dead associate. "And today has been more difficult than most," I said, hoping to convey sympathy to the man.

"And tomorrow won't be any easier," said the Chief Inspector, his tone bleak. "There is so much at stake?"

"Isn't there just?" said Mycroft Holmes, his profound grey eyes filled with determination and unfathomable apprehension.

Watching him, I felt as a swimmer must who has gone out into the sea beyond his strength to return.

FROM THE PERSONAL JOURNAL OF PHILIP TYERS

The Chief Inspector left half an hour before Sutton arrived. The CI was still feeling his wine, but had passed from the most inebriated state to truculent recovery. He was surly to the jarvy who picked him up. By the time Sutton came, I had had time to clear away the things in the parlor and ready the flat for a night of work. The sitting room has been turned into the center of activity for the late hours. G has been trying to persuade MH to reveal his purpose in goading CI Somerford more than once with remarks so far from his true character and convictions that G has gone from being perplexed to annoyance at MH's continuing refusal to explain his intentions.

Arrangements have been made with the Admiralty to have the courier deliver tomorrow's dispatches to MH's club across the street, another ploy that has made G exasperated, and who can blame him for this?

A formal message sent round from the Palace and the PM informs MH that the Swedish Ambassador declines, for diplomatic reasons, to make the safety of Prince Oscar his responsibility. He has reminded the government that his country was assured of Prince Oscar's safety and therefore entrusted His Highness to the British Crown and people, and will hold both accountable if any harm should come to the Prince during his stay. MH was less distressed by this communication than I supposed he might be. All he said was, "Damned Cecil," and went about his business.

Chapter Five

EDMUND SUTTON FLOURISHED a bow to the applause that Mycroft Holmes and I offered for his stirring recitation of an amalgam of Hialmar's speeches from the third act of Ibsen's *The Wild Duck*. "It's a good part—a bit over-blown in its way, but—" He shrugged, relinquishing his posture and appearance of Hialmar and becoming Edmund Sutton once again. "It was a good run, but I was growing weary of it, and all the carping from Irving."

"Very good, very good, very good; I don't know how you do it, turning into someone else, but I am damned grateful." Mycroft Holmes approved. "As always, I am astonished that you are not renowned for your talent, but appreciative for the same, since if you were as recognized as you deserve to be, I would not have you as my double."

"And you would never have had to play Macbeth in my stead," Sutton reminded him with a faint smile.

"That only confirms my point," said Mycroft Holmes.

"My first and last great lead." Sutton laughed aloud as the clock struck the half hour. "There are compensations everywhere, aren't there?" He sat down in the high-backed chair next to our employer's, his face settling into a youthful version of Holmes' habitual expression. "I am a fortunate fellow. Thanks to you"—he nodded to Mycroft Holmes—"I am well-paid and need not take roles simply to keep the wolf from my door; I may venture into new plays that have not yet reached popular acceptance, and I can commit myself to revivals of forgotten works. If this condemns me to remain a character actor, then well and good. There are many wonderful roles I can play in that capacity. I will be glad that my abilities have done more good than entertained a full house for three hours of an evening."

"Your dedication undoes me," said Mycroft Holmes with such an appearance of humility that I was surprised. "Truly it does."

"Nothing like that," said Sutton. "I chose my way, and I have no regrets." He slapped the arms of his chair. "So what is this urgent business you mentioned in your note?"

"I will need you to go round to the Admiralty for me tomorrow, and to maintain my schedule for the next several days." Holmes coughed decorously. "I believe Guthrie and I will be out of town for a short while, and it is most essential that no one learn of it."

"But including the Admiralty—you rarely do that," said Sutton, rubbing his chin in the same way Mycroft Holmes did when he was struggling with a problem.

"In this instance I must," said Mister Holmes, glancing in my direction. "Since Guthrie will be gone with me."

I started, although by now I should have been accustomed to these abrupt announcements. I began to realize that I was learning why he had been singing in the bath. "We're not accompanying the Prince, are we?" I could not stop myself exclaiming.

"As far as Scotland," said Mycroft Holmes as if it were the most obvious thing in the world.

"Scotland? Are you serious?" My own native burr grew stronger just speaking the word. "My God, why? More to the point—how?"

"By rail?" Edmund Sutton guessed.

"But you have been saying by sea!" I blurted out at the same instant. Instantly the recent headlines of the great train race came to mind: Holmes had disappeared twice during those record-setting runs. At the time I had thought my employer was off making the first steps toward some new treaty. Eventually I had learned otherwise—Mycroft Holmes had gone to Scotland for reasons of his own: the trains to Edinburgh were the cutting edge of engineering. Some were said to have achieved speeds over one hundred miles per hour, an astonishing and frightening prospect. The speed had fascinated Holmes, for he perceived at once the strategic implications of such rapid transport, and he had determined to assess its potential for himself. He told me upon his return that a train could reach Edinburgh in half the time of any steamship. "By rail," I repeated less confused and more intrigued.

"Surely, my dear Guthrie, you recognized that for the stratagem it was." He cocked his head in Sutton's direction, and I was struck again at how much alike they could look, Sutton seeming a younger, paler version of Mister Holmes. In the near-decade that I had known him, I had seen the first signs of age settle on Sutton's features, making his resemblance to Mycroft Holmes more marked than when we first met in June of 1887.

"I supposed it must be," I said, "but if it is, why do you begin with the police? There must be better means of establishing false leads than through the police."

"The building from which the assassin took aim had been searched by police," Mycroft Homes reminded me. "Therefore I must presume that someone within the police is connected to the assassin, someone in a position of importance."

I nodded twice as the full import of what he had said was borne in on me. "But the police being involved in something so heinous—" I stopped again, recalling Constantinople. "Well, not *British* police."

"Your fealty does you great credit, my boy, but you cannot afford such admirable sentiments in this instance. Or in many others. The Brotherhood is only one of many enemies of Britain we must be wary of. You know that once the guards are corrupt the castle is doomed." He reached for his port.

"Consider *Lear,*" Sutton recommended, quite confusing me, for

I could not comprehend his intention in this context. "Well, he gave power to the dishonest daughters because they seemed more sincere than the unvarnished affection of his true one."

"Not an unapt analogy in its way," said Mycroft Holmes, making his praise as generous as he could. "The police are being diligent and busy, but it may mean nothing. Spencer and Winslowe are still trying to protect themselves ahead of the Prince. We shall see."

"That wasn't all you told the Chief Inspector," I warned him, and was cut off by the loud report of a rifle. I jumped up, already moving before I had realized precisely what had happened. Mycroft Holmes was ahead of me, out the door of the sitting room and into the corridor with a speed and energy that still had the capacity to astonish me.

"Sutton! Stay here! Tyers! Watch the back!" he ordered sharply, as he reached for his topcoat. "Guthrie, do you have your pistol?"

"In my topcoat pocket," I assured him as I grabbed for the garment as Mycroft Holmes flung open the front door and surged out onto the landing, as I hurried after him, pulling my coat on as we pelted down the stairs to the street where half a dozen uniformed policemen had gathered around the front of the Diogenes Club, two with pistols in their hands—a rare enough sight in the stews of Soho, but absolutely unheard of in Pall Mall. As it was starting to mizzle, the streetlights looked fuzzy and the pavement shone. As we rushed across the street, a naval commander appeared in the door of the Diogenes Club, his hands slightly raised to show he was unarmed and not the prey these police sought.

Mycroft Holmes hurried up to Commander George Winslowe, taking an instant to let the nearest constable declare he was not dangerous, a sentiment I knew was open to question. "Commander," said Holmes in authoritative accents, "where did the shot come from?" I remained near the invisible line established by the constables while my employer issued his first orders.

The Commander pointed across the street to the building two doors down from the one where Mycroft Holmes kept his flat. "The roof, I should think."

"You constables," Mycroft Holmes said sharply to three of the policemen. "Go secure the place. Now."

"Right you are, sir," said the nearest of the three; he motioned to the others to move off with him.

"And you," Mycroft Holmes went on to another of the constables, "find Chief Inspector Somerford as quickly as may be. He must know of this."

Commander Winslowe came down one more step and spoke quietly to Mister Holmes; I could not hear what was said, but I saw Holmes give a grave nod and frown as he did. Then he said something quietly to the Commander before calling out, "Guthrie. Follow the constables, if you will. I want to be sure nothing happens to any evidence they may come upon."

I wanted to remark I should have gone with them from the first, but this was not the time to question him. "Very good, sir," I said, and hurried off in the direction the constables had taken. When I glanced back over my shoulder I saw Mycroft Holmes and Commander Winslowe go up the steps and into the Diogenes Club, the constables stationed close to the steps in anticipation of the arrival of other authorities.

As I reached the building in question, the doors of the flat at the ground floor opened and a red-faced man in robe and sleeping cap stepped indignantly out. "What in the name of all that's merciful is going on?"

"That is what the police are trying to determine," I said, prepared to start up the stairs.

"Shooting!" the man expostulated. "In Pall Mall!"

"Yes. It is shocking," I said, hoping that concurrence would keep him from trying to detain me.

"Something must be done," he insisted.

"That is our intention," I said, already three steps up. "Please go back inside and lock your doors. We haven't yet apprehended the criminal."

That was sufficient to send the fellow back within doors; I heard the bolt of his lock snick home before I reached the landing at the first floor. Running up the stairs increased the ache in my hip, but not so much that I was unable to continue my climb, and speedily. I passed it and the second floor without incident and arrived on the roof to find the three constables using bull's-eye lanterns to inspect the roof. One of them heard me approach and swung around, the beam of the lantern catching me full in the eyes and dazzling me.

"Who's this, then?" one of the constables demanded. "This is a police investigation. Be about your business."

"I'm afraid this is my business," I said. "I am Mycroft Holmes' confidential secretary. You saw me with him down on the street."

Another of the constables said, "That's right, Daniel. He came down with Mister Holmes, all right."

The blinding light swung away from my face. I blinked, but spangles, like echoes, distorted my vision. "Have you found anything?" I asked as I groped my way forward, trying to peer through the blobs of glowing purple obscuring my vision.

"It's possible," said the constable who had identified me. "Here at the edge of the roof, there appears to be a new groove cut. Nice, clean work. Done in a single stroke, I should think," he went on as he turned his lantern on the place he was describing.

I could not yet see clearly, but I could make out the place the beams of the lanterns were turned well enough to know it was like the groove I had seen on the roof above St. Paul's. I squatted down to inspect it more carefully, and squinted to keep my sight as sharp as possible. A curved chisel had cut the groove, and as the constable had said, in a single pass. I touched it lightly, as if some secret to the identity of the assassin might linger in the groove. Nothing. "Did you find anything else?"

"Not yet," said the first constable. "I would have mentioned it right off."

"Well, if you do, make sure I am informed at once," I said as I rose to my feet. "You and your men will need to check the stairs and the rear entrance to the building to ascertain if anyone has seen or heard anything. If our shooter has left something behind, we should know of it." I thought of the shell-casing, and hoped we would be fortunate enough to find another such clue to link the two events beyond cavil.

The constable called Daniel came up to me. "You should tell Mister Holmes that there is something damned wrong about all this. They're saying us coppers haven't done our job proper, but that's a lie." He sounded resentful, which I supposed I would be in his position, with my own force facing the chance of implication in these crimes.

"True enough," said his other colleague, who had been silent until that moment. "The rumors are that the police helped the bastard take a shot at the Swedish Prince, but it's not true."

"There are all sorts of rumors about," I said, in the hope it would quiet their indignation sufficiently for us to get some work done. "I have heard that the Russians were behind it or the Turks." This was not entirely accurate, but I had some experience of rumors, and I knew that it would not be long before someone made these claims, if that had not happened already.

"They're saying the Austrians had a hand in it; at least that's what I heard at the pub this evening," the first constable said, taking my meaning to heart. "They could have done it, couldn't they? They're not over-fond of the Swedes."

"Well, someone did," I replied. "And it is up to us to find out who that is. We can leave it to longer heads than ours to find out why." I bent to look at the groove one last time—the rawness of the scar was already being obliterated by the soft rain. I could feel the drops of water on my face and I knew we would have to get brollies or indoors very shortly if we were not to be soaked.

"Very good, sir. We'll secure the roof and set a guard at the access so no one can come up later. That'll keep the scaff-and-raff away." The first constable shone his lantern in the direction of the roof-door. "If you want to go ahead of us?"

Although I doubted many scaff-and-raff would find their way to Pall Mall, I applauded their efforts. "Of course; you must do. Thanks. Good of you," I said, as if these men had overheard the discussion between the Chief Inspector and my employer and I was left with the work of making amends on their behalf.

Daniel shook his head. "Very cool, this cove. Very cool indeed." He took a last glance back at the roof and the increasing fall of rain. "Too bad the weather didn't change an hour earlier."

"It is a very wet night," one of the others said. "It'll be wetter before morning."

My hip confirmed it, the small sliver of metal imbedded in bone throbbing like a sore tooth. I did not bother to limp—the ache was constant no matter how I walked or sat. "We'll have rain for two or three days," I remarked.

"It's spring," Daniel protested as we closed and secured the lock on the door. "The rain will slack off."

"Not for two days," I said, disliking this dispute I was being dragged into as the result of my own folly. "But nothing we say will change it," I went on in a less belligerent tone.

"That's the God's own truth," said the first constable. "Do you, Childes, stay here. You'll be relieved at dawn. No unauthorized person in or out, not even if he lives in the building. Is that clear?"

"It surely is," said Childes, taking up his post with a self-conscious care that made me wonder how long he had been on the police force.

We began to make our way down the stairs, our footsteps echoing in the stairwell, magnifying the sound until it seemed a regiment might be descending instead of three tired men. What troubled me was how totally the sound covered any other noise. If the assassin were in the building, he might be doing anything and we would not hear it.

As we reached the ground floor, the first constable came up to me and saluted smartly. "Tell your Mister Holmes that he'll have my report on his desk by noon. I'll make a copy for Chief Inspector Somerford as well." He was about to turn when I stopped him.

"I'll be proud to do that, Constable, but it would mean more if I knew your name." I waited for his response.

He laughed. "How lax of me. Of course. I am Constable Desmond Bernard; Mister Holmes will know the name." Touching the edge of his helmet with two fingers, he turned smartly but without military exactness and went toward the door and the rain beyond. Daniel trailed along behind him.

I watched him go, doing my best not to feel too uneasy about leaving this place with only one constable to guard it. No doubt my employer would know whether or not a second guard was needed. I hitched up my coat and brought it over my head enough to keep me somewhat dry; then I bolted from the building and made my short way down the street to the building where Mycroft Holmes had his flat. As I went, I saw the number of men posted at or near the Diogenes Club had increased to nine.

Sutton opened the door to my knock. "Come in, Guthrie," he said, sounding very much like our mutual employer. "Mister Holmes will be back shortly. He sent a messenger to Tyers about ten minutes ago. Tyers has left on an errand and will return shortly."

"Perhaps I should go down again," I suggested, not wanting to leave the flat again until I went to my own rooms in Curzon Street.

"Mister Holmes would like you to stay here. He asks you to prepare a report on what you observed on the roof and to organize any other accounts that might be presented tonight." He had set the lock once more and was gesturing in the direction of the study. "You'll want to take off that wet coat and warm yourself."

"So I might," I agreed, glad to be persuaded to do the very thing I wished most to do. I handed my coat to Sutton and went into the study. I plopped down on the chair nearest the hearth, letting the warmth from the smoldering logs go over me like the massage of angels' fingers. I had not realized until that moment how cold and wet I was.

"There's brandy," said Sutton, indicating the fine old bottle on the table near the shuttered window. "Have some. It will warm you."

He poured a finger into one of the snifters and handed it to me. "Go on. Take it."

Ordinarily I would have refused, but the events of the day, compounded by the alarums of the night, had left me jangled. I took the snifter with a grateful nod. "I doubt my hands will warm it much," I said in feeble jest as I gave the liquid a swirl in the snifter.

"When Mister Holmes returns, you can switch over to tea." Edmund Sutton gestured extravagantly, as if to have the movement carry all the way to the balcony. "It should not be much longer. He said he would not be long."

I nodded, remarking, "It's late," before I allowed myself a bit of the brandy.

"After one," he agreed before he splashed brandy into a second snifter for himself. "Sometimes I miss touring," he said just to fill the silence, which actors abhor. "Those four years I and my company roamed about the Midlands doing Molière and Shakespeare and Ibsen and Sheridan and all the rest, they were wonderful. We went as far as north as Northumberland, and as far south as Oxford and Saint Albans, going up and down and across on trains, our scenery and costumes riding with us in the baggage car; we were this century's version of strolling players, perpetually on tour. We kept to a strict schedule. Five performances a week, with a matinee on Market Day, whichever day it was in that town. Traveling on Sunday, dark on Monday while we set up for Tuesday night." He sighed. "There's no substitute for it. Not if you want to make the most of your talent."

"Did you like the Midlands?" I asked to show I was listening.

"Well enough. There was plenty to sketch; I'll say that for the place. Kept my eye sharp and my hand steady." He grinned, looking now like a slightly over-age university student. "I learned thirty-seven roles in those four years. We did six plays a year, and in a few I played more than one role."

"Was that difficult?" I asked, having had to sustain a persona other than my own while engaged in doing the work Mycroft Holmes required of me.

"Not usually, though in one or two instances, it was." He was standing beside the fireplace, one arm resting on the marble mantle, the other holding the snifter with elegant nonchalance. "We were doing *She Stoops to Conquer,* and my change between roles required a skin-out new costume and completely redone make-up. It was always a rush." He looked up as the sound of the knocker reverberated through the flat. "Excuse me," said Sutton, abandoning his superior pose and going to answer the door. He reappeared almost at once, looking mildly shocked. "Mister Guthrie, you're needed below."

I sat upright, aware from the tone of his voice that something was amiss. I set my snifter aside and went to retrieve my coat. "Do you know what the matter is?" I asked as I pulled on the sodden garment that now seemed intolerably clammy.

"No. But the note is from Mister Holmes and it is urgent." He handed the paper, clearly torn from a notebook, with my employer's familiar, spiky scrawl angled across the half-sheet of paper: "Sutton, Send Guthrie down at once. Secure the flat against our return. MH."

"Not much information," I remarked as I prepared to leave.

"Secrecy may be paramount," Sutton said. "Go on. And watch yourself."

Little as I wanted to, I had to fight off a sudden fear that ran through me. "I shouldn't be long," I said before starting down the stairs. It was raining in earnest now, and the wind had picked up so that the water came at an angle; shortly it was running down the inside of my collar and sliding along my neck and back. The sensation was eerie and unpleasant.

Mycroft Holmes was standing within the line of constables in front of the Diogenes Club, his long, clever face set in a powerful frown. Police Commander George Winslowe and Police Superintendent Roland Spencer were standing in a huddle with him, their demeanor as somber as his. As I came up to them, stopping a respectful five feet and two stairs away, Mister Holmes caught sight of me and waved me closer to the three of them. "I apologize for bringing you out a second time on a night like this, but we must speak with these two men."

"Of course," I said, wondering if I still had my notebook and pencil in my inner waistcoat pocket.

"Nothing written down," Mister Holmes said sharply as if discerning my thoughts. "We have agreed upon a solution to our problem. It is a difficult one, but it has the greatest chance of success." He sighed heavily. "I will have to call upon the men in question." He lowered his voice still more. "Two of the Directors belong to this club. I have no apprehension about them. But the rest . . . well, the PM must add his weight to our petition if we are to succeed."

"Shall you need me on this errand?" I asked.

"I don't know yet. Besides, that is hours away." He dismissed it with an impatient wave of his hand. "What we must settle is far more urgent. Guthrie, what did you find on the roof?"

I knew what he wanted. "The same kind of chisel cut as was on the building by Saint Paul's. Properly cut in a single, practiced blow so that the groove is utterly smooth. Recent enough that the wood was raw with the mark. If there had been more light or it had not come on to rain, we might have found more; but as it was, neither the policemen nor I were able to discern anything remarkable other than that groove. I managed a cursory measurement, and it appeared to have been the same size as the other, although I could not swear to it absolutely." All three were listening closely. When I completed my brief account, I added, "For the moment, I must suppose both shots were fired by the same man."

Commander Winslowe spoke first. "You have no doubts? The groove could not have been caused in some other way? Could it not be older than you reckon?"

"Well, if it is, Commander," I replied, "then we must suppose the assassin has been practicing here, readying himself for yesterday's attempt on Prince Oscar's life. Or something more dire." I indicated the Diogenes Club door. "Many illustrious men pass these portals. Their loss would be disastrous."

Superintendent Spencer endorsed my concern. "That very thought had crossed my mind. What if the assassin knew nothing about Prince Oscar and was seeking instead to kill one or more of the members? It is always possible, Mister Holmes, that his target was not the Prince at all, but you."

I had a quick, nasty recollection of the footman's blood spattering on me, and recalled that Mycroft Holmes was only a few steps away from me. "I believe we should factor such a potential into our plans."

Mister Holmes, who had been silent until now, spoke in a low rumble. "You may do as you must, but our first purpose must be to protect and preserve Prince Oscar, for his death at this crucial time could shift the whole of Scandinavia to Germany, and we would be at a disadvantage, should that be allowed to happen. Put your energies there, gentlemen. Guthrie and I know how to look out for ourselves." He glanced at me again. "The roof is guarded?"

I pointed to the building in question. "A constable is posted inside the door to the roof and the door itself is locked."

Superintendent Spencer heard this with slight approval. "Somerford's men, no doubt. He feels the attempt on the Prince's life—if that is what it was—keenly. Very dedicated fellow. How did your discussion with him go, Holmes?"

"Well enough," my employer answered; his manner told me he was holding something back.

Commander Winslowe, already straight, stood a little straighter. "We will depart at noon, according to plan. We have found a young ensign who resembles the Prince enough for casual observation, and he is willing to embark for Belgium and thence to Stockholm, with a small naval escort. He knows the perils of this undertaking, but he is willing to do it." His face looked a bit ruddier in the lampshine, but that might have been from the rain on his face.

"Good man," Mycroft Holmes approved. "We will hope that the men I must persuade will agree to our plan." He held up a finger. "Do not discuss this with anyone not directly involved. If you do not have to include him, do not. Err on the side of caution, gentlemen. For tomorrow—or today, isn't it?—*bon chance*." He nodded at the two then said to me. "Come, Guthrie. We have much to do before dawn." With that he turned away and trod across the slippery cobblestones in long, steady strides.

I went after him rather more carefully. I caught up with him on the sidewalk. "If you are sending a double to Stockholm in Prince Oscar's stead, where are you taking the Prince? Has there been a change of plans in his destination? Other than somewhere by rail?"

"All in good time, Guthrie," said Mycroft Holmes as he made his way up to the first floor, pausing there before going on. "Is Tyers back yet?"

"Not when I came down. He may have returned since. Where has he been?" I asked before I could stop myself as we began to climb once more. I was cold enough to begin to shiver, and it was an effort to keep my teeth from chattering in the treacherous spring storm.

"Why, with the Prince, of course," said Mycroft Holmes with a smile any Cheshire Cat would envy. "He had one other message to deliver, but after that he has been with Prince Oscar."

"Who is where?" I demanded in a tone I would have never used to my employer even a year ago.

Mycroft Holmes stopped before using his own knocker. "Why, Guthrie, my dear boy, I thought you had surmised it all: Prince Oscar is in Baker Street at my brother's flat—where else should he be as safe as there?"

FROM THE PERSONAL JOURNAL OF PHILIP TYERS

Spent an hour in Baker Street with Prince and when I complete this entry I will make a full report for MH. The Prince is not discouraged, although he is upset about the footman. Another man, less rigorously trained, might become overwhelmed by these events, but Prince Oscar is made of sterner stuff, as indeed all royals must be.

CI Somerford was not available to take the memorandum MH prepared for him, but judging the state in which he departed, and the engagement he spoke of, I am neither surprised nor anxious in his regard. . . .

The Swedish Ambassador has declined MH's request for an interview.

Chapter Six

THREE MUFFLED CHIMES marked the hour as Mycroft Holmes looked down at the maps spread out on the study table. "Gentlemen, it is late and yesterday was eventful." He stretched, joints cracking audibly. "Time to get some sleep. Guthrie, you need not return until eight. I need you rested and fresh."

"Much appreciated, sir," I said, rising from my chair and preparing to depart.

"Dress for a formal business meeting." It was an order; he and I both knew it.

"That I will. Thank you, sir," I said from the doorway.

"Very good," said Mycroft Holmes as he bent over the sheets of paper with their endless scrawling. "I'll need you to copy these when you first arrive, while I breakfast. Make sure you allow enough time to do it well."

"Certainly, sir," I said, trying to decide if I should come half an hour earlier; Mycroft Holmes' specific instructions in regard to the hour made me decide that I had better arrive at the time he stipulated or risk interfering with some other aspect of his plans. As I reached for my coat, which was only slightly less damp than the last time I had worn it, I said, "Do you know where I might flag a cab? With the police about—"

"The Admiralty should have a trap across the street, not elegant but utilitarian enough to serve." He yawned. "Our trials are not yet over, my lad. I rely on you to continue your splendid efforts."

"I'll do my best, sir," I told him as I let myself out of the flat. Descending the stairs, I thought of Tyers, who would be up before six, which now seemed barely half an hour away. As I stepped onto the pavement, I saw the trap waiting in the service alley beside the Diogenes Club, a fellow in a heavy naval cloak sitting on the driving box. I waved to him as I crossed the street and noticed four constables emerging from their posts in the shadows. "Mycroft Holmes tells me you'll drive me to Curzon Street," I called out, a bit too loudly to be polite at this hour.

"Yes. I know about you," said the driver from the depths of his muffler and cloak; his voice, I supposed, was gruff from waiting in this inclement weather.

Climbing into the trap, I thought, but for the voice, he might have been anyone under that mass of clothing—he might have been a bear. "Sorry to keep you up so late."

"Nothing to worry about," he responded, and gave his chestnut the office.

I sat still for the journey, trying to find some obvious flaw in Mycroft Holmes' plans; he had taught me to do this almost eight years ago and I continued the practice ever since. I was too worn out to think clearly, so most of the exercise was in vain, but at least it kept me awake until we reached Curzon Street. As I got out of the trap, I managed to thank the driver.

"Duty, sir," he explained. "Your usual driver will fetch you tomorrow morning." With that he kissed the air noisily and his chestnut walked on.

I made my way up to my rooms and all but staggered to my bed. Fatigue had made my muscles taut from my long hours of forcing myself to remain awake and attentive. As I undressed my hands trembled, a sure sign I was past my limit. Once my clothes were hung up, I found my nightshirt, drew it on, washed my face and toweled my hair and then got into bed, certain I would not relax enough to fall asleep for some time. I heard the clock in the parlor beneath me ring the half hour, but nothing more until an urgent pounding on my door brought me awake just as the night sky was beginning to lighten with the promise of dawn. I must have been dreaming, for I was momentarily disoriented, my thoughts back in Bavaria that was also Constantinople, and the members of the Brotherhood were preparing to burn down the Houses of Parliament, which was also in this fantastical dream-landscape.

"Mister Guthrie!" I recognized the voice of Mycroft Holmes' jarvey. I flung back the blankets and rushed to the door, imagining the worst had happened. I unlocked the door and pulled it open so quickly that I nearly overbalanced Sid Hastings as he strove to rouse me.

"Sid!" I exclaimed. "What is the matter?"

"Mister Holmes wants you at once," he declared in a tone that did not encourage dawdling, or many questions.

"I'll get dressed," I promised him, making an effort to open my armoire to retrieve my clothes. "What time is it?" I had not intended to ask, knowing whatever he told me, I would dislike his answer. I felt groggy and faintly dizzy, a sure sign I had not slept enough to relieve my fatigue.

"It's gone half-five, sir. Sun'll be up in a couple of ticks." He turned around so I could get out of my nightshirt without embarrassment.

I poured water from the ewer to the basin and managed a cursory wash before I began to shave, doing the work by touch more than anything my mirror revealed. It was moments like this one that made me long for a burnoose and a beard. I ended up nicking myself once, but got the job done and then pulled on my singlet and my shirt over that. Remembering Mister Holmes' admonition from the night before, I chose clothes a thought more formal than those I usually wore to work. As I fixed my collar in place, I noticed the room brighten as the clouds in the east became luminous; Sid had been right about the sun. I finished dressing more handily now that I could see what I was doing, trousers on before socks and shoes. In less than four minutes I had my tie in place and my waistcoat buttoned. I pulled on my jacket, and swung around to Sid. "All right. I'm ready," I told him.

"Then let's be about it," said Sid, holding my door for me, and waiting on the landing while I secured the lock.

The streets were far from empty at this early hour; delivery wagons and vans made their way with everything from milk and cheese to live chickens and fresh fish. I wrapped myself in the rug Sid provided, hoping to preserve my collar and tie from the weather, but not at all certain I had taken sufficient precautions. The rain had slacked off but the morning was dampish, and the paving was slicked with mud, spattering as wheels went through it. The pace everywhere was urgent so that the brisk pace Sid Hastings set was not noticeable amongst the rest of the vehicles. As we drew up in front of Mycroft Holmes' building, I saw the clutch of constables had moved from the door of the Diogenes Club to the front of the building from where the assassin had shot. Puzzled, I remarked on this as Sid let the steps down for me.

"Sad, that is," he said, his Cockney accent making the words more brusk than they already were. As I stepped free of his cab, he touched the brim of his hat and moved away toward Charles II Street, where he would wait for my employer to send for him.

Knowing that something had gone very wrong, I hastened up the stairs to Mycroft Holmes' flat on the top floor, my imagination working faster than my feet. Only the knowledge that Prince Oscar was safe in Baker Street kept me from losing heart. Trying to overcome the residue of sleep that held me, I rapped on the door with my knuckles and two breaths later was admitted to the flat by Tyers, who looked fresh enough but for the circles under his eyes. His clothing was impeccable and he greeted me as if this were a usual morning. "Good morning, Tyers," I said as I stepped inside. I saw that it was just after six, and trusted I had been timely enough to suit my employer.

"And to you, Mister Guthrie," said Tyers in unflappable calm.

"Mister Holmes—" I pointed to the corridor.

"—is in the study. He's expecting you," said Tyers as he secured the front door once again.

I left my topcoat on the rack behind the door and went along to the study. I rapped on the door, which was ajar, and said, "Mister Holmes—"

"Do come in, Guthrie, dear boy," he called out from within. "We're about to have some tea and scones. Heaven knows we need something." He was standing near the fire, dressed as if for a day at the Admiralty. His features looked glum, making him appear older than his fifty-three years.

Sitting beside him, Edmund Sutton seemed as always a paler, younger echo of him. "It's too bad," he said, as if I had not yet discerned this.

"It's damnable," said Mycroft Holmes. "It is also most . . . appalling."

"Dear God," I exclaimed, horrible possibilities forming a catastrophic parade in my thoughts. Surely there had not been an assassination at the Diogenes Club? Had some important member been shot? Had there been—I made myself stop. "Tell me."

"The constable—Childes, his name was—guarding the roof where the assassin waited was found murdered this morning." Holmes sighed heavily. "He was shot at close range, high in the back. There is no sign of a struggle."

"It must have been very sudden," I said, shocked to disbelief. I made myself speak the ideas that swarmed my brain. "The devil must have hidden somewhere on the roof, or hung over the side, like Amoud, in Constantinople."

"It rained last night, Guthrie," said Mycroft Holmes quietly.

"Yes?" I spoke more harshly than I had intended.

"He could not have hung over the side of the building. Everything was slick. And the roof was thoroughly searched." He shook his head. "No. Unsettling as it is, we can come to only one conclusion: the constable knew his killer, and trusted him enough to allow him to stand behind him."

It was on the tip of my tongue to say "her," as Penelope Gatspy's lovely countenance filled my mind's eye. I shut such useless thoughts away. "Because he came so close? How close is that?"

"There were burns on the constable's clothes. The killer may have muffled the report with the constable's cloak." He rubbed his eyes with his thumb and forefinger, then pinched the bridge of his nose. "His relief found him at five."

"How long had he been dead?" I was astonished at how quickly I fell into the habits of inquiry Mycroft Holmes himself had taught me. My distress would have to wait or the constable would not be avenged.

"I would say no more than two hours, given the state of the body." He coughed. "I should not have been so sanguine about this whole operation. I have made the mistake of assuming I had assessed the whole, and clearly I have not. I thought because Prince Oscar was safe that we had nothing more to worry about. I hoped we would trap the assassin while delivering the Prince from all harm, and nothing to pay for it." He began to pace, his head sunk down on his chest.

"He's been like this for the past hour," said Sutton, sympathy and exasperation nicely mixed in his delivery. "Holmes, you couldn't have known you were dealing with a bent copper."

I rarely heard Edmund Sutton use such slang and it struck me all the more because of it. "What does he mean, a 'bent copper'?"

"I think the meaning is obvious," said Mycroft Holmes gravely.

"You think a policeman did this?" I wanted to be more stunned by this supposition than I was.

"Who else?" Mister Holmes asked, his demeanor bleak. "One of the police assigned to this case is in league with the assassin, and—we cannot ignore the possibility, can we?—the Brotherhood." He put the tips of his fingers together and pressed his index fingers to his lower lip.

"Do you have any notion yet? Who is the . . . er . . . bent copper?"

"There are three possibilities that I can see." He was preparing to enumerate his suspects when Tyers arrived with the butler's tray laden with tea, scones, butter, and a brandied fruit compote as well as a few slices of cold, rare sirloin.

As he put this down, he said, "I have a pot of shepherd's cheese warming, and diced potatoes browning with the bacon. They will be ready shortly." He offered a quick smile, handing out plates to each of us. "This will serve as breakfast."

"Excellently," said Edmund Sutton, and turned to Holmes. "Come. You'll feel more the thing when you've had something to eat. You're tired and hungry. Nothing ever puts me so off my performance as being tired and hungry."

Mycroft Holmes was about to shake his head in refusal, then saw the sharp look in Tyers' eyes. "Oh, very well. You're probably right." He came back to his chair and tugged the occasional table around to a more convenient angle. "Tea first. I must wake up and clear my thoughts."

"Very good," said Tyers, beginning to prepare a plate for our employer. Edmund Sutton motioned to me to sit down; I complied at once, and not because I was hungry. When Tyers poured tea for me, he put in sugar but no milk, as I liked it in the morning. "If there is anything more you want?"

"Not just at present, thanks," I said, my attention more on Mycroft Holmes than on Tyers.

"It is a very troubling development," said Mycroft Holmes after his first sip of tea. "I cannot but wonder how deep the rot goes."

"And who can root it out," added Edmund Sutton. "You do not want to trust anyone who might be in the other camp." He took his cup of tea with a nod of acknowledgment.

"Precisely," said Mycroft Holmes, some of his usual purpose returning to his visage.

"You will have to learn who the turncoat is," I said. "If he has accomplices, you will have to unearth them as well."

"Very true, and without putting Prince Oscar at any more risk than we already have," said Mycroft Holmes. "Which means we must have not one but two doubles, sent on two different ships, with two different sets of guards. And it all must be arranged today."

I sat bolt upright so quickly I very nearly overset my tea. "Today? Why today?"

"Because tomorrow, dear boy, you and I and the Prince are leaving for Scotland by rail." He must have read incomprehension in my face, for he chuckled. "Well, what is more sensible? I am going to call upon the Directors of the North Eastern today, to arrange for—"

"The *Flying Scotsman!*" I burst out. "Of *course.*"

"If the Directors of the railroad can be made to agree to a few . . . stipulations. They have accommodated unusual situations before—not often, but often enough to give me hope." He smiled at me, an expression a crocodile might want to imitate.

"Those are the Directors you intend to address," I said, relieved to know his purpose. "You want their support for your plan."

"Bravo, old boy. Astute as always, although I want rather more than that," said Mycroft Holmes. He sipped his tea. "We will have to be very careful what we vouchsafe them."

"Naturally. The Prince's safety is paramount," I said, warming to the whole plan.

"The disadvantage is, of course, if the Brotherhood or any of the other enemies of Britain or Prince Oscar learn of this plan, in which case we all become sitting ducks, as the saying has it." He finished his tea, retreating into thoughtful preparation.

"I'll stay here, to cover," said Edmund Sutton, his assurance welcome though it was obvious. "All day and all night, so that anyone watching will not have reason to think there has been a substitution."

I had another sip of tea. "Just so," I said, having trouble swallowing as the potential dangers were borne in on me. If the police could not be trusted, how were we to maintain the ruse that had been successful for years?

"Cecil has already sent a memorandum," said Mycroft Holmes suddenly. "He reminds me that Prince Oscar's protection is my responsibility, and that the Swedes have washed their hands of the problem. If anything happens to His Highness, then I may present my resignation at once, and Cecil will do the rest." He frowned and looked up toward the ceiling. "Spare me the wiles of politicians."

It was rare for Mycroft Holmes to refer to the Prime Minister by his title, and rarer still by his name. I realized that Holmes was as angry as he was irked by the man's interference. "You will yet have his apology, sir," I said.

"From Robert Arthur Talbot Gascoyne-Cecil, third Marquis of Salisbury?" Holmes asked incredulously. "He would rather have leprosy than apologize—to anyone. Apology is worse than scandal to him, and he abhors the necessity of it; I would have had a better chance with Primrose." His reference to the current Prime Minister's immediate predecessor brought another purse of his lips. "When Cecil has made concessions, he has always exacted a price for it. No, no, Guthrie. Better to get out of this neatly and unnoticed, and hope Cecil forgets about it until he's out of office again."

"Whatever is most appropriate," I said, still mildly disconcerted. The half-hour chimed from the clock in the hall, recalling me to our purpose. "What time is our appointment with the Directors of the North Eastern? Do we have that set?"

"Ten this morning. In the Strangers' Room at the club. It's all settled. We will have it to ourselves until noon. That's all arranged," said Mycroft Holmes as if such an arrangement were obvious.

"Do you intend to have me present?" I asked, aware that this meeting was a most unusual one and possibly intended to be wholly clandestine.

"Certainly, my dear Guthrie. I would not attempt this without you." Holmes was regaining his unflappability before my eyes. "Not only do I want a written record, but a second set of eyes and ears, the better to discern anything and everything that might be amiss."

"Not unlike dealing with the Japanese," I said, "or the Imam."

"Exactly," said Holmes, and poured more tea into his cup, adding three teaspoons of sugar and a bit of milk. "There is so much that is hidden, and that we must conceal. It will take careful going to negotiate these waters." He became more brisk, with stronger intent in every word and action. "Come afternoon, I will have memoranda for you to copy and file; for this morning I have the dreary duty of talking with Super-intendent Spencer and Chief Inspector Somerford about the murdered constable."

"Don't you want me to accompany you?" I asked, startled that he would not want me present.

"Not this time, Guthrie. If our appointment were not so early with the Directors, then I might say otherwise; but as this is largely *pro forma,* by necessity, you will be well-advised to remain here." He rolled one of the slices of sirloin and bit it in half. When he swallowed, he added, "Until we know more about the extent of the corruption in the police, I will say nothing of substance to either of those men."

"You surely don't think they could be involved?" I asked, dis-mayed afresh.

"I think we cannot afford to ignore that possibility no matter how remote it may be. And it is possible that if we reveal too much, one or the other may inadvertently warn the real culprits of our scrutiny." He ate the rest of the roast beef slice and reached for another, rolling it as he had the first. "This will be another long day, my friends. And to-morrow will be more so, if we accomplish our purpose today."

"God willing," said Edmund Sutton.

"Amen," said Mycroft Holmes in such a tone of voice that I could not tell whether or not he was joking. He drank down all his tea and took a scone from the basket.

"Tomorrow?" I said as the full import of it sank in on me. "You do mean to go to Scotland tomorrow?"

"I'd do it today if it could be managed," said Holmes as if this was not an outrageous suggestion. "The longer Prince Oscar remains in London, the greater the chance of his discovery, which none of us want. With two doubles leaving, one this morning, one in the evening, we will, I hope, confuse our enemies long enough to get the Prince aboard the train without exposing him to any more trouble. If we can keep our enemies busy watching the ports here in the South, his de-parture from Scotland should be successful." He looked up as Tyers returned with the potatoes and bacon. "Thank goodness. My last in-dulgence until day's end, I fear."

Sutton poured himself more tea then helped make more room on the butler's tray for the small, oval platter Tyers had brought. "I will go along to my flat for my portfolio as soon as you leave to meet with the police," he said, clearly confirming some agreement they had made before I returned to the flat at dawn.

"Um. Thanks," said Holmes as he helped himself to potatoes and bacon. "This is the very thing that will hold me through the day, Tyers."

Tyers nodded to show his acknowledgment of this praise. "You are good to say so." He checked the teapot. "More hot water."

Sutton suddenly stifled a yawn. "Oh, I beg your pardon. It's being up all night after a performance." He looked a bit like a schoolboy caught out after hours. "I'll need a lie-down after I come back from my flat. Sorry, It's beginning to catch up with me."

Mycroft Holmes regarded him indulgently. "Whatever you must do, do it while it does not compromise with your impersonation."

"Thanks. I appreciate that." He leaned back and yawned again. "More tea."

"It's coming," said Tyers, who took up the pot and left the study.

"Guthrie," Holmes said to me, "you might be well-advised to take a nap yourself. You have no duties so urgent that they cannot be postponed for an hour or two. Once we attend our meeting with the Directors, we may have to move very quickly, and I will need you alert and rested."

I was about to say it was not necessary, but I knew that was pride, not good sense talking, so I responded, "Thank you, sir. I will do just that."

"Use the day-bed in the sitting room. You won't muss your clothes too badly on it." He began to eat the potatoes and bacon with gusto, as if the very act itself increased his appetite. I had seen him this way before—in Constantinople especially—and I recognized it for the preparation it was. "You may excuse yourself if you like, Guthrie. I will not impose upon you until you're needed. Sutton can manage to take a few notes for me, and Tyers will make sure you are awake and presentable for the meeting this morning."

I put my plate aside, and put my cup and saucer on it. Six years ago I might have been offended by this suggestion, but I understood it now in the most pragmatic terms: Mycroft Holmes would need me refreshed and vigilant for at least thirty-six hours to come. "Thank you, sir," I said as I turned and left the room.

FROM THE PERSONAL JOURNAL OF PHILIP TYERS

Sutton is off to fetch his portfolio and G is still asleep on the daybed. MH has gone to have his discussion with the police. I have dispatched the memorandum MH prepared for the Swedish Ambassador, giving his assurance that every possible means of protecting HHPO was being employed, the details of which he would furnish upon the Prince's arrival in Stockholm. The flat is quiet but for an occasional shout from the street below. I know what these hours of preparation can mean to the success of an operation, and one of this moment must demand a standard above that used for common occurrences.

Word came from Baker Street, brought by the landlady who was about her shopping, that HHPO is occupying his time there reading some of the more obscure texts. He is well and has obeyed our instructions to the letter. He has not gone near windows, nor spoken above a low voice and always in English. He says he enjoys this chance at invisibility, something that he rarely achieves. It would be as well if his enjoyment of this should last through the journey to Scotland. He has asked for a paper and a notebook, both of which I have supplied, along with MH's instructions that he will come to this flat after dark, and that he should be prepared to leave tomorrow morning early in such clothes as will be provided for him.

The first of the doubles of HHPO has left the Diogenes Club under naval escort, not a lavish one, but sufficient to put our enemies on guard. The killing of that young constable has made the doubles far more chary about their work, but they will do as they must for their country.

It is unfortunate that the young constable should be murdered, but it is a far greater tragedy that the police should have been so much corrupted that this death was possible. I share MH's anguish at the implications of it, and I am determined to do all that I can to aid in eradicating the corruption. Politicians are often venal, and advocates are equivocal; but police must preserve integrity or justice is unattainable. I have seen for myself how swiftly a compromised police erode all the workings of a society. It must not happen here.

Chapter Seven

"ROUSE YOURSELF, GUTHRIE. Sid Hastings will be here in half an hour, and we must be ready to go across to the club while he makes himself busy." Mycroft Holmes' voice penetrated my dozing state as if it had been a clap of thunder, jolting me awake and disorienting me at the same instant. "Tea is coming."

I was very groggy but I was able to sit up. "Just a moment, sir," I said, and felt as if my tongue were sticking to the roof of my mouth. "Sorry. I was—"

"Making up for lost sleep; yes, that is apparent," said Holmes, sitting in the chair directly across from me. "I do regret that this is probably the last real sleep you will have until we arrive in Scotland, but it can't be helped and at least this is not Constantinople, or the Alsace. Or the Duke of York's Theatre, come to that."

"For which we can only be grateful." I was more alert now, and I sat straighter. "Another five minutes and I should be ready for our work."

"Not until you reknot that tie," said Mycroft Holmes in a critical tone of voice. "You have your leather-bound notebook here, don't you? It wouldn't do to appear before the Directors with anything less. The notations must be made in ink. Tyers will supply you an inkwell and a pen, one of those fine Italian glass ones. You've used them before, as I recall."

"That I have," I said, gathering my thoughts. "How much do you want me to write?"

"Whatever seems pertinent." He stood up, clearly restless. "This police matter does not set well with me, Guthrie. The more I think of it, the more troubling its implications become. It smacks of deeper intrigue. If I knew who was the man in the force who has taken the side of our foes—and which foes those are—I would know how to plan to thwart him. But as it is . . ."

"As it is, the Prince's safety must be our first concern," I said for him. "Truly. And if the police are in any way implicated, I own myself appalled." I heard the horror in my voice and saw it reflected in Mycroft Holmes' visage.

"And if this diversion fails to work, I dread to think what will come of it. Not for myself, oh, no. That will be a minor matter should the assassin succeed. What is the greatest calamity here would be the loss of mutual support between Britain and Scandinavia, for German influence would expand to the North as sure as eggs are eggs." He coughed once. "With the Brotherhood supporting Karl Gustav, we must make every effort to preserve Prince Oscar."

"Isn't that a bit self-serving? We support this Prince because he is inclined to deal well with us, and we oppose the advancement of his brother because he is more sympathetic to German interests?" I had never asked such a question so bluntly, but the matter had concerned me increasingly.

"Well, naturally, my dear boy. No one gives support without some benefit accruing to himself as result, and anyone who claims otherwise is a liar or mad." He squared his shoulders and began, "The unification of Germany thirty years ago changed European diplomacy forever. Since the Peace of Wesphalia—"

"In 1648," I supplied.

"Precisely," he agreed, continuing, "the German States, which had not conceived of themselves as a German totality, even when trying to sustain the fiction of the Holy Roman Empire, were principalities, duchies, palatinates, bishoprics, margraviates, electorates, and kingdoms, with varying degrees of autonomy from the Emperor. For more than two centuries the cobbled amalgam limped along. But as Austria's power waned after their many defeats by Napoleon, this changed. At the start of this century these states had a taste of unity when forced to join the French Emperor's confederation of the Rhine. Rather than break up this composite, Prussian leaders encouraged it. The problem was that Saxony or Bavaria had no desire to be part of Württenberg or anything else. Each strove to maintain its separate place in the world. But the pressure of a resurrecting France and the industrialization of the Continent forced all the Teutonic mosaic closer together. The revolution in France in 1848 and Napoleon III's efforts to regain his grandfather's Empire a few years later effectively drove the German-speaking princes to seek unity."

"With excellent reason," I agreed, wondering what the purpose of this review might be, for surely Mycroft Holmes was thinking aloud to some purpose I had not yet discerned.

"Fearful for their very lives, and seeing how Austria was no longer able to protect them, most voted at the Frankfurt Congress to, as they put it rather foolishly, 'merge Prussia into Germany.' Needless to add, it was the Prussian leaders who had Wilhelm IV's ear. For a while Germany struggled to unite and modernize itself. We were all amazed at the efficiency with which they dispatched the French in 1870, a war that also raised the nationalistic fervor of all the Germans to a high pitch and ignited the purpose of the Brotherhood anew. Since then Germany has made every effort to prove itself the equal of the older nations—a rather silly endeavor since no one else seems to discount them as much as they do themselves."

"It is not a mistake any country can afford to make more than once," I said.

"Astute as always, Guthrie," Mycroft Holmes approved before resuming his discourse. "Following the tradition of all Continental powers the German government is quick to use any situation to its benefit;

that makes them especially vulnerable to the Brotherhood. Opportunists are rarely careful about the tools they use."

I was so caught up that it wasn't until my employer gestured at a mirror, without hesitating in his explanation that I remembered to hastily repair the knot in my tie. As I did, I found my thoughts returning to the matter of the police: how could any man on that force permit himself to be enrolled in the cause of Britain's enemies?

Mycroft Holmes went on without seeming to notice my dismay. "So today Germany strives to prove itself to itself and that is most dangerous. The current rage to gain colonies, such as they now hold in East Africa, is a desire that has major implications for the rest of Europe. There are only so many lands out there. And if Germany covets one, it has to be at the expense of whoever already has it in their sphere of influence. I am satisfied our Empire is solid, but those of France and Belgium are proving far less stable. And now every nation is scrambling to position itself either for or against Germany to promote its own place in the greater world."

"So we have seen," I said, having set my tie to rights.

"That is where our risk is keenest, among those struggling for advancement. Britain has the most to lose, for we have the greatest Empire in the world. Our hulls carry half the world's trade. We must maintain stability. When Germany is too strong, we must weaken her. When France pushes too hard we must balance her ambitions by supporting this or that German assertion. You know of the treaties that are being signed and kept secret, and their importance to the Empire: without a strong England, I fear Europe—indeed, the entire world—would be at war in a matter of months."

"And Scandinavia might well swing the balance; hence our concerns for Prince Oscar," I said, repeating what I had been told at the beginning of this venture.

"You are an apt student, Guthrie," said Mycroft Holmes. "I fear it is more complicated than that, for if we cannot protect the Prince, we will lose the integrity of our position around the world, which is precisely what the Brotherhood is striving to achieve. Any failure on our part now would cast other assurances we have made into doubt. So you see, we must consider all our obligations and honor them. With so much at stake, we cannot afford to lose this friend and a most strategically placed ally at that. We cannot permit him to be harmed or be perceived to be in danger. Keep in mind we are playing for higher stakes than a single man's life, or the schedule of trains."

I nodded several times more, and said, "I began to wonder in Constantinople if we were actually doing the task we supposed we were. You've told me that these things are complex; I sometimes lose sight of how complex they are."

"Yes," he said, with a sudden burst of energy. "Come. It's time we were going. Sid will begin to wonder what has become of us."

"Sid?" I finally realized he had mentioned the jarvey when he woke me. "Isn't our meeting across the street? Why Sid?" I asked, wondering if plans had changed while I slept.

"Sid is taking a number of memoranda to the police for me," said my employer glibly.

"You are trying to set a trap," I told him, knowing his pattern.

Mycroft Holmes shook his head. "My dear Guthrie, 'trap' is such a very nasty word. Let us say I am giving anyone of venal inclinations associated with our work a chance to indulge himself."

"Yes. A trap," I said, trying not to smile in spite of my distress at the realization that the police could not be counted upon as allies. "I'll just go get my leather-bound notebook and the glass pen."

"In the parlor, I think, in the secretary." Holmes was already going to don his topcoat and his hat, vigor in every movement.

The items were exactly where he said they would be. I took them and went to get my coat as Tyers came up to me with a bottle of ink with a well in the lid. "Thank you," I said.

"Ta, Mister Guthrie. You'd best hurry. Hastings will be waiting for his messages. Time is fleeting." He made a gesture of encouragement and did not quite shove me out the door.

Mycroft Holmes was half a flight ahead of me going down the stairs; he glanced back once before he reached the street where Sid Hastings had drawn up at the kerb. Here he paused long enough to hand two small leather portfolios to Sid and hurriedly gave his instructions.

Pall Mall was now a very busy street indeed, with carriages and wagons and the occasional person on a horse going by in a steady stream. I made my way across, taking care to make sure that nothing splashed my clothes, for it would not do to present myself to the Diogenes Club or the Directors in smirched garments. As I reached the steps of the club, a somber-faced constable stepped out instead of the doorman.

"Guthrie is with me, Mossleigh," said Mycroft Holmes, coming up behind me.

"Right you are, sir," said Constable Mossleigh. "You're expected in the Strangers' Room." He bowed a little to admit us to the club.

The Strangers' Room was designed to both awe and isolate visitors, with two impressive sets of doors, one of which led directly into the vestibule. These double doors were of a standard size and made of the same dark wood as the bookcases that lined the walls of the room; just now they stood open, indicating, not too subtly, that this was the route for the Directors and their guests to take. At the far side of the Strangers' Room was a second set of double doors. Made of the same wood and fitted with over-sized handles of polished brass, they were covered by deep bas relief in a pattern similar to those on the Acropolis. In the center was an image of the Green Man in his garments of leaves, glaring forbiddingly at anyone who might use this entrance.

The center of the room was taken up with a large table carved from a single piece of oak with padded, leather-covered chairs drawn up around it. Bookshelves from floor to ceiling were filled and divided by subject, one section containing a complete set of medical references, another law, and a third geography and exploration; in one corner were all the completed volumes of the Ordinance Survey. Beyond Mycroft Holmes himself, Guthrie doubted that many members of the Diogenes Club itself made much use of the collected wisdom in the hundreds of somberly bound and gilt volumes.

The men in the chairs looked hardly less imposing than the Strangers' Room itself. Five members of the Board of Directors were in attendance. At the head of the table sat Thomas Wordswell, who could only be described as prim but somehow friendly. His graying hair and large, brown eyes demanded trust. He was relatively new in running the railroad, but had worked at lesser positions for years. His brother had been the man who had kept things going when the engineers had virtually rebelled a few years earlier at the tyranny of Irish Alexander McDonnell; the former General Manager had managed to annoy the line's staff, its engineers, the bankers, and the rest of the board in an amazingly short time. The resulting chaos had been headline news for months. I wondered if there would be a problem with a new and insecure chief approving whatever my employer requested.

With him at the table were men with whom anyone who kept up with the latest technology of our modern railroad were familiar. The large man, his neck and arms were as thick as most men's legs, was Walter Mackersie Smith; his hair was that shade of red found only in Scotland and his skin was surprisingly ruddy. Smith was the Chief Draughtsman and ran the locomotive works at Gateshead. From what the paper had reported during the McDonnell revolt, Smith was not hesitant about speaking his mind, regardless of the company or situation.

Next to Smith was the former Temporary General Manager and Locomotive Superintendent Tennant, who was interested mostly in developing his engines, some of the newest and most powerful ever made; those engines were among the reasons for the recent "Race to the North," so popular with the newspapers between the North Eastern and the Great Northern. Already railroad enthusiasts were calling the new models being introduced on the North Eastern "Tennants." The smallest man at the table by a good measure, his gray eyes constantly shifted to each person in the room in sequence. Neatly dressed and sitting properly with his hands folded in front of him, the accountant and engineer seemed to fulfill all of the jokes about being fussy and demanding. His hair was well-oiled and combed carefully into place; his suit was a very tight tweed. If Mycroft Holmes wanted too much, Tennant would be the problem; such men liked predictability, a quality my employer only pretended to have.

Across from Smith, but leaving a place for Holmes, sat Darwin Bromley. Bromley was almost as large as Smith, but less well-muscled. After years with Mycroft Homes, I knew not to equate his weight with sloth, and did not mistake this man for idle: Bromley was an investor and rumored to be one of the richest men in London. He also owned and managed one of the largest investment houses in the city. The North Eastern had taken a long time to become profitable, and Bromley had been responsible for keeping the line solvent during the trying times before the changes in the Railroad Commission. Normally reserved to the point of being reclusive, Bromley was a different man when speaking about "his" trains. Some of the newspapers derisively, or enviously, accused him and his investment house of "collecting trains" in the way others had begun collecting the models of the great locomotives, for the North Eastern was not the only railroad in which he had invested, although it was now the largest.

Finally there sat Major D. Angus Potter. Almost seventy, he had been on the board the longest of any man there. Despite Smith's middle name, Potter was also the only native-born Scot on the Board. A former major in the Royal Scots Regiment, the longest-serving regiment in Britain, he was considered to be a steadying influence on the often volatile North Eastern board, although some considered him hopelessly old-fashioned.

"You've all received my brief, I think, and have had a short time to familiarize yourself with it," Mycroft Holmes began, his voice no longer his usual rumble, but a strong orator's delivery; I sensed the excellent instruction of Edmund Sutton.

"Mister Holmes, you have a most . . . ingenious plan to protect Prince Oscar, and we know we will benefit from the arrangements with Sweden-and-Norway, so we are at least willing to hear you out, if only out of consideration to the Prince who has offered us such generous terms to aid in the expansion of the railways in his kingdom," said Wordswell, in his position of leadership; his words were supported by grave nods from the other Directors. "Tell us what you would like us to do?"

I made a point of readying my pen, although it was my intention to record the reactions of the Directors rather than anything my employer might say.

Mycroft Holmes unfolded a long sheet of paper and indicated the plan drawn upon it. From the precision of the execution of draughting, I supposed Tyers must have done it, for his early training included such disciplines. I wondered if Tyers was aware that Tennant would be examining his work, and if he had known, if the knowledge had influenced him in any way: knowing Philip Tyers, I supposed he would have done the same precise work, whether it was for a lowly sapper or the Queen herself. "As you can see," Holmes told the Directors, "this plan shows a different array of cars than you usually have on the *Flying Scotsman*. You will see this uses a dining car and one of your half-lounge, half-baggage cars along with a first-class carriage with sleeping accommodations, but not a private carriage, which would call attention to itself. The train is completed with a second first-class carriage bound for Glasgow, and two second-class carriages with bunks in the rear. The first-class carriage and second-class carriage are before the dining car, then the dining car, then the lounge-and-baggage car—"

"Which we will have to lease from another railroad," complained Tennant, his seniority making the rest stare at him.

"You have done so in the past, upon two occasions," said Mycroft Holmes, challenging the man for all his tone of voice was polite. "There would be a first- and second-class carriage in the rear to simplify the change for Glasgow. Glasgow baggage would go in the second-class carriage, as provided by your—"

"Yes, yes, we know these things," said Smith. "Why should we? Profits have been small enough and we have many years to make up for."

"The North Eastern has never hesitated to act in British interests," said Holmes, with heroic mendacity. "You have also made substantial alterations in the cars and their order on four previous occasions in the last year."

"That was to improve speed," grumbled Smith.

"But it has been done," said Holmes, seizing on the salient point. "You have done so and no one will remark that you do so again, which is crucial to our plan." He coughed. "Your passenger list for tomorrow is not full; you are booked at two-thirds' capacity. With Prince Oscar and his minimal escort, and I assure you, the escort will be inconspicuous so as not to trouble your other passengers, you will have reached a comfortable level of profit."

I noticed two of the silent Directors glance at each other, sly as lizards, and exchange a nod so small as to be almost imperceptible.

"Of course, because of what we ask for, we will pay compensation, and owe you the gratitude of the country, as well," Mycroft Holmes went on. "In exchange, we expect our mission to be held in the strictest confidence. I have contrived an explanation for your change that should pass muster with all but the most persistent."

"Is that the farrago in your brief?" demanded the sharp-faced Tennant.

"In essence, it is," said Holmes without a trace of umbrage at Tennant's imputation. "You know that you have the power to make these decisions, and you can put those decisions into effect in hours. This is just such a case."

Bromley scowled down at the drawing. "In the past we have made changes due to exigencies—severe weather, trouble up the line—"

"And threats," said Mycroft Holmes. "You changed the train's schedule and order when you received a threat claiming that the train would be destroyed by explosives planted somewhere along the tracks." He held up his memorandum on the matter. "You took two army carriages with the reinforced frames, and you made the run with half a dozen army sappers in the first carriage." He smiled a bit. "The degree of change in this plan is nowhere near that, is it?"

"No," said Smith grudgingly. "It's not."

"So you will order the train to proceed in the conformation I have specified?" Holmes glanced at me, then put his full attention on the Directors once again. "If you agree, I have a great deal to do this afternoon to prepare to depart tomorrow morning at seven, if you follow my recommendation."

"You?" Potter gasped, his blue eyes seeming to push from his head. "Surely you do not mean to travel to Scotland?" he asked in a thick Edinburgh accent.

"I? That would be the height of folly. To have me escort His Highness would be the same as pinning him in a train's headlight; I am too crucially placed in the government to provide Prince Oscar the obscurity he requires now. *Someone* must accompany the Prince, and whoever those two persons are, they must be made ready for the journey and given what protection we can supply to protect His Highness, who will, of course, travel incognito. Those escorting him will put his protection uppermost in their purpose."

"Of course," said Tennant sneering in my employer's direction.

"Have you even found the escort for the Prince? Do you intend to tell us who is to undertake this work?" asked Smith taking his sarcastic tone from his fellow-Director.

"Oh, yes. There are some minor, last-minute arrangements to be made, but as soon as I have your assurance that you will support this plan and execute it, I will make such accommodations as are necessary for the protection of the Prince while he travels to Scotland. That will be *my* responsibility, as providing the appropriate train will be *yours*." He was able to give them all a confident smile, and I wondered as I watched him if he would appear so confident if the Directors discovered that he—Mycroft Holmes—and I would be the escort taking Prince Oscar north. I doubted the Directors would be as sanguine as they were if they were privy to this intelligence; I also suspected that my employer would not present himself in this manner had he intended to inform them of his intentions.

"Mister Homes?" Bromley asked as if suddenly aware of a new danger, "What do you think will be the greatest danger to the Prince while on the *Flying Scotsman*? The journey from London to Edinburgh should take eight hours, and much can happen in that time. We must hope that such an unmasking does not occur, but should it happen, how do you intend it to be dealt with? And how would such a disaster reflect on the North Eastern?"

Mycroft Holmes almost smiled; he must have anticipated the question. "If any of the Prince's enemies, or Britain's, should discover him on the train, we will have to do everything in our power to remove him from danger, which would mean evacuating him from the train in some manner. There are actually several possible places to accomplish this without raising further suspicion, and I am prepared to take advantage of any or all of them. Each station is, of course, an opportunity for our opponents as well as for us. Stations will be watched, and we must suppose stops for coal, sand, and water will be under surveillance as well."

Pointing at the pertinent parts of Tyer's drawing of the train, Mycroft continued, "With the configuration I've requested, we can leave the train at any point without being seen by the other passengers, here and . . . here. It is very unlikely the assassin will actually venture to strike on the *Scotsman* itself. He would be at a great disadvantage, outnumbered and unable to retreat easily from any failure. The trained assassin prefers to have three means of escape; you can be most certain we are facing an accomplished assassin. Our concern must be discovery and an ambush awaiting us at Edinburgh Station."

"Why do you believe this is the case, Mister Holmes?" asked Wordswell, his keen, fussy features showing his full attention.

"Experience, and a comprehension of the rail route." With nothing more than a cursory glance my employer reached behind him and drew out a copy of the Ordnance Survey. Turning to a page in the middle, he placed the book in front of the Directors. "As you are aware, a typical train has to slow to almost a walking pace to safely pass the 'S' curve at Portabello before reaching Edinburgh Station. If there is the slightest indication that anyone awaits us in the station, we will be able to depart at this point without undue hazard. There will be special men from Scotland Yard in every station along the route and a substantial number available on call. If anything untoward is noted we will leave the train, an advantage not readily offered to those traveling by ship, and thus avoid any unpleasantry. All we need is an appropriate warning. You have your profit, the government's gratitude, and the gratitude of the future king of Sweden-and-Norway."

"You have that wonderfully pat," said Smith.

"I have, have I not?" My employer then granted the five Directors his most sincere smile. They were all comrades and patriots, it said, and they would profit from their patriotism as well.

"So there must be some way to feign trouble on the line, and some way to signal the need for it." He looked around at the Directors. "I suppose I must tell your managers my plans in this regard and will do so at the earliest opportunity."

"Do you doubt our willingness to help, Mister Holmes," said Tennant, "when we have granted you this extraordinary meeting?"

"No, I do not doubt it, nor do I doubt your patriotism; but, gentlemen, I submit to you that we are facing a subtle and ruthless opponent whose agents might be much nearer to you than you suppose." Mycroft Holmes leaned forward, his height making him more imposing than a shorter man would have been, or a slighter one. "Do not deceive yourselves. If word of this gets out at all we stand to lose everything Her Majesty's government has worked so hard to achieve in its relations with Scandinavia."

"The enemy you describe is subtle: the so-called Brotherhood is unknown to us," said Smith. His chin jutted out in stubborn disbelief.

"If they made their presence known, they would not have the power they possess. Secrecy is their most potent weapon. Their very obscurity gives them potency they would lack if they were subjected to scrutiny. Those who have tried to bring their activities to light have paid high prices for their altruism." He paused a moment. "Only those willing to work in the same shadows they inhabit have the least chance of any success in putting an end to the nefarious ambitions of the Brotherhood."

Bromley gave a ponderous sigh. "I've been a banker and invested on the Continent for years and never heard of this conspiracy. Don't you think you may be making too much of this Brotherhood, and the threat to the Prince? Having him travel incognito in such a harum-scarum fashion—well, it is demeaning, don't you know? Fellow like that deserves better, some proper recognition of his place in the world." His hand was large and his fingers thick, with white hairs sprouting from the backs of them like miniature, exotic ferns; he slammed his palm down on the table. "Why should we believe that such elaborate— we must call them shenanigans—are required? Disguises, doubles, misdirections."

"Because the footman was killed yesterday morning, and a constable before dawn today, both assigned to the Prince of Sweden-and-Norway," said Mycroft Holmes in a blunt kind of laconic style that held the Directors' attention because it was not as aggressive a response as the challenge he had been issued. He modified his delivery and diminished the edge in his voice. "Two men have died within twenty-four hours, their common link is Prince Oscar, and we know the Prince has had his life threatened before. It would be unpardonably remiss of England to neglect his safety after the calamitous events of the past days." He looked from one Director to the next. "I may be over-cautious, but suppose the Prince should be killed following one of his established itineraries? What then? When you know that this deception of ours might have saved him? What will this do to railroading in Sweden-and-Norway, and how can you accept the harm this will do Britain?" He was silent then, not prodding them by word or gesture. "I will await your answer in the Reading Room," he said, and signaled me to withdraw with him through the vestibule door.

I knew the Reading Room was the last place we would be allowed to speak, so I hesitated there. "What do you think, sir?" I asked, keeping my voice low as much for respect to the club members as any fear of eavesdroppers from the other side of the door.

Mycroft Holmes angled his long head and contemplated a place on the far wall. "Patriotism and greed: they should be enough. If Tennant and Smith will support the request, we will have nothing to worry about. If they do not, then this may have been in vain." He made a gesture of resignation. "We can but hope, Guthrie, we can but hope."

FROM THE PERSONAL JOURNAL OF PHILIP TYERS

What a frenzy of activity we are in since the Directors of the North Eastern consented to MH's plan to take HHPO to Scotland on the train. It is the more chaotic because we must preserve the impression that no change beyond that which is accountable has taken place. Sutton has already taken up his post in the parlor, a vast number of books piled around him in case any villain is observing this flat through a glass; his sketches are already tucked into their portfolio ready to be taken in the morning to the train where G may claim them for his own.

MH has sent Hastings round to Baker Street to collect the Prince while he puts the final arrangements for the train into effect with the support of the Directors. As soon as MH returns, there will be a rehearsal for the personae all are to play on their journey north. Guthrie has been memorizing a series of codes for sending and receiving messages along the way, as have I.

There was some discussion in the lobby, which I happened to overhear when I brought the Admiralty memoranda to MH there: apparently some scandal about a race horse. It seems the animal, a great favorite, was deliberately injured on its way from the stable to the track and the jockey was thrown and killed as a result of this injury. This was seen as a sign of social decay, when so honorable a sport as racing should be compromised by such a deed.

CI Somerford has stopped by to deliver a report on the death of the constable and to express his thanks to MH for his concern in regard to the policeman's sacrifice. . . .

Chapter Eight

LISTENING TO PRINCE Oscar speak English, Edmund Sutton's frown deepened. "That accent of yours is as much a problem as Guthrie's eyes. The trouble is, you might fool an Englishman, but anyone truly familiar with German would know you are neither German nor Austrian." He began to pace, our employer's clothing now looking inappropriate on him as he revealed himself as he was.

I did not want to concur, but could not deny that Sutton had a point. "I speak German, and I can hear that this man—no offense intended, Your Highness—does not sound truly German. And there is no disguising that my right eye is green and my left is blue."

"No offense whatsoever," said Prince Oscar, clearly enjoying himself, like a schoolboy who has escaped his instructors for the day and is on a romp. "Tell me what I must do and I will make every effort to comply."

The sitting room was shuttered against the falling night; the fireplace was ruddy with new-lit logs, and the gaslights lent their glow to our work, softening the harsh purpose of our preparations. Tyers had removed a lavish tea and had put out the port and Stilton, and had promised a supper at midnight. Now, with nine approaching, we all sensed the urgency of our endeavors, and increased our efforts.

Mycroft Holmes rubbed his chin, his deep-set grey eyes distant with contemplation. "Do you think you could pretend to have a cold?" he suggested suddenly. "You know, cough now and then and talk as if your head was stuffed up?"

Sutton grinned. "That's just the ticket!" he enthused. "Can you do that, Your Highness?"

Prince Oscar nodded vigorously and gave a demonstrative cough that made Sutton hold up his hands. "Too much?" the Prince asked, crestfallen.

"I'm afraid so. You'll scare the other passengers off the train if you do that," said Sutton. Then he displayed a series of coughs. "Something along those lines should do the trick. And speak like this," he went on, *speag lyg dis.*

Prince Oscar tried it, and looked for approval. "Is that better?" *Dad bedder?*

"You will need to practice a little more," said Sutton, "but it isn't bad." He went pale. "I'm sorry, Your Highness."

"Not at all, not at all. I must get this right, and without correction it will not happen," he said with a winning smile. For a stiff-rumped Swede, Prince Oscar was more of a regular chap than you would think. I began to see why he had spent time in Sir Cameron's company: he had been kicking over the traces.

Mycroft Holmes came up to Prince Oscar. "We must discuss something more, Your Highness," he said very carefully.

"I am sure there are a great many things we must discuss, including how I am to address you." He looked around as if he expected to see lists everywhere. "Money, for another. I've never carried money, you know. I suppose I will on the train."

"Yes, you will have to, and we will make appropriate arrangements. That we'll address later," said Mycroft Holmes. "There is something far more pressing, and considerably more hazardous." He waited until he had Prince Oscar's full attention, then he said, "Your titles."

Prince Oscar nodded several times. "Yes, that occurred to me as well. You cannot say 'Your Highness' and expect to maintain our little deception, can you?" He clapped his hands together. "You will need another name for me altogether, won't you?" From the way he said it, this was a delicious treat. "Let me think. I may have a nick-name you can use." He tapped his fingers on the buttons of his waistcoat. "My Uncle Einar used to call me Skynda er"—*sheundah air*—"because I was always telling everyone to hurry up. I would answer to that readily. I would not have to think about it, or remember it."

"It is a bit cumbersome," said Mycroft Holmes diplomatically.

"Schere?" I suggested. The sound was similar I thought. "Is that near enough? There is no 'n' in it or 'd' but—"

"Schere?" Prince Oscar tested it, saying it several times. "Yes. I think that may do. And you will remember it easily, won't you?"

"And," Mycroft Holmes declared, "we have a code word that is marginally safe. We can use 'scissors' instead of anything more obvious." He made a sharp sign of approval. "Excellent work, Guthrie. Now to a first name; something unobvious."

"Osrich?" said Edmund Sutton. "It's enough like Oscar to catch his ear, but Englishmen, hearing it, will think of *Hamlet* and not this Scandinavian Prince."

Holmes actually laughed aloud and clapped Edmund Sutton on the back. "Inspired, dear boy. Inspired."

"Osrich Schere?" The Prince tried out the name, his good-natured features wreathed with an affable smile. "Osrich Schere it is. From now until I leave Scotland, I am Osrich Schere, and you will call me nothing but that."

"Thank you very much, Herr Schere," said Mycroft Holmes, watching the Prince narrowly to gauge his response to the name.

"I am most grateful to you, Mister Holmes," Prince Oscar went on. "You find a way to protect me that is nothing like anything I have done before. I am going to enjoy this very much."

"So I hope," said Holmes with great purpose.

"And remember, you have a cold," said Sutton, taking on the manner of a seasoned instructor. "You will want to keep a muffler about your throat at all times, and you will be able to excuse yourself from conversation by coughing, or claiming a sore throat. It will also make any absences we must impose on you explainable. You will help us if you complain about your condition. And keep in mind, your speech must be thickened."

"I will do it," said Prince Oscar, his energetic stance enough to make it clear he was in the best of health.

Mycroft Holmes gave a little sigh. "Work with him, Sutton, will you? Guthrie, come with me. You, I, and Tyers will finalize our codes." He plucked at my sleeve and all but dragged me from the room, saying under his breath once we were in the hall, "He will be more biddable if we do not watch."

"Sutton will manage handily," I replied, knowing how well he had tutored me.

"That he will," said Holmes as we stepped into the study where Tyers was composing what seemed to be innocuous telegram messages. "The Prince is 'scissors'," our employer announced. "Herr Schere to you."

"Osrich Schere," I added. "Osrich was Sutton's idea."

"Very good. I will mention this to no one," Tyers declared. "And I will use whatever name you designate for our communications. I will send the memoranda you have prepared to the police in the morning after you have left for the station. I will give them to Sid Hastings to deliver." He was reciting in that strangely sing-song way that I had come to realize was his way of committing things to memory.

"Very good," Mycroft Holmes approved. "While Sutton works with Herr Schere, we will make our last arrangements. I want all that in order before supper is served, for Herr Schere will need to get some sleep tonight, to be alert on our long journey. You have the route of the *Flying Scotsman,* and the schedule it is supposed to keep?"

"I have," said Tyers. "A pity the old route isn't still in use," he added. "Even a year ago, you could put Herr Schere on a ship at Boston, or Newcastle and no one the wiser, but"—he shrugged—"The East Coast route isn't used by the *Scotsman* anymore, not in the last few years, and those trains using that route would be too vulnerable to attack."

"Precisely. There is no use in mourning the past, for it cannot be recalled." Mycroft Holmes spread the maps open. "So. In our various aliases we depart from King's Cross at—"

"The Directors confirm that the train will leave on time, and in the confirmation you requested." Tyers held up an envelope and its heavy cardboard case. "It came half an hour ago," he went on.

"Any new information from the police?" asked Holmes, a careful tone in his voice.

"Only a short note from Chief Inspector Somerford that came while you were busy with Sutton choosing clothes for this journey; he says someone has been found who may have seen a fair-haired man of medium height running from the house where the constable was shot a little after four. He is putting five men on it, though he doesn't expect much. Nothing from Superintendent Spencer yet."

" 'Someone who may have seen . . . ' Not very specific, but safe enough in its way. They're all going to ground," said Mycroft Holmes with grim satisfaction. "Not one of them is going to expose himself to any criticism. The police are pulling in, wanting no scandal to touch them, and so they will wash their hands of this as much as they properly may."

"Then you will have the glory when we succeed," I said, laughing enough to show that I had no expectations of reward for my employer.

"No doubt, if we manage to get the Prince home without harm or incident, Cecil will find some way to show he had masterminded the whole." He sighed again. "I would not mind his relentless hunger for credit if he would be more willing to accept blame. But it is hardly surprising a man of his character should be so—so unscrupulous."

I had been aware for some time that Mycroft Holmes had a more than usually precarious association with the Prime Minister, the history of which I had never learned. My curiosity about their dealings was piqued again, but I knew it was unwise to pursue the matter now. "What about the Swedes?" I asked, intending to turn the subject.

"I do not blame the Ambassador—indeed, how could I? He was given the assurance of Her Majesty's government that Prince Oscar would come to no harm here, and the Ambassador took us at our word. A shocking turn of events." His mock horror ended in a faint smile. "But we have a train to catch. Let us be about our plans."

"I have marked those stations where the train halts long enough to send and receive messages," said Tyers, pointing to the red ticks on the map. "A pity the *Scotsman* no longer goes through Hitchin and Peterborough, but there it is."

"Bedford is the first halt with time to send or receive telegrams," said Holmes thoughtfully. "Guthrie, I depend upon you to tend to that duty. I have no wish to let the Prince out of my sight."

"I will do anything you require, sir," I said, my voice firm and my posture worthy of a Guard. The police might fail him, but I would not; it was an honor to be worthy of his trust, an honor I would not betray.

"Very good, very good," said Mycroft Holmes, not quite dismissing my fervid avowal. "Guthrie, you have long since proven your dedication. You need not make such a display for my benefit." He put his finger on the map. "So Leicester after Bedford, and Sheffield after that." He sighed. "Leeds is the next stop we must pay attention to, then Kirkby Stephen—it is the smallest and therefore the most hazardous—then Carlisle, where the Glasgow cars will be shifted over from yours. At Saint Boswells, you will have your last chance before Edinburgh to send word of what has happened. That stop is for fuel and water, and is twenty minutes long. Some of the passengers will leave the train." He recited this as if it were nothing more than a packing list.

I looked down at my notes. "You have outlined our travels. What do you think the Prince will expect?"

"In what regard, my boy?" my employer inquired with a blandness that indicated he was willing to think about what I said, but would not welcome an ill-considered recommendation.

"In terms of having to support our sham. This is going to be a long ride for him—eight hours—and he will be in danger most of the way. He thinks it is an adventure now, but who is to say how he will react when he is put to the test of riding the train like any common person, and possibly with an assassin hunting him?"

"If you think that the Prince will discover that he is not as willing to undertake the task of mixing with ordinary folk, then his supposed cold will provide him the excuse he will need to make himself unavailable to the people in his company. You have anticipated my strategy." He gave me a quick half-smile.

By now I knew better than to assume this praise was more than it appeared to be; I was accustomed to his ways and had learned to recognize some of his devices. Mycroft Holmes had every reason to take precautions before setting out on this excursion. "We will have our codes, and we know where we may send and receive telegrams. I suppose this is to assure Tyers, and through him, the Admiralty, that nothing untoward has happened—which we must hope to be the case—and to receive any information that may have been discovered relative to the men desiring to kill the Prince."

"Yes, that is the main thrust of all our design, of course. But we have also the question of the murdered constable, and what role his death may or may not play in our current situation." He motioned to me, showing me the map once more. "We take on water and sand at most of those stations, when the train itself will be exposed. That is when we must be most alert, for that is when the assassin may be most likely to strike, in order to make his escape without detection. I would like to think that notifying the police along the North Eastern line would be advisable; but with the doubts we must have about the police, it would be too much of a risk to ask their assistance, for fear of alerting the assassin through whomever is the agent of Prince Oscar's enemies— and ours."

I nodded, taking it all in. The worst problem was the police, beyond question, but I could not completely forget the extent of the danger we were dealing with if the Brotherhood was part of the plot to be rid of Prince Oscar. "How much do you suppose the Prince should be told?"

"It would be folly to keep him in ignorance, but we must also take care not to frighten him so much that he does not want to take on the risks of our journey." Mycroft Holmes fingered his watch-fob, a sure sign of concentration and apprehension. "He could still change his mind and demand that he be protected by his own embassy and given escort by his own navy, which would mean a profound embarrassment to Her Majesty's government."

"He could, but he will not," said Prince Oscar from the door. Behind him, Edmund Sutton stood somewhat awkwardly. "You are not asking me to do anything that dishonors me, or I would refuse. But your worry that I would not be willing to encounter danger, well, that is absurd. I was born to royalty, which is a kind of danger by its very nature. I have been guarded and protected and hemmed about since I was in my cradle. If I must be in danger now, at least I will be on my own."

"Not quite on your own," I said, with a glance at my employer.

"Compared to what I have encountered before, I will be free of all but the most minimal encumbrances." He sighed a little. "When I was young, I loved to read those stories about Princes going about the world incognito, without guards or other companions, passing as one of the folk, and having adventures just like most men would. I loved to dream of what could happen if I had such an opportunity. Then I grew older and discovered that those stories were just fables, and I had to put them aside."

"Your Highness," said Mycroft Holmes, his voice serious. "This may seem like an escapade worthy of some novel, but the men seeking you have deadly purpose: you will be in danger while you are in our company. Those men who are hunting you are not villains from some play, as Sutton can tell you. They intend to do you harm, and they will if they have any opportunity. Be certain you know this hazard is genuine before we leave for King's Cross."

Prince Oscar laughed. "What has Osrich Schere to fear? He is a German fellow with a cold. Sutton has been showing me how to deal with this." He gave an experimental cough and muttered something that was distorted by the apparent illness. "You see?" He beamed.

"Yes. And you will do very well so long as you keep in mind how very serious the situation is." Mycroft Holmes regarded the Prince, saying slowly, "A fair-haired man of medium height. The description of the possible assassin might suit the Prince himself. How perplexing for us all." He indicated the maps spread out. "Would you like to see the route of the *Flying Scotsman*?"

"Yes," said Prince Oscar, his blue eyes brightening still more. "This is going to be a grand bird, isn't it?"

"I think you mean lark, sir," said Sutton from behind him. He made a kind of apologetic gesture to Mister Holmes, his expression discouraged. "He *would* come."

"Nothing to fret about, Sutton, dear boy." Mycroft Holmes gave him a quick, reassuring pat on his shoulder. "You're doing uncommonly well given the constraints of time and—er—circumstances."

"Thank you," Sutton said, bowing his head as if to acknowledge applause.

"I have learned much," Prince Oscar declared as he looked around at the confusion of maps. "Which one must I examine?"

Holmes showed him the map of the routes of the North Eastern line and said, "The *Flying Scotsman* follows this track." He traced the course with his finger, pausing once to say, "Here there is a transfer of cars—some go to Glasgow, while the main part of the train continues to Edinburgh."

"And how long shall this journey take?" Prince Oscar asked, as fascinated as a child with a toy.

"Between eight and nine hours, if we have no trouble." Mycroft Holmes was somber now. "It is far more important that we deliver you to Scotland in good health than in good time; even nine hours is good speed, one that ensures our enemies cannot catch us. Our arrangements, once we are there, are easily managed. I hope both promptness and safety are possible; but if they are not, I will put in my choice for your successful escape from danger instead of a record-breaking run."

"But wouldn't it be delightful if we could do both?" Prince Oscar enthused. "I would be overwhelmed to think I had participated in two great occasions." He chuckled while Sutton and Holmes exchanged looks of dismay.

I decided to try to talk sense to the Prince. "You are right: it would be a great thing, but that very accomplishment might throw light on something you may prefer not to make public. You know how easily retelling magnifies an event—you have only to listen to the rumors about your footman's death to know that in no time your ride on the train would take on embroidered details that would render the whole little more that titillation for the common love of gossip."

"Yes, yes," said Prince Oscar impatiently. "But it would be wonderful." His expression was wistful. Then he pursed his lips. "Then Sutton will teach me to fold shirts. If I am an ordinary man, I must know how to do this."

"It is not so difficult, Your Highness," Sutton promised him.

"I suppose not. My valet does it all the time." He concentrated on Mycroft Holmes' description of the train route once again, saying, "I am sorry we will not get to cross the Forth Bridge. I am told it is a marvel."

"A great accomplishment," Holmes agreed. "But the very men who designed that bridge will be able to assist your engineers when our agreement is put into effect."

"That will be most welcome, for I know Sweden-and-Norway will improve the state of their commerce once such bridges are built and our railroads expanded." He rubbed his hands in approval. "Very good. Now, Sutton, let us deal with the shirts."

Sutton nodded. "Certainly. I will also show you how to pack your trousers so that the crease will not be lost and the fabric will not wrinkle."

"You actors know such startling things," said Prince Oscar as he nearly dragged Sutton from the study.

"He is determined to make the most of this," said Mycroft Holmes as the door closed behind Sutton and the Prince. "I only hope his yen for excitement doesn't lead to more hazard than we have already undertaken."

"Which is not unlikely," I could not keep from adding.

"We will have to be on the alert for what he may do," said Mycroft Holmes, his face looking longer than it was. "If only there were some workable distraction we could provide that would not hamper our task." He shrugged. "Well, if we had more time, no doubt we could arrange it. As it is, we will have to be doubly diligent."

"And that may prove more difficult than we would like," I said, thinking back to the train ride out of Germany with Cameron MacMillian in tow. That had been a journey no one could envy; it was also my first experience in the world Mycroft Holmes so covertly inhabited. Now that I had been in his employ somewhat longer, I knew that I had been luckier than I deserved to be on that mission; I could not suppose that I could count on such luck to follow me now. I vowed I would not repeat the mistakes I had made then, or since.

"I think when we return to London, we had best not travel on the *Flying Scotsman* again. We don't want to leave ourselves open to retribution, or to the animosity of the Directors." Holmes' smile was mildly sarcastic, but I understood his sentiments. "It will take a bit longer, but I think we had best come down the west side, don't you?"

I felt moved to remark, "You are assuming, sir, that we will reach Scotland without trouble and will depart from there unnoticed."

"Oh, Guthrie," he chided me. "You forget: I never assume." He reached out and began to fold his maps. "It's time we were packing. There will be much to do between now and our departure for the station." He raised a heavy eyebrow. "Best to make a good supper. I doubt we'll have time for a proper breakfast."

"Very well, sir. I will keep my peace for now. But we will have to review our plans at least once more before we leave." I nodded to show I was not trying to contradict him.

"Yes, and you will need a sketching lesson from Sutton before we depart. We must account for your drawings without too much incident." He began to put his maps away, pausing a moment to add, "It is fortunate, isn't it? that Sutton has so many talents."

"That it is," I said, thinking it would be a hopeless task to try to teach me how to do sketches in an hour or two.

"Do not despair, Guthrie," Mycroft Holmes advised. "Consider it a performance, and learn what Sutton can teach with a performance in mind."

His recommendation puzzled me, but I gave a sign of compliance as I gathered up my notes and went to arrange my valise and portfolio.

They are having supper and I have just completed the copies of the codes we are to use in communication between the Flying Scotsman *and this flat. MH has said he does not want HHPO to have a copy of it, for fear he would not hold it as carefully as MH would wish.*

The personae of MH and G for this journey have been decided, and if all goes well, they should be dressed and prepared by first light. Satchel's Guides *will provide credentials for MH, G, and HHPO for the journey, which MH is certain will be all they will need to maintain their dissemblance. It is reassuring that G has picked up the basic skills that Sutton has taught him in regard to the appearance of sketching. Sutton has loaned G his portfolio of drawings of major castles along the North Eastern line, so that he will have something to display to account for his supposed work as an illustrator of travel guides. Luckily the memoranda that MH sent yesterday have gained some fairly convincing credentials for himself and G that should withstand anything but close scrutiny.*

The scandal at the races the men were talking about earlier has knocked all speculation about the assassination attempt off the front page of the earliest morning papers; the death of the constable has not yet come to the attention of the editors in Fleet Street, and when it does, it may well receive little more than a paragraph among the back pages.

HHPO is still approaching this journey as a romp, and MH is afraid his exuberance may well cause trouble while they are bound northward. For all his prudence, HHPO reminds me of a good Hunter that has never been given more of a run than a canter round the paddock. It is not surprising that he is readying himself for a thrill.

There are a dozen or so messages I must deliver once MH and the rest are aboard the train: I have instructions to pursue the trouble of infiltration and corruption of the police, which may bring some resolution to this unhappy turn.

I must finish preparing the luggage, and make sure that the banknotes MH requested are in his billfold. G has been provided £20, certainly more than he will need for the trip, but enough to help if there is trouble requiring a sudden expenditure of cash. At least he will have this at the ready. MH has a total of £55, and HHPO is being allotted £10, for small expenditures. Fortunately MH has access to such discretionary funds that these amounts are minor. . . .

Chapter Nine

AS WE HAD agreed, Mycroft Holmes and I arrived at King's Cross Station in separate cabs; he in Sid Hastings', I in one I had flagged down on Regent Street. Prince Oscar rolled up in a handsome coach, as suited his good luggage and slightly top-lofty bearing.

We must have made quite a picture gathering there in front of the simple elegance of King's Cross Station. I hoped we were not attracting too much unwanted attention among the other travelers. I glanced about, trying to determine if we were observed and was caught up again in astonishment for this splendid building: even after forty years the buff walls of the elegant station and curved windows were admired. Directly behind and above where the Prince was descending from his carriage, the central tower struck the hour. The large, arched windows brightened the interior, and the high ceiling kept the steam and smoke high away from the crowds. We had some time yet, but the sound of warning bells urged us to hurry under the wrought-iron supports and the patriotic blue, red, and white bunting onto the platform where the *Flying Scotsman* was waiting.

"It's grand," exclaimed Prince Oscar, stifling a cough as he had been taught to do.

The streamlined engine was visible at the far end of the train; its dark metal and brass fittings were recently polished, as was usual for the *Scotsman*. Puffs of steam occasionally escaped the new pneumatic brakes. Some still preferred the old mechanical breaks, but my employer had once explained the deadman's system that stopped the train if the pressure failed; since then I have always felt more secure when the train I rode in was so equipped. Around us a jumble of passengers of all sorts hastened to reach their cars. Most were well-dressed, which was hardly a surprise since there were no third-class cars even in the *Flying Scotsman*'s standard configuration.

"What on earth—?" Prince Oscar blurted out as a scuffle erupted nearby.

A dozen steps from where we stood there was some disturbance as a hard-hatted bobby struck the pavement with his baton while holding tightly to a small man who struggled weakly to escape.

"A dip," Mycroft commented relieved that the problem would draw no attention to our party. "Such denizens haunt places where travelers gather. Note the loose clothing, the many pockets, and the way he protects his hands even while resisting."

A second and then third bobby arrived, and the man submitted to being led away. Mycroft used the distraction to push ahead of the gaping crowd and drew us after him in his wake. Thirty steps farther and we were approaching the car we had reserved. The large windows in the first-class cars were slightly open to allow the air to circulate. A severely uniformed conductor waited by each car eyeing the passengers and looking for the inevitable scaff-and-raff who were attracted by the departure of the most prestigious train in Britain.

"Go ahead and make sure that the compartments are prepared as instructed," my employer ordered quietly while pulling the Prince into the shelter of a large baggage cart.

I sauntered down the platform as if nothing motivated me but restlessness, yet all the while I was examining the train, making sure the configuration was just as Mycroft Holmes had requested; I signaled to my employer, then made my way to the first-class car at the front of the train, showed my ticket to the conductor standing by the car, and went to settle my things in my compartment—number three in the middle of the car.

As with all the first-class compartments, the seats were a plush maroon color and the dark wood stained almost black. Compared to many other modes of transportation my work for Mycroft Holmes had required, this was luxury indeed. I put my portfolio by the door and secured my valise in the rack above the seat that would become a bed if one was needed on the journey north. I was still trying to remember to let my Scottish burr be more apparent than I had schooled myself to have it. On a Scotland-bound train, a few burrs should be apparent. Sutton had fitted me out in a fine suit of houndstooth brown-and-white wool, with a natty tie and a dashing wing collar that made me look like more of a sporting gentleman than I am. I knew that I was expected to behave with an easier demeanor than I usually displayed, and I reminded myself that I should be ready to boast of my travels if the occasion seemed appropriate.

I heard a noise just outside my window and I swung round to see what might be its cause, for someone was shouting and there was a flurry of excitement among the porters. What kind of lout could be causing such a ruckus, I asked myself. A moment later I had my answer as Sir Cameron MacMillian, drunk as a proverbial lord, swaggered up to the car, his valet in tow, and a veritable school of porters behind them. I backed away from the window, my heart sinking into my shoes. "Good Lord," I whispered at this terrible development. We had not planned on having anyone who actually knew us—and Prince Oscar— be aboard the train. And now, Sir Cameron was, and drunk. He could be disastrous for our purpose. I began to wonder how I was to warn Mycroft Holmes when I saw him come aboard, bowler at a jaunty angle on his head, a cigar in his mouth, a stylish cane in one hand, and his double-caped coat open enough to show off his expensive, if slightly garish, suit of dark mallard blue. He was the very picture of a successful traveler and journalist; Edmund Sutton had truly out-done himself.

At Holmes' instructions, a small trunk was put into the baggage section of the lounge car, and two valises were carried to his compartment by two porters, Mycroft Holmes coming grandly after them, handing each a shilling for their service, twice the customary gratuity, and for which the porters thanked him profusely. I had not been so generous, as we had planned.

I was about to go out and warn him of the intrusive element in our plans when Sir Cameron saved me the trouble by reeling aboard, trudging along the corridor to his compartment—the first in the car—swearing at his valet. I heard the porter leaving Mycroft Holmes offer an apology for this disturbance.

"A great hero, Sir Cameron, but a great boozer, too, if you know what I mean," he said as he prepared to leave the car.

Holmes stopped him. "Is he going all the way to Edinburgh?"

"Yes, sir. That he is." The porter tipped his cap and departed.

I wanted to step into the corridor and have a word with Mycroft Holmes but I hesitated, for if Sir Cameron was drunk enough he might not recognize me or Holmes. That was hoping for a lot, I knew, since Sir Cameron had been in our company for several hectic days when I first went to work for Mycroft Holmes. I remained where I was, waiting to hear the door of the first compartment slam—as I was sure it must—before venturing out to speak with Holmes. As soon as I heard the door bang closed, I slipped out and rapped on the door of compartment two, where Mycroft Holmes was. I did not wait for Holmes to open the door, but stepped inside quickly, taking care to shut it before I spoke.

Mycroft Holmes was standing by the window adjusting the shades; he barely looked around as he spoke. "Yes, I know. It can't be helped. We will have to keep Herr Schere in his compartment most of the time, for Sir Cameron will seize upon him and reveal him as soon as he catches sight of him. There is no turning back, Sir Cameron or no. We're committed now and if we delay we lose all."

"But Sir Cameron knows Prince Oscar and—" I began.

"Yes. Sir Cameron. We must pray he remains drunk or asleep from here until we reach Scotland. Something will have to be arranged. I must say, it is useful that he is in compartment one. We will not have to go past it except to use the lav, and we might do that in the lounge, as I recall."

"True enough," I said, wishing I might share some of his remarkable composure. "What if he should recognize us? Or the Prince?"

"You mean Herr Schere?" Holmes asked with mild incredulity. "Why on earth would such an important person as Prince Oscar travel in such an undistinguished way? No doubt Sir Cameron is too far gone to be relied upon for any identification."

"I hope you are right," I said with feeling.

"So do I, dear boy; so do I." He patted my shoulder. "Speaking of Herr Schere, he should be here any minute. He is in compartment four, as I believe."

"Do you know who is in compartment five?" I asked, wanting to reassure myself that we had not just made a mull of our attempt to keep the Prince safe.

"No, in the dispatch that came before we left the flat the compartment had not yet been reserved." He began to twirl his watch-fob. "Perhaps it will remain vacant. That would serve our purpose very well."

"Do you think so?" I could not rid myself of the conviction that something would happen, that someone would come and our planning would be for nought. The very presence of Sir Cameron shook me to my soles.

"Try not to despair, Guthrie," Mycroft Holmes said in heartening accents. "And go along to the lounge car in the next half hour, if you will, just to see what manner of company we have. You will know what to look for." In his ostentatious clothes I felt as if he were trying to sell me optimism rather than inspire it. "Then we will meet, and you will remain Guthrie, and I will be Micah Holcomb. In fact, to all intents and purposes I probably am already."

"I'll do my best, sir," I said, and slipped out into the corridor and down to my own compartment where I ended up fretting until I heard Prince Oscar come aboard, coughing to make the most of his tutoring. I stepped out into the corridor as the Prince's bags were carried on. The porter loaded his valise into compartment two and did not complain when the Prince tipped him half a crown, his hand closing on that lavish amount quickly, in case the Prince should change his mind. I noticed the activity around the train was more hectic as those riding in the second-class carriage strove to get on. A short while later the first warning whistle sounded, signaling the train would leave in five minutes. I became aware of a scramble at the end of this car as the porters struggled with the bags of a late arrival, and I swore under my breath. Compartment five would be occupied after all.

"Would you let me join you?" Prince Oscar asked as he came into Mycroft Holmes' compartment.

"Of course, Herr Schere," said Holmes with the appearance of enthusiasm I understood from my years in his employ was less than wholehearted.

The bustle of porters and passengers made one last surge; then the departing whistle sounded and the big engine began to huff and chuff, and slowly the *Flying Scotsman* pulled away from King's Cross Station, en route to Edinburgh where we expected to arrive in less than nine hours.

It took some time for the train to pull out of the city. London sprawled for miles and it tended to extend along the train lines as well. Almost immediately after leaving the station, the train passed through the first of three small tunnels. None were so long that there was more than a momentary darkness, and our review of the route had prepared us for them. Even so, as the light disappeared briefly I was startled to see Mr. Holmes had moved silently from his seat to stand by the door to the corridor. After the third tunnel he sat down without a comment and stared out the window. The Prince and I exchanged glances and then smiles, his suitably nervous. We passed through the stations at Finsbury Park and Wood Green without pausing; the stations looked small after the grandeur of King's Cross.

The train halted at a third station near the edge of the city. Here the houses had thinned and the brown pall that often blanketed London had been left behind. Again my employer moved to look first out into the corridor and then the window.

"A mail stop," he observed, after a few seconds of studying the scene outside. "Most likely mail for the Far North gathered at the last minute. It should be no problem. Yes, three, four, five, all the gentlemen who entered with the bags have left again. One was likely a sergeant in the service. He has the walk and was more neatly dressed. Good solid yeomen are what make England great."

"All that for a postman?" Prince Oscar marveled, as much amused as shocked.

After the stations we entered a deep cut and for quite a time the view was that of brown stalks and dirt.

Realizing there was no time like the present, I decided to brave the lounge car, where Mycroft Holmes had suggested he and I might pass some of the time in the company of our fellow-passengers, not only to assess them, but to keep an eye on Prince Oscar without seeming to be obvious about it. I remembered my portfolio and the box of drawing pencils Edmund Sutton had loaned me; it was to be part of my disguise.

As I prepared to step into the corridor, I heard a commotion from the head of the car. "Sir Cameron," I told myself with gloomy satisfaction: Sir Cameron MacMillian, son of the MacMillian, was drunk, and had been drunk, I suspected, since the débâcle of a reunion with his German wife. Doubtless Holmes found his presence an annoyance, but would find a way to weave the sodden Scot's presence into his plans.

A moment later my suspicions were confirmed as I saw his valet hasten past in the corridor; I decided to follow along and learn what I could. The corridor of the second-class carriage was very like the one in first class, but there were eight of them instead of five and the seats did not make up into beds; which were instead fitted with curtained bunks at the end of the car. Sir Cameron's valet was still ahead of me, his body moving with the kind of restless urgency of one fearful of punishment, which working for Sir Cameron encouraged. The connecting platform from one car to the next was swaying from speed, and I saw the valet steady himself; I followed his example. In the dining car the napery was in place and the silverware set, but there were no other signs of readiness to serve. We went through it quickly, passing the galley where the sound of banging indicated that preparations were underway for meals; across the next swaying platform we went, the valet six or seven paces ahead of me. I held the door as it began to swing shut and stepped into the lounge car.

The far end of the lounge car that I entered narrowed to provide a large storage area for supplies and baggage. The door was outlined by a brass strip that contrasted with the heavily stained wood panels that lined the car; the full luxury of the lounge was now visible. While studying the lounge's other occupants and trying to determine if any were potential threats, I began to enjoy the opulence of my surroundings. There were curtains on the windows of the lounge car, blocking off the view of the fields beyond the tracks. These curtains matched the fine linen that covered the seven tables lining one side of the car. Near the window adjoining each table was a small vase containing a spray of blue flowers. The train swayed around a curve and I wondered how the tall, thin, cut-glass vases remained upright. Then I noticed a small collar had been fitted to each table to contain the fixtures and that the linen cloth stopped just short of it. Certainly those who engineered the marvels had forgotten nothing. Absently I wondered if any of the Race to the North runs had included a lounge car in their configuration.

I approached the bar that occupied the last several yards of one side of the car; two men tended it. The wall behind them was lined with shelves, each containing an array of the finest liquors; I was particularly impressed by the brandies, including a bottle that was seventy years old. There was also, not surprisingly considering our destination, a selection of Scotch whiskies, including a single malt I knew to be superior but I rarely had the opportunity to enjoy. I stood a moment studying the selection.

I watched Sir Cameron's valet take a bottle of brandy from the barkeep, and a snifter, then turn around to leave the car, presumably bound for compartment one in the first-class car. I nodded to him and received no response whatsoever from the harried gentleman's gentleman. I let my attention wander.

The valet's departure left only five of us in the lounge car. The two men behind the elegantly outfitted bar, myself, and two others, seated at the window table, apparently strangers, for they were discussing the weather and the new extravaganza at the Hippodrome, as those who are chance-met do. One man was stoutish, square-faced, between forty and forty-five, of moderate height, with short, blunt fingers that were stained with ink. His companion was somewhat older, an angular chap in good Scottish tweeds, with a subtle air of success about him that his table-partner lacked.

"—don't hold with cutting women in half. I don't think it's seemly," said the stouter man, his accent a nice mix of Northumberland and London.

"But it isn't as if anyone were really hurt," said the Scotsman.

"Still. If anything went wrong, think of the scandal," the first persisted.

"If anything went wrong, the police would set it to rights in a trice, with an audience of witnesses." He reached into his pocket and extracted a pipe and a pouch of tobacco. He went about the task of filling the bowl and tamping down his mixture with the absentminded ease of long practice. His face was calm. "Cutting a woman in half, done by a fine magician, is a harmless entertainment."

"But with those horrible murders of eight years ago, and it still unsolved," the first man exclaimed. "If nothing else it is poor taste to have such a performance until the Ripper is brought to justice. Better to catch a bullet with one's teeth than remind the public of those murders."

I went to the bar and signaled the 'keep. "Quinine, if you please."

"And what in it?" the barkeep asked, as he lifted a glass. "Gin?" He was in his thirties, sandy-haired and hale, his moustache neat and turned up with wax. He looked as if he fancied himself a dashing sort.

"Nothing just yet. The sun's too high in the sky." I held out payment and a generous tip. "I need a steady hand in my work."

"And what would that be?" The barkeep had asked this so routinely that the words were almost without sense. He was bored but knew what was expected of him.

"I illustrate travel guides," I said. "For Satchel's."

"Travel a lot then, do you?" said the barkeep, marginally more interested than he had been. "A job like that, I think you would do."

"A fair amount. I was in Constantinople a few years ago. I've been to Bombay, as well." I salved my conscience with the reminder that I had, indeed, been in Constantinople in 1889, but for Mycroft Holmes, not for *Satchel's Guides*.

"You couldn't pay me to go there, either one," said the barkeep. "Not with all the wogs and heathens. No, thank you." He opened a bottle of quinine water. "Dare say you need this because of your time in the East."

"Thank you," I said, taking the glass and holding it carefully as the train rattled and swayed in response to its increasing speed. I went to sit down at the end of one of the upholstered benches, keeping my portfolio with me. I listened to the two men continue their sporadic conversation and waited for more of the passengers to drift in. Despite Mycroft Holmes' assurance, I doubted I would automatically recognize anything or anyone who came into the lounge as suspicious.

"They say it will rain again tonight," the stout man said suddenly with authority. "There isn't much in the sky to make that likely."

"We're bound north," the Scotsman reminded him. "It's wetter in the North."

"So it may be," the stout man said, and reached for a copy of *The Scotsman* from beside him on the stool. He opened it and began to read with the determination of one trying to remove the print from the page with the power of his eyes.

The Scotsman lit his pipe at last and the smell of port-soaked tobacco filled the air. He was content to sit and drink his "wee dram," as my Uncle Bethune used to say when he had his.

In very little time, a Glaswegian in clothes more appropriate to bird hunting than travel came along from the rear of the train, his dour expression daunting for anyone but a fellow-Scot. He leaned on the bar, glowering forbiddingly down at its surface, and ordered Scotts' whiskey neat, lifted it, announcing, "To the ruddy Queen, save her," tossed his drink back, had it refilled and went to a seat as far from the three of us as he could get in the lounge, and proceeded to demonstrate his unsociability by pulling the curtain aside and pointedly staring out the window. I had rarely seen such an unappealing man as he, in his buckskin breeches and high boots. I could understand why the Scot and the Englishman would try their hand at conversation—as you do when you travel with strangers—but I could not imagine anyone trying to strike up any talk with this Glaswegian.

I continued my observation, making the quinine last as long as I could, waiting for the luncheon chime. My lack of sleep very nearly caught up with me, for the rocking of the train was soporific and the sound of the wheels became as soothing as the babble of a brook. Were it not for the grim certainty that we were not safe, I might have dozed off. As it was, I tried to clear my head by opening my portfolio and pulling out a few of the sketches Edmund Sutton had so obligingly provided to lend verisimilitude to my role. He had included a few new ones, half done, of buildings of interest along the North Eastern tracks, so that I could claim I had works in progress.

"Not bad," said the barkeep, as I held up a fine drawing of the front of Durham Cathedral. "Not bad at all."

"Thank you," I said, changing for one of the incomplete ones, of Stanford Hall in Leicester. The basic form was recognizable, but almost all the details were absent. The Hall was near where that dare-devil Pilcher kept trying to emulate a bird; most often his efforts in powered flight had so far resembled that of the dodo or the ostrich.

"Have to do some work on it while I have the chance."

"While the train's in motion?" The barkeep was much astonished.

I realized my mistake as soon as I made it. "Not the finished work, of course; in my business, you often have to work while traveling."

The barkeep grunted a kind of acknowledgment and busied himself polishing the bar while the lounge fell silent again, but for the click of the wheels and the rattle and engine bellow of the train. I took out one of the pencils and did what little I could to make it appear I was working on the illustration, but as soon as the luncheon chime sounded, I was johnny-on-the-spot to put away my pencils and drawings and buckle my portfolio closed.

"Ah," said the stout man. "In good time. I am feeling a bit peckish." He tossed off the last of his drink, folded his paper, and prepared to leave the lounge. "After you, sir," he told me.

"No; please," I said, standing aside to let him open the door onto the platform.

We trooped out, the stout man, myself, the pipe-smoking Scot, and the curmudgeonly Glaswegian, across the platform and into the dining car—now redolent with savory odors of mulligatawny soup, potatoes in onion gravy, grilling lamb, and baking cod—where a dozen or so passengers were already seated, Mycroft Holmes and Prince Oscar among them.

"Guthrie!" sang out Holmes in the accent that had never known a public school education. "There you are. Come join us." He waved me toward him with large gestures, which, from a tall, portly man, were nearly overwhelming.

"Coming, sir," I said, clutching my portfolio and heading for their table, which was laid for four. I had to jostle by a young couple from the second-class car and murmured my excuses as I did. Reaching the table, I endured a hearty handshake worthy of an American, and did my best to look accustomed to this treatment.

"I don't know about you, Guthrie, but I am famished," Mycroft Holmes exclaimed. "Didn't have time for much of a breakfast; had to show Herr Schere here some of the sights before we left. Too bad he isn't quite up to snuff." He sat down and motioned Prince Oscar and me to do the same; Prince Oscar had the seat next to Holmes, on the window, which, after long debate the previous night, we had decided was safer than the aisle seat would be. He nudged Prince Oscar. "I dare say you at Satchel's in Vienna don't often enjoy a ride like this one?"

Prince Oscar coughed experimentally and mumbled, "Not often," in German. He fumbled with his chair, the space being limited and the Prince unused to such treatment. "The countryside is very nice." He remembered to continue to muffle his voice.

The Glaswegian was seated across the aisle from us, with the two other men from the lounge car. He looked decidedly bilious, his face an underlying shade of green, as if he had spent the night in hard drinking and was not yet wholly sober. The two whiskies had not helped that, I thought as we settled in for our lunch.

"Two soups, an omelette, lamb, or fish. Very nice," Mycroft Holmes enthused in his Fleet Street accent. He seemed to have taken on the nature of his clothing, and he sat in his place with his shoulders thrown back, arms overlapping his chair, for all the world like a large, extravagant bird displaying his feathers. I was reminded yet again of Sutton's remark that Holmes was a loss to the theatre—"He'd give

Irving and Beerbohm-Tree something to worry about, especially in the Scottish Play, if his performance was any indication"—and at this moment I was prepared to concede Sutton was right.

"The fish is cod," said Prince Oscar. "I dislike cod."

"Then have the lamb," Mycroft Holmes recommended, before he swung around to the table across the aisle from us and held out his big hand. "Good afternoon. I am Micah Holcomb, a writer for *Satchel's Guide*. Since we're traveling together, we might as well be acquainted. This is my illustrator; his name is Guthrie. And our companion is the from the Viennese bureau of Satchel's, Herr Schere."

The stout man looked slightly offended at this open display, but he put out his ink-stained hand at last and said, "Heath. Kerwin Heath. Printer by trade. I don't know these gentlemen's names, or I should introduce you."

Such was the strength of Mycroft Holmes' force of character that his hearty good-will was sufficient to require a response from both men. The Scot with the pipe spoke first. "Angus Dunmuir. Pleasure." The brevity of his handshake belied his cordial word; he volunteered nothing about his profession.

The Glaswegian growled his response. "Camus Jardine." He hunched his shoulders so that he would not have to shake hands.

"Well!" Holmes said genially. "Well met, gentlemen. I hope we may wile away the hours in pleasant conversation." His determination earned him the careful scrutiny of the three across the aisle; undeterred by this beginning, Mycroft Holmes rose from his seat and went about the dining car, introducing himself to all the passengers who were waiting for their luncheon. When he had completed this self-appointed task, he returned to our table in time to order the Scotch Broth and the cod for his lunch and a bottle of claret for our table, which made me stare— ordinarily Mycroft Holmes would never drink a red wine with fish. But, I reminded myself, Micah Holcomb would. I joined Prince Oscar in selecting the mulligatawny soup and the lamb, wanting to compliment the wine.

The waiter brought goblets of water and a basket of crescent rolls and butter before returning to the galley for our soup. I noticed the swaying walk he had developed to compensate for the movement of the train. He brought the Scotch Broth first, took the luncheon orders from the opposite table, and went back for the mulligatawny. As he did, a middle-aged couple came from the lounge car; they were seated behind us and were immediately subject to Mycroft Holmes' ruthless affability.

"Fine day for a journey," Holmes declared, as soon as he had learned the names of the couple, James and Missus Loughlan, just back from America; they had returned from Baltimore some four days since and were now venturing home to Leeds. "Fine place, America. Full of travel possibilities."

Until that instant I was unaware that Mycroft Holmes had ever been to America; he had made reference to Americans, but that was not the same thing. He had also confessed to having been in Canada, but that was hardly commensurate with visiting the United States.

"We were glad of your travel guides," said Mister Loughlan. "I had no notion that country was so big."

His comfortable wife laughed. "Now, don't play the noddy, Mister Loughlan," she said, giving him a shove in his elbow. "Not that the guides weren't helpful, but we did spend many weeks planning our travel."

James Loughlan was delighted to be distracted by the waiter. He managed a nod that was quite cordial, then pretended Mycroft Holmes had vanished like a conjuring trick.

"I see nothing worrisome," said Prince Oscar, clearing his throat as if against pain.

"Ah, Herr Schere, if we could see it, it would not be worrisome," Mycroft Holmes agreed, making a sign of approval to our patient waiter as he served the other two bowls of soup and offered to open the wine.

"Good idea," Holmes said as if it were a novel one. "Wine does better when it's opened awhile, just as stew is always better the second day." As the waiter took out his corkscrew, Holmes went on, "Custard needs to set a bit before you eat it, too."

"So they say," the waiter agreed as he drew the cork and handed it to Holmes, who, wholly unlike himself, pocketed it instead of sniffing it or examining it for dryness.

"Let me have a taste of it," Mycroft Holmes requested, holding out his glass and watching as the waiter poured a bit into it. He drank it straightaway, without looking for color or legs or sniffing its bouquet. "It'll do," he announced. "Give it ten minutes and serve it." He winked—actually winked—at Prince Oscar, saying slyly to the waiter, "Can't have the Viennese think we're complete savages, now can we?"

"No, sir," said the waiter woodenly, and went about his duties as the dining car continued to fill.

"How's the mulligatawny?" Holmes asked when I had tasted mine.

"Very good," I said, thinking they had done a good job, although the intensity of the flavors had been lessened to accommodate English tastes. "It could use a bit less salt."

Across the aisle, Mister Heath was jostling uncomfortably in his chair, exchanging uneasy looks with the taciturn Mister Jardine. Mister Dunmuir seemed oblivious to it all, sipping his Scotch Broth and occasionally looking out the window at the passing scenery. At one point Jardine said something under his breath, and Heath's color mounted in his face to a shade of plum I knew could not be healthy.

Our soup bowls were removed and our main courses brought. I was pleased to see side-dishes of potatoes with minced onions and green peas in butter; and as soon as all three of us had been served, I settled down to my meal, realizing for the first time I was famished. I noticed that Prince Oscar appeared slightly perplexed when neither Mycroft Holmes nor I waited for him to begin, but then he recalled his role and fell to, taking as much pleasure in our food as the rest of the passengers.

Shortly before we were finished, an abrupt oath uttered sotto voce came from the table across from us. Mister Jardine pushed to his feet and stumped out of the dining car in the direction of the lounge. Mister Heath squared his shoulders and watched the fellow go; while Mister Dunmuir paid no attention whatever but continued to enjoy his cod.

"Oh, dear," said Missus Loughlan behind us.

Her husband did his best to make light of the unpleasantness. "We might as well be in Texas," he said, and chuckled.

"As you say," his wife agreed. She pointed out the window. "Oh, look Saint Albans. A mail drop, isn't it?"

Prince Oscar remembered to cough and beg pardon for doing it, while Mycroft Holmes poured out the last of the wine.

FROM THE PERSONAL JOURNAL OF PHILIP TYERS

I have had two notes returned to me in response to the memoranda that MH had dispatched this morning, and I am not sanguine of their results. I cannot help but believe that this investigation is more hazardous than any of us supposed. The police have closed ranks, which is to be expected; but in their solidarity, they are protecting a criminal whose purpose is the ruin of them all.

I must shortly prepare my first telegram to send to MH to be received at Bedford.

Sutton is about his impersonation, remaining in the parlor with papers spread around him, which only he and I know are pages of a play he is memorizing. I have already been treated to his animadversions on Henry Irving's unfair and unreasonable dislike of Mister Ibsen's work, and his own conviction that the plays of Ibsen will one day number among the classics. Fortunately his next part is in an English play. The role he is currently learning is in Volpone *by Ben Jonson, a far remove from the work of Mister Ibsen, in which Sutton is to play Mosca, a character who assists Volpone in his machinations. Mosca, Sutton tells me means "fly."* Volpone *means "fox."*

I cannot say I will regret having to leave Sutton to his task while I carry out MH's instructions. I find my capacity for Mister Jonson's humor is less than his provision of it. Still, during these difficult times, I am grateful to be able to laugh now and again. . . .

Chapter Ten

"I THOUGHT THAT went rather well," said Prince Oscar as we crowded into Mycroft Holmes' compartment after lunch. His fresh, open face was so full of optimism that I did not know how Mycroft Holmes would have the courage to tell him otherwise.

"If you mean we were not set upon by assassins in the middle of the dining car, yes, I would concur," Holmes told him. He did not let the Prince's downcast air keep him from going on. "I am still trying to decide if the contretemps we witnessed at the table across from us was intended as a distraction or was really nothing more than what it seemed—not that that is readily determined." He rubbed his chin. "Guthrie!" He rounded on me. "Find out more about that trio, if you will. It may send you back to the lounge, but do it. I will follow you in a short while."

"And I? Shall I come, too?" Prince Oscar asked eagerly.

Mycroft Holmes shook his head. "Until we know more, it would be best if you remain here. I am sorry, Herr Schere, but I do not want to tempt fate."

Prince Oscar did his best to conceal his disappointment. "I understand."

"What should I look for?" I asked, wondering what I had missed.

My employer gave a sigh of exasperation. "To begin with, I should like to know why Mister Heath is lying about his occupation; he is no more a printer than I am."

"He is not a printer?" the Prince exclaimed.

"What makes you say so?" I asked in almost the same instant.

"You observed the ink on his fingers—well, you were supposed to see it. But you will notice it was only on his right hand, and the color was dark blue, such as one might find in any inkwell in the country. Printers have ink on all their fingers, not just on one hand, for they must touch their machines with both hands; and traditionally it is black, not blue. Also, no ink was apparent under his nails or on his cuticles. His sleeve on his right arm has a slight dusting of what I suppose must be chalk, for which few printers find use. Therefore I must assume the man is lying about his occupation." He was standing and had to reach out to steady himself on the luggage rack as the train swung around a bend in the track. "We're increasing speed," said Holmes dispassionately. "We'll reach Bedford shortly. I'll put a message together for you, Guthrie, and you will send it from the telegraph office and retrieve any sent from Tyers or anyone else who may require my attention."

"Of course," I said, reaching for my portfolio. "Do you need me further or shall I—?"

"Back to the lounge car with you, and keep your eye on Messieurs Heath, Jardine, and Dunmuir. There is something going on there that I do not like." Mycroft Holmes glanced down at the Prince. "If Guthrie discovers nothing troubling, then in a while we should go along to the lounge car, as well. You will have to continue your performance, sir."

"I will enjoy it," said Prince Oscar, enthused at the prospect. "This is most instructional, traveling this way."

"I should think so," Mycroft Holmes said without a trace of irony.

"Very well, sir," I said to my employer as I rose and picked up my portfolio, patting it just below my embossed initials. "My faithful companion and I will go see what is happening in the lounge. And I will leave the train at Bedford to send along our initial report." With a nod, I let myself out into the corridor and started along it in the direction of the lounge car. I had traversed the second-class car and was in the platform connecting it to the dining car when the door opened from the other direction and a trim woman in a most fetching traveling ensemble in dark, steel-blue twill came through. I started to stand aside, and wished I had worn my hat in order to tip it, when the woman took hold of my elbow. Surprised, I supposed she was unsteady on her feet, but as I looked her fully in her face, I knew I had erred.

"Guthrie," said Miss Penelope Gatspy without preamble, "what on earth are you and Mycroft Holmes up to this time?"

My breath stopped in my throat and I must have blushed, recalling our last encounter two years since. How could she behave as if none of that had happened? Not that I was ungrateful, for to experience the castigation I most certainly deserved would not have helped our mission. "That is no concern of yours," I said as if it were only a day or two ago when I had last seen her. No doubt the woman would demand an explanation of me in due time and an apology that I should certainly offer.

"Oh, Guthrie, of *course* it is my business. I shouldn't be here if it were not." Her laughter did more than an accusation would have done to convince me I was not hallucinating the whole episode.

Delayed shock coursed through me. I discovered I was unable to speak. I stared into her mesmerizing blue eyes and remembered how she had looked the first time I had met her; we had been on a train then, too. I was in a compartment that she, too, occupied. I had not realized then that our meeting was far from chance. In the intervening years since that first encounter, I had come to regard any association with her with ambivalence; for although she was a most lovely and self-possessed young woman, she was also an agent in the Golden Lodge, whose purposes were ambiguous at best. Our last encounter was still vivid in my memory, to my chagrin. Finally I said, "Miss Gatspy. It *is* you. I suppose I should not be surprised."

"No, Mister Guthrie," she said with purpose. "You should not."

"How am I to respond to that?" I asked, feeling stupid for challenging her.

"You are usually a sensible man, Mister Guthrie," she said impatiently. "You know that the Brotherhood seeks to place Prince Oscar's brother, Karl Gustav, on the throne. Why should it astound you if the Golden Lodge takes an interest in Prince Oscar's welfare? Particularly now that your English police have a highly placed agent of the Brotherhood among their numbers?"

"Good God," I swore without apology. "How do you come to—"

"Guthrie, we haven't time for this. We might be discovered at any moment. Tell Mister Holmes that I am traveling as a nurse, should he need someone to help with protecting Prince Oscar. Or should I say Herr Schere?" She smiled winsomely at me and went on her way, opposite to mine, pausing once the door closed to turn back and wave to me.

I stood on the swaying platform for the greater part of a minute, trying to order my thoughts. Miss Gatspy often had that effect on me, and I told myself I should be accustomed to it by now. But with every attempt at reassurance, new questions arose, so that what should have led my comfort in fact resulted in more turmoil. I made myself turn and continue on through the dining car—now nearly emptied of diners, one of whom was the second bartender—and into the lounge where nine passengers were seated taking advantage of the friendly air of the place.

"How're you doing?" The barkeep glanced at me with concern that went beyond the demands of his service; if having his partner gone was an imposition, he showed no discomfort because of it. "Not my place to say it, but you look as if you've seen a ghost."

"I suppose I have," I said blankly, and gave myself a mental shake. "Nothing to worry about, though. Not that kind of a ghost."

"Travel can do it to you," said the barkeep and poured a brandy-and-soda for me. "A lot of you artist-types like this." He accepted his payment and tip with a quick smile, and I saw him put the brandy bottle down in the carton behind the bar, although it was less than half empty. There were four other partially filled bottles in the carton as well. He noticed my attention and said, "I always like to hold a little back, you know how it is—looks better to some if the bottles are fairly full."

"Ah," I said, supposing he knew what he was talking about. It was his profession after all.

"How do you think we're doing? Are we making good time?" It was a common enough question on a train famous for its speed.

The barkeep glanced out the window and then at the clock behind the bar. "About average. We won't break any records on this run, not at this rate." He gave the polished surface of the bar another wipe-down, frowning either at the gloss or the speed we were traveling.

I was about to make a remark on how fast English trains were when Mister Jardine, who was sitting alone at the end of the lounge, lurched to his feet, clutched his neck, took two horrid gasps as if through a severed throat, and fell heavily onto his side.

There was consternation in the lounge car almost at once; oaths and outcry competed with the shriek of brakes and the clank of cou-plings as the train slowed in answer to the barkeep's tug on the emer-gency cord, which brought the train to a shuddering halt.

Almost before the train was stopped, three conductors converged on the lounge ready to berate the barkeep for his actions, and all fell silent at the sight of Mister Jardine, now lying dead with an unques-tionably cyanotic tinge to his distorted features.

"Oh, my God," said the eldest of the conductors, and he did not intend this profanely. "What happened?"

Knowing what was expected of me as Mycroft Holmes' secretary, I stepped forward. "The man appears to have been poisoned," I said as calmly as I could. "He died swiftly, and his coloring suggests it."

"Are you a physician?" one of the conductors asked me sharply.

"No, but I have seen a man done to death this way before," I answered carefully and offered no other qualification.

"Poison," the youngest of the conductors scoffed. "How could he have been poisoned?"

The passengers in the lounge car had gone suddenly very quiet, listening to this as if it were news from the front. Two of them set their drinks aside; another swallowed his whole.

"That, I suppose, is a matter for the police," I said. "And the sooner they are notified the better." I realized some of my drink had splashed onto the arm of my suitcoat, and I daubed at it with my pocket handkerchief.

The barkeep nodded twice. "He's right. When any suspicious event takes place aboard a North Eastern train, the authorities are to be summoned at once." He saw that the conductors were nodding in re-sponse to his recitation.

"Then I suppose we'd better put him in the luggage compartment for the time being," said the senior conductor, and was about to reach for the body when I intervened.

"I don't think you're supposed to disturb the body when a crime's been committed," I said. "The police usually want to examine the scene as it is." My tone was deferential, but my determination was apparent. I put myself between the conductors and the corpse. "I have been called upon to draw crime scenes before, and always the police have emphasized the importance of leaving the site undisturbed."

"That's true enough," said one of the passengers whose name I did not know. "Coppers want things left alone. Not that I want to drink with *that* for company," he added and was given a grumble of support from a few of the rest.

The conductors hesitated, and it was while they were muttering among themselves that Mycroft Holmes came into the lounge car.

"I say there, Guthrie? What is this all about?" He sounded more inconvenienced than worried, which I knew was far from the truth.

I stood back. "As you see," I told him, indicating the body.

"Gracious!" he declared, and went toward the fallen man; such was the force of his presence that no one attempted to hinder him. He stopped a foot or so from the body and bent down to examine him. "This man has been poisoned," he said calmly. "You must inform the police at once."

The senior conductor was willing to agree now. "Just what I thought myself. We must make a full halt at Bedford and wait for the authorities to tell us what next to do."

"You should also secure this car," Mycroft Holmes went on. "If not, the murderer might well be able to escape."

This brought a buzz of consternation from the other passengers, one of them calling out, "You don't think any of us did it?"

"No," said Mycroft Holmes bluntly. "But neither do I know that all of you did not." He let the implications of his remark sink in before continuing. "Until the police tell us otherwise, I should think you would all want to wait for them to do their job. You would not want suspicion to fall upon you by mistake, would you?"

A few of the men exchanged uneasy glances, and then Mister Dunmuir spoke up. "I don't like the dead for company, but I'm willing to let the constables do their work." His reasonable tone was enough to persuade most of the rest to comply with this requirement.

"Bedford is not far, and once the police have finished with this unfortunate occurrence, I am sure we will be on our way again quite handily," said Mycroft Holmes, looking at the conductors for agreement. "I don't know how we do this, gentlemen. One of you should surely remain here, and I am certain one should notify the engineer of what has happened, and one should probably make whatever arrangements are necessary for when the police come aboard." He looked about. "I will be glad to keep order here, with my illustrator Guthrie, and help in any way we can."

"But Herr Schere?" I protested, knowing we would be leaving the Prince exposed. For all we knew this was a diversionary tactic to leave the Prince unguarded.

"Oh, he is in good hands, Guthrie," said Mycroft Holmes in a tone I thought bordered on smug. "There is a nurse aboard, a Miss Gatspy? I think you may have encountered her already. She has agreed to watch Herr Schere for us."

"How good of her," I said, feeling an unaccountable stab of jealousy go through me. Inwardly I told myself this was absurd, an emotion unworthy of me and having nothing to do with my past dealings with Miss Gatspy. Still, it rankled. The very notion of Miss Gatspy alone with Prince Oscar was enough to set my thoughts racing, and along lines I found most disquieting, for after all, the Prince had had a night on the town with Sir Cameron. I had to fight the irrational impulse to protest this arrangement. Which was ridiculous. I reminded myself that Miss Gatspy was an accomplished player of these difficult games and that under these unexpected circumstances, we should be grateful for a young woman of Miss Gatspy's talents to protect Prince Oscar.

"Yes, it was. No doubt she will look after him quite well while we are occupied here," said my employer.

"No doubt," I said tonelessly. "Then we should proceed on to Bedford. The longer we delay the more chance the culprit will have to protect himself."

"True enough," said Mycroft Holmes. "Then it is as well that the conductors should be about their tasks at once." He made a gesture that sent the three hurrying. Then he looked toward the barkeep. "The police will most certainly want accounts from each of you of what you did or did not see. The same is true of all the rest of you. If you discuss this among yourselves, you may not have as clear a recollection of the event. Therefore I propose to sit down with you," he said to the barkeep, "and get what information you have to give. Then my assistant and I will do the same for each of you in this car, at which time I will stand each of you a drink. Lord knows, we could all use one."

"Mighty high-handed," muttered one of the passengers.

Mycroft Holmes heard that and spoke up at once. "You cannot

be compelled, of course. But the clearer and more complete an account we may give the police, the less time we are apt to be delayed." He knew this observation had an impact on all of them. He lowered his eyes. "A man is dead. It is the least we can do to help in bringing his murderer to justice."

"True enough," said Mister Dunmuir quite suddenly. "I don't like murderers roaming about the countryside, and I don't like to dishonor the dead."

This unlooked-for support seemed to encourage the rest. In a matter of a few minutes the men had sorted themselves out, and I was perched on one of the three barstools, my notebook out of my pocket and my pencil sharpened and at the ready.

"My name's Cecil Whitfield," said the barkeep. He struck me as being much of his type—regular-featured and accommodating. "I live in London. I've worked for the North Eastern line for seven years." He cleared his throat and began, "I noticed the . . . the deceased when he came into the lounge before luncheon was served. He kept to himself, very dour and moody. He took his drink and sat at the end of the divan, as far from others as he could. The same when luncheon was over. He came in with those two"—he pointed to Dunmuir and Heath—"ordered his drink with them, said a few words about the food, and then he took his whisky and went off by himself."

Several of the men in the lounge were nodding their heads in agreement, although one, a beanpole of a fellow in a modish tan suit that didn't become him, said, "They talked longer than that."

Mycroft Holmes swung around and looked at him. "You will have your chance to give your account. In the meanwhile, please say nothing. I want every account to be individual, to aid the police in making a complete picture of the event. If you disagree with what has been said, tell me when it is your turn." He glanced toward Mister Jardine, whose lips were now decidedly blue.

A man with a Midlands accent grumbled at Holmes' high-handed ways, but did nothing to challenge him.

The barkeep finished his account, read my transcript of it, signed it, and poured himself a generous tot of gin. "I'll manage the drinks, sir," he said, looking a bit restored.

"Well and good," said Mycroft Holmes, and signaled to the man who had been sitting nearest Mister Jardine.

"You understand I had my back to him. I saw very little until he rose and . . ." His expression was confused.

"Then this will not take long," Holmes assured him. "Which seat were you in? Guthrie, draw a scheme of the lounge, so each can mark his place. We know Whitfield was behind the bar and Jardine was in the last chair before the corridor to the next car and access to the baggage compartment. We need to place all the others as well."

I did my best to sketch the lounge as ordered, and did not acquit myself too dreadfully. When I was done, I let Mister Olwin mark his place on the drawing, and I wrote his name to the side of it, then prepared to take down his statement. It turned out to be quite brief and delivered in neat, organized declarations that would surely be useful to the police. When he had signed his account, he ordered West Country cider for his tipple.

The third account was given by the man who had been seated across from Olwin, and he had more of a flare for the dramatic. To improve his account, just as he was describing how he saw Jardine clutch at his throat and stagger out of his chair, the train began to move again, punctuating this account with a lurch and a groaning of metal that created a most alarming effect in the lounge. Mister Wrougtham continued his narrative as the train picked up speed, as if carried along with its movement. Aside from dramatic elaboration, his tale added little to the information we had already compiled. He accepted a split of champagne for his efforts.

The beanpole was the seventh man to render his account. He gave his name as Fitzwilliam Carstairs, his occupation as a solicitor who was returning to Sheffield after completing a transfer of deed for a client. "I am sure of what I saw," he said as if daring Mycroft Holmes to deny this.

"Which is why we are at such pains to get all of you to tell what you observed. You, Mister Carstairs, say you saw Mister Dunmuir and Mister Heath talking for more than the few moments the rest have described?"

"Yes," said Carstairs indignantly. "I cannot account for what these others have said, but I know what I saw."

"Yes. You have said so," Mycroft Holmes said calmly. "Will you be good enough to let Guthrie take down your words?"

With an injured sniff, Carstairs gave a hitch to his shoulders and began, "I was behind the three gentlemen when they came in from the dining car, where they had been seated together. The Scot with the pipe—I'm sorry, I don't recall his name—was saying to the dead man that some arrangement would have to be made, at which time the dead swore and told the other man that he would never agree. When they reached the bar to order their drinks, the portly fellow said that the dead man could be compelled, at which the dead man swore again. They ordered their drinks and exchanged a few tense pleasantries; and then, just as the dead man took his whisky, the Scot grabbed his arm and said they were not finished yet. The dead man said, 'Be damned to you,' in an ugly whisper, shook the man's hand off, and went to be seated by himself."

Several of the men protested this account, claiming that nothing of the sort had taken place. This threatened to turn into a general squabble, which was only ended when Mycroft Holmes called them to order once again. "Each shall have your chance, and each shall say what he saw and heard. It is rare when witnesses all agree about an event; and when such a thing does happen, it is also suspicious." This served to pacify the men in the lounge car.

When Mister Carstairs had finished, I read back what I had taken down, and while he signed it, marked his place on the plan of the lounge car. He drank tea laced with rum.

We had just completed Mister Dunmuir's account and had three statements to go when we began to slow for Bedford, where I would send a telegram to Tyers and, with luck, would find one waiting. I did not want to hurry this process, but I knew the others in the lounge were as restless as I. With a warning look at Mycroft Holmes, I said, "The police should be here soon."

"So they should. I imagine the conductors will take care of summoning them. We had best remain here." He seemed unflustered at this recommendation.

"But if we are delayed, shouldn't I inform Satchel's?" I asked, meaning Tyers.

"Of course. A very good idea. But we will want to let them know how long a delay they might expect. We may not know that for a short while once we arrive. Still, we will have to tell them something," Mycroft Holmes said, thinking aloud. "Well, as soon as we are dismissed from here, you will send a telegram to Satchel's to tell them we may be detained and for what reason." His smile was faint and faintly sarcastic. "If we do not have a long wait for the police to do their duty, we may not be so very late into Edinburgh."

"True enough," I said, with more hope than conviction.

The train was pulling into Bedford now, going no faster than a trotting horse. Bedford Station was a long, narrow building along the eastern side of the platform. It was built of the dark brick common in the area. Clustered around the edges of the platform as it extended beyond the station were a number of kiosks and push-carts manned by a dozen or so men waiting to sell a variety of sausages, boiled nuts, and bottled drink to passengers on each train as it passed through, and this train was no different. Nearer the edge of the platform there were hand-carts and a clutch of passengers waiting to board. A thick row of un-painted walls of warehouses lined the back of the western platform, their windows reflecting darkly the bustle across from them.

"Let everyone stay as he is," Mycroft Holmes announced. "We have good reason to remain where we are, with doors closed, until the police have done with us." His reminder was delivered in firm accents. "Guthrie," he went on, his voice much lowered, "make sure no one leaves, if you have to confine him by force. All we would need would be for Schere to be harmed now, when we are aware of danger, for the whole attempt we have made to end catastrophically."

"Yes," I said, looking about as the passengers in the lounge car stared out the window as the *Flying Scotsman* stopped, jerked, and stopped again amid a splendid hissing of steam.

"Why not be seated, gentlemen?" Mycroft Holmes proposed. "The sooner the police do their work, the sooner we will be able to depart."

Surprisingly, the barkeep agreed. "Listen to the man. He's making sense." He began to set up glasses on the bar. "On the house, gentlemen. On the house." With a flourish, he started to fill the glasses, recalling almost every drink ordered. "Come. We can drink to the poor man who has died."

It was well-nigh impossible to refuse such an overture; one or two of the passengers in the lounge hung back, but the rest were eager to accept the offer. As I joined the others at the bar, I saw one of the conductors leave the train and hurry off in the direction of the station-master's office, his step hurried, his demeanor harried. "Not a task I envy him," I remarked quietly to Holmes.

"No, indeed." He had his snifter in hand and he moved away from the crowded bar to take a position near the corridor to the rear of the train. As I went up to him, he said, "I would not like anyone to leave through the baggage compartment."

"Of course not," I said, keeping an eye on the slice of platform I could see through the window beyond the bar. "Not a lot going on."

"Give it a moment, dear boy," he said, still maintaining his superior shopkeeper's accent. "We do not have long to wait."

"How do you mean?" I had an uneasy vision of the train being surrounded by armed constables ready to fire upon anyone attempting to leave.

"The police will come and very likely a physician as well," said my employer. "And they will want to deal with this as handily as they may." He shook his head slightly. "Chagrined though I am to say it, thank God for your Miss Gatspy."

I had long since given up trying to persuade Mycroft Holmes that she was not *my* Miss Gatspy. All I did was shrug. "If we may trust her."

"In this instance, I think we may," Holmes said, glancing into the corridor behind him as a loud noise came from the luggage compartment. "Trunks being loaded, by the sound of it," he told me as if to reassure himself.

"Why should we trust her?" I asked before I had wholly realized I had spoken at all. I began to apologize for this unseemly outburst only to be silenced by Holmes holding up his hand. "I am sorry—"

"There is so much we have to do here," he informed me. "I will discuss this with you later. For now, we must ready ourselves for the police." He cocked his chin in the direction of the window. "Keep a look-out. When the police arrive, we must not falter."

"Why would we do that?" I could not imagine he intended to extend our disguises to the point of hindering any investigation.

"My dear Guthrie, think a moment," he said with great patience. "Think of what Tyers is doing."

I held my tongue this time, remembering that Tyers was continuing Mycroft Holmes' efforts to discover the man or men in the police who was also a member of the Brotherhood. "You mean the solidarity of—"

"Precisely," said Holmes, and folded his arms while the conversation in the lounge car became more anxious. "I hope we will not have long to wait. There's no point in continuing our questioning now. These men are restive enough as it is," he added in an undervoice.

"That they are," I said, and went back to staring out the window, both anticipating and dreading the arrival of the police.

FROM THE PERSONAL JOURNAL OF PHILIP TYERS
My first telegram has been sent to Bedford and the memoranda that MH said were to be delivered as part of the second round of communications are ready. I will leave Sutton alone with his sides and Ben Jonson's occasional

vulgarity. By the time I return the first telegram from MH or G should have been delivered, and I will know which set of instructions I am going to be expected to obey. What a predicament to be in—having to identify a corrupt official without exposing ourselves in the process. In these days of so much distrust of the police, it is prudent not to raise any more public sentiments against them than is necessary. By the same token, it is also necessary to redress any wrongs committed by members of the police as quickly as possible. When the repercussions are such as may be in this current case, circumspection is more essential than ever, so that any findings are capable of supporting the most thorough scrutiny.

The second double for HHPO is about to depart from the Diogenes Club under naval guard. Unless something has gone very wrong, I believe MH can take justifiable pride in protecting HHPO from the danger of assassination. . . .

Chapter Eleven

"MISTER HOL—COMB," I exclaimed, wanting to be sure I caught my employer's attention in the midst of all this turmoil; I saw two uniformed constables running down the platform, one of them in the company of the conductor. "The police have arrived."

"At least the first wave," Mycroft Holmes said, and addressed the men in the lounge car. "Gentlemen, as you can see, your ordeal is coming to an end."

One or two of the gentlemen in question were beginning to show the effects of drink, and I could see they would not make a very good appearance when the police spoke to them; it was a fortunate thing that Mycroft Holmes had insisted that they provide their accounts before they bolstered their nerves with strong spirits. One or two were regarding Mister Jardine's body with growing uneasiness, as if they expected it to do something untoward.

A few moment's later and a constable came into the lounge car, his expression wary, as if he was apprehensive about what he might encounter. He looked at the men at the bar, at the body, and then to the barkeep. "Anything been touched?'

Whitfield snorted. "O' *course* something's been touched. But if you mean the body, Mister Holcomb and Mister Guthrie have kept us away from it." He pointed out Mycroft Holmes with a mixture of relief and satisfaction.

The constable came up to Holmes; he was nearly a head shorter and five stone lighter, but he gamely gave my employer a long, skeptical scrutiny. "Oh, yes?" he said at the end of it, implying a world of doubt.

"Yes, Constable, I did," said Mycroft Holmes, thrusting out his hand. "Micah Holcomb of *Satchel's Guides*. This is my illustrator, Paterson Guthrie. Glad to have been of service."

A second constable arrived, there was a hurried, whispered conference between the two, then the second rushed off again and the first assumed a stance of authority. "This is how it is. We have to wait until the Inspector comes aboard with the medical man. They will decide how we're to deal with . . ." he let his gaze, wandering in the direction of the corpse, finish his thoughts. "In the meantime, you're to remain calm and go nowhere. I'll begin taking your statements now." He reached importantly for the notebook in his sleeve.

"Holcomb's already done that," said Whitfield. "He's been taking down statements from everyone. That fellow with him has done most of the writing." He was almost smug as he made this announcement.

"Guthrie," Holmes supplied, going on, "It seemed a good notion to record as much as possible while the impressions were still clear. Once men begin to talk among themselves, they will tend to try to reconcile their impressions with those of others. I did not think that would benefit your investigation." He motioned to me. "Let him look over the notes, Guthrie. I am sure he will find them interesting." It was more disconcerting than I had anticipated, hearing that accent from him, though I had heard him use a great many others. They had been foreign accents, not English ones—this was rather like hearing the Prince of Wales speaking broad Suffolk, or Cockney.

"Um," said the constable grudgingly. He squinted at Holmes, sniffed, and took the pages I held out to him. "I'll have a look at these."

"There are still a few more to be had. Would you like to get their statements now?" Mycroft Holmes indicated the men waiting on the upholstered bench. "It would be more convenient for those men, no doubt."

"No doubt," said the constable, squaring his shoulders and advancing on the last witnesses as if to overwhelm them with the magnitude of the case. "Now, which of you was next?"

As the constable began his job, Mycroft Holmes said to me, very quietly, "We must be careful with this chap. He's carved himself a niche and he does not want it ruined. If it is at all possible, do not challenge him on any issue unless I begin it."

"Why are you so worried about a constable?" I asked.

"Because police are no different than anyone else. Those in their profession talk among themselves. They boast and they complain, as men of all professions do. This man will want to make the most of his part in this investigation and he will say far too much to his cronies, and word will get out." He shook his head ponderously. "If only we knew how far the corruption has spread, I would be more sanguine. As it is . . ." He coughed delicately. "Say as little as possible about Herr Schere."

"I am not wholly a novice, sir," I said a bit stiffly.

"No, Guthrie, you are not. Forgive my maladroitness. I meant nothing to your discredit." He lowered his head and added, "We must finish this case quickly."

"Herr Schere?" I asked, not following his thoughts.

"No, Guthrie; this murder. If it is connected to our mission—which I am beginning to believe it may not be—we must determine what part it plays." He rocked back on his heels as if the train were moving. "It is easy to think it a diversionary tactic, but it may, in truth, be something else entirely. And we had better know which as soon as may be. A pity you had to hand those notes over to the constable. Nothing for it, though." He turned away, and managed another expansive gesture. "Mister Whitfield, I am most impressed by how well you have handled this tragedy."

Cecil Whitfield, being only human, grinned, and his very ordinary face reddened with pleasure for the praise. "Well, you know, sir, we try to do our bit."

"And so you have," Mycroft Holmes enthused. I watched him, bemused, wondering what he was up to. "You must have had experience before in dealing with awkward situations."

"You know how it is, sir, on trains," Whitfield responded, basking in flattery.

"And no doubt you have a keen eye for trouble," Holmes went on.

"I like to think so, sir," said Whitfield, his face serious and his manner bordering on obsequious.

"Well, then—just before that poor man died, did you happen to notice anything about him that suggested he was afraid? If he was, could you tell what frightened him?" He tossed the question out as one might speculate on the number of dried beans in a jar.

"He were a sullen sort of man," said Whitfield, making a great show of thought. "Nothing seemed to please him. That could have been fear, but it could have been surliness just as well."

"Well, yes," Mycroft Holmes conceded. "But take that man"— he pointed at a thin gentleman with graying hair wearing a tweed jacket—"what can we discern about him?" Without waiting for a response, he went on in a near-whisper to me, "I recommend that you don't try your pose as an artist on him."

I waited, knowing that I'd understand in a moment; Mycroft Holmes made these observations as a kind of mental exercise, as another man might take a daily constitutional. He said it kept his mind limber.

"Unlike our companion at luncheon, this man *is* a printer. There is printer's ink under his fingernails, but only on his right hand. Also, his right forearm is slightly tighter in his jacket's sleeve. That indicates he works with one of the new high-pressure presses or more likely the sheets of highly detailed illustrations they produce. The ink is the wrong shade for the poor stuff used in a newspaper, so I surmise he works at printing those woodland scenes so popular lately or perhaps even an illustrated magazine. Since he is too well dressed to be one who regularly operates the presses, he likely owns or manages such an establishment. I have always observed that the owner of a business is often much more willing to engage in the actual work of the place than are his managers. Perhaps that is why they are the owners. I also suspect his cannot be too large an establishment or he would not be concerned about pressure, perhaps a deadline, for he has been nervously regarding his watch, which you will see he has placed on the table beside his drink. You may observe he has two pens in his jacket. I am willing to wager that we will find one contains red, or some other distinctive color of ink. Since he lacks a pencil box, it is unlikely he is an artist himself. Hence I deduce he is the owner or editor. Let us wait a moment. His movements reflect someone who is reluctantly about to finish a task he can no longer avoid. His posture shifts, his fingers and wrists have tensed three times in the last minute, and his eyes keeping darting around and then settling on the table in front of him as if he is already looking at what he antici-pates—much as you behave as you approach doing my accounts."

I had not realized my discomfort with those accounts was so ob-vious; in spite of my years with Mycroft Holmes, I found it intimidating to attempt to prepare records for someone with the eye for detail and analytical mind my employer possesses. I resolved to try to put on a more cheerful air the next time I approached that monthly chore. I had just made my resolve when the fellow we were observing reached under his seat and brought up a sheaf of papers. These proved to be proof prints of illustrations of military activity during the Siege of Port Arthur. Within minutes he had circled in red several parts of the first illustration.

"An editor," Mycroft Holmes said, satisfied at what he had dis-cerned.

There was a sudden commotion among the men at the bar as the constable snapped to attention and a man dressed for hacking with prematurely white hair came into the lounge car, followed by a rabbitty little man in an out-at-the-pockets-and-elbows suit carrying a physi-cian's bag. The white-haired gent stopped and looked around the lounge. "God have mercy," he said as he caught sight of the body.

"The Inspector has arrived," said Mycroft Holmes, not quite making a public announcement.

"That he has," said the white-haired man, declaring, "I am In-spector Jasper Carew of the Bedford constabulary. The man with me is the coroner for our investigations, Norton Rollins. He will conduct the examination of the body, if you will clear a path for him?" His manner was faintly laconic, as if he wanted no part of bustle and strife, but he had a look in his deep-set blue eyes that told me he was someone of powerful will. I hoped that he and Mycroft Holmes would not lock horns, for such a contest would surely take on epic proportions.

There was a shuffling of chairs, stools, and feet as the coroner made his way toward the corpse. Most of the men in the lounge car were still unwilling to look at Mister Jardine. I stayed near Mycroft

Holmes, anticipating his need of my abilities, although I could not determine which he might request.

He surprised me yet again. "Inspector, my illustrator has made a rough drawing of the state of the lounge car at the time the man died, if it would be useful."

I shot him a quick look. "The quality—" I reminded him, hoping there would be no opportunity to compare my schematic with the finished drawings Sutton had provided. I must surely be found wanting if that were done.

"Of course, Guthrie," Holmes soothed. "You know how artists can be, Inspector—not wanting the world to see their work until they have had time to polish it, making it as flawless as possible. Guthrie is no different. The sketch he has made of this scene is quick and without finesse. But working on a moving train is hardly the best of drawing circumstances; I know you will make allowances."

The white-haired Carew swung around to look at us, then held out his hand. "Thank you. That will be useful." As he took the sheet Mycroft Holmes held out to him, he added, "Perhaps your illustrator will add to his civic virtues and consent to draw the body as it lies."

I could feel myself go pale. "I . . . I . . . this isn't the sort of . . ." I looked around at Holmes, hoping he would find some way to excuse me from such a disastrous duty; my drawing classes were twenty years behind me, and I had been taught to use charcoal, not pencil, for drawings. It was one thing to add a touch here and there to Sutton's excellent work, and quite another to prepare a record of a crime. My previous sketch had been for purposes of detailing persons' locations, not the disposition of the corpse.

"He isn't in the general way of drawing dead bodies, of course, although he has done so," said Mycroft Holmes blandly, "but I'm sure he can provide you with a quick sketch that will suit your purposes." He put his big, long hand on my shoulder. "Don't fret, my boy. The dead cannot hurt you."

With gratitude I seized on this one bit of salvation he had offered. "Yes," I told the Inspector, "I have an aversion to dead bodies."

Carew sighed. "So many do," he said to the air, ignoring the slight mutter of discomfort that swept through the occupants. "Well, Mister Guthrie, I am grateful to have you aboard. Let Mister Rollins finish his preliminaries and then I will tell you what to draw."

I took my portfolio and made my way back in the car to where Mister Jardine was lying. I could feel my hands shaking and chastised myself inwardly for being so lax that I could not control myself; after all, I had walked to my own execution in Constantinople and remained unshaken. But the thought of having to attempt to draw this scene unnerved me. "Sorry," I mumbled as I nearly bumped into Mister Rollins, who was bent over Mister Jardine, nodding and sucking in his cheeks as a sign of thoughtfulness.

"You don't have to bother with the face; I'll have that at the morgue and I'll photograph it," said the physician in a testy manner. "I need to know how he is lying, how the furniture is disposed around him," he went on, then looked up at Inspector Carew. "Do you need anything more?"

"Not with this excellent schematic," said Inspector Carew. "Don't worry about the aesthetics," he advised me. "Just a sketch with the pertinent information is needed. Otherwise we'll be here for hours more, and the North Eastern would not be best pleased." He made a quick gesture. "If we're given the go-ahead from London, we will ride along to the next stop. That way we may be certain no one leaves the train, and we can anticipate being met by a proper escort for the victim." He patted the breast of his hacking jacket and drew out a brass case from which he removed a long, thin cigar. "If anyone wishes to smoke, I find it makes the air less oppressive." He indicated the body.

A few of the passengers hastened to take advantage of this kind offer. Pipes and cigars and a few pouches of tobacco and papers were brought out, prepared, and set alight.

"I'm a trifle nervous," I said, vastly understating the case. "I doubt the work will be very good."

"Very good isn't necessary," Inspector Carew assured me. "Barely adequate will suffice." He studied Mister Jardine's position intently, then stepped back, tapping Rollins on the shoulder indicating he should give me access to the corpse.

A number of passengers in the lounge made a great display of trying not to watch what I did, all the while struggling covertly to observe me at work. I took out the pencils Sutton had showed me how to use only hours ago—how I wished I had a stick of charcoal instead!—chose a clean sheet of paper, and using the back of my portfolio to steady the paper, I did what I could to sketch the end divan, the table, and Mister Jardine fallen between the two, one hand still to his chest, the other flung out as if to seize something in his rigid fingers. I looked at what I was doing and thought it woefully disappointing, but kept gamely on, knowing that until I had achieved some semblance of accuracy, Inspector Carew would cordially-but-inexorably keep me at this task.

"That will do well enough for my purposes," said the Inspector after what seemed an eternity. "We will be underway again in a minute or two."

As if to confirm this there was a hiss from the front of the train, and the cars gave a kind of shudder, as if readying themselves to resume our journey. The men in the lounge car looked about uneasily, as if they thought something intrusively dramatic were about to happen. Several of them gulped down their drinks and one of them went so far as to put his just-lit cigar out in the last of his stout.

"Do we ride along?" Rollins asked, his voice low and rumbling, not at all the kind of sound one would suppose could come from such an unprepossessing chap.

"Yes, Rollins, we do," said Inspector Carew. "And we remain with the body until it is removed. God willing, we will depart with our culprit in tow." He sighed, looking through the paper Mycroft Holmes had given him. "I shall review these. Any of you gents need the necessary room, use the one in this car at the end of the corridor beside the baggage compartment once the train has left the station. There'll be constables at both platforms, so don't try anything foolish." He took hold of the edge of the bar as the train heaved itself forward a few inches.

"Once the train is moving, may we go to our compartments once again?" Mycroft Holmes asked. "I am traveling with a Viennese gentleman, Herr Schere, who is unwell. I have left him in the care of a nurse, and I would like to see how he is faring."

"A very reasonable request," said Inspector Carew after he had given it some consideration. "I will do myself the pleasure of accompanying you to inquire into the condition of your Viennese traveling companion." He smiled with no trace of warmth. "Will that suit you?"

The train was moving again, going more slowly than was usual. I had a moment of panic when I realized we were leaving Bedford without sending or receiving telegrams. Undoubtedly Tyers had one waiting in the station telegraph office, but it might as well have been on the moon; I could not reach it.

Just north of Bedford we passed another train pulled off on the siding in order to allow us to go on undelayed; I thought how intricate a task it was to keep trains in motion without more catastrophes than we had. I had to reassure myself that the North Eastern line did not often make mistakes in adjusting their schedules—I hoped this would be another such successful run. We had more than enough to worry about without wondering if the North Eastern were doing their part of the work.

"Tell me, Guthrie," Holmes said in a low voice as I made my way back to where he stood at the end of the bar. "What do you think Mister Jardine did that made someone willing to kill him?" He began to toy with his watch-fob. "This is more my brother's area of expertise than mine, but let us apply his methods."

"All right," I said as I watched Inspector Carew begin to pour over the plan I had done of the lounge, occasionally consulting the statements Mycroft Holmes had prepared for him. I had no doubt that beneath that aloof façade, the man was thorough and dogged.

"Ah, yes," Holmes said following my gaze, "Inspector Jasper Carew. You would think that he saw corpses on every train coming through Bedford for all the response he has made. Too cool by half, if you ask me." He folded his arms and braced his shoulders against the wall, accommodating the movement of the car. At this reduced speed, we swayed and jostled more than we had done at our earlier, faster pace. "He bears watching. And, of course, he is watching us."

"Yes," I said. "I'm aware of that."

"Good for you, Guthrie. You have learned to hide your awareness, which is a very great advantage in our work." He glanced toward Mister Dunmuir, who was staring out the window, nothing in his demeanor to suggest he was upset. "I wish I knew more about that man."

"Why? Why Dunmuir more than another?" I asked a touch more sharply than was called for. I did not like to see fellow-Scots accused or even suspected of criminal activities.

Mycroft Holmes answer was bland. "Because he had a greater chance to observe Jardine than most of us did."

"I suppose he did," I allowed, recognizing how accurate his state-ment was. "That is assuming he paid any more attention than necessary. You saw how they were during lunch—Dunmuir and Heath exchanged perhaps a dozen words with Jardine, most of them about salt and pep-per." I was not going to be put off my guard quite so easily. I swayed as the train pulled around the long, gentle, westerly curve leading to the straightaway into Wellingborough and Kettering beyond.

"They were not very expressive," Holmes agreed. "I cannot help but find it puzzling." He twirled his watch-fob some more, like one of those eastern mystics with his prayer wheel. "Why did they sit together at lunch if they had nothing to talk about."

"Perhaps they preferred solitary—" I broke off as Inspector Carew got to his feet and came toward Mycroft Holmes.

"You did a very good job, Mister Holcomb—a very good job. Which still puzzles me, but let that pass." He turned toward Rollins. "How much longer do you need with the body?"

"Five more minutes and then he can be placed in the baggage compartment," Rollins answered.

Behind the bar, Whitfield looked up sharply. "I'd better go and make sure there's room for him. We can't have him rolling about on the passengers' cases." He slapped his palm down on the bar. "Closed for ten minutes, gents." He bent down and picked up one of his crates, then made for the inner door into the luggage compartment where his supplies were also stored.

"Conscientious," said Inspector Carew. "Don't see that too often nowadays." He held up the papers. "Rollins, will you keep these with you? That's a good fellow." He handed the papers to Rollins then regarded Mycroft Holmes. "Shall we deal with your sick friend? You will have to run the gamut in terms of questions from other passengers. If you would prefer to wait until after Leicester, I can well understand."

"I think it would be best to look in on Herr Schere," said Mycroft Holmes crisply. "He is in charge of the Vienna office. I wouldn't want him thinking I was lax in my duty to Satchel's by neglecting him."

"Is he aware there is a body in the lounge?" Inspector Carew inquired.

"I suppose he must do," Holmes answered, frowning. "I trust he will not develop a dislike of travel in England because of this." He shouldered his way to the door. "Inspector, if you will be good enough to come with me. Guthrie?"

"At once, Mister Holcomb." I clutched my portfolio and followed after the two taller men, going past the constable on the platform to the dining car. I found the wonderful odors of roasting capon unappealing as I made my way between the tables, trying not to disturb the waiters who were changing napery and glasses; the second bartender was alone at his table, the last of his meal before him. The second-class carriage was oddly quiet, the occupants of the various compartments busying themselves with reading papers or other private activities. I wondered what the constable said that had had so daunting an impact on them all.

Arriving at Prince Oscar's compartment in the first-class car, I held back as Mycroft Holmes knocked on the door. "Herr Schere? It is Micah Holcomb come to see how you are doing."

The door slid open and Miss Gatspy appeared. "Good afternoon, Mister Holcomb," she said with a demureness I knew was not hers. "Herr Schere is resting. If you must speak to him, then let me make him more comfortable." With that she closed the door again, leaving the three of us standing in the narrow corridor.

"A most personable woman," said Inspector Carew with a speculative shine in his eyes.

I bridled in her defense; luckily no one saw me. "Nurse Gatspy is most capable," I said, trying to sound approving and coming off pompous.

"Guthrie is right," said Mycroft Holmes with a slight smile. "Her skills are beyond question. That she is fair and conducts herself well recommends her the more." He looked back at the door as Miss Gatspy opened it again. Obedient to her signal we crowded into the compartment.

Prince Oscar lay on the wide bench that had been made up as a day-bed. He wore his smoking jacket, surrounded by pillows. On the pull-out table was a tray with a teapot and the rest of the service for tea, as well as a small bottle of Benedictine that had only just been opened. The Prince waved languidly to us. "Good afternoon, gentlemen. I am sorry I cannot rise to shake your hands."

"How are you feeling, Herr Schere?" Mycroft Holmes asked. "May I present Inspector Jasper Carew? Herr Osrich Schere of *Satchel's Guides*, Vienna."

"A pleasure to meet you, Inspector. As you can see, Mister Holcomb, I am the better for Miss Gatspy's help," he replied, with such a look at her that I longed to tell him how offensive I found his behavior. Perhaps Princes were allowed such liberty, but no man of good character would so compromise the—

"Guthrie has been assisting Inspector Carew here deal with the dead man in the lounge," said Mycroft Holmes, laying his hand warningly on my shoulder.

"Oh, bravo, Mister Guthrie," said Miss Gatspy, her blue eyes alight with mischief. "I should like to see your efforts."

"And so you shall," Holmes promised her before giving his attention to Prince Oscar once more. "Herr Schere, I fear we may be delayed; our arrival in Edinburgh will be later than we expected. I trust you will not be too inconvenienced?"

"I presume you can make alternate arrangements for me?" His brows were pale so the lift he gave them was not so noticeable as it would have been had they been dark. "I am sure you will work out something."

"Of course," said Mycroft Holmes heartily. "We can't have the publisher of Satchel's Vienna left to fend for himself like a tradesman."

Inspector Carew seemed satisfied. "I'm sorry to have disturbed you. I hope you make a full recovery."

Prince Oscar remembered to cough. "I think Miss Gatspy has made me better already," he said with another of his knowing glances; I recalled again that the Prince had gone carousing with Sir Cameron during his stay in London, and I had to force myself to listen with composure. "Still, I think it is best if I remain here in my compartment, under her care, for the rest of the journey."

Miss Gatspy's smile could only be called a smirk. "Why, thank you, Herr Schere; you're much too kind." She shot a glance at me from under her lashes that made me want to throw something. I reminded myself this was an excellent way to guard Prince Oscar now that this unfortunate murder had taken place, and that Miss Gatspy was helping us, but it made little difference to my conviction that she was deliberately provoking me.

A loud bellow from the front of the car claimed all our attention, and a moment later we heard a timid voice raised in dismay, "But Sir Cameron, I *can't!*"

FROM THE PERSONAL JOURNAL OF PHILIP TYERS

Word should have come from Bedford by now, but no telegram has been delivered. I have said nothing to Sutton regarding my concern, but he can read the clock as well as anyone and he knows it is past time that a telegram should have come. Which leads to two questions: has a telegram been sent and intercepted, or has no telegram been sent? If intercepted, by whom, and in which direction? Was mine purloined, or was MH's? If the telegram was never sent, why was it not? Both possibilities are troublesome, but both in very different ways.

Without the telegram from MH, I do not know which of his instructions to follow, which is especially distressing now, for one or the other plan must be put into effect soon or we will lose what little advantage we have secured for ourselves.

. . . I suppose I should prepare telegrams for Leicester and pray they are received. If nothing occurs to hurry me, I will try to hold off taking any action until my second round of instructions arrives. . . .

Chapter Twelve

"OH, GOOD LORD!" Mycroft Holmes exclaimed over a renewed outburst from compartment one, "Sir Cameron MacMillian."

Inspector Carew was immediately interested, more in our reaction than in the altercation in compartment one. "How do you know that?"

"Well, how do you think?" Mycroft Holmes demanded impatiently. "I have seen him before, of course—"

"Yes. He does like to have himself before the public eye," said

Prince Oscar, with a fastidious expression that eloquently displayed his disgust of such antics.

"That he does," Holmes seconded, adding, "I saw him come aboard this morning," he told the Inspector. "He was not what you would call sober, and he demanded more drink at once."

"Can't think how he can stomach it, on a moving train and all," I added.

"Guthrie, don't be cheeky." Mycroft Holmes swung around. "For the sake of Herr Schere's health, would you be good enough to go down and see what is wrong?"

I was astonished that Holmes would suggest such a thing, for it was possible that Sir Cameron would recognize me and put an end to our subterfuge. I was about to protest when a new, louder roar was set up. "Oh, all right. I only wish I had a quarterstaff," I said.

Miss Gatspy spoke unexpectedly. "I have something that will work as well," she said, adding, "I'll just go along to my compartment. I shan't be long." She did not wait for permission but slipped out of the room.

"Excellent nurse," Prince Oscar approved and I wondered if I saw something sly in the way he praised her. It was distressing to think that the Prince might use his high position to take advantage of her.

"Yes; that is our understanding," said Mycroft Holmes. "She would probably blush to hear us praise her so."

From what I knew of Miss Gatspy, blushing was the last thing she would do; her demure manner was a calculated performance, and her porcelain skin and limpid blue eyes created an impression that was far from the truth. I knew Holmes expected me to say something to support his observation, so I said, "She is not often given all the credit she deserves."

"Nor, I suspect, would she take it if it were offered." I knew my employer was enjoying himself hugely; I hoped that Inspector Carew would not become suspicious.

Prince Oscar spared us all any more awkwardness by saying, "I reckon it would be a wise precaution to have nurses on all trains."

"A most novel idea," said Inspector Carew, his expression lightening. "There are physicians on ships, aren't there? A nurse on a train might be a good safety measure."

"Tell the railroads, if you think it would be useful," Holmes recommended as the door slid open and Miss Gatspy returned, a screw of paper in her hand.

"I'm sorry this took so long, gentlemen; I had to measure from a bottle, and on a moving train, this is not easily done." She managed a shy smile and went on, "This is a compound that causes lethargy. Those who have indulged as Sir Cameron has tend to sleep long and soundly under its influence." She put the screw of paper in my hand. "If you add it to his drink, he will be snoring in twenty minutes."

Inspector Carew regarded her in mystification. "Do you always travel with medical supplies, Miss Gatspy?"

"Why, yes, of course," she said as if hers was the most ordinary conduct in the world. "I find I need to be prepared. Nurses are often more readily to hand than physicians in emergencies, don't you think?"

"True enough," said Mycroft Holmes, swinging around to look at me. "Well, Guthrie, good luck. If there is anything we can do to assist, you have only to inform us."

"Yes, sir," I said, dreading facing Sir Cameron again.

Inspector Carew spoke up. "You have had experience with this woman before? You have reason to trust her?"

"We have met on our travels and seen her deal with more than one emergency," was the last thing I heard as I left the Prince's compartment and went along down the corridor to Sir Cameron's. I knocked on the door only to have it nearly skin my knuckles as it was opened with considerable force.

The valet, his face quite pale, stood ready, it seemed, to apologize. He did his best to block the way into the compartment, but over his shoulder I could see the place was in disarray. I could just make out Sir Cameron's shoulder, hunched as if to hide, near the window. "The trouble is, Sir Cameron wants another bottle of brandy, but the constables won't allow it." His long, narrow face had all the features crowded into the middle, seeking the shelter of his long, prominent nose, the only distinctive feature he possessed.

"Is Sir Cameron without . . . without anything to drink?" I asked, recalling his demand for brandy as we departed King's Cross. He had been a sot when I had encountered him in Germany, he had been a sot in London five years ago, and he continued a sot in the years since; but it appeared that his vice had worsened.

The valet nodded and whispered, "It was the wedding, sir—at Saint Paul's?—there were four receptions and a few more occasions Sir Cameron was moved to attend. He became caught up in things, and, as you see . . ." He dared not finish his thoughts.

"I see he is fairly far gone," I said, quietly but bluntly. "Do you think he should drink anything more?"

Before the valet could answer, Sir Cameron surged up energetically if unsteadily and hove himself around to face the door. His features, always ruddy, were now florid; and his ginger mutton-chop whiskers bristled like a tomcat's; his hair, I noticed with ungracious satisfaction, was all but gone on his pate, and the pouches under his eyes were more pronounced. He squinted in my direction. "Who the bloody hell is that, then?"

"I'm sorry to disturb you, sir; we were wondering if anything were wrong?" I knew Sir Cameron well enough to know it was folly to suggest anything was actually amiss. "We heard shouting, and considering there has been a murder on this train, we thought it best to check. Inspector Carew is with us, the officer in charge of the investigation."

"No murder here, no murder here," said Sir Cameron. "But there might soon be if I cannot get some brandy." He directed a fulminating gaze at his hapless valet.

"You see how it is, sir," the valet said quietly. "Sir Cameron— he'll be better once he is home, if you understand me."

"I certainly do," I said, and added a bit more loudly, "I'll talk to Inspector Carew, to see what we can arrange." With that promise I took a step back, the screw of paper in my pocket feeling as if it were afire.

"Well?" said Mycroft Holmes when I went into the Prince's compartment once more.

"He wants brandy," I said. "The constables will not allow his valet to get any; he would have to go to the lounge car for it." I shrugged. "He will start yelling again soon, I fear."

Inspector Carew scratched at his cheek; it was clearly a nervous gesture. "What if I arrange for him to have his brandy—what then?"

"I think we can get Miss Gatspy's powder into it. He will sleep all the way to Edinburgh." Mycroft Holmes made a gesture to show he did not want anything to do with Sir Cameron.

Inspector Carew made a snort of agreement. "I will get the brandy, and a snifter for him. Then Guthrie here can take it to him, all prepared, as it were." He made a polite nod to Miss Gatspy which Prince Oscar answered with a curt one of his own just as the Inspector closed the door; I hoped he had not seen Prince Oscar's response, for it might set him to thinking in ways that could not help our mission.

"So, tell me about this murder?" Prince Oscar tried not to look too curious.

As quickly as possible, Mycroft Holmes summed up the events in the lounge car, choosing his words with care so as not to alarm the Prince unduly. When he was finished, he added, "The police will remove the body at Leicester, and I hope we may be allowed to leave the train there in order to send and receive messages. I fear if we do not find the murderer, we will be detained on this blasted thing until we reach Scotland."

"Well, then we will have nothing to fear from other assassins," said Prince Oscar.

"You assume there is no new culprit aboard," Holmes corrected him, doing his best to show respect although he was becoming impatient. "We have not received Tyers' report from London." It was a significant admission for Mycroft Holmes to make, and I could not help but feel sympathy for him.

Miss Gatspy, who had listened in close attention, said, "I can tell you a thing or two that may help you."

"And what might that be?" asked Mycroft Holmes sharply.

"My . . . my organization," she said, apparently deciding not to mention the Golden Lodge by name, "has some information on assassins that might prove interesting to you. We assembled it when we learned about some of Prince Karl Gustav's new supporters." She looked in Prince Oscar's direction. "I do not mean to offend you in saying any of this, Your Highness."

"Carry on," he said indulgently. "What does Herr Schere care about such things?" It was a gallant attempt to conceal his dismay and it very nearly succeeded, but his hands trembled as he reached for his cup of cold tea.

"What have you learned?" Mycroft Holmes demanded.

"That there are, in fact, two assassins working, each using the same methods so that you will assume it is one person." She spoke with little emotion beyond a trace of exasperation, yet I could sense the indignation that seethed beneath her calm exterior; the pale line around her lovely mouth gave her away. "The Brotherhood does this as a common device—they train two to behave as one, and then assign them to act in such a way that it is impossible to connect the crimes, or to determine the correct times for the crimes, since one person cannot be in the same place at once."

"I've heard about that device," said Mycroft Holmes, sounding a bit down-cast. "They did that in Prague, didn't they?"

"And in Constantinople," said Miss Gatspy with a nod in my direction.

"Good Lord!" I expostulated. "Then *that* was how—" I saw Mycroft Holmes' warning gesture and fell silent.

"How can you be certain that this is what is going on in this instance?" Mycroft Holmes asked Miss Gatspy; he had lost his Fleet Street accent and now he looked very odd to me, dressed as he was.

"Because one of our sources was killed before he could report to us. He was assigned to look for breaches in the Prince's protection. He was supposed to meet with me yesterday morning, as soon as he was relieved of duty." Her blue eyes grew very cold. "I am certain he knew who the second assassin is."

"Was that Constable Childes?" I asked, suddenly convinced I could not be wrong.

She looked down at her hands, her expression sufficient confirmation. "He was trying to find out how many of the police have fallen under the influence of the Brotherhood. We knew that some of the men were, but we did not know who or what positions they occupied."

"Are you suggesting that one of the assassins may be a policeman?" I demanded, and felt Holmes big hand close on my lower arm. I swung around and stared at him. "My God! That *is* what you're suggesting isn't it?" I glanced at Miss Gatspy. "I'm sorry if my language offended—"

"Oh, Guthrie," she said in exasperation. "As if language means anything at a time like this."

"Then what about Inspector Carew?" I demanded. "What are we to think of him?"

We heard Sir Cameron swear loudly from compartment one, and a distinct bang as something of moderate size and weight—such as a boot—struck the wall.

Mycroft Holmes pointedly ignored this interruption. "For the nonce, dear boy, we must be very careful with Inspector Carew. Even if he is wholly blameless and honorable to a fault, he may inadvertently let slip something to one of his colleagues that could have dire repercussions for our efforts now." He patted my shoulder. "Keep your wits about you, Guthrie." This last remark was spoken in the journalist's accent, and for a moment I was jarred.

"I'll do my utmost, sir," I assured him.

"I am certain of it," he said, and cocked his head in Prince Oscar's direction. "You will have to be very careful with Inspector Carew. If he even suspects that there is any deception being practiced, he will most assuredly proceed to investigate our mission, which could be disastrous. It is bad enough that our arrival in Edinburgh is delayed, we must—" He broke off as the door opened and Inspector Carew came back into the room with a tray in hand, a sealed bottle of brandy and a snifter set upon it.

"What about the Edinburgh delay?" he asked nonchalantly, as he handed the tray to me. "I thought it best that the valet should see the bottle sealed, so that he will suspect nothing when his employer falls asleep and cannot be wakened."

"A sensible precaution," Mycroft Holmes approved, adding, "With Herr Schere not feeling well and his connection to the Continent lost, we will have to make arrangements for him to have special accommodations. As we are going to arrive later than scheduled, that may be difficult." His explanation was glib and had I not known Holmes as well as I did, I would have been convinced, as I hoped Inspector Carew was.

"Most inconvenient," he agreed. "Even if Herr Schere were feeling well." He looked at me as if he was surprised I was still in the compartment. "Well, get on with it. We have to return to the lounge car as soon as possible."

"So we must," said Mycroft Holmes. "Mister Jardine's death is still a mystery."

I understood the meaning of that last remark; I hefted the tray and prepared to leave the compartment.

The train was still traveling at a reduced speed, no more than thirty miles an hour, and it rocked like a smack in fresh seas. I used my elbows to steady myself against the walls and windows of the car as I made my way to compartment one. I tapped the door with my foot. "Brandy," I called, hoping that the screw of paper in my pocket was not as visible as I feared it was.

The valet opened the door; I could see the distinct impression of a palm on the side of his face. Sir Cameron had not improved his conduct toward his servants since those few, wretched days more than eight years ago when I had served him as valet. "Thank God," said the valet with genuine piety.

"I'll bring it in, if you like, and help you get it open. From what I heard, you've had something of a ruckus here." I thought my intentions must be completely transparent, but apparently they were not.

"Oh, thank you, sir, thank you so much. Do come in." He pulled the door open for me and I had my first clear look at Sir Cameron MacMillian; I strove to avert my face without being too obvious about it.

"At last," he said, from where he sprawled on his day-bed, for his compartment was made up very much as Prince Oscar's was, but in far greater disarray. "Do something about this place," he ordered his valet. "The compartment is a shambles."

I pulled out the table from its niche in the wall, set the tray upon it and went about opening the brandy. "Have a look at it, if you like," I said, holding out the bottle.

The valet was busy picking up boots, two valises and a pillow from the floor; he paid no attention to me. Sir Cameron inspected the label on the bottle, scowling before signaling his grudging approval. I took advantage of the moment to pull the screw of paper from my pocket and empty its contents into the snifter. I wondered, as I did, if it had any taste. Miss Gatspy had not mentioned any, but with so determined a sot as Sir Cameron, any slight change would be detectible. I took hold of the bottle and poured out a generous amount, swirling the snifter in the approved method of warming the brandy, only to have Sir Cameron snatch it away. "Never mind that," he growled. Then he grew very still, staring at me.

My courage all but deserted me as I endured his scrutiny. "What is it?" I asked, expecting to have him denounce me.

"I thought I saw aright. Left eye blue, right eye green. Most unusual." Sir Cameron made a gesture to ward off misfortune, then lifted the snifter. "Not the best they make, but well enough." And with that, he took a long swallow.

The valet had stowed the items he had collected in the overhead rack, and he said, "Thank you. You've been most kind."

"A pleasure to help a fellow-traveler," I said with what I hoped sounded like automatic courtesy.

"He isn't often so . . . so demanding," the valet went on. "He has been so much in the lime-light, even in the company of royalty, that he is now despondent. To hear him now, you would think that he and the Prince of Sweden-and-Norway are bosom chums."

"All this travel and official functions can put a strain on a man." I did my best not to sound too sarcastic, and I supposed I had done a fairly good job, since the valet said nothing more.

Sir Cameron took another swallow, not so large as the last, and squinted at me again. "Damme, you look like someone . . . I'll bring his name to mind in a minute. A scoundrel, as I recall . . ."

It would not be wise to leave too hurriedly, I knew, so I spoke to the valet again. "If there is anything more you need, I will lend you whatever assistance I can." I held out my hand—an egalitarian gesture that made the valet blink.

"Much appreciated, sir, I'm sure." He edged me toward the door.

I had no wish to linger; I took myself off, pleased that the danger Sir Cameron could represent had been successfully reduced. As I was reassuring myself that all was well, I stepped back into Prince Oscar's compartment. "He took it," I said, and saw that this was of little or no concern to anyone in the place.

"—if you think that the two sitting with him at lunch murdered him, whether or not Heath is a printer," Inspector Carew was saying, taking issue with something Mycroft Holmes had said. "How can they be associates? You have no reason to think they are."

Mycroft Holmes leaned back against the windowframe, blocking out the glowing afternoon light. "If I did not, I would not say so," he informed the Inspector. "I suspect that Heath is a bookie—the ink on his hand, the chalk on his sleeve, and the fact that he has been reading about that scandal at the races—"

"As have half the men on this train," Inspector Carew interjected.

"—and has been in the company of a horse-trainer. Mister Dunmuir has quite a reputation for training champions," Holmes said emphatically. "You've heard of him; you simply did not associate him with the precise Mister Dunmuir. If you will take the time to review the various accounts of winning races, you will see his face in many reports on winning horses."

I watched in some surprise. I was unaware that Mycroft Holmes had any interest whatsoever in horse-racing; he had an eye to a good animal, and when he rode, he had a good seat; but he had never so much as mentioned any of the races, famous or not. "Why do you think Mister Heath is not a grocer, chalking his prices? Or a . . . a . . . ." I began to flounder.

"Would you buy so much as a vegetable marrow from that man?" Mycroft Holmes inquired sweetly. "No. He has the manner of a bookie, and if he is not carrying betting slips, you may call me an idiot."

"Then we shall see which of us is more deserving of the name," said Inspector Carew. He motioned to Holmes. "Shall we put your notion to the test? If you can convince me that there truly is an association among those men, that would provide motive for a murder."

Prince Oscar's eyes were shining; under other circumstances he would have followed us out of his compartment and back through the train to the lounge. But for the sake of his disguise, as well as his safety, he had to remain closeted with Miss Gatspy. Had it been possible to do so without earning Miss Gatspy's scorn, I would have remained with her and the Prince.

"Hurry up, Guthrie," Holmes said impatiently as we passed through the second-class car. "Your observations may be crucial. Can't have you lagging behind now."

"No, sir," I said, lengthening my stride and clasping my portfolio while Mycroft Holmes summed up his thoughts to Inspector Carew.

FROM THE PERSONAL JOURNAL OF PHILIP TYERS

Still no word from MH or G. I do not know whether I should report this to anyone, for with MH's suspicions, it may play directly into the hands of the conspirators to inform the police of this development. The devil of it is, I cannot reach MH either, and so I cannot inform him that one of the two decoys used for Prince Oscar has been shot as he reached Dover. The second double remains unharmed, at least so far. This only confirms MH's certainty that HHPO is in danger and is likely to remain so.

Sutton has suggested that we keep on as we were instructed. He will go to the Diogenes Club on schedule, and maintain the illusion that MH is following his habitual routine. Sutton believes if anyone is party to the conspiracy, he will betray himself when MH appears to be keeping to his routine. I do not know that I am wholly in accord with Sutton; but as I cannot yet determine what is best to do, I will run along to King's Cross and see if I can learn anything about the Flying Scotsman. *There may have been word received at the station, and if there is, I will discover it.*

The shooting of the double worries me, for it suggests that the assassin is still at large. The only consolation I have is that so long as the shooting took place in Dover, the assassin cannot possibly be on the train to Edinburgh. I wish I could so inform MH. It would not be much assurance, but at such a time, it would undoubtedly be welcome news.

Chapter Thirteen

WHITFIELD WAS LOOKING white around the gills when we came into the lounge car. He greeted Mycroft Holmes like a long-lost friend, holding up a pony of sherry as a kind of welcome. "It's the best we have—shooting sherry. Dark as a nut." He glanced at the men in the lounge car and the ominous vacancy where Mister Jardine had lain.

Mycroft Holmes accepted the sherry and sipped it, making a sign of approval. "Good of you, Whitfield," he said.

"Ta, sir. It's been thirsty work." He held out a drink to Inspector

Carew, a glass of pale, wheaten ale. "I've taken the liberty of giving Mister Rollins a brandy—riding alone with a corpse and a compartment full of baggage cannot be"—he made a gesture to show how little the notion appealed to him—"I am sorry we have not kept order as much as you might want," he said more quietly. "I must tell you, Inspector," he went on, unable to lower his voice much due to the noise of the train, "some of these men are taking a nasty turn, surly-like."

"Hardly surprising," said Inspector Carew, his white hair shining like a halo as the light struck it. "Have the constables been able to maintain order?"

"Yes; now that the passengers are free to use the necessary room. That was becoming something of a problem." Whitfield did his best to look amused at his own feeble wit.

"Just so," said Inspector Carew. "Well, perhaps we can liven things up. It appears Mister Holcomb has a theory about how Jardine came to die. You must all want to hear what it is, mustn't you?"

There was a general sighing from the men at the bar, by the look of them I would have thought this was the last thing on their minds, but then, who was I to cast aspersions upon them? I sat down on one of the upholstered stools near the window, opened my portfolio and drew out my notebook, as Mycroft Holmes had instructed me to do as we went through the dining car.

"How is it that you listen to that windbag from Satchel's and not to any of us who have done as you've told us to and not pressed for advantage?" This came from a man named Albert Whipple, who was a property agent from Sheffield; he was plainly much distressed by the delay as by the murder.

"I have listened to him because he was willing to do the work I should have done had I been here at the time of the murder," said the Inspector bluntly. "You would do well to take a lesson from him instead of carping at the slights you imagine." He nodded in Mycroft Holmes' direction. "So, if you would like to listen while he propounds his theories, I will listen along with you, to discover what I can. It may prove useful." He went and ordered a whisky, saying, once he had his drink in hand, "You may begin, Mister Holcomb."

Mycroft Holmes strode two steps forward to the center of the lounge. "I have my illustrator, Guthrie, to thank for the observations I made. He came into the lounge before luncheon was served and he had occasion to see Mister Jardine, Mister Heath and Mister Dunmuir. He had the impression that Mister Heath and Mister Dunmuir, who sat together—where?"

I pointed out the table the two men had occupied. "They spoke occasionally, as strangers will when traveling. Mister Jardine arrived after I did and seemed disinclined to seek any society but his own. His accent and his demeanor were Glaswegian."

"And he sat in roughly the same location where he died, did he not?" Holmes asked as if to punctuate the manner in which Mister Jardine had continued his self-imposed isolation.

"At the far bend in the angled settee, yes," I said, and saw Whitfield nodding in anxious agreement.

"Are you certain he sat there the whole of the time?" asked Inspector Carew. I could see he was paying keen attention, and had formed a few notions of his own. This was his means of measuring his deductions against those of Mycroft Holmes.

"Certainly it was his only place before luncheon," I said, and heard Mister Heath clear his throat.

"I had little occasion to regard him, and the end of the bar prevented a direct look at him, but I am quite certain that he did not rise from that place. I should have seen it." His cheeks were ruddy, and a certain roughness had come into his speech, but he was quite presentable.

"Mister Whitfield," Mycroft Holmes said to the barkeep, "does this tally with what you saw?"

"Yes, it truly does," said Cecil Whitfield. "The dead man sat there by himself and making no sign of wanting any company but his own." He looked about the bar and said, "Had more of you gents been in here then, I might not have noticed so clearly, but with only the four, his behavior was easily discerned." He seemed proud of himself for knowing so impressive a word.

"So," said Mycroft Holmes. "We have four men in this lounge before luncheon—Mister Dunmuir, Mister Heath, Mister Guthrie, and, shortly after, Mister Jardine. None of them behaved as if they were acquainted. When the chime rang for luncheon, they all went into the dining car, where Mister Jardine was seated with Mister Dunmuir and Mister Heath across the aisle from Guthrie, Herr Schere of Vienna, and myself. They spoke little during their meal. When I introduced myself to them, Mister Heath was the most voluble of the three, displaying a good deal of bonhomie not shared by the other two at the table."

"Well," said Mister Olwin, "two of them are Scots, aren't they?" His cheeky wit gave everyone in the lounge an excuse to laugh.

"Camus Jardine was more than taciturn, from what I saw at luncheon," said Mycroft Holmes, cutting off the laughter. "He was a very frightened man. It would appear he had good cause to be."

At this announcement, Inspector Carew leaned forward, his attention sharply focused on Mycroft Holmes. "Why should you think that?"

"For one thing, he stank of it. He wore country clothes, to be sure, but the odor that came from him was fear, not the stable. That, and the nature of his silence, which was not unlike a hare hiding in a bush while a fox is prowling." Holmes looked at each passenger in turn as he continued. "No, gentlemen, there can be no doubt; the man was terrified of something—something near at hand."

"Or someone," said Mister Loughlan, who was looking tired; I could hardly blame him.

"True enough. Or someone," Mycroft Holmes concurred. "But what should so frighten this man? Who was he and what had he done, to be so distressed?"

"I have an answer to that," said the Inspector. "Camus Jardine was a horse—"

"A horse-trainer," said Holmes at the same time. "Yes. His riding boots were well-worn, with stirrup chafes on the inside of the leg, yet the heels were worn down from walking; therefore a trainer or a game-warden. If he were a game-warden, he would have worn other clothes than the ones he had on, whereas a trainer would have excellent reason to dress for the stables while traveling. There was a bulge in his jacket pocket and a bit of oat-chaff clinging to the fabric, where he kept his rewards for the animals he was training. He wore a cap such as stable-men wear; therefore I must suppose that he had been in London, or near London, to work with one of the horses he had trained."

"That seems a bit of a leap to me," said Mister Olwin, folding his arms to emphasize his skepticism.

"Not at all," Holmes said in amiable contradiction. "Think about this, if you will. This man, who was clearly more at home in a stable than a train, was returning home from some event in a state of great agitation. Losing a race would be cause for disappointment, not terror. Assuming he lost."

"Unless there was more at stake than winning," said the man with the Yorkshire accent.

"Exactly," Holmes agreed. "If he had more at risk than the race. As a trainer, what would that be? What could a horse-trainer do that would make him so frightened?"

Whitfield had an answer. "He could try to fix the race." He looked about, proud of his answer.

"Very astute, Mister Whitfield," said Mycroft Holmes. "You have hit upon a most promising line of inquiry. Wouldn't you say so, Inspector?"

Inspector Carew had been following this in thoughtful attention, and he finally made a gesture with his hand. "Assuming everything you have said thus far has any basis in fact."

"Oh, Inspector, I never assume. In my travels I have learned that assumptions are far more trouble than they're worth." Holmes lowered his eyes, making it apparent he did not want to become engaged in a dispute. "Let me continue along these lines if I may?"

"Please do," said Inspector Carew.

I watched this intellectual sparring with some trepidation. Holmes was making himself very visible and could attract more questions than would be easy to answer, but if I tried to communicate my apprehensions to my employer, I would tend to worsen the very problem I sought to correct. So I made notes in a desultory fashion and hoped nothing would happen to make the two men confront one another more directly.

"If Mister Jardine had agreed to do something to change the outcome of a race, then those with the greatest interest in the race—an owner or a bookie, for example—might feel moved to demand compensation from the man." Mycroft Holmes glanced about the lounge. "Poison is a sly weapon, not a passionate one. It is a weapon of deliberate malice, a weapon of clear intent. A man seeking revenge might well use it." He chuckled unpleasantly. "And, as we all know, its use and source can be hard to detect."

"But I poured the drink for Jardine, and he carried it himself," said Whitfield, no longer as sure of himself as he had been.

"Ah, you are assuming the poison was in the drink he obtained here," said Holmes. "Yet he had just come from the dining car, and had eaten and drunk immediately before. If the poison required a short while to act, or was taken in a form that needed a little time to become potent, then the drink here is the least of our worries. I have heard . . ." He let the provocative tone of his voice make its impact.

"I have heard that there are many ways to disguise poisons, to slow or hasten their action, usually with food and drink."

Inspector Carew nodded slowly. "I think I'll have one of the constables go along to the kitchen of the dining room."

"All the dishes are probably washed by now," said Whitfield.

"But probably not the napery," said the Inspector. "That could tell us a thing or two, if we can find the napkin and the tablecloth from Jardine's meal." He looked directly at Holmes. "I am impressed, Holcomb. Who would have thought a man from Satchel's would turn out to be so keen an observer?"

"Observation is an essential part of my work," said Holmes in what seemed a modest manner. "No one who travels as I do can afford to be unobservant."

"As soon as I return, you may carry on with your theory," Inspector Carew informed my employer. "Gentlemen, I am afraid I must ask you to remain in the lounge for a short while longer. Rollins," he said, signaling to his coroner, "you can help find the—"

"Napery," the fellow finished for him. "I am coming." And so saying, he followed the Inspector out of the car to the platform leading to the dining car.

"At least we'll soon have that body gone. It's bad luck to travel with a corpse," Olwin declared. "Kettering is a mail drop, and then we're on a straight course for Leicester. I leave the train at Leicester." He looked at the place Inspector Carew had stood.

Mycroft Holmes did not argue. "All the more reason to settle this here and now. None of us wants this nagging after him. Unsolved murders leave the police in a bad light. They pursue murderers diligently, and this case is no exception." Holmes saw the men exchange glances.

"They never caught the Ripper, did they?" Mister Heath countered.

Holmes was unflustered. "No, they did not. But this is not a Ripper killing; it is a murder aboard a moving train, which means that there are a specific number of possible killers, for the murderer must be aboard." He paused to let the men in the lounge consider this in all its possibilities.

"How do you mean?" asked James Loughlan, suddenly more apprehensive. "Surely they cannot think any of us would do this."

"Well, *someone* killed him," I ventured. "Those in his company are the ones most likely to be investigated."

"Gracious!" Mister Olwin looked genuinely shocked at the suggestion. "You can't think that we would have done anything to that poor man."

"Well, he is certainly dead," Mycroft Holmes pointed out.

"What about suicide?" Mister Heath looked nervous as he suggested this, as if it were a lapse in taste.

"Then why should he be frightened?" asked Whitfield.

Before an argument could erupt, Mycroft Holmes interrupted. "I believe it is wise for the police to err on the side of murder, for whom among us would like a such a killing to go undetected and unpunished?" As the men in the lounge exchanged uneasy glances, Holmes went on. "Poison is, as I have said, a sly weapon. Perhaps the most insidious thing about many poisons is that their effect is remarkably difficult to detect."

"Do you think this was such a murder?" Whitfield was looking more frightened, and his voice had risen.

"It would certainly seem so," said Mycroft Holmes. "But we must keep in mind the victim and how he came to be poisoned." He cleared his throat and rocked back on his heels. "Poisons are not all alike; there are a number of poisons that simulate heart failure or apoplectic collapse that no method known to science can detect. Those are the favorites of the true professionals."

I saw the barkeep go quite still, as if stricken with worry.

"To me the best poison has always been that which kills hundreds in Britain every year: food poisoning." He looked about, knowing everyone aboard had at one time or another eaten a dish that was not wholesome.

Inspector Carew had returned in time to hear the last of this; he stood watching Holmes through slightly narrowed eyes. Only when there was silence again did he speak. "We may be in luck, but I doubt the chemist will think so. He has several days' work ahead of him."

The train began to slow down, not greatly, but enough to attract attention. As the men looked about in apprehension, Whitfield spoke up. "We've got behind the Ipswich to Manchester train—that'll be it. It'll take the switch to Derby just after Loughborough."

"We'll be behind it for such a distance?" Mister Heath sounded distressed.

"You have no reason to complain of it," said Inspector Carew. "We will be put on a side-track while the body is removed, and the poor man's luggage. He had a second-class ticket in the rear of the train, and would have gone to Glasgow, not to Edinburgh, had he completed his journey."

One of the men looked disgusted. "The only speed record we'll be breaking this run is the one for tardiness."

His tone was taken up by several of the others, but not quite so boldly. This time Inspector Carew responded, addressing the men before Mycroft Holmes could speak. "I know you don't like being late. It's inconvenient and annoying. But think of Mister Jardine. He has experienced something far worse than lateness. You will at least arrive at your destinations; he never will. If he were your son, your brother, your husband, your father, wouldn't you expect more than shuffling his body off with no more ado than if it were a sack of meal?" He gave the men in the lounge car a short while to think about that. "Whether or not you have sympathy for him, show a little to his family."

I would have liked to say, "Hear, hear," but I suspected it would not sit well with the Inspector if I did.

"Didn't mean no disrespect," said the square-faced man, who had a wife and three children in the second-class car bound for Edinburgh. He wore a mourning-band on his sleeve, and I recalled he had said something about having to attend a funeral when he was questioned.

"Of course not," said Inspector Carew. "It has been a difficult time for us all. And as I must ask your continued indulgence until we have finished our tasks, I apologize for the delays and any inconvenience it may cause you." He directed his gaze toward Mycroft Holmes once again. "Have you any more ideas about who might be involved in this?"

"As a matter of fact, yes, I do," said Holmes evenly. "It will be my pleasure to tell you what they are. Speculation, of course, but that is to be expected. I may have misread the situation entirely, in which case, I will owe at least two men an apology: you and the man I suppose might have done it. Would you rather we discuss it here, or—?" He gestured to the platform.

"A fine notion," said Inspector Carew. "Very well; the platform will do. And in the meantime, Constable Washbourne will inspect the tickets of all the men in this lounge. Only those who purchased a ticket to Leicester will be allowed to leave the train there. We will require your names and where you may be reached, of course. I am confident you will all assist us to your utmost capacity, and so I will tender my appreciation in advance of your service." His cordiality was belied by the cold light in his pale eyes.

"Shall I remain here?" I asked Holmes very quietly.

"Better do. I need a reliable witness in this car." He raised his voice. "If anyone else has a theory, my illustrator will take down your ideas, or make sure you have the opportunity to speak with the Inspector."

I very nearly cursed him then, for I could see four of the passengers just bristling with notions they could not wait to elucidate. The next few miles promised to be hectic ones for me unless Holmes and the Inspector could hit upon some astonishing revelation. I resigned myself to the task to taking down every theory offered to me, and consoled myself with the thought that one or two of them might possibly be right.

FROM THE PERSONAL JOURNAL OF PHILIP TYERS

There has been a death on the Flying Scotsman, *as the telegraph operator at King's Cross informed me when I presented my letter of authorization from the Admiralty. The police from Bedford have taken the investigation, and no one has been allowed to leave or board the train, which is now on its way to Leicester. The telegraph operator gave me his word he would inform me as soon as the train's arrival at Leicester is confirmed. I must hit upon some means to get word to MH if he is not allowed to send his telegrams to me. It would probably be wise to send duplicates of the Bedford message, as well, and to send them and any new information to Sheffield, so that if I am unable to reach MH at Leicester, he will still be kept fully abreast of what has taken place thus far.*

Sutton admits he is relieved. This long wait for information has taken a toll on him as well. For nearly an hour he abandoned his study of Jonson's play and reviewed all our railroad notations in case he might hit upon some means of using any associates of his from the theatre who are touring in the Midlands to get a message onto the train. That is one approach that never occurred to me; and although it seems somewhat far-fetched, if communication remains precarious, I will have to consider Sutton's alternative. At least HHPO is safe; that much I have been able to establish.

CI Somerford sent word that a spent shell has been found on the roof of the house where Constable Childes was killed, apparently matching the one on the roof from the first attempt on HHPO's life. Whoever this assassin is, he has left his mark like a calling card, perhaps to taunt the police, perhaps to signal his accomplices. . . .

I am off to King's Cross again, to learn what I can about the Flying Scotsman.

Chapter Fourteen

AFTER THE MAIL-SACKS had been exchanged at Kettering—somewhat less frenetically than usual, owing to the slower progress of the train—Inspector Carew and Mycroft Holmes returned from their discussion to find the lounge awhisper with speculation, each passenger regarding his nearest traveling companion askance. I had been observing this and was still not as certain as my employer that it would be possible to unmask the culprit before we arrived at Leicester. Constable Washbourne had checked all the tickets and made notes of his observations in his memo-book. I busied myself pretending to sketch the interior of the car.

"Why bother with this place?" Whitfield asked suddenly, leaning over the bar to talk to me. "It's nought but a lounge car."

"It's a lounge car where a man was murdered. I might find a paper that would pay well for it." I shrugged. "Not that I can do much until we're standing still, but I can make a beginning." I thought I sounded plausible enough. "When we reach Edinburgh, I'll do a proper job on it."

"If you think so," said Whitfield, looking in Mycroft Holmes' direction. "Strange fellow, that Holcomb. Too clever by half."

"It's the travel," I said, hoping he would make more sense out of my remark than I could.

"All that talk about poison. Quite puts me off." He polished the wood automatically, his attention on Holmes and the Inspector. "Don't like to think about how he comes to know it."

"Now then, gentlemen," said Inspector Carew. "I am sure you are all anxious to have this unfortunate event behind you, and Mister Holcomb has persuaded me that he might be able to show how the murder was done and who did it. I have discussed his theories with him, and I am satisfied that they may well offer the solution to this crime. Therefore, I ask you to listen to him and answer any questions he may put to you." He gave a nod in Mycroft Holmes' direction. "There you are, Mister Holcomb. The rest is up to you."

"In other words, you are permitting me to damn myself if my conclusions are incorrect." Holmes' tone was dry. "Understood." He straightened himself up to his considerable height, took a deep breath, and began. "When Mister Jardine first came into the lounge car, Mister Heath and Mister Dunmuir were seated—there." He pointed to the table they had shared. "My illustrator was at the bar. Have I got that right, Whitfield?"

"That you have, sir," the barkeep answered promptly.

"In other words, Mister Jardine sat as far away from Dunmuir and Heath as he possibly could," Holmes declared. "He could have been trying to hide from them."

"You might say that," Whitfield said, as if the notion were new to him. "He didn't seem the sociable type."

A few men made noises of agreement. I saw one of the men point to Heath and whisper something to his neighbor.

Holmes rocked back on his heels. "Did none of you think it

strange that the man should be wearing clothes more suited to the paddock than to travel?"

"Thought the fellow was rude and inconsiderate," said Mister Olwin.

"He was dressed for the paddock," Holmes went on as if Olwin had not spoken, "because he was trying to escape." He paused for effect, just as Edmund Sutton would have done. "He had left the track without taking more than his bags. He packed and fled. You may imagine his dread when he stepped into this car and found the men he had been hoping to elude sitting together as if they were waiting for him."

"Just a minute here . . . ," Heath began. "I never met this man before today"—he indicated Dunmuir—"and as for the dead man, aside from sharing a table with him at luncheon, I have no acquaintance with him whatsoever." His face was growing pink and his eyes glittered.

"In a moment I shall demonstrate that isn't true," Mycroft Holmes said confidently. "You, Mister Heath, not only knew Mister Jardine, but you and Mister Dunmuir were part of a criminal ring fixing horse races. You, sir, are a bookie, and Mister Dunmuir is a breeder, one of the most respected in the North. But of late affairs have gone against you, have they not, Mister Dunmuir?"

Mister Dunmuir was packing his pipe and gave Holmes a long stare. "You're the one telling tales, laddie, not I."

Who, I wondered, was Mycroft Holmes' source for information in the racing world. In an instant I realized he had had recourse to his brother's formidable files. When had he perused the material on horse racing, and why had he bothered? There had been some word of a scandal in the papers, but why should Mycroft Holmes have any reason to pursue the matter? I would have to ask him when the occasion permitted.

"You, Heath, and Jardine have been feeding horses—often your own, so you could profit by betting against them—various substances to compromise their performance on the track. Only it went wrong this last time, didn't it?"

Heath started forward only to find Constable Washbourne at his side. "You have no basis for these accusations."

"You think not?" Holmes asked, and gave Heath a long time to answer. When nothing more was said, Holmes went on. "There was a mishap at the track, wasn't there, one that brought inquiries too close to you, and which caused Jardine to panic. When you discovered he had decamped, you set out to get him, and to silence him."

"Preposterous!" Heath bellowed.

"He was the weak link in your chain. He, being a trainer, was distressed by how the horses were being treated. I am guessing he wanted to end the . . . er . . . enterprise, and you would not let him. With this scandal, you were convinced he would turn against you and give your scheme away to the authorities." Holmes set down his empty pony on the bar; Whitfield took it promptly. "There have been rumors for the last two years about tampering with the races, although there was no proof. But with the jockey dead, there is going to be an intense scrutiny, and you all were aware your activities would be revealed."

"Assuming there is any truth in this farrago of yours, sir," said Dunmuir, pausing to light his pipe, "why should we maintain so elaborate a ruse on this train? Why should we not travel together, the better to plan how to avoid the consequences of our reprehensible acts?"

"Because, as I have said, Jardine bolted. You had originally planned something of the sort, I suppose." Holmes looked over at Heath, whose face was now mottled red and white, declaring either guilt or the righteous indignation of an innocent man. "You had to get away, and Mister Dunmuir could provide you a place to go to ground at his estate in Scotland. Jardine was on his way home to Glasgow. I believe Jardine thought he had a one-day lead on you."

Inspector Carew spoke up. "On Mister Holcomb's suggestion, I have gathered a number of newspapers from the passengers on this train, and there is indeed much attention given to the death of the jockey. The police are investigating it, and a number of irregularities from the track." He held up a number of newspapers, rolled into an untidy tube. "It is all here. Scotland Yard have begun their inquiries."

"What makes you think that has anything to do with us?" Mister Dunmuir seemed almost bored. "Why should either of us know Mister Jardine, let alone kill him? Your story would probably do very well in the theatre, but it will not answer in court."

"But it will, you know," said Mycroft Holmes. "The police will hold you in Leicester while they search your home in Scotland and your office in London. It is likely you will have left some note or other evidence of your plot."

It took Mister Dunmuir a shade too long to respond. "I will demand restitution for any invasion of my privacy."

"It will be forthcoming, of course, if nothing incriminating is found," said Inspector Carew. He noticed Mister Heath was sweating. "Washbourne, take the two of them into the lav, will you, and keep watch at the door? I have a few more questions for them once they compose themselves."

A few of the passengers were looking relieved; one of them offered to buy a round of drinks, and in an instant a hectic melioration was spreading throughout the lounge. Whitfield hopped to his job as Constable Washbourne escorted Heath and Dunmuir to the lav. I watched them go with a degree of bafflement; I had not thought the matter would be so swiftly concluded. I admitted as much, sotto voce, to Mycroft Holmes, who replied, "The Inspector needs a good reason to hold the train at Leicester until he can get instructions from the Yard. This provides him one."

"Then it was a ruse?" I asked, shocked at the notion.

"Possibly; although I am certain those two men were behind Camus Jardine's murder. I may have the details wrong, and it may be Heath and not Dunmuir was the instigator, but I doubt it. Dunmuir has the right demeanor." He accepted another pony of shooting sherry. "I don't want the police aboard the train any longer than necessary, for Schere's sake." He took a sip of the fortified wine.

I had declined more drink, knowing I might easily become sleepy and inattentive if I allowed myself anymore such indulgence. With the strain of the last two days, I knew that I would not be able to resist the sweet seduction of rest if I had stronger drink than tea, so I ordered a pot of Assam from Whitfield, explaining myself by saying, "I had wine at luncheon."

"Very abstemious sort, aren't you?" He signaled the kitchen for the order, adding, "You want milk and sugar with that?"

"Sugar only," I said, knowing I would want the full benefit of the tea. I had come to marvel at Mycroft Holmes' capacity for drink, which seemed to have little or no impact on him. Some men had such constitutions, and my employer was undoubtedly one of them; I was not made of such hardy stuff—when tired, drink invariably made me sleepy.

Inspector Carew made a point of putting a light touch on the moment. "Those of you who need the necessary room, use the ones in other cars. For the moment, the one in this one is engaged." It was a feeble enough joke, but one the men in the lounge car were glad to laugh at.

Beside me, Mycroft Holmes said quietly, "No inspection of the train. We have something to be grateful for."

"Amen," I said with feeling. "And perhaps in Leicester we can use the telegraph station to reach Tyers."

"I should think so," said Mycroft Holmes, his long face appearing jovial now. "No doubt Tyers has enlightened himself as to our predicament."

I knew better than to ask how he might accomplish this; instead I regarded Holmes with an inquiring eye. "Have you discerned who among the police has been working against us?"

"Not yet. I am lacking two crucial pieces of information. Once I have them in hand, I will be prepared to tell you all." He laid his long, straight finger aside his nose, as if he actually were a journalist who made his living writing about his travels.

"As you say," I responded, then added, "Do you think one of us should visit the first car?"

"Yes, but not yet. We do not want to draw any more attention to the car than is necessary. We have to remember that part of a disguise is being unnoticed." He smiled a bit. "When one or two of the men here have gone off to the lavs in the other cars, then one of us will be able to leave without being conspicuous."

Inspector Carew made his way to Holmes' side. "Constable Washbourne knows his duty. You need not fear that those men will bribe him. If they attack, Constable Snow is on the platform and ready to assist." He looked at Holmes carefully. "I must say, your assessment of the crime was most astute."

"Well, m' father was a magistrate in Swindon. He taught me a great deal about crime and criminals." He had a smile worthy of a Cheshire Cat. I tried not to stare at this clever fiction.

"How does it happen," the Inspector asked, so nonchalantly that I, for one, was instantly on guard, "that the son of a magistrate is a journalist? Wouldn't you have trained for the bar?"

"No talent for it, and no money to pay for it," said Mycroft Holmes, with the bluntness of one long used to such questions. "As it was, my brother has filled that place, while I have become a kind of professional vagabond, going about the world and reporting on what I find." He winked at Inspector Carew. "You learn a lot, going about the world."

"No doubt," said Inspector Carew drily. As Whitfield handed him a second glass of ale, he added, "Had some run-in with criminals in your travels, haven't you?"

"What traveler has not?" Holmes countered. "I have seen my share of skulduggery, I believe."

"Which accounts for your knowledge of poisons," said Inspector Carew.

"Inspector, any man traveling on his own in foreign climes had better be alert to these things or he will never live to file his report. Foreigners are often targets for certain criminal elements. This is true in London, or Paris, or Rome, but it is the more so in regions beyond our usual travel. One must be on guard against poisons, against thieves, against murderers, against the greedy and the zealous. A man in my position has to tell the readers of *Satchel's Guides* where it is not safe to go as well as where it is, and what the dangers are as well as the sights."

"Very likely," said Inspector Carew, and turned his interrogation on me. "Have you had the same experience. To illustrate the publications, you must go to many of the same places as Holcomb here has gone."

"My travels are not nearly as extensive, but I agree with Mister Holcomb." I did my best to be amiable, but I was beginning to feel some exasperation as well. "Before you ask, I am a Scot, as you probably can hear in my voice, though I have called London my home for nine years and more. My mother is a widow with other children, so when I could, I went out to earn my own way in the world." It was true enough for broad strokes, although it conveyed an impression that was not accurate, as I intended it should.

"Have you encountered any trouble with poisons in your travels?" His inquiry was so bald that I spoke in haste.

"In Constantinople, some time ago, a fellow slipped one of those devilish Chinese rice-sprouts in a tiny bag into my food. It would have sliced my guts to ribbons had I eaten it. That might not be a classic poison, but it is close enough for me," I said, the burr in my words stronger than usual, clear indication of my emotions. Even thinking of that ghastly moment when the tiny bag was discovered had the capacity to make me unpleasantly giddy. "What Mister Holcomb tells you is true."

"Would Herr Schere say the same thing, I wonder," the Inspector ventured, his eyes dreamy.

"I should think so," said Mycroft Holmes at once. "He has the Balkans near enough to make him cognizant of the risks as well as the benefits of travel."

"Um," said Inspector Carew, indicating he was withholding judgment for a time.

"And if you have anything more you would like to ask us, why not do so directly? Mister Guthrie and I understand how important it is for you to do this, and we will gladly answer your questions." He put his empty pony back on the bar; Whitfield took it at once.

"I am satisfied. For the moment." He looked over his shoulder. "I am still surprised that you should be able to discern so much from such minuscule amounts of information."

"The trained reporter's eye, Inspector. I daresay you would have seen as much yourself, had you been in Guthrie's position, or in mine." Holmes pointed to my portfolio. "Remember that those who illustrate must see before they can draw. And observing the men through lunch-eon persuaded me that something was amiss among them."

"You've made that very clear, Mister Holcomb. You need not repeat it for my bene—" He broke off as a loud crash and the sound of splintering glass came from the rear of the car, followed at once by a loud cry from Constable Washbourne. Inspector Carew was in motion almost before the sounds had died in the rattle of the train.

Mycroft Holmes was barely a step behind him, and I followed after him, shoving my way through the men who had gathered in the narrow entrance to the corridor that led past the baggage compartment to the lavatory. Shouts of consternation came from Constable Snow on the platform beyond, compounding the confusion around us.

By the time we reached the lavatory, Constable Washbourne had opened the door and gone in; the Inspector stood in the doorway. "Best fetch Rollins from the luggage compartment," he said heavily.

Looking over Mycroft Holmes' large, square shoulder I could see the window of the lav had been broken. As my employer took a step forward, I saw that Mister Kermit Heath was crumpled on the floor, a great, bloody welt on the side of his head. Blood had run from his nose and ears; it was apparent he was dead.

Constable Washbourne rose from the side of the body and mut-tered, "Excuse me, sir," to Holmes as he went to bring the medical man to view the corpse.

"Dreadful, quite dreadful," said Holmes with feeling. "I gather Dunmuir has escaped?"

"Constable Snow says he threw himself out the window; he saw him land on the embankment, but nothing more." Inspector Carew indicated the door onto the platform. "I sent him back out. He was about to be sick."

"Small wonder," I said as I stared at the body.

"What was his weapon? Such a blow could hardly come from his hand," Mycroft Holmes remarked as he approached the remains of Mister Heath.

"I must suppose he had some weapon secreted about his person we did not find." It was clear from the tone of his voice that he held himself responsible for Heath's death.

Holmes was close enough to bend over the body. "Something small, I should think. One of those shot-loaded saps, perhaps, or—" He stopped and scowled. "What a bloody fool I've been!" Since he rarely swore, this strong language surprised me.

"In what sense?" Inspector Carew asked wearily, rising as Rollins came through the door.

"It was right under our noses all the time," Mycroft Holmes exclaimed. "The pouch of tobacco. It was larger than most and left a heavy bulge in his pocket. I took this as a sign of long use, but that was not the cause; it was the weight of the sap concealed beneath the tobacco!"

Mister Rollins knelt down beside the corpse. "A sap is very likely," he agreed after a cursory examination of the wound. "The skull is broken right at the temple. The skull is thin there and more readily cracked. The killer knew his business." He put his hand on the dead man's face. "Probably happened too quickly for him to feel it."

"Small comfort," said Inspector Carew. "Still, I suppose it meant something to Heath."

"He had no notion what he was caught up in. At least Dunmuir 0understood," said Mycroft Holmes. "Which was why he fled."

Inspector Carew leaned over Rollins to look out the shattered window. "We should be able to have police after him as soon as we arrive in Leicester. He's on foot. They'll snap him up before the dawn."

"Possibly," said Holmes, his voice sounding fatigued.

"But—" Inspector Carew began.

"You don't know whether or not he had other accomplices. He had dragged Heath and Jardine into his coils—why should they be the only ones?" Mycroft Holmes moved back to the lavatory door where I stood. "Set your hounds after him, by all means, Inspector, but do not be dismayed if they cannot find him."

Inspector Carew's light blue eyes narrowed. "Do you know more than you are telling me, Holcomb?"

"Undoubtedly," was Holmes' answer. "But none of it pertains to this case."

The nod that Inspector Carew gave had more than a bit of skepticism in it. "I will want to know how to find you. I may require your testimony in court." It was a facile-enough explanation, but his intent was plain—he intended to check up on the fictional Mister Micah Holcomb.

"Satchel's will always know where I am. And where Guthrie is, for that matter," said Holmes easily.

Rollins got to his feet. "We'd best put this one in with the other," he advised. "I'll stay in the compartment until we reach Leicester."

"That shouldn't be too much longer," said Inspector Carew. "That's Market Harborough up ahead. Once past it, we have less than twenty miles to Leicester. Even following another train, we should be in Leicester within the hour." He stood aside for his two constables, who were set to carry the body into the baggage compartment. "Mind how you go," he advised his men as they struggled with the large, inert mass that had been Mister Heath.

As Mycroft Holmes and I moved out of the way for the men, Holmes said to me, "The police will probably not detain us for very long at Leicester. They have their work cut out for them, hunting Angus Dunmuir. The man is a greater scoundrel than they know at present; I am convinced of it. No doubt my brother could tell us more of the man, were we able to inquire of him. I imagine that a careful examination of his life would reveal some very troubling things."

"Then you were suspicious of him from the start?" I had been unaware of it, had that been the case.

"Alas, no. I was too concerned about Herr Schere to pay much attention to Dunmuir. In retrospect I can point to many signs that would have excited my notice at another time." He glanced behind him to see James Loughlan peering at the constables bearing the body of Kermit Heath, Norton Rollins completing the cortège. "A little respect, man, if you will."

Loughlan withdrew at once, to be replaced by Olwin and the print editor still clutching his portfolio. The whole thing struck me as shabby and sad.

"Move back there!" Inspector Carew ordered, and this time the men obeyed, retreating to their chairs and stools and places at the bar, a few with the demeanor of schoolboys caught peeking into the master's study.

Mycroft Holmes swung around to look at the Inspector. "Are the passengers restricted in their movements still?"

Inspector Carew thought it over a short while. "No," he said finally, the suggestion of a sigh in his voice, "I suppose there is no reason." He faltered. "I—I'll make an announcement. That should ease them all somewhat."

"And what are your instructions for Leicester?" Holmes continued. "Some of the passengers will be leaving the train there—"

"My men have their names," said Carew.

"And some—like myself—have messages to send and to retrieve." He stared directly at the Inspector.

"Once the bodies have been removed and the constables have checked the train, you will have a short time to send necessary messages. You are not the only one who will have to make alternate arrangements for travel." He appeared mildly annoyed by these minor inconveniences. "For example, I will have to arrange to get the constables and myself back to Bedford."

"At least you can return with the satisfaction of having completed your investigation," said Holmes by way of encouragement.

"Perhaps. I would be better satisfied if we had Dunmuir in hand as well." He tugged at the lobe of his ear. "I must alert all the constabularies in this vicinity."

"Still, you have done excellent work, Inspector Carew," Mycroft Holmes told him.

The Inspector laughed once. "You would think so."

FROM THE PERSONAL JOURNAL OF PHILIP TYERS

Still no word from MH. I am informed the train will arrive in Leicester shortly; I will have to send my telegrams at once if all my information is to be available when the train arrives. If I do not have communication from MH then, I will have to alert the Admiralty.

Poor Sutton is nervous, but he does his best not to show it. I know this is a struggle for him. He is getting ready to assume the persona of MH and pay his habitual visit to the Diogenes Club across the street, although he has plenty of time before he will be called upon for that service.

No further word from the police, either in regard to the assault on the double or to the trouble within their ranks. There is also no additional word about the assassin, which is the most troubling development of all. I had hoped to have more to impart, but that may have to wait for Sheffield. . . .

Chapter Fifteen

"THREE TELEGRAMS FROM Tyers!" I exclaimed as I entered Mycroft Holmes' compartment in the first car of the train. "And only one a copy of the one he sent to Bedford."

"Matters must be moving more swiftly than I anticipated," Holmes said, worry making his face more serious.

"Or they are more confusing than anyone anticipated," I added.

"And you sent—" Holmes said as he took the messages I retrieved from my portfolio and held out to him.

"Everything you gave me, and my own report as well. The telegraph operator asked questions about a few of the phrases. I said it had to do with business dealings. I don't know whether or not he believed me. I asked him to forward any more messages to the Sheffield and Leeds Stations. Cost me nearly three pounds." This outrageous sum would have been inexcusable under less hazardous circumstances.

"A tidy amount," said Holmes as he began to read the first. "How appalling," he said as he perused the account of the assassin's work on Prince Oscar's double. "The information given to the assassin comes from a very well-placed source, one whom we must assume has some knowledge of our plans. The corruption goes higher than I feared." He slapped the flimsy yellow message down on the seat. "I should have managed this better, Guthrie, had I known—" He stopped himself. "Well, there is nothing to be done now. I suppose I must resign myself to dealing with Herr Schere first, and settling the rest of it later."

"Are you planning to tell Herr Schere?" I asked with an uneasy glance in the direction of his compartment. Miss Gatspy was still with him, maintaining the stratagem of his indisposition to make his isolation in his compartment unremarkable. I understood the necessity of this, but still thought it unseemly.

"Not just yet. I see no point in upsetting him," said Holmes as he went on to the second telegram. "So. Tyers says another spent casing has been found on the roof of the building where Constable Childes was killed, a casing matching the one from the site of the first assassination attempt. How very . . . convenient. I can understand an assassin being clumsy once, and leaving behind a casing, but twice?" He read the message through a second time. "Well, put this back in your portfolio, Guthrie. I will want to review it on our journey back to London, when I can give it my full attention."

"Do you expect you will find something—" I began only to be interrupted by my employer.

"It's all so *pat*. That's what bothers me; it is set out like a trail of crumbs in the forest, a trail that is never disturbed, and leads inevitably to the very thing I am intended to find." He laced his long fingers together and extended his arms. "This assassin is supposed to be very clever, capable of vanishing as if he had magical powers. Yet he twice leaves an important clue behind. This suggests to me that this may not be a clue at all. He would seem to disappear in a puff of smoke. Which is patently impossible. Therefore he is doing what magicians have always done—he is misdirecting our efforts, making us search where he wishes us to search, not where he is."

"How do you intend to go about finding him, then?" I asked, for although I was by now familiar with Holmes' methods, I did not see how he would apply them in this instance.

"The best way," my employer reminded me, "to detect such a man is to look for someone doing a normal thing in an abnormal place or way. We must see who doesn't fit, whose pattern of actions is slightly different from the usual, while appearing to be the most normal. Guthrie, my lad, we must never forget that this is a killer; he is not an ordinary man. When placed in the appropriate situation, he will kill, whatever the pose he has assumed. And that is supposing that we are dealing with a male assassin, which I believe to be the case now due to the absence of women at the earlier attempts, the selection of weapons, and the physical strength he demonstrated when killing the unfortunate policeman."

I could not help but feel a jolt of relief on behalf of Miss Gatspy.

Mycroft Holmes paused and looked out the window at the passing countryside. "Sadly, the most likely opportunity to expose this assassin is when he makes his next attempt on the Prince's life. If we can prevent its success, then we will have him. He believes he has made no mistakes, which is the greatest mistake of all."

I put my hand to my eyes and said, "Then you think he will try to strike again?"

"If he has the chance." He steadied himself for a moment as the train rocked with unusual vigor. "I think we must also prepare ourselves for the possibility that the assassin has an accomplice."

"Do you mean among the police?" I asked.

"Unfortunately, I do," he said. "Someone is helping him. How should he have gained access to those rooftops without the contrivance of the police? How else did he—or his accomplice—know about the movements of the double? And once the assassin learns he has failed to kill his target, where will he strike next?" He sat down, his face glum. "At least the police are no longer on this train, for which I am profoundly grateful. We may now act without regard for their scrutiny." He fell silent as there came a knock on the door. "Yes?"

"Mister Holcomb? Will you be wanting tea?" The waiter's voice was automatically servile. "There is a choice of China or India, green or black, and scones, biscuits, cheese, or cake with clotted cream, com-

pote, or preserves. And there're watercress-and-cucumber sandwiches."
He had repeated this so often that he rattled it off almost too quickly
to make sense of it.

Mycroft Holmes pondered a moment, then replied, "My illustrator, Mister Guthrie, is conferring with me; we will both take our tea in this compartment. I will have China, black, and my illustrator India green—gunpowder, if you have it."

"We do," the waiter declared. "And the rest?"

"Scones, biscuits, cheese, and compote, I think," he ordered, glancing at me for my approval, which I promptly gave. "Oh, and two baked eggs, if you would be so good. I'll pay the three shillings extra for the special service."

"Of course, sir," said the waiter. "Your tray will be brought in fifteen minutes."

When he was gone, I said, "I must confess, sir, that I have no appetite."

"That does not mean you do not need something to eat. Come, Guthrie. Remember how difficult it is to try to think when the body is famished. You have said yourself that hunger impinges on thought more than fatigue." He gestured toward the window. "At this rate we shan't be in Sheffield much before dark. And the reason we took this train was its speed! Any villain on the London to York train could readily overtake us at the rate we are moving." He began to play with his watch-fob. "I don't know what to say to Herr Schere. We are entrusted with his safety, and thus far all occasions contrive to compromise it."

"Then we must find ways to restore it once again," I said, with full awareness that I had only the vaguest notion of how this was to be done.

"So we must." He cleared his throat. "I hope you are not too distressed by my employing your Miss Gatspy as Herr Schere's guard? It seems a dreadful waste to have a woman of her talents available to us at this time and not to make use of her to the fullest. I trust you understand."

"I have told you often and often that she is not *my* Miss Gatspy. You hardly need my permission to employ her in this or any other capacity you see fitting. I only hope she will not deceive us as to her purpose." I heard how stiff I sounded; I tried to laugh in order to mitigate this severity. It came out more of a bark than I had intended, but it would have to suffice. "As an agent of the Golden Lodge, she must surely be watched; for the aims of the Golden Lodge, and hence

Miss Gatspy's do not always march with ours. Still, if the Brotherhood are behind these misfortunes, then she is the staunchest ally we can find, and for that reason alone I am certain we can rely on her to protect . . . Herr Schere."

"That was most impressive," said Holmes. "I would almost suppose you had prepared it ahead of time." He put his hand on my shoulder. "No, dear boy, do not bristle at me. I only want you to know that I am not insensible to your feelings in this instance, and I regard them as much as our predicament permits." He fell silent as a kind of roar erupted from the first compartment of the car. "Oh, dear. Why did the waiter have to assume Sir Cameron wants tea?" he asked the air.

"—bloody arse! Bring me brandy, not your damned cat-lap!" There was a bang from the compartment door sliding closed. An instant later the door opened again. "And scones with clotted cream." Then it slammed shut once more.

"Where is his valet?" I asked, thinking sympathetically of the poor man.

"Probably getting a brandy of his own. He probably thought Sir Cameron would not waken yet. As, I confess, did I." Mycroft Holmes sighed and paced the limited confines of the compartment. "I must hope we have no more trouble from Sir Cameron. Perhaps he will doze after he eats. Brandy with scones and clotted cream should send anyone into the arms of Morpheus in a matter of seconds, although we cannot be certain in his case."

"He sounded sleepy; that's in our favor," I said. "I don't think we can drug him again, not without injuring him."

"There is a certain temptation in that," Mycroft Holmes confessed.

I had to concede him the point. "Yes. There is." I did my best to put a good face on our situation. "If he has more to drink, he will probably go back to sleep."

Holmes nodded distantly. "If he keeps on this way, he will never see sixty."

"If he ruins our mission, he might not see tomorrow," I reminded him. "If he should recognize you—"

"He didn't recognize you," Holmes said, as if this was encouraging.

"When you sent me to look after him and his treaty in Germany, I was in disguise and wearing an eye patch. The times I have encountered him since, I was nothing more than a functionary, and therefore invisible. If he ever made the association, we—"

Holmes interrupted me again. "In his current state I should think we have little to fear; I doubt such cognition is within his capabilities just now." He waved his hand in dismissal. "This is jumping at phantoms. I should rather put my attention on the real troubles we face and leave Sir Cameron to his own devices."

The tap on the door this time was more authoritative. "Mister Holcomb? It's Inspector Carew. Might you spare me a moment of your time?"

Mycroft Holmes thrust his telegrams into his valise. "Certainly, Inspector. Guthrie and I were just trying to work out how to deal with this delay." He offered a slight smile as the Inspector entered the compartment.

"Very good of you to see me, Mister Holcomb. I have come to thank you for all you did to make my work here less protracted. I confess I still cannot follow how you came to suspect Dunmuir on what seems such minor considerations, but I am grateful that you did. I have dispatched telegrams to all the constabularies up and down the line as well as those in the towns to be on the look-out for the fellow. I have no doubt that he will be in hand by tomorrow morning."

"I hope you may be right, Inspector," said Holmes, extending his hand and gripping Inspector Carew's firmly. "I would like to ask you to send me word of how it all turns out. A note to Satchel's in London will reach me wherever my work has taken me."

"Under the circumstances, I should think it is the least I can do." Inspector Carew then extended his hand to me. "You were most helpful also, Mister Guthrie. I never thought I should be grateful for an illustrator, but your efforts were most welcome."

"Pleasure to have been of help," I said.

"Well, I am going to release the train. The North Eastern line will be glad to have the *Scotsman* flying again." He chuckled at his own humor. "They say the train will pick up speed after Loughborough and the turn-off to Nottingham and Lincoln; and after Leeds, it will move at its usual pace." He gave Holmes a side-ways look. "I will not be filing my reports until morning, I think. The copies will not reach London until tomorrow afternoon."

"Indeed," said Mycroft Holmes as if he did not care.

Inspector Carew smiled thinly. "Well, I hope your journey will be unencumbered, Mister Holcomb. You may still reach Edinburgh before midnight."

"I should hope so. But there are other trains on the tracks. Not like the old days when half the trains stopped at sundown," said Mycroft Holmes as if he missed those times.

"No, not anymore." He sketched a salute in our direction. "If only other Englishmen were as willing to do what England Expects," he said, grinning at his own wit. Then he was out the door and gone.

"Finally," said Mycroft Holmes. "If he is right, we should do well the rest of the way."

"If he is right," I echoed.

"Oh, Guthrie, such pessimism," Holmes chided. "One would think you anticipate the worst."

"If I do," I said, "it is only because I have learned, in your employ, that the worst happens." I heard the waiter pass in the hall and knock on Sir Cameron's door.

"The Inspector knows more is going on than the crime he investigated," Holmes was saying. "Which is why he told me when his report would be filed. If only I knew what he suspects, I—"

"Brandy, Sir Cameron," the waiter said, as if calling a hound to a joint of lamb. The door opened.

"About bloody time," Sir Cameron growled.

"Dreadful chap," said Mycroft Holmes.

"Your valet will bring you your tea," the waiter went on just as the door closed again; the waiter retreated down the hall.

I patted the wall separating compartment one from compartment two. "I hope you were not planning to sleep tonight."

"I had not, no," Holmes replied. "We may now assume it will be a certain thing." As he spoke the train made an initial lurch as the sound of the engine grew louder. "Well, Sheffield next, and a coaling station and water tower there, then on to Leeds and Carlisle, and finally Edinburgh. Water a final time just beyond the station at Leeds, as well as sand. We will be most vulnerable in those places, for we must now suppose that our foes, whomever they may be, know that we are on this train and are making moves to stop us. Mail drops and pick-ups need not concern us."

"Unless someone puts a bomb in a mail-sack," I added, disquieted by my own thoughts. I felt as much as heard the train begin to move. My conjectures were caught up in the dangers ahead as we slowly slid out of Leicester Station, resuming our northward journey, so that the waiter's knock on the door sounded as loud and lethal as the discharge of a pistol.

"Come in," called out Holmes as if he had not noticed my start at all.

"Tea, Mister Holcomb, Mister Guthrie." He stepped into the compartment and pulled out the table on its folded hinges, set it aright and put down the tray. "I'll pick it up in half an hour, if that is satisfactory. Oh, and I would recommend taking the second seating for supper; the families traveling with children usually prefer the first seating." He caught the shilling Holmes flipped him with the ease of experience.

"Most prudent. Put Guthrie and me down for the second seating. I will ask Herr Schere if he will be well enough to join us. We have plenty of time to inform you, haven't we?" Mycroft Holmes indicated the tea. "We will not dine before eight, I presume."

"Eight-thirty, the maître d' says," the waiter answered. "For second seating. Barring any more unforseen events." With that he was gone, preparing to bring yet more tea to Herr Schere. I thought the Prince must surely be awash with all the liquid he would have consumed this day.

When we had gone a mile or so in silence, Mycroft Holmes said, "I will wager you five pounds that the police will not find Angus Dunmuir. I predict he will be away from England, possibly from Whitby or Hull before sunrise tomorrow."

"You assume he has accomplices," I said. "Shall you inform Tyers of these events?" I touched my hand to the side of the cozy covering my pot of tea; it was very warm.

"I had better. I will have to improvise regarding codes." He muttered the last.

"Why not give the account without codes?" I recommended. "It would not be thought remarkable that one who played so signal a role in solving the crime should report upon it. In fact, should you fail to mention it, there might be scrutiny paid to the whole of your message." I righted my cup on its saucer, set the strainer in place, and prepared to pour, trying to match my movements to the motion of the train.

In compartment one, just ahead of us, Sir Cameron was starting to sing: I think he meant it to be "Where Did You Get That Hat?" but I could not be sure. Periodically he would exclaim, "Hello!" which is why I thought it might be that song: "Where 'ere I go, they shout Hello! Where did you get that hat?"

"The drink will tire him in a while," said Holmes.

"Wishful thinking, sir," I said, and managed to get half a cup of tea poured without mishap.

"Just a moment," said Mycroft Holmes, taking a thin ivory shaft about four inches long from his breast pocket. He reached over and stirred my tea with it, studying the ivory for more than a minute. "No change. Your tea is safe."

I shuddered in spite of myself. "You do not seriously suppose someone will try to poison us?" I noticed my hand hardly shook at all as I lifted the cup; this pleased me enormously.

"No, but that is how men in our line of work come to die. You must suppose that there is malice around you and take the necessary precautions." Mycroft Holmes lifted the cozy from his teapot, opened the lid and thrust his ivory stick into it, stirring thoughtfully. When he drew it out, he waited a short while, then nodded his approval. "If Sir Cameron had had one of these, he might not have slept so much of his journey away. We can only be grateful that he did not, and we were free to put Miss Gatspy's powder in his brandy." He sat down and poured himself some tea, adding sugar and milk to the dark liquid before he was willing to taste it.

"Tell me, if you would," I ventured, "if you truly believe it is the Brotherhood who are behind these terrible acts."

"I am fairly certain they are, but I also assume they have help of a sort; and as a result, there are more who have taken it upon themselves to act against our charge than we supposed when this began." He sipped his tea. "I do not think the Dunmuir question is part of this, but it is convenient for the Brotherhood and their allies. And the worst of it is, we are condemned to this train as far as Edinburgh. I thought it would protect us with misdirection and speed, but neither has been sufficient to keep Herr Schere from harm."

"So it would seem," I said, reaching for a scone. "But our work has not been entirely for naught, has it?"

"No, I would not think so," said Mycroft Holmes. "I am certain, however, that our greatest danger now comes from the police. If we are to deliver Herr Schere to safety, then we must avoid any further contact with the police." He set his cup down with such force that I feared he had cracked it. "Damned deception."

"The police?" I poured in more tea.

"Just the one or two who are in the hands of the Brotherhood. I think we may have been too lax in our investigation following the assassination attempt." Holmes glared at the wall between this compartment and compartment one, where Sir Cameron had got onto "Tah Rah Rah Boom-tee-ay," making special efforts on the "boom." "I do wish he would go back to sleep."

"We can but hope," I said, thinking it quite marvelous to hear how far out of tune the man could sing. "What do we do if Sir Cameron does not go to sleep?"

"Then I shall have to have a discussion with his valet, and I fear we will have to make a few arrangements." Mycroft Holmes sighed. "A pity his family didn't send him to Australia or India when he was young, so he might have made something of himself or fallen to bits by his own efforts. Here he is at liberty to blame his family and his duty to them for what he has done to himself. That débâcle with his wife was just another example of his inability to assess his actions." He had a bit of a scone. "Not as fresh as I like them, but well enough, considering."

I waited a bit, then asked, "Would you like me to check on Herr Schere?"

"And his lovely companion?" Holmes asked with an impish arch of his heavy brows.

"You *will* have your joke, I assume," I said, somewhat stiffly. "I am concerned that—"

"My dear boy, you need not fly up into the boughs. I meant nothing to your discredit." He lifted the lid on the porcelain cup in which his egg had been baked. "Not too bad for railway fare, though I like mine with a bit more butter." He reached for his fork.

"Shall I check on them?" I persisted.

In the first compartment Sir Cameron fell silent.

"As soon as you are through with your tea by all means do so. It will reassure us both," said Mycroft Holmes as he bit into the soft egg on his fork.

"Very good," I said, and had a taste of a scone and then a small wedge of good English cheese. This suited me very well indeed, and I wondered who supplied the North Eastern line with such fare.

"Make sure you do not scrimp on your tea, Guthrie. Supper is some hours away and anything might happen between now and then." Holmes was having a wedge of cheese himself, savoring it and nodding to show his approval.

"Will we have to be as careful with supper?" I asked, knowing we would attract unwanted attention if we went through the kind of testing Holmes had done here.

"I think not," said Holmes as he considered his situation. "Service in the dining room is public enough to afford us some protection."

"How do you mean?" I asked sharply. "Surely you do not think there will be another attempt? After the Dunmuir incident, it would be foolish for the assassin to make a move, I should have thought."

"Ah, but Guthrie, what better time? We are off our guards; we have assumed the worst is over. Our defenses are lax and the assassin may act with impunity." He cut two wedges of cheese and offered me one. "Tell me, what do you make of this situation we are in? We should be at Leeds by now, but we are not. The sleeping berths may have to be made up for the second-class passengers if we are delayed any longer, as I begin to fear we may be. If the Brotherhood has learned of our intentions, then we are little more than moving targets in this train. And the trouble is, we must stay with it or risk the very kind of incident we are seeking to avoid." He studied the countryside flashing by the window for a short while. "I must try to believe we have not led our charge into a death trap."

"No more do I," I said, my voice as somber as his. I drank more of my tea and tried to find comfort in its familiar savor.

"I hope we have news from Tyers that will more fully reveal what I most fear." He finished his baked egg—I had not tasted mine yet—and put his fork down. "It is going to be a long evening, my boy. Sustain yourself as best you can."

I heard him with trepidation, for I knew from previous experience that he had a suspicion he was not yet prepared to voice that bore on our predicament. It was useless to urge him to reveal anything of his thoughts; he would do so when he was ready. I dutifully began to eat my baked egg and wondered if I should order a second pot of tea when Sir Cameron once again began singing. "Too much to hope for."

"You never miss the water until the well runs dry," he caroled.

Mycroft Holmes sighed. "He has the most perverse stamina."

"So he does," I agreed, listening to the maudlin sentiments become bathos in his drunken rendition.

After listening a short time longer, Mycroft Holmes broke off half a scone—there were now only two left on the plate—and began to eat.

I finished my tea without doing more than shaking my head at the more painful of Sir Cameron's outbursts. I took consolation in noticing that his words were now slurred beyond definition and his pursuit of melody had been abandoned for a kind of meandering chant. I reckoned he would not be able to continue this way for much longer.

FROM THE PERSONAL JOURNAL OF THE PHILIP TYERS

CI Somerford has brought by a copy of his report on the police assigned to the investigation of the attempt on HHPO's life; he has given the original to Superintendent Spencer, who is vetting the investigation and who has handled all the efforts to protect HHPO during his stay in Britain. Somerford told me that he is aware of three other Chief Inspectors reporting to Superintendent Spencer as well as he himself. This concentration of information must either protect or incalculably weaken this investigation, for if the Chief Inspectors are all loyal, which as yet has not been established, then the Superintendent must become a suspect, and his superiors as well, a supposition that can only bring the gravest apprehensions. Against this possibility, the Chief Inspectors are planning to share their information, preferring to protect themselves rather than run the risk of being made scapegoats by those above them. CI Somerford confided in me his growing apprehension about the corruption that he is now certain pervades the police and his determination to see an end to it.

While Somerford was here, Sutton remained in the parlor behind closed doors. It would not do for the police to know of MH's double while we have not yet determined the full extent of police corruption. I will review the report and send along the salient points to MH at Sheffield or Leeds.

Commander Winslowe has sent word that no further actions have been taken in regard to HHPO's double. Apparently the attack on the one is the full extent of what may be done. The Royal Navy has increased coastal patrols in case anything untoward may be attempted in regard to the remaining double.

I have reports to prepare for the Admiralty and for No. 10, which I must deliver shortly if I am to have full information to send on to MH. Sutton is willing to help me, and he writes a fine hand, so I will not hesitate to use his skills.

If only that train had remained on schedule, so many of the difficulties we must deal with would not enter into the picture at all. We must all be doubly vigilant with these delays exposing us to so much more than we had anticipated at the first.

Chapter Sixteen

IN RESPONSE TO my rap on the door, Penelope Gatspy opened it carefully, one hand deep in the folds of her skirt. "Guthrie," she said and stood aside for me.

"You will not need the pistol," I told her, and watched her put it back in her small beaded handbag and close the door, securing its lock. "Your Highness," I said to Prince Oscar, who was still lounging on his day-bed.

"Herr Schere," he corrected me with an affable smile. "I have been spending a delightful afternoon with Miss Gatspy," he went on, motioning me to sit on the stool Miss Gatspy had just vacated.

I remained standing, as should any gentleman. "I trust she has taken good care of you?"

"Most excellent care," said Prince Oscar with a look I could only describe as lascivious.

"And you are pleased with what she has done for you?" I could feel my collar tighten around my neck; I strove to mitigate my emotions. "I hope the . . . impromptu concert has not been too unpleasant?"

"You mean Sir Cameron?" Miss Gatspy asked, and laughed a bit. "At least he has fallen asleep again. We must hope he will remain so for the rest of our journey." She indicated the tea-tray which was still to be claimed by the waiter. "Aside from using the lav from time to time, I think we will remain here until journey's end. I will not fall asleep or allow myself to be distracted, and so you may assure your employer."

I could not like the notion of her staying alone with Prince Oscar for so long. I decided to approach the matter obliquely. "Mister Hol . . . comb would like to know if you will dine with us this evening, Herr Schere?"

"Assuming my health permits, I would be delighted," he said, a gleam in his eyes that I did not entirely like. "I presume the invitation extends to Miss Gatspy?"

"A woman traveling alone is usually wisest to remain in her own company, or she might attract the sort of attention she would not like," I said, trusting Miss Gatspy to take my meaning.

"But the whole train must know I've been nursing Herr Schere," said Penelope Gatspy, a most adorable and unexpected dimple appearing in her cheek as she smiled. "It would probably be more remarked upon if I did *not* dine with you than if I did. You do not want the passengers questioning Herr Schere's illness, do you? That speculation would be far worse than any scandal that might be incurred by our dining together. After all, this is a train, not a hotel. It is expected that passengers should be thrown together in unconventional ways."

The worst of it was, she was right. I nodded two or three times as I strove to gather my thoughts, and then I said, "I will inform the dining car there will be a fourth at our table. We are going to do the second seating." I regarded Miss Gatspy narrowly. "Are you sure this is what you would like to do?"

"Yes, Guthrie, it is," she said, sounding exasperated.

I offered her a short bow and gave my attention to Prince Oscar. "It may be boring for you, but my employer is still recommending you remain in your compartment as much as possible; Miss Gatspy is wise to recommend such a precaution. We have new passengers aboard since Leicester, and that may or may not mean anything, but it is a chance we are unwilling to take unless you insist."

"With such charming company, how can I object to remaining in my compartment?" said Prince Oscar, so pleased with his answer that I wanted to shout at him. The extremity of my response I attributed to strain and fatigue. I knew I ought to apologize for my intentions, but before I could form my sentiments, Miss Gatspy interrupted.

"You are very gracious, Herr Schere, but Guthrie is right: traveling with only one person for company must be boring for you." She did not look at me, but I could see how her words were as much for me as for the Prince.

"In fact, it is something of a relief not to have an entourage to concern me. I rarely have the opportunity to do much alone. I am not alone now, of course, but I am more on my own than I have been since I was a boy. It is a treat and I am making the most of it. You cannot know how vexing it is to be always surrounded by those dedicated to your service and each one hoping for a reward for their dedication." He sighed. "To have so few around me for company and not one of you seeking advancement from me, that is a pleasure I had not hoped to encounter." He made a sign to Miss Gatspy. "Had you seen my guards at home, you would know why I am so enjoying myself now."

I had to admit it was a splendid little speech, and one I might have enjoyed more had the circumstances been different. "I am pleased that you can find entertainment in so dire an embroilment as the one we face now."

"Oh, Guthrie," chided Miss Gatspy, "don't be such a prude."

"If concern for those entrusted to my employer and me makes me a prude, so be it." I was appalled at how I sounded, and I shuddered to think the impression Prince Oscar must have of me now.

"Miss Gatspy, I believe Mister Guthrie is worried on your behalf," Prince Oscar declared. "It is reassuring to know a man in his line of work still considers the reputations of women he works with."

"Um," said Miss Gatspy, looking at me with the air of one who has been given a dubious gift.

"What sort of man would I be if I did not uphold the honor of my associates, for then mine would be less than nothing." I looked at her again, wishing I could discern her thoughts.

"Mister Guthrie," said Prince Oscar. "You may rest assured that I will in no way trespass on Miss Gatspy's good-will."

I had to be content with this. "Certainly. Well, now that our plans are set, I will go along to the dining car and amend our reservations for the second seating." I turned to let myself out, but Prince Oscar had one more observation to add before I was released.

"A most fortuitous thing, that Mister Holcomb could so handily discern the miscreant in the lounge car." He smiled to show he attached no greater significance to it than the whim of fortune.

"It is a skill that runs in his family," I said, and slid the door back.

"Guthrie," said Miss Gatspy, "before we go in to supper, if you will be kind enough to relieve me for ten minutes so that I might go to my compartment to . . . make myself ready to dine?"

"Of course. It will be my pleasure." I did not look at her as I answered, afraid her glowing smile would detract from my purpose. It was perplexing to think how such a woman could influence my thoughts and throw my perceptions into turmoil. I told myself that my single lapse with her was in the past, to be forgotten: no doubt it was her occupation that so unnerved me, for a woman skilled in espionage and assassination was a rare creature in this or any time.

"Thank you. I will knock on your compartment when I am ready for you to take my place," she said.

"Very good. I will be at your service," I said, and left her alone with Prince Oscar.

In the dining car, the maître d' took the reservation and promised a table where we might look into the kitchen. He was middle-aged with deep-set lines in his face and a nice capacity to judge the social importance of travelers. He treated me with courtesy but without the deference he would show to someone of greater social standing. "It is strange you should want that one," he told me as he studied my initials on my portfolio. "Most passengers would prefer not to see what goes on in the galley."

"Perhaps, but since Mister Holcomb and Herr Schere are employed by *Satchel's Guides,* you will understand their purpose in this request." I spoke with the kind of easy negligence that suggested that such an insistence was standard for Satchel's.

"Of course," said the maître d', whose rolling gait that rocked with the train, along with his nautical use of the word galley made me suppose he had once worked for a steamship line, and had continued his work in the rails as he had once on the sea.

"Thank you. We'll see you at the second seating," I told him, trying not to be too grand in my demeanor, for I sensed this would not gain the high opinion of this maître d'.

"Very good," he said, and went back to his duties in the dining car.

Passing through the second-class carriage I noticed that the compartments were still all full, which led me to suspect that there were many reasons for us to remain alert, for we could not adequately observe all those who had boarded at Leicester. I kept a mental tally of those passengers I was certain were new and considered returning to the lounge car to listen to gossip. That was not what I had been instructed to do, however, so I continued on to the second compartment of the first car. As I came up to that door, I noticed Sir Cameron was finally silent.

"Come," said Mycroft Holmes in response to my coded knock. I slid the door open and stepped inside. "Are we ready for the evening yet?"

"Miss Gatspy will be joining us at supper," I told him. "The reservations are for a party of four."

"Very good, Guthrie," said Holmes. "I was troubled that we had not thought to include your Miss Gatspy. I am glad Herr Schere remembered to do so." He had lit a cigar and the aroma of the tobacco filled the compartment.

"Are you joking me, sir?" I asked rather more curtly than I should have.

"No, Guthrie, at least not this time." He indicated a place I might sit. "You are a stickler for good form, as I tend to forget. It is one of the reasons I hired you, for you know to a nicety what is proper to do."

This praise took me by surprise. "I had not thought you would find much use for—" I almost said *my prudishness,* but stopped myself in time.

"My dear boy, I know protocol, but that is not the same thing as good manners and a sense of decorum." He took another draw of his cigar and blew out the fragrant smoke slowly, letting it wreathe around his head. "You have those skills I lack, and I rely upon you to augment my knowledge when such becomes necessary."

"You have only to ask me, sir," I said to him, still mildly astonished by what he had just confided.

"Tonight I suspect we will need more than two pair of eyes to adequately assess our situation. Miss Gatspy is no amateur, and she will bring her keen attention to assist us in our work. I am very grateful that she is willing to extend herself on our behalf." He saw something in my face that made him add, "I realize her interests are those of the Golden Lodge, Guthrie, and not necessarily those of Britain; but when their purposes march with ours, I am not above making the most of it. The Brotherhood has certainly not allowed such minor matters as national alliances to influence their work. In situations such as this one, the enemy of my enemy is my friend."

"I take it, sir, you do not believe we are out of danger." I had seen him in such a state of mind before, and I could not make light of it. "What do you anticipate?"

"Trouble, of course," said Mycroft Holmes. "I am not yet wholly sanguine about our journey, the less so because the police have been brought into it, will-ye, nil-ye."

"But Inspector Carew said his reports would not be ready until tomorrow, and by then we shall be finished with our mission," I reminded him.

"Ah, but Inspector Carew isn't the only man having knowledge of these events. There is Rollins, the coroner, and any number of constables. Men in that profession gossip as much as any, and word can spread like fire if the case is significant enough for the men to boast of it." Holmes tapped the ash from the end of his cigar. "The gossip is not the same as the rumors of crowds; it changes less in the repeating, for it must convince men who are familiar with the work the police do. In this instance I could wish for wild retellings for the sake of having the whole dismissed as fabrication."

"Do you think that the word could reach London quickly?" I asked, and knew the answer as I did. "The telegraph. Of course it could."

"And it could find its way to ears and eyes not working to our advantage." Holmes glared at the swiftly passing scenery. "If only Tyers has unearthed some information that we can use as regards the police.

But if we are not kept informed, then this journey is still fraught with peril for Herr Schere."

"Do you think Herr Schere is aware of it?" I listened for his answer most attentively, bearing, as it did, on Miss Gatspy.

"He would be a fool if he is not, and I have no reason to think him a fool." He took his handkerchief from his pocket and buffed the toes of his shoes. "We must keep up appearances, mustn't we?"

"If you require it," I said, recognizing that he would not say much more on the matter of danger until he had received his communications from Tyers.

"You will want to neaten your tie, and then go along to the lounge again. You will not appear too obvious if you wait twenty minutes before making your appearance there. I want to know what the new passengers are being told about the murder, and the lounge is the ripest place to hear such things. As you participated so much in the apprehension of the criminal, questions may be directed to you." He held out his cigar. "When I am done with this, and have finished readying one or two items for you to telegraph when we reach Sheffield, I will come along to join you."

"Very good, sir," I said, rising and taking up my portfolio again.

"You needn't sound like my butler, my boy, nor need depart upon the instant. Sit. Sit," said Mycroft Holmes with the trace of a chuckle. "I shan't keep you away from your Miss Gatspy all evening."

"That was not my concern, sir," I said, disliking the tone I had taken but unable to keep from being condemning in my thoughts. "I am going to take her place with Herr Schere before we go in to dine, so she might freshen her appearance; I trust you will not object to this? It is in our best interests to do this." Obediently, I sat.

"If you say so, Guthrie; if you say so." He continued to smoke in silence for a short while. "I will have more telegrams for you to send at Sheffield, as I mentioned, including one to Tschersky at the Russian embassy, that, perforce, cannot be in code. Then there is the Admiralty. You will have to make the most of the time we have there, as Tyers is not the only one we must report to."

"Very good, sir," I said, finally relaxing my hold on my portfolio. I wondered if I had left impressions in the leather above my initials.

"We must also plan for what we will do in Carlisle, when the Glasgow cars are taken off from this train. We will be more vulnerable there than in Leicester, and that now concerns me very much; for in the confusion of a rail yard, an assassin might strike and get away without so much as a constable's whistle to mark him." He folded his hands, continuing, "The problem with any yard is the combination of sound and movement. There is simply too much of it and too many things happening we have no way to anticipate. There will be a maze of open and closed cars of all types. Freights from Newcastle and all of the mills will be arriving hourly and their cars switched onto a dozen different engines. If we are trying to be alert to any threat, the noise level will be such that we will hardly be able to hear a shot, much less a shout. Our analytic eye will be sorely tested, and so it is where we will be most exposed."

"How can you and I, with or without Miss Gatspy, deal with such risks?" I was appalled at what Mycroft Holmes had said. Leaving Constantinople had been easy by comparison, and that last desperate rush through the streets of Bucharest a game.

"Because we must," said Mycroft Holmes quietly. He was almost finished with his cigar. "Go along to your compartment, Guthrie, and do something with your tie. I will come to the lounge within the hour."

"As you wish," I said, getting up again and going to let myself out. I wished I could think of something to say that would lighten the burden he carried, but nothing came to mind that did not also trivialize what was at stake. I nodded as I closed the door and went along to the third compartment where my valise waited, large and lumpish, faithful as a hound.

One glance in the mirror made it apparent that Holmes' advice was more than needed: the knot was askew and the stick-pin was thrust to the side at a rakish angle. I could not recall how or when I had become so disheveled, but I set about putting myself to rights, not only fixing my tie but brushing my hair back into place.

On my way to the lounge car I stopped in the lav and noticed that the frosted window was partially open; about seven inches at the top were open to the air. I tried to close it and discovered it was jammed. As I had not used this facility in the first-class car before, I supposed it must have been that way since before we left King's Cross. I was confident that few men could squeeze through such a small space and in such an inconvenient location, so I did nothing more than make a mental note of it and continue on my way to the lounge, where Whitfield greeted me like a long-lost friend.

"So much excitement," he said, speaking as much to the dozen or so men who were enjoying their drinks. "And Mister Guthrie here right in the heart of it." He handed me a small whiskey—one of his better ones, by the smell of it—and told me it was on the house. "You earned it, Mister Guthrie. That you did."

"Thank you, Whitfield," I said, thinking Mycroft Holmes had been right and I would be answering questions until I went to take over Miss Gatspy's place with Prince Oscar.

"Very helpful you were, Mister Guthrie. The Inspector said so," Whitfield continued to enthuse. "I'm sure they could not have done as much as they did without you to help them. You and Mister Holcomb, of course."

A man somewhat older than I, with an air of prosperity and a very fine suit, came up to me. "About that horse that killed the jockey, they were saying. Some sort of conspiracy, according to the barkeep."

"As much as we could determine, yes, that would appear to be the cause of the killing." I noticed that two or three other men were listening attentively, and so I made an effort to elucidate my part in the whole. "Mister Holcomb was adept at discerning how the poisoning was done; I merely supplied an occasional drawing to help clarify—"

"It's a shocking thing, what racing has come to," said another newcomer, a skinny, knobby gent, with a nose that overpowered his face and seemed to have pulled his two small eyes near to it by magnetic force.

"That it is," I said, adding, "The horse is not to blame, of course, but the men who plotted this are to be condemned for turning an innocent animal into a weapon."

"Shameful," said the hatchet-faced gent. "The name is Burley, by the way—Arthur Burley. A pleasure to meet you."

"Paterson Guthrie," I said as we shook hands.

"They tell me you and Mister Holcomb work for Satchel's. You like the work?" His manner was genial, perhaps, I thought, a bit too genial.

"Well enough, if it is any concern to anyone but myself," I said sharply.

Burley chuckled. "Habit, asking questions. I work for the *Sheffield Intelligence;* you've probably never heard of it, as it is not much known outside of Sheffield. It is a small weekly, devoted to local politics and business."

"Interesting work, I expect," I said blandly, while my thoughts raced: good God, we had a reporter aboard, one dealing in business and politics. This story had most certainly whetted his appetite for skulduggery. What could be more disastrous than this? If the slightest whiff of what we were doing should reach him, how could we keep the whole of this incident from being bruited aboard? And then what would become of our treaty, let alone our efforts to protect Prince Oscar not only from harm, but from scandal?

"Sometimes. Often it is bread-and-butter reporting, utilitarian and dry. Once in a while we happen onto something a bit more exciting, but those occasions are rare. Nothing like what happened here today. I'm sorry I missed it." He sighed. "I should have realized that when the *Flying Scotsman* was late and arrived on a side-track with constables hovering about that it was more than a minor mishap aboard." He downed the last of his whisky. "So if you do not mind, I will ask a few more questions. I might as well file some sort of story about this when I return to my desk tomorrow."

I realized he had volunteered so much to put me off my guard; it had quite the opposite effect than the one he had intended. I did my best to smile and look as if I were willing to be interviewed on this subject, all the while responding with senses alert, not only to Arthur Burley, but to the men in the lounge, most of whom seemed eager to listen. "If you believe it will be of any interest to your readers, ask away," I said, ready to deal with the man as best I could.

"You make this very formal, Mister Guthrie. Still, it's worth a try, I'd think." He pulled a notebook from his pocket and a pencil with a sharp point. "Can you describe what happened here?"

I took a deep breath and began to expostulate on the events surrounding the murders of Jardine and Heath, taking care to be accurate and all the while doing my best to make it seem that such an occurrence was normal enough, deserving of no special attention. Burley listened, taking notes and occasionally prompting me with questions while the other passengers in the lounge listened with that embarrassed curiosity reserved for calamities and scandals.

FROM THE PERSONAL JOURNAL OF PHILIP TYERS
Word has come from the Admiralty that no attempt was made on the other double; in fact, there is some doubt among the highly placed officers that the ruse was successful, and that there was no attempt made because it was known the man was not HHPO. This could mean that the assassin might have learned of the change in plans that put HHPO aboard the Flying Scotsman, which is a development that can only be viewed with alarm.

Between reading the lines of Mosca and fretting about MH, Sutton has voiced concern for something that has me even more dismayed—that there may be two assassins working in concert, with the same intention as our use of doubles: to throw us off the scent of the primary assassin and his target. Sutton is afraid that the assassin may be aboard the Flying Scotsman *with MH, G, and HHPO, an idea I can only view with utmost horror. Little as I may wish to, I realized I should inform MH as soon as possible, which would mean sending a companion telegram to the one I have already dispatched to Sheffield where G will retrieve it when he sends on the report from aboard the train. . . .*

No further reports from the police, although I have noticed a constable patrolling the street rather more frequently than is the usual custom. What this may indicate I cannot be certain, but I am determined to use the backstairs and the service alley if I have to leave the flat anytime today or tonight.

The butcher has delivered a rack of lamb which I shall set to roast with onions and herbs shortly, so that when Sutton returns from across the street we may dine straightaway, so that should any more complex problems arise, we will be ready to deal with them. . . .

Chapter Seventeen

MYCROFT HOLMES ARRIVED in the lounge just as I was finishing my account of his revealing the murderous plot of Heath and Dunmuir. "The police determined to hold the two in the lav, certain that with a constable to guard the door, it must serve well for their confinement until they could be taken along to jail." I looked directly at Holmes, saying, "Ah, Mister Holcomb. This is Arthur Burley of the *Sheffield Intelligencer.* He has taken an interest in the case you did so much to solve."

"A reporter, you say?" Holmes beamed, holding out his hand. "A pleasure to know you, Mister Burley. I think of ourselves as brethren in type." He beamed at this labored witticism. "Quite a change, seeing a journalist seeking to present the facts of an event instead of a more sensational fable. If I may assist in any way to present an accurate picture of the events in question, I would be honored to do so." He signaled to Whitfield. "A brandy please, in a snifter."

"Right away, Mister Holcomb," said Whitfield, and I saw him put down the bottle he had previously opened into one of the storage crates before he unsealed a new one. This seemed to be something of a ritual with him, and I wondered again what its purpose might be.

"You seem a most astute fellow, Mister Holcomb," Burley went on. "But how you were able to hit upon such salient points with so little opportunity for observation impresses me."

"Well, you know how important it is to notice as much as possible while traveling," said Holmes as he went to fetch his brandy; his crown was waved away by Whitfield. "Since traveling is my stock-in-trade, no doubt I have honed my capabilities more than most men."

"No doubt," said Burley. He glanced back at me. "You told me he lacks false modesty. I see you were right."

Mycroft Holmes inclined his head. "Guthrie has worked with me long enough to appreciate my character."

"No doubt," said Burley again, as if preparing to dismiss Holmes from his work after all. "I wonder that you should be willing to be caught up in such work as unraveling a murder."

"Mister Burley," said Mycroft Holmes with an air of exaggerated sympathy, "you cannot think that murders on a train are good for travel. Since travel is my livelihood, I felt it incumbent upon me to do my utmost to end the mystery quickly, so that there would be no growing apprehension about rail travel." He gazed up at the ceiling as if seeking inspiration. "You may not recall how sharply rail travel and holiday-making dropped off in Cornwall after that freak rail crash in eighty-one? The rumors surrounding the tragedy were soon laden with specters and the most dire of manifestations, and all because it could not be determined who had left the switch open, or why. I should hate to see such a plight befall the *Flying Scotsman.*"

Mister Burley scribbled a few notes, I suspect because he was being closely observed. He was still watching Mycroft Holmes narrowly, mea-suring him with canny attention. I was increasingly aware of the tension in the room and the attitude of—I must almost call it predation—that filled the lounge. At last Mister Burley achieved a sour smile and said, "No doubt it would be bad for *Satchel's Guides* to have people take their holidays close to home."

"Precisely," said Mycroft Holmes, and sat down at the very table Heath and Dunmuir had occupied. "You see, Satchel's is revising its guide to rail travel in Britain, which is why Guthrie and I are here. Guthrie has prepared some excellent drawings of interesting sights that might be seen on a rail holiday." He motioned to me. "Show them your work, Guthrie. No need to hide your light under a bushel." He tasted his brandy and made an affable gesture to the room at large, inviting one and all to view Edmund Sutton's drawings, which I dutifully displayed.

"One doesn't see many left-handed illustrators, I fancy." Mister Burley remarked as I finished collecting the drawings I had shown.

"I have not thought much about it, sir," I responded. "I recall my first teachers strove to train me to use my right hand, but I had not the aptitude." That much was true; I had spent three years trying to work with my right hand only to fail, although I was rather more capable with that hand as a result than many another left-handed man. "I cannot say whether or not it has affected my work. How can I know without learning to write and draw afresh?"

"A telling point, I'll give you that. Self-effacing, aren't you?" Mister Burley inquired testily some while later. "One would think these drawings were the work of another, for all the pride you show in them."

Mycroft Holmes responded for me. "Illustrators are not like gallery painters, don't you know. They are not as moved by passion as those who style themselves artists, and they view their work more pragmatically than their more self-absorbed brethren." He rose, handing the nearly empty snifter back to Whitfield, along with a shilling and thr'pence. "For your excellent service," he said grandly.

Whitfield took the tip and chuckled. "You're as generous as an American, sir, and no doubt about it."

"Well, a traveler like me learns to show appreciation for good service," he said magnanimously. "If you can tear yourself away, Guthrie, I would appreciate your company for a short while. We must prepare a telegram for Satchel's to explain our delays."

I slid the drawings back into my portfolio and prepared to follow him, but I was detained by Mister Burley, who had one more question for me. "Mister Guthrie, where may I find other examples of your work? I should like to acquaint myself with it."

Fortunately I had anticipated his question and gave my answer without stumbling. "Until last year most of my illustrations were done for newspapers, most of them English or Scottish. I have been employed by Satchel's for nearly a year, and my first work for them will appear in a guide to the *Orient Express*, which is due to appear in Europe in two months. If you contact *Satchel's* in London, I am sure they will supply you a copy when the publication is available."

"What kept you?" Mycroft Holmes demanded, as he stood on the platform between the second- and first-class cars at the front of the train.

"Mister Burley wanted to do a bit more fishing," I replied. "I thought it best not to avoid answering him."

Holmes nodded. "Very wise. Damn the man! To have a journalist on this train is the worst possible luck. Our attempts to make our passage undetected by our enemies have not been sufficient. We should have ridden in the rear car of a freight train and traded comfort for safety. But I thought speed would—" He scowled out at the hedgerows flashing by. "Burley may be able to recognize Herr Schere, which would be—" He stopped himself before he revealed the whole of his anxiety.

"But he will leave the train at Sheffield," I pointed out.

"And send telegrams to half the newspapers in England, or I do not know the breed. Journalists are more curious than the police and often more dogged. Mister Burley senses all is not as it appears, which moves him to look more closely. A man of his profession is always on the alert for a story that will make his reputation and none more so than a journalist working in a routine publication doing routine work. Journalists are easily bored, and when they are bored, they can do mischief." He sighed. "I know *Satchel's* London will endorse our credentials; but if Burley pursues the matter, as I fear he might, we cannot rest assured that we will remain . . ." His words trailed off. "I hope we do not end with a débâcle."

For a long moment I could think of nothing to say, but then I suggested to him, "Can Chief Inspector Somerford do anything to throw Burley off the scent?"

Mycroft Holmes rubbed his chin, his large, long fingers outlining his jaw. "Chief Inspector Somerford," he mused aloud. "Perhaps. If we can reach him without causing an upheaval. That may prove to be an excellent notion, Guthrie."

I saw at once that my employer had more in mind than I had had when I had offered my word of advice. "You will want to prepare another telegram," I said, knowing what was to come.

"No, my dear Guthrie, I will prepare two more, and I'll supply you the money for full delivery." He very nearly smiled. "I think you may have hit upon something very useful."

"I wish I knew what it was," I complained, and followed Mycroft Holmes into the first car and along to compartment two.

"We will be in Sheffield shortly," said Holmes, pulling his valise down and extracting his writing supplies. In no time he was at work on his additional telegrams, handing them to me with the previously prepared ones, and two pound notes to pay for messenger delivery upon receipt.

"Are you expecting communication from anyone but Tyers?" I asked as I put the telegram texts into my portfolio.

"Not at this stop. At Leeds perhaps—certainly at Carlisle." He rubbed a spot of ink from the tip of his finger. "Tschersky should have something to tell me by then."

"Carlisle," I repeated, recalling his apprehension regarding the place. "But we will have more time there, won't we?"

"That may or may not be to our advantage," Holmes murmured. "We will have to be very careful; when we arrive in Carlisle it will be full dark, which is not to our advantage. We will have to make preparations."

I nodded and glanced at the wedge of corridor I could see beyond the drawn shade. There was Sir Cameron's put-upon valet, making his way down to the rear of the car. I once again had a fleeting impression of the short time I had served Sir Cameron in that capacity, and my sympathy for the man welled anew. Recalled to Mycroft Holmes' remark by a clearing of his throat, I said, "Beg pardon, sir. You were discussing the preparations we will need to make for our arrival in Carlisle."

"At least you were not wholly wool gathering, my boy." Holmes took another of his cigars from his silver case, which he kept in his inner breast pocket. When Sutton had given it to him, I noticed he had had it inscribed to his "most highly regarded mentor." Now, as Holmes prepared to return the case to the inner breast pocket, he paused. "I trust I have not placed Sutton in danger again. My conscience still smarts when I recall he was shot in my stead. And kidnapped, as well."

"Sutton is a brave man," I said, aware that until I met Sutton, I had never thought of actors as brave; Sutton had long since taught me the error of my ways. "He will not begrudge you a risk or two."

"Very like you in that way," said Mycroft Holmes as he snipped his cigar and went through his little ritual of lighting it. "Don't imagine I am unaware of my good fortune in that regard. But I would just as soon neither of you got shot again, if you don't mind." He blew out the smoke. "Given how long it has taken us to come this far, we will probably have to take on water at Sheffield, as a precautionary measure."

"How long will that take?" I asked.

"It's hard to say. Perhaps no more than five additional minutes, but it will mean pulling onto a siding to do it, and that could create a delay by itself. The York-to-Birmingham is due through Sheffield at about the time we will arrive; and if we must take on water, we will have to wait for the other train to pass before resuming our journey. Assuming we have no other delays, this run will take half again as long as it was supposed to."

"It may be possible to continue on without further mishap," I said, with more hope than conviction.

"Possible, yes, but I fear it is not likely." He motioned to me to get down his valise. "I will have to prepare one more telegram. If you like, go along to compartment four and see how Herr Schere and Miss Gatspy are managing." He gave a rumbling sound, which I knew to be a chuckle.

I accepted this dismissal with alacrity, excusing myself at once and hastening to knock on the door to Prince Oscar's compartment. I noticed that the Prince remembered to cough as he called out, "Come in."

"Hello, Guthrie," said Miss Gatspy as I closed the door behind me.

"Miss Gatspy," I replied. How fetching she was, I thought, and reminded myself that she was also very dangerous. "I hope I find you doing well?"

"Actually," she said with the hint of a smile, "I am a trifle bored. These long journeys, no matter what the circumstances, have a sameness that wears on one, don't you think?"

"I hadn't noticed," I said somewhat mendaciously, for I had felt very much the same after the police left the train.

"When our only entertainment is Sir Cameron's antics, it is a sign that all is not going well," said Miss Gatspy.

Just then there was the sound of someone stumbling against the door, and I moved swiftly to see what was the cause, hoping as I did that Sir Cameron had not wakened and was making his perambulations about the narrow corridor. As I slid back the door, I saw Sir Cameron's valet, his face a bit ruddy. He did not smell of spirits, but his manner suggested he had been drinking. I noticed his eyes were lacking that shine of inebriation. "Well?" I said sharply.

"Beg pardon, sir, I'm sure," said the valet. "Tripped. Foolish thing to do. I don't like riding on trains."

"Well, hold onto the outer rail. That's what it's there for," I recommended, unwilling to berate the poor fellow; Sir Cameron did that to excess in any case.

"Yes, sir," he said, and continued on his way back to Sir Cameron's compartment.

"The valet," I said as I once again closed the door.

"Yes, Guthrie. We heard," said Miss Gatspy. "I wonder why he was listening at the door. Do you think Sir Cameron suspects anything?"

"I think Sir Cameron is in a drunken stupor," I said.

"If his singing was any indication, I can think nothing else," said Prince Oscar.

"I think he was listening," said Miss Gatspy.

"I think he was coming back from the lav and stumbled, just as he said, for I did not see him in the corridor as I came along, which I must have done if he had been stationed here to listen," I countered. "You must always suspect everyone."

"In a situation like this one, only a fool would not," she snapped back.

"Guthrie, Miss Gatspy, please," the Prince intervened. "Whatever the cause of the valet's presence, he had only a minute or two to listen, and all he could learn was our unflattering opinions of Sir Cameron. I see no danger in that."

Miss Gatspy nodded, her fair, shining hair catching the light from the window. "It's having to be confined," she explained. "I begin to be apprehensive when my world is limited to a corridor and a compartment." She stood and stretched. "Do you think, Guthrie, that you could give me a moment or two to use the lav?"

"Of course," I said, knowing it was expected of me. "If you want to step into your compartment for a moment as well, I will be glad to continue on here."

"How kind of you," she said, smiling at me as she left the compartment.

As soon as she was gone I secured the door. "When she returns is there anything you would like me to get you?"

"A deck of cards, to pass the time," Prince Oscar said.

"Cards. Of course," I said, a trifle disconcerted that it had not occurred to me to make such an offer myself. "I should find a deck for you."

"I cannot ask you and Miss Gatspy to amuse me all the time," he added with a hint of an impish smile.

"Amuse you?" I echoed.

"Well, you do fence so endlessly, I wonder you have not married the girl," said the Prince.

I could feel heat mount in my face and I stammered out, "Marry? Miss Gatspy?" I managed not to take umbrage at this provoking remark. "I fear you mistake the matter, sir. Miss Gatspy and I have passed one or two adventures together in the nature of our work, but nothing more, I assure you." I could feel color mounting in my cheeks as if to give the lie to my protestations. "The railing you perceive is our way of testing one another, nothing more."

"If you say so, Guthrie," said Prince Oscar. He looked toward the window. "We must be nearing Sheffield. There are more houses."

"Yes. We must," I said, obscurely grateful for the nearness of the town. I supposed we should soon arrive at the station, where I would be busy tending to Mycroft Holmes' instructions regarding telegrams.

"While you are in the station, would you be kind enough to pick up a paper or two for me? I have nothing to read but the reports I was provided when we signed the treaty, and frankly, Missus Radcliffe would be welcome to me now." He laughed once to show he was exaggerating.

I knew I was expected to laugh, and I did my best to comply, although to my own ears I sounded most false. "I will try to oblige you, sir."

"Thank you, Guthrie," said the Prince, and resumed watching out the window as we moved more deeply into Sheffield.

The farm cottages and estate houses amid the gorse rapidly gave way to mills, factories, and the tight rows of narrow-fronted homes. There was a slight haze over the entire town, a combination of dust and the smoke from thousands of coal fires. The streets, when I could see them as we rushed by, were bursting with traffic, mostly wagons filled with goods. We went past a wagon piled so high with wool I wondered it didn't topple over. A few seconds later Irish laborers in their distinctive caps came into view, loading machine parts into a wagon that must have been specially reinforced to handle the weight of the steel. Everyone we passed moved energetically.

"I know many English purport to dislike industrial towns, but I think they must be very proud of such a place as this, and Manchester, and Birmingham," said Prince Oscar, as we slowed still more, approaching the station.

"They are places to be proud of," I agreed, feeling a trifle apprehensive as I would soon have to report to Mycroft Holmes and Miss Gatspy had not come back to her post. I could not help but worry on her behalf.

"One day we will do as well in Scandinavia," the Prince said, making his assertion sound like a vow.

"No doubt; and this treaty will help to make it all possible," I said just as a knock sounded on the door. I very nearly jumped at the sound and went quickly to answer. "Miss Gatspy?"

"Whomelse were you expecting?" She sounded vaguely annoyed, and I opened the door at once, relieved to discover she was unharmed. "I am sorry I took so long," she said before I could speak. "I had a minor matter to attend to."

"Well, you are back and no harm done," I said, adding, as I retrieved my portfolio, "I must go along to compartment two—"

"Your employer must have work for you to do in Sheffield," Miss Gatspy agreed, and let me step past her into the corridor. As she closed the door, she said, "Do not fret, Guthrie. We'll get through this. We've survived worse."

"That we have," I said as the door closed.

The train was now moving quite slowly, and the station was not far ahead. I hurried along to Mycroft Holmes' compartment and knocked my identifying pattern as swiftly as I could.

"I was beginning to worry where you had got to," said Holmes, as he admitted me. "How is Herr Schere?"

"He says he is bored. He would like a paper to read and a deck of cards." I saw a sheaf of papers on the pullout table. "Are those for me to send?"

"Yes, Guthrie, and I am afraid you will have to rush to get them all on their way." He picked up the sheets and handed them to me. "Read them carefully and make sure the telegraph operator does his work well."

I made a sign of agreement that had the intention of showing I would waste neither words nor time. "And I will fetch Tyers' messages for you."

"I expect no less," said Mycroft Holmes. "We will be in the station directly."

As if to confirm this, the train lurched as brakes became more imperative. I steadied myself before tucking the sheets Holmes had given me into my portfolio. I turned and went toward the rear of the car so I would not have to pass Sir Cameron's compartment, for surely this energetic slowing would disturb even his slumbers. The platform was just coming into sight as I reached the steps that would be allow me to descend. Glancing down the train, I saw that Mister Burley had taken up a similar position at the end of the second-class car.

Steaming like a monster of legends, the *Flying Scotsman* halted at last in Sheffied amid a flurry of activity to which I contributed in my rapid sprint through the slanting sunlight of late afternoon to the telegraph office in the station-house, only to discover a salesman from Harrogate was ahead of me with three telegrams to send. All my chafing did nothing to hurry this genial gent, who spent a good five minutes gossiping with the telegraph operator; apparently the two were somewhat acquainted. As if to add to my complaint, the old wound on my hip began to ache, making me less patient than I ought to have been.

"Damned awkward, missing the 3:27 out of Leeds, but it can't be helped," the salesman said at last. "I'll have to hope the Red Ram will hold a room for me when my telegram is delivered."

"I should think they would do," said the telegraph operator. "Mind how you go along, now." He very nearly waved as the salesman stepped away. "What can I do for you then?"

"Do you have any messages for Guthrie? Paterson Guthrie?" I asked as I handed him the various sheets of messages Mycroft Holmes had entrusted to me. "These are for immediate dispatching."

"Guthrie, Guthrie," said the telegraph operator, speaking slowly as if to shame me for my demand for prompt action. He leaned toward his receipt boxes and pulled half a dozen of them from the pigeon-holes behind him. "There you are, sir. If you'll just sign for them" "

I took them and handed him a shilling. "For your trouble," I said as I scrawled my name on the line he indicated on his telegram register. "And there is another for you if you will hasten to send these." I put the telegrams in my portfolio, unread.

The telegraph operator glanced at the sheets. "We heard you'd had a murder on board," he said as he began to tap out the first message; I knew the more I told him, the faster he would send the texts.

"Two of them. The first was a man who had sought to escape the men with whom he had undertaken a crime, which is what brought the police into the matter. Then, once they were apprehended, the leader of the criminals killed one of his accomplices," I said, hoping the police would not regard any of this as compromising, although I was convinced it would be in every Midlands paper by tomorrow.

"They say one of them escaped," the telegraph operator said, encouraging me to explain more.

"He certainly threw himself out of a moving train, if you can call that escaping," I said, trying to make it sound as if the whole issue were settled.

"That's criminals for you," said the telegraph operator. "You want this sent to the Russian Embassy in London? Is that right?"

"Yes, it is," I said. "My traveling companions and I are all employed by *Satchel's Guides,*" I confided as if this would account for the contact with the Russians.

"Oh, *Satchel's,*" the operator said wisely, willing to accept this without cavil. In a matter of a minute, that had been sent. There were three more to go. I saw the activity on the platform increase, and I knew I had very little time to complete my errand. I handed payment to the operator, saying, "All the telegrams will have to be delivered. This should cover the amount, and any left over is yours for swift service." With that, I turned away and went to purchase a paper and deck of cards for Prince Oscar, striding hastily back to the train as the warning whistle sounded. I was mildly surprised, thinking that the time had been very short. Swinging myself aboard the train, I noticed that Sir Cameron's valet was doing much the same thing at the other end of the car. There was still sufficient light for me to be confident of my identification of the man; in another twenty minutes it would be too dark for easy recognition. It struck me as odd that he should have left the train for he held nothing in his hands and had not sent a telegram. I wondered if he might have been disposing of something—but what? I frowned as the conductor closed the door and signaled the engineer to begin moving. Taking this as my cue as well, I went along to compartment two, aware that the valet had already ducked back into Sir Cameron's compartment.

"What do you have for me?" Mycroft Holmes asked as I entered his compartment; the first powerful strokes of the train's great pistons began, and, jerking a bit, the train inched forward.

"Telegrams, sir," I said, drawing them out of my portfolio and handing them to him. "Two from Tyers, one from Superintendent Spencer, one from Commander Winslowe, one from the Admiralty— I think the latter may be giving you a report on the shooting of the double."

"That's five, and as you can see, there are six," said Holmes, continuing before I had a chance to speak, "Well, let me have a half an hour to study these. We'll review what we can glean from them when I know what that may be."

"Very good, sir," I said. "They should be starting the first seating in the dining room shortly."

He looked toward the window. "Oh, yes. It is getting late, isn't it?" He sighed heavily. "And we have to wait until we're through Leeds, I suppose."

"That should be about the right time, providing we have no other impediments to our travel." I was about to go to my own compartment when I decided I would do well to mention seeing Sir Cameron's valet on the platform.

"He sent no telegram?" Holmes asked when I was through.

"Not that I saw. I reckon he was disposing of something, or posting a note perhaps, but I cannot say so as fact." I shrugged. "I just thought you should know."

"Very true, Guthrie, whether or not it comes to anything, you're right—I should know of it." His heavy brows drew downward. "Keep an eye on him, if you will. Nothing too obvious, and nothing that will prevent you from attending to our primary purpose. He may be doing nothing but sending gossip to a crony, or there could be something sinister in his activities. It would relieve me if we were just jumping at shadows."

"And I, too, sir," I told him before leaving him to peruse his telegrams.

FROM THE PERSONAL JOURNAL OF PHILIP TYERS

Sutton is putting the finishing touches on his ensemble for his walk over to the Diogenes Club, and I am waiting for the next telegrams to arrive. This uncertainty is nerve-racking. I know it must take a toll on Sutton as well, but he expresses himself by other means than I do. . . .

I cannot rid myself of the fear that the information that ought to remain confidential has been spread about in a most dangerous way. Far too many of those who should know little or nothing about the destination of HHPO appear to have not only the general plan but some of the particulars as well. The only consolation I have is that once the source of the information is identified, it will be possible to root out the corruption that has so compromised the police.

I have had some dismaying news come my way through an old friend at the Admiralty—that an Admiralty agent has been placed aboard the Flying Scotsman *to "lend support" to MH and G. This is the very kind of well-meaning interference that MH will find most unwelcome. I cannot help but think it is my duty to notify him of this action taken by the Admiralty, although I realize it will make the work MH does much more difficult. I must prepare a report to reach him at Leeds and hope that nothing untoward happens because of this rash decision made by someone at the Admiralty with more hair than wit. . . .*

May the Flying Scotsman *not become a moving cage, trapping MH, G, and HHPO as surely as any snare made for game.*

Not more than half an hour ago, Sutton reiterated his concern that there may be more than one assassin in this plot, in which case I should warn MH to continue on his guard no matter what the Admiralty may tell him. I was pleased to inform him that I had already sent such a warning to MH, and that when next he retrieved his messages—at Sheffield, we must anticipate—he would find that supposition numbered among the various inferences that might be made when their potential risks are assessed. . . .

Chapter Eighteen

"I LOOK FORWARD to Tschersky's response to my telegram; given our current speed, he should have more than enough time to send it," Mycroft Holmes said as he came into my compartment; his tone reflected his exasperation with still more delays. The train was once again proceeding more slowly than usual due to other trains ahead of us on the track. "I cannot but hope he will be able to fit a few more pieces of the puzzle for us." He was looking a trifle tired, and his voice was a bit rough. I decided that his heartiness with the other passengers was catching up with him.

"Why should he know what you cannot discover for yourself?" I had not yet reached a point where I felt I could repose any real trust in the handsome Russian in spite of his usefulness in past years.

"Because he has knowledge of parts of the world where our inquiries would be conspicuous. His experiences have given him access to certain persons and organizations that are beyond our reach. He has made it a point to learn the activities of many rogues—not of the same cut as those my brother pursues, for Tschersky's interests are more political, which suits my purpose admirably. Fortunately, I have served much the same function for him from time to time, and he is sufficiently in my debt to be inclined to extend himself on our behalf." He held out three of the telegrams. "Read these, Guthrie, and tell me what you think when you have done."

I took the flimsy sheets and stared down at them. "Which shall I start with?"

"The first is from Tyers. Read that one, if you will." He managed to pace, while the train rattled on through the gathering dusk.

I adjusted the lamp over my settee, squinting to make out the faint letters. I had to remind myself of our code phrases, but once I had done that, I was able to get through the message without difficulty. "Two assassins? Is that likely? Could the Brotherhood have sent more than one, anticipating just such a ploy as we have undertaken?"

"I have thought it possible that we had to deal with more than one foe, but I did not allow for the possibility that they would be acting in concert. It is bad enough to have two men wanting to harm Herr Schere—that they have coordinated their efforts is far worse. That is most distressing in its ramifications." He waited while I read the next, from Commander Winslowe, informing MH of the disaster with Prince Oscar's double. "What perturbs me most in regard to Commander Winslowe's message is not just the shooting, but the fact that he knew our ploy and was well enough to be able to reach us means that someone is talking about this tactic of ours far more than he ought. By all rights, he should have notified Tyers and allowed him to pass such news on to us." He clapped his big hands and locked them together. "If I could discover who told him, then we might be in a fair way to unmasking the traitor."

"Traitor? Isn't that rather strong language?" I had been thinking of external opposition and enemies, not foes within.

"What else can I call it?" He looked distressed. "Read on, dear boy. There is more for you to see."

Dutifully I examined the telegram from Superintendent Spencer, and I noticed that he was aware of the delays of the train, seeing sinister intent in this as well as what he represented as conclusive proof that his police were beyond suspicion in the danger to Prince Oscar, whom he insisted on calling "the foreigner," as if such a designation were a sufficient disguise. "Not very encouraging," I said when I put it down. "If he will not look to his men, where are we?"

"We will find a way," said Holmes with great determination. "And late though we are, it may prove to our benefit if our enemies are not wholly aware of our new schedule, which may yet be subject to change again."

"Do you suppose such a thing will happen?" I asked. "Why should we be delayed?"

"There might be any number of causes, all perfectly natural: there has been considerable rain in the last few weeks; as a result I would not be surprised if there are numerous washouts under tracks, which continue to appear solid but bend or give when the locomotive passes over them. There is also the chance of a tree down, or mudslide blocking the track farther up the line. I was once delayed because a bull had gotten loose and chose to try its horns on the locomotive engine itself. The train might have continued on without delay, but pride and concern for the good opinion of the passengers required most of the carnage be removed before the next station. And, of course, there is always the possibility that someone left a gate open for a large herd of sheep to amble slowly across the tracks in front of another train farther ahead of us. As to wrecks and other mischance, we are rather more familiar with the possibilities, from a crash to a sleeping switchman. The companies rarely choose to announce their mistakes."

"I take it you have no plans of informing either Superintendent Spencer or Commander Winslowe of any changes of arrival times?" I handed him the telegrams.

"No. I will leave it to the Director of the North Eastern to do that, or so I shall say if I am questioned in this regard. They are the ones responsible for the safety of their passengers, and they have stated they place safety above speed." He rubbed his chin. "These are the places where we must be diligent. If we are to assume that we were undiscovered until we boarded, then the run to the first station must be safe because there is no way to board before then. I anticipate the locations where we stop may be hazardous, Leeds and Sheffield the more so as we will be taking on water, sand, and coal, which will lengthen our halt."

"We will be hard-put to observe all who come aboard, or leave," I remarked.

Mycroft Holmes nodded. "In addition, there are those curves where the train must slow dramatically. One is very close to Edinburgh and Waverly Station; that may be turned to our advantage. But there are a series of curves after Leicester and more some distance before Edinburgh that will force a reduction in speed that could allow access to the train by anyone waiting nearby and determined enough to risk the jump."

"That would be a desperate act, sir," I said.

"Our enemies are desperate men, Guthrie." He went on, as if thinking aloud. "We must assume that at some point we will be faced with opposition in the train itself. That is, if there is not already an assassin on board. Within the confines of the train we must be alert to any disturbance or distraction. There is no way to know what ruse may be employed to distract us and allow the killer to reach his quarry."

I did not want to remind him that in the person of Miss Gatspy we already had an assassin on board. "I hope it will not come to that," I said as I touched my stick-pin to be sure it was properly in place.

"No more than I," Mycroft Holmes admitted with a hard sigh. "And there is supper, as well. We must be careful when we dine."

"If you think we must, we shall be," I said, sorry not to have any opportunity to enjoy the meal waiting for us. "I should think that given Jardine's murder, poison would not be the method of choice for killing us."

"Ah, but Guthrie, consider: the poisoner was another passenger, not one of the staff, and poison can be subtle as a knife or a gun cannot; often the victim of poisoning is unaware of what has happened until it is too late, which danger increases when a physician is not available. That is a consideration we must acknowledge. Between Leeds and Car-lisle there are precious few stops where first-class medical care may be found; after Carlisle the possibilities are fewer still, and often what care is available must be summoned from a distance, all of which means the victim has a high likelihood of death. Poison is what we must guard against, although we must be alert to all means of attack." Mycroft Holmes went to stand by the window. "At this speed, reduced as it is, we have little to worry about from an assassin on the ground."

"Except when we are stopped or slowed to a walking speed," I added for him, to acknowledge I understood his anxiety in that regard.

"Yes." he cleared his throat. "I must go. You will have another spate of telegrams to send at Leeds; there may be ones to collect as well." He lowered his voice. "I'm sorry to keep you on the run, but I fear I must."

"No such thing, sir," I said. "I welcome the activity." It was no more than the truth—all these hours cooped up in a compartment, no matter how handsome, weighed upon me; my hip was no longer sore and I was as eager as a race-horse for a good run. I marveled that Prince Oscar could endure this enforced inactivity so well. I had to stifle the uncharitable recognition that he had Miss Gatspy to occupy his attention as unworthy of either the Prince or Miss Gatspy.

"Then, Guthrie, bestir yourself and see how Whitfield is doing in the lounge." He went to the door. "And have a look at the first seating in the dining car. If anything strikes a wrong note with you, I want to know of it."

"Very good, sir," I said, thinking that while this recommendation was prudent, I did not entirely look forward to reciting the details of Jardine's death yet again.

"Of course, you know better than to make your scrutiny obvious," Holmes added as he let himself out of the door.

"Of course," I said, rising and turning the lamp down low—I was not about to leave my compartment in darkness. I picked up my portfolio, neatened my tie, wishing as I did that I had brought a spare collar with me, for the points on this one were sadly wilted. We were nearly five hours behind schedule now, and no one who had boarded the train in London was looking entirely fresh. Had we been on time, we would have passed Carlisle by now and been on the last, fastest leg of our journey; as it was, there were hours ahead of us still.

The second-class car was not much occupied, the reason for which became apparent when I entered the dining car to find it filled to capacity with any number of passengers, including one family of seven that occupied two tables, one parent at each, trying to deal with tired children whose ages ran from two or three to thirteen or fourteen. As I made my way along the aisle between the ranks of tables, a few of the diners greeted me; having no desire to enter into any discussion of the deaths, I nodded my reply and kept moving, trying to present an air of cordiality as I did. Nothing struck me as inappropriate to the place, nor did I feel any inclination to question anyone I saw. Relieved, I went across the platform linking the cars. The lounge car was hazy with smoke from cigars, cigarettes, and pipes produced by a bit more than a dozen men. Making my way to the bar, I saw someone who was not Whitfield tending.

"He's off shift," said the new man, remarkable only for his astonishing ordinariness. Nothing about him was attractive, or odd, or notable: his height was average, his hair was medium brown, his features regular, his demeanor appropriate. Were he not behind the bar, I should never have noticed him. "He works until the first seating for dinner, and then he has four hours off. The name's Quest; you'll be that illustrator fellow, Guthrie. The train's still agog at what you and that Mister Hol—comb did." He held out his hand.

"Pleasure," I said, and noticed how powerful a grip the fellow had; I also noticed that he had stumbled over Holmes' assumed name— was it a slip of the tongue or something worse? Regarding the fellow as closely as I dared, I could not believe that the chap was athletic, but the strength of his hand suggested otherwise. "These long delays must be aggravating to you," I went on.

"Not a bit of it," he replied. "The longer we have to travel, the better business is here. It is inconvenient, to be sure, but thr'pence here and there makes up for it." His reference to the tip he usually received when a passenger left the car made sense to me. "It helps that we don't have to close in the afternoon, as we would if we were stationary. But there you are, then. What's your choice?'

I considered a moment, then said, "I'll have Assam laced with rum, if you can make it? In a glass."

"Sounds Russian," said Quest. "Wanting it in a glass."

"If you had vodka, it would be," I agreed with a laugh.

"Been there, have you?" Quest asked over his shoulder, tending to the kettle that steamed over a small gas ring.

"To the Crimea, very briefly," I said; I had been there hardly thirty-six hours before I managed to get aboard an Italian merchant ship bound—thank goodness—for home.

"They say the women are passionate in Russia," Quest prompted.

I could not help but smile. "Foreign women are always passionate. In Rome or Cairo or Moscow they probably say the same thing about Englishwomen."

Quest chuckled. "Point taken," he said, and put a strainer filled with black tea in the mouth of a good-sized glass and then gingerly poured in the near-boiling water. "Dark or light rum?"

"Dark, I think," I said as he finished making the drink for me; he filled a jigger with dark rum and poured it through the tea leaves before removing the strainer from the glass. I could smell it across the bar and was relieved that the heat would burn off a little of the alcohol. "There you are," he said, using his polishing rag to place it in front of me.

"Smells wonderful," I said, and was about to move away from the bar so I could eavesdrop on the various conversations in the lounge when Quest motioned to me.

"You see that man with the nose? He's been asking about you and Mister Holcomb. Just thought you ought to know." Quest moved back quickly and easily, once again suggesting a degree of athletic prowess.

I gazed over my right shoulder in the direction Quest had indicated, and saw that Arthur Burley was deep in conversation with an elderly man who might be a solicitor or a schoolmaster. "What the devil?" How had he got onto the train? He had said he was leaving at Sheffield, and here he was, riding on to Leeds. I supposed he must have been ordered to stay aboard, or had taken it upon himself to remain in the hope of finding more information. I wanted to curse, for I knew Mycroft Holmes would be annoyed to learn of this. Perhaps, I thought, the man would leave the train at Leeds, having got as much as he could on the murder. He would still be able to catch the Lancaster-to-Bristol night train and be back in Sheffield around midnight. It was a comforting thought, but I knew better than to rely upon it.

"I trust you will not mind my saying to you that you have done a very great service to the peace of this country," said a man who had come up on my left side. I turned rather suddenly and saw a well-set-up fellow of about my own age; I recalled him from our earlier encounter when Inspector Carew was conducting his inquiries. The man's name was Jeffers, or something similar to that.

"I think you overestimate what I have done," I said, studying his face in the hope of discovering any guile he might reveal. "In my position you would have done the same."

"Shortly before you came in, I said as much to Burley there. Can't have those newspaper johnnies carrying on as they do about the lack of duty that is becoming rife in these modern days." He looked at my glass. "I'll be pleased to stand you another."

"Thanks," I said. "No need. This is my limit before supper. It is kind of you to—" I did my best to look grateful for his offer, but I could tell he was mildly annoyed that I would not accept his hospitality. I tried to undo any poor impression I might have made by my refusal. "It has been a trying day, and I suspect much more drink would go to my head. You know how it is; Old Scratch fiddles on a drunken tongue. Can't have that when there will be a lady at the table with Mister Holcomb, Herr Schere, and me."

"Indeed," said the fellow, and turned away.

"Don't mind him being huffy," said Quest, who had overheard the exchange. "You know how these former army types can be."

"Former army?" I asked. "Why do you say that?" I supposed the man might have had a military background; I thought it more likely his father might have been an officer. I waited for what Quest might say.

"Stands like he's got a broom up his bum," the barkeep said, commonly and succinctly. "He has a very good opinion of his own judgment as well."

"Very likely," I agreed, balancing the glass on my portfolio as I adjusted my fingers on it.

"Takes all kinds, they say. Still, stuffy sorts are not as pleasant as those that likes a good time." His attention was demanded by another passenger, whose ruddy cheeks revealed his mild intoxication.

I continued to take small, burning sips of my black-tea-and-rum while I did my best to listen without seeming to be listening.

". . . too late for the coachman. I'll have to walk the two miles . . ."

"How can I explain to my wife about the killing? She's been asking questions. She's a delicate creature . . ."

". . . thirteen or fourteen hours to Edinburgh! Scandalous, I tell you. I shall demand a refund of my fare."

". . . left in the baggage, so I cannot reach it . . ."

". . . since my man of business advises against it."

"The most marvelous whores in London, give you my oath . . ."

". . . prices on cotton from America . . ."

"The whole village came out for it, made an occasion of it . . ."

"Not that you could expect anything else from the Americans . . ."

". . . in terms of settlements, of course, I could not advise anyone to agree to such terms, let alone a friendless widow . . ."

". . . but I wouldn't want my name in your paper . . ."

". . . against regulations, they told me, to let a passenger into the baggage compartment while the train is in motion; they don't want to . . ."

"Just what I was telling you. The fellow will be in custody by now . . ." This was the military chap whose name I recalled as Jeffers.

". . . the lad's at school, of course, and will go on to Brasenose in . . ."

". . . hardly something for the Prince of Wales to deal with—more along Cecil's line, I should have thought . . ."

". . . and a sweet omelette to finish . . ."

"Nothing to do with me, old man, but if my daughter . . ."

". . . another scheme for the Norfolk broads . . ." I recognized Arthur Burley's voice, very smooth and plausible, as if he were steadying a skittish horse.

"If I left my bags at the station, the coachman could fetch them tomorrow . . ."

Nothing caught my attention as requiring my immediate concern. I took a bit larger sip of my drink, burning the roof of my mouth as I swallowed.

"Is it to your liking?' " Quest asked, trying to appear concerned for my good opinion.

"It is very good," I told him, more out of courtesy than any sense of the quality of the drink. "Thank you."

"Not the sort of thing often asked for; I shall remember your tipple, sir, that I will." He thumped the bar with his knuckles to register the promise with the old Druid oak-gods. A summons from the other end of the bar from the fellow who had been talking about his son who would be going to Oxford demanded Quest's attention, and he went to replenish the drink.

I went back to listening, hoping to learn something of use, but not at all sanguine that I would, or that I would know it when I heard it.

FROM THE PERSONAL JOURNAL OF PHILIP TYERS

The telegrams have been sent and Sid Hastings is standing by at King's Cross to receive any communication from MH, which he will deliver to me at once.

I am still much perplexed by the stance taken by Superintendent Spencer regarding the investigation of his men. Nothing I have communicated to him has shaken his conviction that there can be no member of the police willing to compromise the rest of the force in this way. If he is being willfully blind, I can only marvel at his assumptions and his ability to view the world on terms that are so influenced by his own loyalty. He insists he is satisfied that no police have knowingly helped enemies of Britain or her people. This impasse is at a most inopportune time, for I cannot partake of his beliefs without signally failing in my duty—a duty that S Spencer sees as unforgivable. I do not wish to occupy myself with disputes involving this most well-meaning man, but I am committed to do the task MH has given me.

Sutton is at the Diogenes Club, fulfilling MH's habitual daily visit. He offered to have a word with Commander Winslowe, who is also a member, but upon reflection decided it might be risky to speak with someone who has worked with MH, no matter how superficially. Sutton believes we must identify the Admiralty spy aboard the train, not only to provide MH the identity of a possible ally in time of difficulty, but to inform him what passenger has been sent with instructions to observe him. I concur, but I would like to have more confirmation of this before I add it to the other information that must cause anxiety to MH when he learns the whole. With so many unexpected intrusions upon a fairly simple plan, I can see no good coming from adding unnecessary apprehension to the mix. I will wait until I have more solid information to impart.

No further word from CI Somerford, which does not give me the comfort it ought. I may be too superstitious about these matters, but his absence at this time strikes an ominous note within me; and although I can give no rational account for it, I fear that the explanation for his silence may have sinister implications. . . .

Hastings has just arrived. I'll continue when I have seen what he has brought to me. . . .

Chapter Nineteen

SIR CAMERON HAD started singing again; I could hear him as soon as I entered the first car, and I shuddered at the sound he made. I wondered if he intended to visit the dining car for the second seating, in which case the maître d' should be warned of what his staff might have to accommodate. Passing compartment five, I realized I had not seen its interior. Not that I should have done, since Miss Gatspy occupied it; but with Prince Oscar in the compartment ahead of her, I could not help but be concerned.

The valet appeared in the door of Sir Cameron's compartment, his skimpy hair disordered, his face filled with repugnance and dismay. "I'll try . . . to arrange . . ." he stammered to Sir Cameron, then hurried in my direction. "I won't be more than five minutes, Sir Cameron." He faltered as he neared me; I took sympathy upon him.

"Not an easy employer, by the sound of it." And as I knew from experience.

"Just so, just so." The valet glanced nervously back over his shoulder. "I should have been suspicious," he added.

"Should have been suspicious about what?" I inquired, doing my best to detain him without actually laying hold of him.

"The salary was very good. Too good. I needed the money, you see, and my former employer had died six months since, so I accepted this post as an interim one," he muttered before he broke away from me and hurried away toward the rear of the train. I watched him go with curiosity, hoping to make sense of what he had only now told me. He was not a long-time servant of Sir Cameron's—and I doubted Sir Cameron had many of those—but what of his circumstances of employment might be significant, I could not tell.

Leeds was not far ahead; another twenty minutes and we should be on the platform. I would have to sprint to the telegraph office, collect the messages that had arrived, send those my employer wanted sent, and return to the train without attracting the attention of whomever was tracking our progress. I trusted the platform would be well-lit, enabling me to see everyone who left the train for whatever reason. If it turned out to be dark, I should have a much more difficult time of it. That the same would be true of the assassin gave me scant comfort.

Sir Cameron's messy attempts at "Sweetheart, Remember" finally trailed away in a wailing cadenza. I thought the valet would be pleased to return to find his charge had fallen asleep once more. As I knocked on the door of compartment two, I thought it was fortunate that Mycroft Holmes did not have to listen for such a small sound against all that bellowing.

"Come in, Guthrie," he called.

"How was the . . . concert?" I asked, as I stepped through the door, jerking my thumb in the direction of compartment one.

"Don't be cheeky, my boy. It doesn't become you," said Mycroft Holmes with a faint smile. The light from the lamps had softened his features so that he looked more like Sutton than was generally the case. "He only started about five minutes ago." He had a small pile of papers in front of him. "I want to go over one or two things with you before you send these off. One, you will see, is to Yvgeny Tschersky. If there is a telegram from him, send this. If there is none, do not send it." He indicated I should pull out the stool and sit. "This one to Tyers is obvious. This to the Admiralty must be handled very carefully. We do not want the telegraph operator puzzled by a journalist for *Satchel's* sending information to such an august body as the Admiralty, so this salutation of 'Dear Uncle' is crucial, as is the wording. I know you are always conscientious, Guthrie, but in this instance you must be doubly so, for it is my intention to unveil a traitor if we can. The same strictures accompany the telegram to Superintendent Spencer. We have to make an effort to discover which service is the source of the duplicity we have seen in action."

"Hence the various telegrams," I said, indicating the papers he had prepared.

"Obviously. I have a notion that with the right prodding, I can unearth the culprit," he said with that quiet confidence that marked all his actions.

"Rather like poking a stick into a wasps' nest, I should think," I ventured.

"It may be, or it may be more a badger's earth, and my opponent will make himself known in an obvious and belligerent manner." The satisfaction he felt at this prospect would have unnerved me a year ago; now it only made me wince a bit.

"Have you formed some opinion upon it?" I asked, trying to imagine what scraps of information he had pieced together, if this were the case.

"I would be foolish to do so, Guthrie. I am well-aware that, like it or not, I must take the cautious approach and be doubly certain of all my facts before I draw any conclusions. At present, facts are in short supply, a situation that these telegrams are intended to correct. So ready yourself for a hectic ten minutes. I, for one, will be glad of a short respite while you are about your labors." He yawned as if to prove he meant it.

I took the papers he proffered. "Other than Tyers and Tschersky, what other responses are you expecting?"

"I am *expecting* none; I am envisioning two or three different possibilities, which is another matter entirely." Mycroft Holmes sighed heavily. "If we were not on this train, matters could be handled very differently indeed. But we are here and here we must stay, so I will deal with our problems within the limitations imposed upon us." He fiddled with his watch-fob. "How is our . . . our invalid?"

"I did not stop in compartment four returning from the lounge. I must assume it is much the same as before." I heard that stuffy note come back into my voice again and was about to apologize when Mycroft Holmes stopped me.

"Don't fash yourself, dear boy. The lady is safe as houses." He beamed at me. At another time I might have questioned his motive, but on this occasion I did not, for I was convinced of his kindly intentions.

"Yes; I understand that." I had to steady myself as the train began to brake.

"Good. By the way, what news from the lounge?" He gave me his polite attention.

"Nothing that seems of bearing on our work," I said, and outlined what I had overheard.

"Um. Just as well." He clapped his hands together. "We'll be in Leeds Station shortly. Make yourself ready, Guthrie. This may prove to be our most crucial stop."

"Very well," I said, and readied myself by putting the texts for the telegrams into my portfolio.

"Damned useful thing, that portfolio of yours," Mycroft Holmes remarked. "So very obvious it is unobvious." He gestured me to the door and put his hand to his forehead. "I am more than ready for my supper; I admit it readily."

I had little appetite but I knew it would be prudent to eat, so I nodded. "The second seating will begin shortly after we leave Leeds. I will take Miss Gatspy's place as soon as I have delivered the telegrams to you," I reminded him.

"Yes, yes." He looked toward the windows where houses and undecipherable buildings flashed by, some showing well-lit windows, some dark as tombs.

I felt the train continue to slow and heard the signal bells as we approached the station, now going quite slowly. I swung around toward the door. "I am ready, sir."

"That you are, my boy, that you are," said Mycroft Holmes looking far more relaxed and confident than I would have thought possible. "We'll have a pleasant time at supper, no doubt of it." With that he motioned to me to leave his compartment.

I complied at once, sensing that he was filled with more concerns than he would impart to me until he had read the next installments of telegrams. I had come to know when he was holding himself in readiness and saw that now was just such an instance. As the lights of the station platform struck me, I saw that a number of policemen were waiting, apparently for the arrival of the *Flying Scotsman,* for as the train braked itself at last, I saw two of the uniformed constables move forward, one of them carrying a truncheon. What on earth required such preparation? I was puzzled, for I supposed that the police were finished with the passengers. Then a more sinister possibility struck me—if the police were here to intervene in Prince Oscar's journey, there was clearly something very much amiss.

The conductor bawled out the name of the station from the platform between cars; the engine hissed and billowed masses of white steam into the evening air, and the sound of opening doors was heard throughout the train.

As soon as the steps were down, I was off the train and moving quickly to the telegraph office. I did not run, for I knew it would draw attention to me in a way I would find most inconvenient. It was an effort not to watch the progress of the constables over my shoulder, but I managed.

"Guthrie?" said the telegraph operator with a stunning lack of attention; he was a pudding-faced man nearing forty and grown lackadaisical. "No, I don't think I—"

"Look again, man," I said sharply. The last thing I wanted was to deal with a clerk who was slipshod in his work. My first impression of this fellow was that he was just such a one. "Guthrie. P. E. Guthrie," I repeated, leaning on the high counter between us.

He shrugged to show his lack of concern, but went through the motions of looking, and this time feigned surprise when he put his hand on four telegrams. "This will be what you want, then?" He held them out to me, plainly waiting for a tip for his service.

I took the telegrams and glanced at the various returns on them, and selected the appropriate message for Tschersky. "Thank you," I said absently.

"You're a busy lad, having so much to do." He tapped his finger like a musician warming up.

I ignored his implied slight. "I have a few to be sent," I said sharply, handing him the papers Mycroft Holmes had just entrusted to me. "Put them on your wire at once. The train is badly behind schedule and there are those in London who must be notified of our delay."

"Patience is a virtue," the man said with a show of unconcern that annoyed me.

"And sloth is a vice," I added for him as I put the telegrams into my portfolio. "Your superiors would not like to receive complaints of you, I am sure."

His posture grew straighter. "You have no cause to do that."

"Not if you set out to send the telegrams at once," I said, ignoring his look of ill-usage. As the man began to work his key, I said, "Plenty of constables about."

"Oh, aye. They're here at the behest of some brass-buttons in Bedford. They're looking for a barman from the train. Something about a murder on the train. But you'd know more about that than I, I suppose." He was glad of this interruption and would have taken more advantage of it if I had not made a point of pulling out a five-pound note and holding it where he could see it. He sighed and went on with his task.

The policemen were milling about now, and one of them began to rap out orders I could not hear. The constables were clearly distressed about some aspect of what they had discovered. In a short while, the Sergeant came into the station and went toward the Stationmaster's office, closing the door forcefully.

"I wonder what that is about?" the telegraph operator said speculatively. He glanced in my direction, but I did nothing to encourage him.

"I haven't a notion," I said, hoping I did not sound as curious as I, in fact, was. "Keep on with your work."

The fellow scowled, and I did my best to ignore his evident displeasure. Only when he had keyed the last of the messages did I pay him for his efforts. I then prepared to return to the train only to hear the Stationmaster announce that the train would be delayed for twenty minutes while the police conducted a thorough search of the cars for the other barman.

So Whitfield was missing, I thought, and decided it alarmed me to hear this. I decided Mycroft Holmes needed to be informed of this at once. With that intention in mind, I went back across the platform and climbed aboard the train once again.

Mycroft Holmes was pacing the confined space of compartment two. For a man of his height and size, the compartment provided very little room for an outlet of his strain. I paused in the doorway until

Holmes came to a halt. "I have telegrams, sir," I said, patting my portfolio just above my gold initials.

"Good." He held out his hand for them even before I had closed the door behind me. "How many?"

"Four. Tyers, Commander Winslowe, Superintendent Spencer, and Tschersky. Nothing from anyone at the Admiralty," I said as I gave them to him.

"Too many, with or without the Admiralty; we might as well head a parade," he grumbled. "Well, let's have a look at them." He opened the first, from Tyers, and read through it swiftly. "Damn," he said conversationally.

"What?" I asked nervously; he was apprehensive, and I caught it from him.

"There seems to have been a problem." He sat down and pinched the bridge of his nose.

"How . . . how bad is it?" I did not want to add to his distress, but I could not deny my apprehension. "What does Tyers say?"

Mycroft Holmes did not answer at once. "I must assume that Tyers has kept this to himself. Otherwise I am certain we would not be—" He stopped and looked up at me. "Guthrie, we must have a word with Miss Gatspy."

He did not say *my* Miss Gatspy, and that caused me a moment of dismay. Whatever he needed to learn from her, it superceded his good-tempered gibes. "We will be dining with her shortly—surely the matter can wait."

"Yes, but it is hardly an appropriate topic for table conversation." He snapped his fingers. "We will go to Herr Schere's compartment as soon as we are moving again."

I coughed delicately. "That may not be for some time," I said. "It would seem that Whitfield is missing, and apparently there is a search on for him."

"Whitfield? Missing?" Mycroft Holmes slapped the seat of his bench. "How very irregular."

"Does it worry you?" I wanted to hold my breath as I waited for his reply.

"I don't know," he answered slowly. "It depends on whether or not the drink he was pilfering is found. If it is and he is not, I shall be very worried indeed."

"Pilfering drink?" I exclaimed, and at the same instant recalled the cartons of partially opened bottles behind the bar. "You are saying he—"

"Stole from the railroad? Yes, most certainly I am." He smiled at me. "There are probably half a dozen publicans between London and Edinburgh who have a cozy arrangement with Whitfield. He saves an ounce or two at the bottom of every bottle and off-loads them to men along the way. Each makes a small profit in the process, and if it is not too greedily done, the North Eastern turns a blind eye to the enterprise. It is not uncommon, I assure you." He put his hands together, the remaining telegrams held between them. "If it is Whitfield and not the drink that is truly missing, I fear our enterprising young barkeep may have stumbled upon a true villain, not a venal publican."

I felt confusion mount within me. "But why should—" I stopped myself. "If the drink is still on the train and he is not, he has met with more than he bargained for."

"Precisely," said Mycroft Holmes as he opened the telegram from Tschersky. "Oh, poor operator," he exclaimed in mock dismay as he held the flimsy sheet out to me.

Puzzled I took it, and glanced down to see . . . *Ny pravda lhi? Vy pruhvy* . . . "In transliterated Russian and in coded phrases?" I recognized the first—"Isn't it true?"—but I had not had enough time to manage the rest, and the smattering of Russian I had acquired in my travels was not sufficient to make reading such a message easy for me.

"How very like him," said Holmes with a sigh of approval. He was silent as he read, occasionally pausing to study the words carefully. "Most illuminating." He folded the telegram and put it in his inside waistcoat pocket; whatever Yvgeny Tschersky had said, Mycroft Holmes regarded it as singularly important. Looking up at me he went on. "He has answered my question, for which I am grateful, and it is now more imperative than ever that we speak with Miss Gatspy. Little as I like the idea, she may hold the key to our situation."

As high a regard as I had for Miss Gatspy's capabilities, I did not see that it followed that she held the solution to our quandary. "Why should she—"

"Guthrie," Mycroft Holmes interrupted patiently, "I make full allowance for your enthrallment, but in this case you must permit me to do as I think necessary in regard to your Miss Gatspy."

I could feel my cheeks grow red. "It isn't like that at all," I began, then saw his heavy bow arch and gave up. "You *will* have your joke, sir," I said, and waited.

"Those fellows in the Golden Lodge have access to all sorts of material that you and I cannot readily obtain." Mycroft Holmes tapped the telegram with his finger. "I hope she might be able to procure a few smidgens of information that will simplify our search for this would-be assassin—or assassins, if what Tschersky tells me is correct."

"Assassins?" I repeated. "There *is* more than one?" The idea had seemed improbable when it was first proposed; but if Tschersky endorsed it, I had to reconsider the situation.

Holmes nodded heavily. "From what Tschersky tells me, there is a pair of them, working in tandem, one functioning as a decoy, the other as the killer. I had hoped this was not the case, but there can be no doubt. Tschersky has a great deal of information about them. They do not always take the same roles. They are said to be resourceful and capable of improvising if all is not as they expected. And they are quite ruthless. The Russians believe the pair have accounted for more than fifteen highly placed individuals in more than a dozen countries. If the Russians have such knowledge, I must suppose the Golden Lodge does, too. And it would explain Miss Gatspy's presence on what should be ordinary escort duty." He opened the third telegram from Commander Winslowe, reading it quickly and nodding once when he was finished. Then he opened the telegram from Superintendent Spencer and his expression darkened. "The bloody fool!" he exclaimed, and read through the telegram a second time. "Fool!" he reiterated.

I watched in some dismay at this dramatic change in demeanor that overcame my employer. I could not imagine what Winslowe had said that would so affect him. Finally I held out my hand for the telegram, hoping that if I read it, I might learn something to account for this change. "Sir?"

He thrust the telegram into my hand. "Go ahead. Read it." He glowered at the page.

I held the sheet near the light:

HOLMES: MUST INSIST YOUR INQUIRIES GO NO FURTHER STOP POLICE ARE NOT TO BLAME STOP NO INVESTIGATION WOULD REVEAL CORRUPTION STOP PERSISTENCE WILL BE TREATED AS ATTACK STOP WINSLOWE.

"I'd expect something of this sort from Spencer, but Winslowe?"

Mycroft Holmes shrugged. "They work on each other's behalf. I reckon they thought I would accept orders regarding the police more readily if they came from Commander Winslowe. Not a bad assumption, as far as it goes, but a trifle simplistic."

"They're closing ranks," I said, somewhat unnecessarily.

"That they are, and at the worst possible moment." He folded his arms. "If he had waited just a few hours before he sent this, our work would be easier. But no aid for the wicked, as my old French granmama used to say."

"Are you going to comply with this . . . ultimatum?" I asked, holding up the telegram.

"Of course not," he said. "But we can no longer be assured of help from the police, not with such a shot across our bow." He lowered his eyes. "I wish I knew how much he has been told and by whom."

"Do you suspect Winslowe?" I wanted to be more shocked than I was. What better position for a man determined to corrupt the police than a Superintendent? He might do vast amounts of damage without serious risk of exposure and with the power to quash all but the highest reviews of his decisions.

"It is very tempting, and it would provide a degree of satisfaction that has eluded me in this mission, but it may be a bit too soon to cast that particular gauntlet," said Mycroft Holmes, looking up as the sound of men climbing aboard our car came through the corridor. "And speaking of police, that will be the ones looking for Whitfield, I would think. I wish them luck with Sir Cameron." This last was said with a wry smile.

A short while later there was a sharp rap on the door to this compartment. I opened the door, and held out our ticket stubs to the fresh-faced young constable who stood there. "Please come in. And you may search my compartment as well. I'm in the next along, number three. We are traveling in company with Herr Schere in compartment four; he is unwell."

"Is he?" said the young constable, his accent placing him from the Yorkshire dales. "Well, we'll not disturb him more than we must."

Holmes and I waited patiently while the constable searched for Whitfield in a few unlikely places, then ushered him out of the compartment.

As soon as the constable was gone, Mycroft Holmes said, "Guthrie, we'll be here for a short while, I fear. I'd like you to have a look around—you know, check the platforms and the baggage compartment to see if there are any indications of what happened to Whitfield. I can accept one set of criminals being aboard as coincidence, little as I may like it and inconvenient as they may be, but two such events pushes credulity beyond my limits. Whitfield being gone is a signal that strikes me as particularly ominous. At our next stop, I will have to find out who this Quest chappie is."

"Then you think something may have become of Whitfield?" I shared his alarm.

"Dear Guthrie, do you not? I should have thought he would have bid us adieu when he left, if only on the hope of garnering another tip. I trust the avarice of men in his position far more than I trust these unplanned events. Do not tell me you haven't had similar suspicions."

I sighed. "Of course."

"Cheer up. Think of this as earning your dinner," Holmes suggested with a wink.

I handed him my portfolio. "You'd better keep hold of this," I said, and went out of the compartment. I noticed the constable leaving Miss Gatspy's compartment and so I waited, as if I was about to make my way to the lav or into the next car. As I began to walk, the constable raised his billy to me in a kind of salute or casual threat before he left the car. What on earth had he learned from Miss Gatspy that he should respond to me in this wise? I thrust my apprehensions from my thoughts and put the whole of my concentration to finding any signs that someone had been forced off the train.

On the platform I saw nothing indicative of a struggle—not scrapes nor scratches, nor patches of skin, nor blood, and no odor of strong drink. I continued on through the second-class car, where the constable was just beginning his search. At the end of that car I again inspected the platform with the same result as before. The dining car was in confusion as the waiters tried to ready it for the next seating while a pair of constables looked under the tables and through the kitchen in an effort to discover where Whitfield might be.

I reached the lounge and saw that the bar had been closed down while the police were at their tasks; Quest stood behind the bar, idly smoking a churchwarden's pipe and gazing at some distant point known only to his memories. I nodded, and continued on a bit farther to the platform leading to the second-class car behind the lounge-and-baggage car. If I were to discover anything of significance, it would be here. Resolved to take greater care inspecting this site, I dropped down onto my knee, making the most of the light-spill from the platform.

On impulse I got down from the platform to look at the ties between the tracks, thinking that something might have fallen from

Whitfield's pocket if he had been thrown from the train. I peered into the dark, wishing I had a bull's-eye lantern. I used my fingers, discovering a bent ha'penny and a small link of tarnished silver that had once been part of a heavy chain, but nothing that persuaded me that Whitfield had been harmed here. I moved back and peered under the shadow of the platform, trying to see if anything had been hidden there. The odor of oil and coal was so strong that I had to clench my jaw to keep from coughing, stopping the spasms in my chest, and making a dull sort of hacking sound.

Which may have been why I did not hear my assailant come up behind me until an instant before his truncheon struck me on the back of my head and I toppled into unconsciousness; as my eyes closed I had an impression of a bloody hand reaching out of the platform shadow, but it may have been nothing more than a response to the blow that knocked me out.

FROM THE PERSONAL JOURNAL OF PHILIP TYERS

Finally word from Leeds. I was beginning to fear for MH's safety, but his report indicates that all is well at least superficially. HHPO is in no apparent danger; and aside from the demands of local police, the train has not been delayed beyond another half hour, which still means it will arrive in Edinburgh much later than was prepared for. As soon as I am finished with this entry I have half a dozen errands to run and a sheaf of instructions to hand to Hastings. It appears that Sutton's notion about two assassins is not as far-fetched as I thought it had to be, and if certain telegrams confirm MH's fears, there will be more work for all of us to do if HHPO is to arrive safely in his own land once again.

I have in the last ten minutes been handed a report brought by a fellow with a Russian accent, with a note—unsigned, of course—saying that the contents in the sealed envelope are private and must be destroyed as soon as they have been read. The Russians are the most leery folk on earth, always certain of spies and plots. Still, with their history, who can blame them?

Sutton is just back from the Diogenes Club and has sworn to disguise himself afresh and help me in my errands, and I am inclined to accept his help. He may be an actor, but his probity, at least in regard to his work for MH, is beyond question. He has a dozen personae he may adopt quickly and turn to advantage. A young man in the uniform of a foreign navy bringing a dispatch to the Admiralty would attract less notice than I would at this point, if anyone is monitoring the actions of Commander Winslowe.

That will allow me to carry the messages MH has asked me to prepare to CI Somerford and Superintendent Spencer. Whatever has transpired in the last hour or so aboard the train has prompted MH to reassess his thinking in regard to this mission.

A constable came here not ten minutes since with news for MH that he will not like. Inquiries regarding the assassination attempt in front of St. Paul's have been suspended on order from the PM, who has declared that this investigation is causing friction between Britain and the great countries of Scandinavia. He has ordered Scotland Yard to hand all material they have gathered to his Secret Service men, so that they may handle the matter less publicly. MH will have something to say about that when he learns of it. I must include a report of this development for my next telegram which should reach him at Carlisle.

I have much to do before I send that report and less than ninety minutes in which to do it all. Sutton is in the kitchen smearing his face with soot so he may leave by the back stairs as a chimney-sweep. His enthusiasm for verisimilitude is laudable, of course, but in this instance I am inclined to temper my praise. I must attend to getting him on his way before the flat is dusted in charcoal.

Chapter Twenty

I CAME TO myself as steam hissed and a last flurry of activity indicated the train was about to depart. Dazed, I sat up holding my head with my hands. I did not realize until that moment I had scraped the flesh of my palms as I fell. I had been pulled a foot or so away from the tracks and perhaps half a car length toward the front of the train, so that I would be in the shadow of the platform—or so I guessed as I attempted to put together the fragmented recollections I had of the attack I had sustained.

Slowly I stretched out my arm and flexed my hand, reassured that I could do so much without succumbing again. I blinked several times and moved experimentally; I knew I had to board the train or be left here alone.

The engine bellowed again and the train began to inch forward. In my befogged state I tried to compel myself to move, to make some effort to return to the train, but it took four or five seconds before I could will myself to try to stand. By then the train was moving at the same pace as a brisk walk and in a moment or so it would pick up such speed as I would not be able to catch it. More from desperation than thought, I reached out to the brace beside the baggage door. I did not expect to catch it, and therefore almost wrenched my shoulder when I managed to grab and hold the long metal bar. I swung heavily against the train, landing just where my old wound on my hip was: the pain went through me like a bolt of lightning, and only my grim determination kept me from releasing my hold on the train. Much as my hip ached, I knew it was nothing compared to the terrible injuries I would suffer if I let go and fell, for I risked being crushed by the metal wheels.

I was half-running now to keep up with the train, and to any observer I must have appeared comical, a man dangling in ungainly fashion off the side of the *Flying Scotsman:* for me, it was grim business, my head ringing and dizzy, my arm aching, and the possibility of serious injury or death waiting for me at any mischance. We crossed a broad street, and I feared for discovery or perhaps an assault from the denizens of the town who preyed on the unwary. From my position, I would be unable to fight off any toughs who might decide to bedevil me. I had to get aboard the train now or drop off before the speed increased to a fatal rate. I knew I would have one chance and one chance only.

With a single, tremendous effort, I hauled myself up the bar and onto the narrow lip where the sliding door left six inches of purchase. I took hold of the door handle and clung to it, promising myself I would pull the door open slowly and get safely inside the car as soon as we were out of Leeds.

The scenery fit my darker mood. The comfortable rolling hills of the southeast had given way to stonier and broken lands. Large patches of ground were still enclosed, showing spots of bright green among the gray-green of prickly weeds and the first thistle. The stone here was a creamier color, less grey than that around London and a lot more prevalent in the fields. The track itself was lined with three- or four-year-old plantings of a silver-leafed tree and another shorter tree whose foliage was so dark as to appear almost black as the lights of the train struck them.

I was frightened and sore and famished. After ten minutes I was weary as well. My hands, mauled and cold, fixed on the metal bar like claws. My hip felt as if I were being mangled by a tiger from within my flesh. I cursed when the first spitting rain promised to chill me to the marrow. The sound of the train rolling over the rails was mesmerizing, and I had to force myself not to be lulled by its seductive repetition. I deliberately pressed my lacerated palm against the wood of the door, letting the splinters bite enough to shake off any lassitude the clicking and rocking might impart.

After working on the door for some time—I would hazard no more than five minutes, although it seemed nearer an hour—I realized that it was probably locked from the inside, which meant I would have to get back on the platform or hang onto the bar from Leeds to Skipton, where we would have to stop for water, or so I recalled. The resistance I encountered when I tested the door suggested a chain on the inside, which puzzled me, for if the lock was in place, what need was there for a chain? It made me more aware than ever of how desperate my situation was. Now that I was in this position, I did not know for certain how far it was to Skipton and if it was truly a water station; the schedule of the train was so compromised, I dared not assume that all the halts would be fixed. Besides Skipton was twenty-five miles ahead, the rain was increasing and I would be soaked through in less than five minutes. I knew there was a kind of service ladder on the side of the train that allowed the maintenance men to service the roof of the car; it should be next to the rod I was holding onto. But I did not relish climbing to the roof of this moving train car in the rain and the night.

I was so caught up in trying to sort out how to proceed that I did not notice the stone bridge just ahead until it scraped along my back and shoulders, shredding my coat and leaving me a vaster collection of bruises than I had accumulated thus far. Now my shoulders vied with my hip for monumental pain. I made myself think of what was ahead. This part of the North Eastern line was littered with such bridges, narrow and tall-sided. I now had no choice, for the next bridge might easily batter me to pieces or knock me from my perch to the rails where I would be cut to ribbons in seconds. I swallowed hard against the image formed in my mind at this. No, I told myself over the agony of my shoulders and hands, it was the roof or a coffin. I reached out and began to feel for the shallow rungs, hoping all the while that I could reach the roof before we crossed another bridge.

At last I found a rung and grabbed hold of it as if it were a life-ring in a stormy sea. This left me sprawled across the side of the car like some preposterous insect flattened on the headlight of the engine. I had to move, but I found it nearly impossible to summon up the courage to swing away from the door and pull myself to the ladder. My shoulders and my hip made such a notion preposterous, for the effort would be a strain even if I had no injuries. With my body hurting with every movement, the very idea of climbing over the car made my gorge rise. I had to chide myself with all the remembered rebukes of the schoolyard before I could gather determination enough to make the attempt, for I knew it would have to be successful or I was lost.

I pushed out and tugged myself at the same time, scrabbling with feet for purchase on the lower rungs, and reaching for a place with the other beside my one fixed hand. Occasionally I find my left-handedness an unexpected blessing, and so it proved in this instance, for my left hand was the one already holding the rung, and as I flailed about with my right, my left held true, and at the end of interminable seconds, I caught the rung above my left hand, and I knew I would not fall, no matter how wind and rain buffeted me. My hip flared, sending agony up my body like a flame. With grim determination, I began to climb to the roof, reaching it less than two minutes before the train swept over another narrow stone bridge. I clung to the roof and breathed deeply for a short while.

Not wanting to have to account for myself to anyone in the lounge, I made my way forward on the car, crawling along the roof, being battered by wind and drenched by rain while I crawled—I am not too proud to admit it—along toward the other access ladder. I was shaking from effort and cold by the time I reached my goal. Moving with exaggerated care, I finally climbed down the outer ladder to the platform between the dining car and the lounge. My hands were shaking, and it was not entirely from cold, as I opened the door to the dining car.

The maître d' saw me and instead of admonishing me to wait for five minutes before being seated, he rushed to my side. "Good Lord, sir. What happened?" From the expression on his face, I knew I looked as bludgeoned as I felt.

"It's a long story," I said, and was shocked at how thin my voice was. I cleared my throat and went on. "I shan't bore you with it now. Suffice it to say that I shall have a word or two for your Directors when this journey is over." I trusted my indignation covered my relief. For several heartbeats my bones felt like cold aspic.

"Just so, sir," said the maître d', all but saluting. Once again I found myself wondering how long he had been at sea before he took to the rails.

"I must be a fright," I said, trying to pull myself together. I busied myself with getting out of the ruin of my coat; the condition of it shocked me afresh. I had not realized how comprehensive the destruction was. I dropped the remnants to the floor, unwilling to touch them any longer. "Do you perhaps have a jacket you could loan me until I can return to my compartment and change my clothes? For I fear these are quite ruined."

"Indeed, sir," said the maître d'. "Shall I put that in a sack for you?"

My first impulse was to tell him to throw it out, but I knew Mycroft Holmes would probably want to inspect the garment, in case any useful clues had survived the onslaught. "Yes, if you would," I said, and put my hand to my temple as a wave of nausea swept through me.

The maître d' observed this impassively. "How fortunate you may rely on the nurse in your car to tend to the worst of your hurts."

I realized this was more an order than a suggestion, but just for a moment I could not imagine whom he meant. Then I recalled Miss Gatspy's current ruse. "Just so," I said, and waited while the maître d' secured a white jacket for me. "Thank you. I shall mention this in my report."

"Very good, sir; I shall have your coat ready in a sack when you come to dine," said the maître d', and turned to shoo his waiters back to their tasks as I staggered along toward the next car while I tugged on the white jacket.

I made my way through the second-class car without incident, for which I was grateful. My condition was frightful and I was limping heavily. Apparently no one noticed or was inclined to inquire as to the cause. As I entered the first-class car I nearly collided with Sir Cameron's valet, who was just emerging from the lav, a basin of water balanced between his hands. I swore, and he yelped, and we both stopped stock-still.

"Good God, sir," said the valet.

"Yes, very likely," I said, trying to make light of what I was by now fairly certain must be a horrific sight.

"Are you . . . all right?" He leaned against the wall to keep from spilling any of the water. "I would like to help, but Sir Cameron—" His shrug was an apology, and one I accepted readily.

"Of course." I moved enough to allow him to get past me, then followed him as far as compartment three, which I opened and slipped into with the relief of reaching a haven. I had a brief, wholly irrational urge to weep, but I set my teeth and began to undress, putting the white jacket where I could easily reach it when I left.

I was down to my singlet when there came a drubbing on the door, and I jumped at the sound. "Yes?"

"Guthrie!" Mycroft Holmes ordered sharply. "Let me in."

By the tone of his voice he would willingly have broken the door down, so I put my fresh shirt aside and went to obey.

He stood staring for perhaps five seconds before he came in and shut the door. His deep-set eyes were studious. "Dear me; Miss Gatspy was right," he said as he contemplated. "Not Whitfield, I should guess." He held my portfolio in his large, long hands, and his grip tightened on it as he surveyed the sum of my injuries—at least those he could see. "I heard you blundering along the hall and the slam of your door, but never supposed you had entered into a contest with a battering ram."

"A stone bridge," I told him. "The remains of the coat are in the dining car. I shall hand it to you when we go to dine." I removed my singlet, noting it too had been torn; there was some blood on it but not enough to make me worry. I took down my valise and pulled out clean clothes as I summed up what had happened to me since we left Leeds. Mycroft Holmes listened without interrupting until I fell silent.

"Have you any thought of who might have struck you?" He might have been asking about the latest successful novel or a musical revue.

"No. I wasn't expecting anything of the sort, not there next to the platform with constables about," I said, feeling sheepish. "That was a mistake, of course," I went on before he could point that out to me. "The most successful attacks are carried out when the attention is diverted or when confusion is high. I forgot that."

"Well, it is easily forgotten," said Mycroft Holmes, a frown creasing his long forehead. "I am puzzled that the baggage compartment door should be so tightly secured, however. The doors are most usually locked, of course, but from what you describe—I must surmise that you are correct—a chain was used on the inside. Because of picking up the mail and dropping it off, the baggage compartment door is on a single lock, not a double one, certainly not a chain." He turned away as I continued to dress and went on. "I do not like so much uncertainty. But if I speak up, I could bring our mission into more risk than it already has, which may prove intolerable."

"How do you mean?" I asked as I began to fasten my new shirt; my back was painful but not unendurable. My hip had begun to subside.

"It is as if we were being driven into the open. I cannot feel reassured in any way." He turned to study my face. "You are a rare sight, Guthrie. You must let me warn Herr Schere and Miss Gatspy before they see you, or their dismay could draw attention to your condition in a way you would not like."

"Part of being driven into the open?" I suggested as I fixed a fresh collar in place.

"Exactly." He watched me pull on the second coat I had brought on this journey. "Best take care of that one."

"If I ruin this one, I could ask Sir Cameron for the loan of one of his. It would fit well enough." I managed to smile at this absurd idea.

"Good lad. I knew from the first you had bottom. Miss Gatspy was right to be concerned when you did not report to relieve her guardian duties." He put my portfolio down and went back to the door. "Come along in a few minutes. We'll all be the better for our supper." With that he closed the door and a moment later I heard him knocking on the door of the next compartment where he was admitted promptly. I took that as my cue, picked up the white jacket and went along to the lav to wash up.

Inspecting my face in the mirror, I wondered if I ought to go into the dining car. I had a bruise forming over my left eye—the blue one— that was bigger than the palm of my hand and might excite no little interest from the other passengers. My lip was cut and swelling a bit as well, and my torn hands were puffy and discolored, although the scraps were superficial. I knew I would be stiff and sore tomorrow. But I was expected and my absence might be more conspicuous than my presence. And I was hungry, and in need of genial company, I realized. I neatened my face to the best of my limited ability, ran my pocket-comb through my hair, shrugged, and went off to the dining car, my portfolio in one hand, the white jacket in the other.

I gave the jacket to the maître d', who accepted my thanks with a hint of a smile, then led me to the table where Mycroft Holmes sat with Prince Oscar and Miss Gatspy. Mycroft Holmes was facing me, and the chair beside him was empty. I steadied myself to face the other two as I approached.

"There you are, Guthrie. Looking improved already," Holmes cried out. "Quite a tumble you took out there."

"Yes, it was. I was clumsy," I said as I sat down and met Miss Gatspy's cerulean gaze; her expression flickered but nothing more, so I knew Holmes had warned her about my appearance.

"Still, no real harm done, thank goodness." He laid his hand on my shoulder. "After such a journey as we have had, this is all of a piece."

"That it is," said Prince Oscar, appearing a bit subdued or perhaps bored. He looked directly at Mycroft Holmes. "Mister Holcomb, I am worried about our arrival in Scotland. We will be much later than we had anticipated, which must change our plans."

"Yes, I have been thinking about that, Herr Schere," Holmes replied, sounding so urbane that I almost laughed aloud. "I have a secondary arrangement we may use if it becomes necessary."

The waiter approached the table and asked which of the appetizers we wanted: Holmes ordered the broiled salmon, as did Prince Oscar; I ordered the paté, and Miss Gatspy asked for the deviled eggs. A dry French white was selected by Holmes to start, with a rich Bordeaux for later in the meal.

"I am glad to see you are not badly hurt," said Prince Oscar, his face somber but his eyes oddly wistful. "You had quite a run for it."

"That is certainly one way to look at it," I said, doing my best to seem unbowed by the events that had left me so cudgeled.

"What were you doing off the train?" asked Miss Gatspy, a sharp note in her question that warned me she would not accept a trivial answer.

"I thought I might help the police in their search," I said blandly, meeting her sharp look with a steady one.

"Your employer sent you to find something," she said with certainty, and added, for the benefit of anyone who might be listening, "How very like *Satchel's* to want every tidbit of information, favorable or not, about travel."

"Yes. Very like," said Holmes and prepared to taste the wine.

Our appetizers were replaced by soup—an oxtail in heavy broth or a creamed carrot soup in the Belgian style—and then a tureen of chicken in custard before our main courses. I found myself ravenous and queasy at once, inclined to eat and abstain in the same instant. Hunger won consistently, but I could sense that I would be wise not to indulge overmuch. By the time my entrée—a pork loin with turnips and mustard—was served I had slowed my consumption and was dawdling over the meal.

"Have a care, Guthrie," said Miss Gatspy. "After so much ill-usage, you may not want to indulge too much." She smiled, so I could not be sure whether she was genuinely concerned or joking.

"Possibly not," I conceded. "I appreciate your concern."

She chuckled. "Nothing of the sort, Guthrie," she said, mischief brimming in her eyes. "You think I should mind my own business, and you would be very much more comfortable if I would tell you precisely what that business is."

I had been cutting a bit of turnip, but her acute remark so caught my attention that I arrested myself. "Are you willing to tell us what—"

"I have already said what my intentions are, and you prefer to disbelieve me. Well, if that is your desire, so be it. I will do my best to attend to . . . Herr Schere. I trust you will do nothing to impede my efforts." She had ordered the sole, and she stopped talking to try the fish with her fork.

"So long as that is truly your intention, there is no reason for us to be at odds," I said, strangely relieved that I had put my portfolio between my back and the back of my chair. Not that there was anything in it at present more strategic than Sutton's sketches, I reminded myself, feeling a bit discomfited that I should be so suspicious of Penelope Gatspy.

"You would have a better use of your time if you would try to find the assassin—" she began only to have Mycroft Holmes interrupt her.

"Yes, and it is something that merits more study, but not, perhaps, here?" He poured a bit of the Bordeaux into her glass, saying, "It is not proper with fish, but unless I order a white for you—"

"My dear sir," said Miss Gatspy archly, "if an inappropriate wine is the worst I have out of this journey, I will think myself very well satisfied."

"Very good," Mycroft Holmes approved, as he poured the Bordeaux into her glass. "Never let it be known that I did this."

"Certainly not," she said, and returned her attention to me. "And you, Guthrie. Does Holcomb's lapse trouble you? You must work with him." She lifted her glass in an ironic toast.

I felt an unreasonable inclination to shake her. This was no game we were engaged in—the danger we faced was real. At the same time I admired her courage, knowing she was a woman in a thousand, a recognition that made me more conscious than ever of our mission. I seconded her toast, unable to think of anything else to do. "He is never dull, I will say."

Mycroft Holmes laughed aloud. I found myself thinking how much he shared Sutton's talent, performing with all the verve of those who trod the boards. "Guthrie, I am deeply complimented that you should say such a thing of me." He sipped his wine.

"Well, why should I not?" I asked, feeling caught in a contest I did not entirely understand.

I had no answer from Holmes or Miss Gatspy; my employer glanced around, saying, "At least Arthur Burley has left the train. That is one thing we can take comfort in knowing." His visage was ironic and his smile was a bit sour, but he toasted the journalist. "Good luck to him."

We all echoed this sentiment and went on with our supper.

I ate only half of my entrée and I refused the sweet at the end of the meal, for I realized it would not sit well with me. The most immediate pain had passed, a dull, relentless ache taking its place. The conversation of the others remained innocuous, and ordinarily I would have done my part, but this time I could not summon up the banter that was called for. I told myself the strain of the journey was telling on me, but I knew it was more complicated than that. We had so much at risk, and if we failed to protect Prince Oscar, our failure would be exposed for all the world to see. As I drank my tea, I noticed the train was slowing down. "Good Lord, what now?"

"Something of importance," Prince Oscar suggested as the buzz of conversation among the other diners increased.

"Haven't our travels been eventful enough?" I asked, making no excuse for my petulance.

"It's Skipton just ahead," said Holmes. "There may be a train waiting for water, as we shall be, for there is a junction at Skipton as well as the water and we are very late coming through." He looked out the window, seeing only the darkness of the spring night with occasional points of light showing the outlying houses of the town.

"We are nearing the long, empty stretch to Carlisle," and Miss

Gatspy. "It is a part of the country that many admire." She finished her sweet and smiled at me. "Do you admire this wild part of England? Before you answer, remember that my own family came from the North."

"I recall," I said, somewhat testily, for I had not yet determined which of the things she had told me were truth and which were mendacities. "And as a Scot, I am drawn to the rugged crags and empty moors."

"How very unexpected," she said, amused by my confusion. "Perhaps we should return to our compartments so we may make whatever plans we might need?"

Mycroft Holmes took her suggestion with alacrity, rising and summoning the waiter. "Give me the bill, if you would."

The waiter hastened to comply, and I levered myself to my feet and turned to take my portfolio as the train stopped.

"There's a freight ahead on the tracks," the waiter explained. "We will be moving up shortly. It's the last water for a while." He waited while Mycroft Holmes paid him and added a tip for service, then bowed and went away.

We were almost to the first car when the train lurched and we staggered as the train inched forward.

"That will be the freight leaving," said Holmes. "We're pulling onto the siding where it was." The car swung as the train turned. "There. You see?" He continued on his way, making sure his hands were ready to brace himself if we should be flung about again.

"When do you think we will arrive in Edinburgh?" Prince Oscar asked as we crossed the platform to the first car. "This will make us more late, will it not?"

"No matter what schedule the train keeps, it must stop here for water," said Mycroft Holmes. "Do not fret about this. If we reach Carlisle in two and a half hours, we should be in Edinburgh by one in the morning, assuming we have no other delays but those necessary ones of switching in Carlisle."

"Ah yes, the two rear cars going to Glasgow," said Prince Oscar.

"There will be baggage to transfer," I reminded them. "That may not go as quickly as we would like." I recalled the resistance of the baggage compartment door and my impression of an interior chain.

"What is it, Guthrie?" Holmes asked, apparently discerning something of my concern from my countenance. We had reached compartment five and Miss Gatspy had just excused herself for a moment.

I reiterated my impression of the chain, and added, "I cannot be sure, but if there is an interior chain, I am baffled as to why they might need one."

"There are any number of reasons, all of them rational," said Holmes, as he indicated the door to my compartment—it being the most central to the car, we had determined we would talk there, for if the train were being watched, we would have to suppose that the watcher had determined that compartment four was Herr Schere's. "It may be that the ordinary lock is in poor repair and therefore something more secure is wanted. It is possible that some of the baggage cannot be fully contained, and therefore the door requires a chain. Or the police may have ordered it when we reached Sheffield." He pulled out the small side stool and sat down, looking like an eagle attempting to perch on a wren's nest; he indicated the Prince should occupy the day-bed. "Lower the shade, if you would, dear boy," he said to me. I complied at once, and then took up my place near the door, my shoulders braced in the angle of the compartment. I was resigned to standing.

Prince Oscar sat down carefully. "Now what was that about two assassins?" he asked, without any preamble whatsoever.

"Yes. Well, that is the current assumption we must deal with," said Holmes, with as little preparation as the Prince had shown. "Our information confirms we are dealing with a brace of them."

A knock at the door announced the return of Miss Gatspy. I hastened to admit her and was mildly annoyed to see her take her place next to Prince Oscar, for I thought it would be more suitable for her to stand.

Just as Holmes began to speak, a rush and a penetrating whistle alerted us that a train was coming through on the main track, bound to the south. We could not see it with the shades lowered, but the clatter of its passing silenced us until it was gone.

FROM THE PERSONAL JOURNAL OF PHILIP TYERS

Yvgeny Tschersky has come to the flat bringing a file filled with reports—most of them in Russian—about a pair of assassins. It is most unusual for him to visit in this manner, so I must suppose he perceives a danger or an urgency in his reports that requires his most circumspect attention. He told me MH would want to see this and that he should arrange to return it clandestinely, since it was not supposed to leave the Russian Embassy. Tschersky tells me that these assassins have eluded police and other pursuers for more than four years that he knows of, though he suspects they have been working far longer than that. I have placed the file in MH's study for his perusal on his return.

Sutton has not yet returned, but I am not yet concerned. No doubt he will be back in time to send his report with my own to MH. I have my telegrams to prepare to be sent to Carlisle, and then it is only a question to hear from Edinburgh that they have arrived safely and the Prince is unharmed. The Norwegian yacht Morning Star *will escort HMS* Imperative *bearing HHPO home, and our part will have concluded successfully.*

I have also received a missive from Commander Winslowe, who it seems is most displeased with MH's conduct in this whole affair. He claims he is going to make a formal complaint, but that's as may be. Whatever has him so upset now might well seem less important once the mission is complete.

Superintendent Spencer has sent no reply to the messages I have had carried to him. I will have to inform MH of this. This may account for my inability to make contact with CI Somerford, who has either removed himself from the mission, or who has chosen to conduct his investigation in as much secrecy as he can secure. With Superintendent Spencer so adamant about protecting the good name of the police, he could have decided that to accomplish anything he will have to act in a covert manner and not with the full scrutiny of Scotland Yard upon him.

Chapter Twenty-one

"AN ASSASSIN, OR rather, two assassins working in concert," said Mycroft Holmes. "According to the information provided by . . . a most knowledgeable source, we must consider that the attempts on Herr Schere's life were made by this infernal team."

"Loki," added Miss Gatspy with such confidence that the three of us stared at her. "Well," she said, "that is the code name they use. We first encountered it some years ago and nothing has happened to change it."

"Yes," Holmes confirmed, as I stared at her in astonishment: how could she have kept this crucial information from us? "Loki is the name." He studied her face. "I assume you in the Golden Lodge have some information on this . . . these men?"

"Yes. We keep records on many of the assassins working in the world, and when we can we arrange for them to be discovered and detained. We have not had such an opportunity where Loki is concerned, for when one is in danger the other becomes his protector in the most vengeful sense. There was an occasion, about eight years ago, when one had been held for questioning, that the other murdered nineteen people to force a release of his partner. The government in Montreal was able to silence most of the reports on the incident, but the Golden Lodge has friends in Canada, just as the Brotherhood does." She did not smile but her pride in this was apparent in every aspect of her demeanor.

Prince Oscar nodded his approval. "I should like to know more of what your organization has found out."

"It is not for me to tell you more than what you must know to protect yourself, Your Highness," she said. "As much as I may tell you, I will."

"And what does this admirable record tell you of Loki?" Mycroft Holmes asked with utmost civility. "Who are they?"

"Two men, medium height, medium build," she said. "They have assassinations to their credit in the United States and South America as well as in Canada and Europe. There are two deaths we have attributed to them—one in Saint Petersburg, one in Bombay—but as yet have no confirmation to number them among their certain acts. From what we have learned, they are accomplished actors, very convincing in the identities they assume for their tasks, with well-rehearsed stories of youth and families to bolster their credibility and plausible enough to move virtually unnoticed through the world. They have managed to be invisible because there is nothing remarkable about them," she went on.

"You could say that of one man in five, I suspect," I interjected. "Any man of moderate height and build is less likely to be clearly recalled than anyone more distinctive."

Holmes looked at me. "Such as having a green right eye and a blue left one?" he suggested gently.

"I am also slightly above average height," I said.

"That is one of the many reasons they can succeed," Miss Gatspy said, for once not inclined to argue with me and to keep our discussion to the purpose. "They may be anything from twenty-five to forty, although we believe that—"

" 'We' being the Golden Lodge," said Mycroft Holmes, his face set.

"Of course," she told him. "We believe that one is at least five years older than the other, and a few in the Golden Lodge are convinced the two men are related—brothers, uncle and nephew, cousins, something of the sort." She glanced at Holmes. "Does your source agree?"

"I wouldn't be surprised," he said drily.

The *Flying Scotsman* began to move once more, the engine sending white billows out into the night as it began to draw onto the main track.

"We know they have spent time in America, not only for the purpose of assassination, but we do not think they are Americans," she said firmly. "We are of the opinion that one of them may have been raised there, but that is far from certain. Our records indicate that one of them was wounded four years ago, and some of our officers think a different man replaced one of the two men afterwards, but that is by no means certain." She looked in my direction. "You have seen how coolly they work."

"I would agree, but for the spent shells," I said, determined not to be too much taken with her description.

She laughed. "Good God, you don't mean that you actually thought—Don't you know that the shells were left to confuse you? Surely you do not think the weapon they use really is a German hunting rifle, possibly one from Mauser, do you? The shells are left to create an incorrect impression, to make investigators wear themselves out searching for a rare weapon when the one in question is not uncommon, but not quite ordinary either. Our authorities say that the weapon they use is an American Sharps rifle. I suspect they are basing this more on familiarity than fact. The Sharps is certainly capable of being the weapon, but is too bulky to conceal and we've had not a single sighting of a man with a rifle anywhere near any of the shooting scenes."

I sat listening in an emotion that was very nearly dismay, for I could not summon up any argument to offer in the face of such persuasion. I was aware that Mycroft Holmes was as convinced as I. "What makes your . . . superiors in the Golden Lodge so sure of these things?"

"I've told you we have records. We have a most interesting file on Loki. When the attempt was made at Saint Paul's and the empty shells were found, the Golden Lodge took up the search for Loki at once. Our files are extensive, Mister Holmes—comb. They are gathered from every place in the world where the Brotherhood has a foothold, and they are reviewed and compared twice each year. I believe we may have the most complete compilation of assassins to be found anywhere in the world." She was not exactly boasting, but she was not showing excessive humility, either.

"A very useful register," said Mycroft Holmes. "And if it is as exhaustive as you claim, I would very much want to see it if such could be arranged." He did not dwell on this unlikely possibility, but went on, "When you came aboard this train, did you suppose the assassin we were dealing with was this Loki?"

"As I have said already, since the attempt in front of Saint Paul's," she said. "It is precisely what Loki did in the Argentine, only there the second assassin was able to strike that evening while the police pursued the first of the pair through the streets of Buenos Aires. The man was the Finance Minister, and his death threw certain crucial mining negotiations into confusion."

"I recall the event," said Mycroft Holmes emphatically. "But as I recollect, a man was executed for the crime."

"Yes, because someone had to have the blame, and both Lokis were gone from the country, well beyond the reach of the Argentines. Not that they bothered to look once they found a man who owned a printing press and a Mauser .30-caliber hunting rifle." She smiled without humor or mirth. "Your use of this train was a masterful stroke, sir," she continued, her whole attention on Holmes so utterly that I might have found it in my heart to be jealous, were I inclined to such an emotion where Miss Gatspy was concerned.

"It would have been if we had kept to schedule. But, as you see, we have been thrown into disorder." He did his best to look unconcerned about this, but I could see how very dismayed he was beneath his sang-froid.

Prince Oscar studied the shaded window. "Do you think I have anything to fear?"

"Probably not, had all gone according to plan," said Miss Gatspy, "but there have been too many delays and misadventures to—"

Mycroft Holmes thumped his fist onto his knee. "This is a most damnable coil. I do not apologize for my intemperate language, Miss Gatspy, for the situation would be made trivial by less forceful words."

"The train has been slowed by more than half its usual speed, and that, in turn, increases the risk of exposure to . . . Herr Schere." She favored me with a look I did not know how to read. "I believe that Loki might have been puzzled or thrown off the scent at the first, but once we were delayed in Bedford and Sheffield, I worried that Loki would know to come after us."

"Do you say that there are spies on this train?" I demanded, feeling foolish, for I knew of two already; yet I would not betray my knowledge to her without learning more.

"No doubt. But I doubt that they suspected your ploy until after the Jardine murder," said Miss Gatspy. "That was a lucky mischance for Loki and their agents."

"Then you think they have pursued us?" Prince Oscar's visage was somber, which was hardly amazing given the circumstances.

"I presume one followed the navy's double," Holmes interjected. "But your point is well-taken; the other may be aboard."

"And may have been from the first," said Miss Gatspy. "You are not the only one to see the advantages of Scotland. If Loki wished to reduce the risk of both being captured, one might well go north while the other went toward the Channel."

"I wish this did not make so much sense," said Holmes. "Since I have read the report from my source, I have wondered if we might have inadvertently put ourselves in harm's way, and given the assassin a new opportunity." He lowered his head, pondering. "Or, more sinister still, if the assassin were informed he would have an opportunity to finish his work on this journey. If the police have been compromised, might not the corrupted officer or officers inform the assassin of Herr Schere's whereabouts? If that is the case, the assassin might have been able to monitor the progress of the damned journey and come aboard to finish his task. Given the delays we have encountered, the man could well catch this train if he departed from London an hour or so after we did." He turned his somber gaze on Prince Oscar. "I must apologize for putting you so much at risk."

"Tut," said the Prince with a jauntiness that startled me. "You had no reason to think you were doing that—in fact, your intentions were quite the opposite—when you arranged this departure and our little deception. A man in my position must understand the game that is played for high stakes." He nodded in my direction. "So far, it appears Guthrie has taken the brunt of our hazards, and for that I am extremely grateful."

We were finally traveling at speed once again, the train swaying in regular rhythm with the click of the wheels.

I felt color mount in my bruised face. "You're most gracious. I am only doing my work."

"Oh, very good, Guthrie," Miss Gatspy approved, her wicked praise ringing sarcastically in my ears.

"And you have allowed Miss Gatspy the time to instruct me in all the nefarious acts of the Brotherhood. If half of what she says is true, my brother has fallen in with villains indeed." The Prince paused. "Do you think Karl Gustav would agree with you regarding his associates in the Brotherhood? Might he not see them in much the same light as you represent the Golden Lodge? Not that I accuse you of deception, Miss Gatspy—that is not the case at all—but you are not a disinterested party, and you have good reason to persuade me to view your work in a favorable light and the efforts of the Brotherhood in a negative one."

"No one is truly disinterested," I said before anyone else could speak. "If they claim to be, they are the most subtle of all, and you would do well to be wary of them. Those who have reason to know these things cannot understand what the issues are and remain disinterested unless they are also wholly removed from the world."

"Very good, Guthrie," said Mycroft Holmes, echoing Miss Gatspy's praise with none of her sarcasm. "I must concur. And so will you, Mein Herr, if you will but think about the stakes for which we are competing." He gestured. "I think it would be best if you and Guthrie changed compartments. You need not move your luggage, but if you will stay here in compartment three, Guthrie will occupy compartment four, ready to deal with any incursions that may arise."

I had expected something of the sort and so I showed no surprise at this recommendation. "That is satisfactory to me, sir," I said.

Prince Oscar shook his head. "You have taken more than your share of risks, Guthrie. It is time I—"

Mycroft Holmes made bold to interrupt. "You will have to face your brother once you arrive home, and all his support within your court and government. Here we are in a position to guard you, and it is appropriate for us to do so. This is a minor thing, and furthermore, it is part of Guthrie's duties to provide this protection. I ask you to reconsider; if you move to this compartment, you will have a degree of protection that we could not otherwise offer you."

I decided to add my observations. "If you think that bruises are enough to make me useless, you do not know what a mentor like my employer can teach. Once we arrive in Scotland, I will have ample opportunity to rest, while you will be entering a more demanding phase of your task as a leader. My bruises will heal. You will need all your steadfastness for many months to come. I am pleased to be able to secure a short respite for you, if you will but allow it."

"By all means," Miss Gatspy put in. "I have seen Guthrie in action before, and I can assure you he has endured worse than this for far less obvious benefits." Her smile in my direction made me bristle with indignation.

The Prince coughed delicately. "Perhaps it would be best," he said, adding as an explanation. "I do want to do my part."

"As well you should," Holmes approved. "In this case your part is to make yourself as hard-to-strike a target as possible. When you reach Sweden, you may throw caution to the winds—although I hope you will not—and take whatever chances you deem necessary in the face of an implacable enemy; but while you are a guest of England and Scotland, let us do our utmost to show you our high regard for you."

"And our treaty," added Prince Oscar, continuing on before Mycroft Holmes could protest. "Oh, do not worry. I support this treaty as much as you do, and I am not reckless by nature, but that does not keep me from chafing."

"Very understandable," said Holmes. "In your situation, I would certainly feel the same." He smiled. "So, Guthrie, bring your portfolio and come along to compartment four. You may leave this compartment for Herr Schere. Miss Gatspy, you will want to occupy your own compartment once we leave Carlisle, or there will be wagging tongues which you would not like and which would bring attention to your being here—"

"Yes, I know," she said quietly. "And you are right. I am in an excellent position to be your sentinel without putting the assassin on alert, if he has managed to board the train. I have my pistol with me, do not fear. I will keep watch from my compartment in case anyone should enter the car from the rest of the train."

"Which, after Carlisle, will move more quickly, having fewer cars to pull," I reminded them all. "The Glasgow leg will be shifted to another engine at Carlisle."

"Damned annoying," said Holmes. "We will have to watch that change as carefully as we can. They will off-load all the baggage going to Glasgow before we resume our journey, and that will put us at risk while the confusion is greatest. Take care not to draw attention to our intention, if that is possible, for that could expose us to far greater dangers than any we may seek to alleviate. We must all remain alert."

"It's a shame," said Miss Gatspy, "that Sir Cameron did not elect to return home through Glasgow."

"Yes, it is," said Holmes, and sighed once. "Why he should be aboard is more than I want to think about. But we cannot forget him, much as we may want to." He put his big hands on his knees. "What can we do to ensure he does not become embroiled in our—"

Miss Gatspy laughed, sarcasm robbing her tone of any lilt. "You cannot anticipate what Sir Cameron might do. He is cumbersome and unpredictable, but do not assume that we are wholly at the mercy of his caprice. He has enough alcohol in him to render him incapable of much action, as his valet must tell you."

At the mention of the valet, I frowned. "Fellow told me he has not been long in Sir Cameron's employ," I began.

"I should think that is the usual situation with Sir Cameron's valets," said Prince Oscar. "A man of his nature does not usually command the loyalty of servants. When I had one evening in his company, I knew he had no respect for others. It was amusing for a short time, and annoying after that, especially since he supposed he would make a favorable impression on me through such methods."

The sound of a crossing bell caught our attention, and I wondered briefly which road we had just passed.

"True," said Holmes. "But I doubt that is the reason for Guthrie's observation." He smiled faintly. "What is it that bothers you?"

"Well," I said carefully, "I am curious about anyone connected with this mission who is a stranger to our fellow-passengers, particularly one situated so near to Herr Schere. Sir Cameron's valet still concerns me. What would Loki—either one of them—make of an opportunity like this?"

"It isn't Loki," said Miss Gatspy, "though the point is well-taken."

"How do you know it isn't Loki?" I challenged her, an irrational spurt of anger making me sharp with her.

"Because he is the wrong build. The man might change his hair or his face—you know an actor so you know how that is done—but he cannot change his skeleton." Miss Gatspy made her pronouncement. "He is too thin and his height is wrong."

"Are you certain of that?" Holmes asked. "You have admitted the two men are resourceful and—"

"If they have discovered a way to change their frames, more than the Golden Lodge will want to know of it," said Miss Gatspy testily.

"Whatever else that valet might be, he is not Loki." She made a quick gesture. "For the security of this car, we must concern ourselves with passengers from the other cars."

"Or the staff," I put in. "The maître d' used to work aboard ship or I know nothing of the sailors' walk. If he brought food or drink to Sir Cameron we could not properly detain him."

"That may or may not be significant," said Mycroft Holmes. "If my brother were with us, he might make something of it, but I would need more than a walk, for it is possible he served on liners as well as in the navy, in which case his earlier employment has no bearing on us."

"Unless his experience as a merchant seaman brought him into the arena of the Brotherhood," I persisted, loathe to give up my second candidate. "In which case he becomes doubly suspect."

"Very true," said Miss Gatspy. "But I will be in a position to watch him, and with Guthrie in compartment four instead of Herr Schere, we may keep our charge as protected as anyone aboard."

"True enough," Mycroft Holmes allowed. "And I must tell you that I am inclined to think the maître d' has held his position for long enough that he ought not to be our first suspect. There could be others—waiters, for instance—who have worked for the railroad only a short while, and who might be considered more suspicious." He rose. "Come, Guthrie. It is time we put ourselves into position."

Miss Gatspy, too, prepared to leave. "If I notice anything that alarms me, I will tap on the wall between compartment four and five to alert you," she said to me. "If I have to leave my compartment for any reason, I will scratch on your door."

"Very good," Holmes approved.

I gathered up my portfolio. "Will you need me to send and receive telegrams at Carlisle?"

"Yes, of course I will. In fact, I am depending upon you to look over the shifting of baggage and the separation of the rear cars. If you time your movements, you should be able to make your observations with a modicum of difficulty." Holmes actually held the door for me. "Be about it, dear boy."

Taking care to keep my face away from the outer window, I slipped into compartment four, glad now that the shades were down. The lamps were low, and I turned them up so that I could have sufficient light to make my notes regarding my climb over the train, which Mycroft Holmes would expect to have in his hands by the time we reached

Edinburgh. I found, as I did my best to be comfortable on the day-bed, that my shoulders were stiff, making my handwriting crabbed. I kept at it, as much to keep from fretting as to finish the report. Sitting was not as easy as I had expected, for some of the soreness in my hip made the constant rocking of the car a trial. I did my best to complete my work in good time.

I was vaguely aware when we passed Hawes Junction, indicating we had less than ten miles to Kirkby Stephen, where we would have a brief halt, but not one long enough to send telegrams. Satisfied that my report touched on all the significant points of the evening, I slipped the pages into my portfolio before I set up the day-bed for resting, telling myself I might have a short nap between Kirkby Stephen and Carlisle, where I would need to be active once again. As I removed my boots, I decided against taking a composer, for that might make me groggy when I would need most to be alert. But that would also mean dealing with aching shoulders and hip, an unpleasant but necessary bargain, or so I convinced myself as I turned down the lamps and lay back on the day-bed.

Tired as I was, I could not quiet my mind, which all but sang with commotion, as if it were a busy train station and all my thoughts were locomotives coming and going in furious enterprise. I chuckled a little at my conceit, which I thought showed a certain aptness to the moment, but I could not will my muscles to relax, for when I tried, I began to fret, thinking I would drift to sleep and be unavailable in an imminent-but-undefined emergency. After a while, I stopped forcing myself to release tension and began to consider the various passengers I had encountered, attempting to discern any resemblance to the assassins who might well be on board. For once I was sorry I had not bothered to look closely at the two rear cars, for now it struck me that they might well provide an excellent place for Loki to hide, where our attention would not be turned while we relied upon the dining car and the lounge to separate us from Glasgow-bound villains. Not that I supposed the assassin would have been obliging enough to put himself on the Glasgow cars, for from what we had been told to that moment, we had no reason to think the man—whichever one it was—was stupid. I kept stopping at the various waiters and other staff of the train, thinking that anyone new among their numbers must stand out to the rest of the staff if not to those of us who were traveling. I did not like to dwell on the possibility that something had become of Whitfield, for it not only cast question on his replacement, but not knowing Whitfield's fate left me prey to many speculations, none of which served to lull me into repose. Wrestling with phantoms of my own invention, I waited for the first signs that we were nearing Carlisle.

FROM THE PERSONAL JOURNAL OF PHILIP TYERS

Not ten minutes ago Sutton returned with some information that, if true, causes me the gravest apprehension. What he has imparted is so weighty a matter that I dare not set the particulars down here for fear such a record would compromise good men if they are shown to be free of any taint of wrong-doing. The name is not so common that it can be dismissed as without meaning, but it is not so rare that it can be pointed to as absolute proof of so unthinkable a connection. I will have to prepare a second telegram for MH and then send Hastings to the station to wire it forthwith. I must hope that it will reach MH at Carlisle; in case it does not, I will send a duplicate of the message to Edinburgh, although I fear if MH does not learn of it presently, he may well be in grave danger. If I had time I would try to include supporting information, but as I haven't received the same, I must act with what I have to hand. Then I shall set Hastings to watching for any activity that will confirm or negate the deduction Sutton has offered to account for what he has stumbled upon, which I have asked him to describe in detail. That must be telegraphed to Edinburgh. MH may dismiss the whole as conjecture or he may have some other means to account for what appears to be most reprehensible in the current light I must shed on the report presented to me. I hesitate only because I fear to blacken a name through a simple error. Honorable and trustworthy as I know Sutton to be, for all he is an actor, I will require closer scrutiny than he has been able to provide; if he is correct, he will be in danger until the guilty party is taken into custody. I should also send word to Scotland Yard as soon as I can determine to whom I may safely present such observances. The scandal this revelation—if revelation it is—could bring is painful to contemplate.

In regard to these matters, I have had word from Commander Winslowe once again, who is standing staunch in his championing the police. Should Sutton's information prove accurate, Commander Winslowe may find he has followed the wrong banner. He demands a report from me regarding the progress of the train and the safety of HHPO, along with full reports of all incidents that might have some direct implication for the police. I have nothing to tell him that he would find acceptable, so I must take it upon myself to postpone his outcry at least until morning. Given the hour, that should not be as difficult as it would have been had the Scotsman run on time. Never did I think I should be grateful for tardiness, but so I am. . . .

I have sent a note around to CI Somerford but have not yet received a reply. Ordinarily this would not cause me apprehension, but after what Sutton has told me, I cannot remain sanguine where any policeman of rank is concerned. There could be serious consequences for MH and his companions if the police are truly as compromised as it now appears they are. . . .

A courier from the Admiralty has provided revised times of arrival for the Flying Scotsman, *as given to them by the North Eastern line. According to their estimates, the* Flying Scotsman *should arrive in Edinburgh at 12:48* A.M., *which may well be its slowest time on record. What matters most now is its arrival, not the time. I trust word will be sent as soon as MH and G are safely at the club and HHPO is sleeping under naval guard.*

No more time. Must get this to King's Cross at once.

Chapter Twenty-two

THE SWITCHING YARDS at Carlisle were a maze worthy of Hampton Court. There was a switch every fifty or so paces. These allowed the cars to be moved between trains most effectively, but meant that there were no through or main tracks, but rather a jumble of possible routes. The whole was choreographed by flags, telegraph, and whistles from a tower in the center, though it seems likely the most they could accomplish in their efforts was the prevention of the worst disasters. Since colored lights over some of the tracks gave an indication of when it was safe to proceed, I gave them my attention as we began our progress through the confusion. As I watched, a small engine belching gray smoke rushed past on an adjoining track that lay only a few feet from ours, shuttling a closed box-car from one train to another. Even now, well into the night, the yard was active, with freights from Newcastle vying with an excursion train from Dumfries for the track to the south, while we were shunted along toward the main station to allow the Carlisle passengers to depart. We were traveling very slowly—I could have walked as fast without undue effort—tracing our way among the rails as we made our way to our destination.

We stopped opposite a newly painted sign: the city's name in blocked black letters over white that hung off the wooden shelter that afforded protection from the rain to those waiting closest to the station's main building. This was a brick-and-wood structure bordered along its impressive length by a long wooden platform. The brick of the station itself had been recently scrubbed and the window frames painted a bright white. Small knots of porters and passengers waited where the cars for their class of service were disgorging passengers. The steam brakes in the locomotive engine spurted loudly, causing a horse harnessed to a carriage nearby to rear and whinny in protest.

I waited, ready to sprint to the telegraph office. My portfolio was under my arm, the texts of the various messages I was to send newly deposited within it. I was still somewhat stiff from my earlier experiences, but not as impaired as I feared I might be. I saw the office I sought at the far end of a number of platforms, and I knew I would have to be quick about my work if I were to do all that I needed to in the time allowed me.

There were men waiting to unload the Glasgow baggage standing next to those clearly waiting for Carlisle arrivals; they did not mill so much as simmer in anticipation, and I was reminded of the quays in Constantinople for the state of readiness I saw. The train signaled its stopping with an elaborate display of steam released into the night, and the whole stopped with a solid jerk that left me glad I had taken hold of the railing.

At once the station was alive with activity as the men waiting to off-load baggage came forward and the process of separating the Glasgow portion of the train from the Edinburgh began in earnest.

I did not linger to watch the process; I headed at a fast walk toward the telegraph office, my senses telling me my telegram texts were vital. Had I a more imaginative bent of mind I might have supposed they were about to burst into flame; as it was, the urgency of my mission kept me moving. At least, I thought as I dodged a handcart laden with trunks and cases, this was not the busiest time of the day, for that would have made my task more difficult. I kept moving, and when I reached the telegraph office, I hurriedly went inside and asked for the telegrams that had been sent to me as I handed over the new ones and a L5 note to expedite the sending.

The telegraph operator, a keen-faced man of fifty or so, handed five telegrams to me without comment beyond, "One came in two minutes since," and began the first of the messages Mycroft Holmes had prepared. He tapped out the letters with the efficiency of long experience, no sign of expression in his eyes in regard to the nature of the message he was transmitting. He finished the first as I put the ones I had received into my portfolio. He began the second with the same expressionless demeanor, glancing at the page from time to time as he continued to communicate the text.

"Any difficulties?" I asked, wondering if I should leave before I saw the whole of them dispatched.

"No. Very clear it is," he answered, a soft Scottish burr in his voice that set me into a nostalgic mood for several heartbeats. "It will be in London shortly."

"Thank you," I said, and prepared to leave.

"You're going in late, aren't you?" he asked, as I reached the door. His question startled me. "How do you mean?"

"Oh, only that the *Flying Scotsman* has never had so slow a run. You're making something of a record tonight." He winked and his face became almost elfin. "I have half a bob on your not making it to Edinburgh before one in the morning." He continued to tap out letters as I stared at him.

"You bet on such things?" I knew I should not be surprised, but I was unable to contain my astonishment.

"Why not? The *Scotsman*'s always good for a bet, but usually not for being slow." He motioned me to go away, and I did, my thoughts in consternation as I went out into the confusion of the station.

The unloading of the *Flying Scotsman*'s baggage compartment was coming along quite well, for the Glasgow-bound baggage had been stored in the same area of the compartment. Those leaving the train had a slightly more complicated situation to deal with, but nothing so involved that it could not be readily handled. I was about to climb back aboard the first car when curiosity got the better of me. I determined to find out why the baggage-compartment door had been secured by a chain when I had attempted to get into the compartment earlier.

A porter was just leaving the compartment with a handcart half-laden with leather-strapped cases. He barely looked at me as I went past him into the compartment, muttering something about a forgotten train-case. The porter tipped his cap and kept on going as I looked about in the darkness to assess the condition of the place.

The supplies for the bar were nearest the narrow door leading to it, kept in place by wide canvas belts that held the cartons and bottles without danger of breakage. I noticed that one of the barman's aprons was draped over the back of this stack, which suggested to me that Quest was not on duty in the lounge. Next to this there was the stowed baggage for the front two cars of the train, stacked neatly and held by rope nets that prevented shifting during travel, a feature the fast trains took great pride in providing. For that reason alone I was somewhat surprised to see a small trunk canted at an angle at the back of the compartment; I assumed it had been knocked aside during the unloading of the Glasgow baggage.

I started toward the trunk with the intention of setting it to rights when I discovered a hand protruding from beneath it. Suddenly I was consumed with curiosity and dismay. Just as I moved closer, the baggage compartment door slammed closed and the first clanking of the un-coupling of the rear cars began with a groaning of metal as dismal as any reputed ghostly wail in Scotland. The darkness was not complete, for a low light burned near the door into the bar, but it provided only sufficient illumination to make it possible for the barkeep to find his bottles; the rest of the compartment was engulfed in gloom.

Holding onto the heavy netting on the Edinburgh baggage, I resolved to make my way to the angled trunk in order to investigate further. I had to feel my way once the shadow of the stacked baggage overwhelmed me. So it was that I realized that the arm belonged to a corpse, and the dead man had not been there long enough for the skin to be noticeably cool. I was torn between the wish to discover the man's identity and the knowledge that the scene should remain undisturbed for the police—for they would have to be summoned.

I could not see or reach the dead man's face, but I was very much afraid I had discovered the absent Whitfield. I stood very still, trying to decide what to do and knowing the authorities had to be notified. But that could mean another significant delay; and with Loki pursuing Prince Oscar—it was an assumption but one I felt it prudent to make—

such a delay could completely undermine the whole of our mission. I did not want to leave the body for the porters to find at Edinburgh, but I did not want to give Loki any more advantage than he already had. Reluctantly I decided to leave the body where it was so that we could continue on. I knew this decision would hang heavily on my conscience, but the death of Prince Oscar would be a far greater tragedy than the death of this poor man. The final clang of separation from the rear cars served as the passing bell for the dead man. I vowed I would return to see him accorded the respect he was owed, and I apologized for leaving him alone once more.

Duty made me rise and step into the bar. Hoping that I would not encounter Quest, I let myself out through the bar-hatch at the end of it, startling a square-faced man whom I vaguely recalled from the dining car; he was smoking a rum-soaked cigar and reading a Midlands paper.

"Have you seen the conductor?" I asked him, as if there was nothing remarkable in any of this.

"On the platform, helping the uncoupling," he replied, goggling. He continued to stare at the side of my face where bruises had formed. "We'll be pulling out shortly."

"And the barkeep?" I wanted to prepare myself for anything. If Quest were aiding Loki—or worse, if he were Loki, he was an ordinary-enough man—I would have to be ready to confront a vicious enemy.

The man shrugged. "After hours. He's probably asleep some-where."

I saw he was becoming curious and would commence asking me questions, which I needed to forestall. "Thank you," I said, and hastened toward the dining car, holding onto my portfolio as if it contained the revelations of all mysteries. I had to account for my decision when I handed the telegrams I carried to Mycroft Holmes, for he would need to be informed about the dead man. I attempted to console myself with the reflection that this timely warning would make up for the impulsiveness of my entering the baggage compartment.

The maître d' looked at me in some alarm as I came through the dining car; he muttered a few syllables of commiseration at the sight of my face but made no effort to detain me. The waiters were cleaning the tables and putting up the chairs for the night, and none of them paid any attention to me as I went on into the second-class car. Here I noticed many of the shades were down, and the compartments darkened, which made the hour seem later than it was; and for a brief moment, I yearned for sleep. Then I crossed the platform into the first-class car and felt the first surge and rattle that signaled our departure. The last leg of our journey was about to begin, a realization that elated and appalled me in the same breath.

Mycroft Holmes did not seem worried when I entered his compartment. "I was beginning to think you had become lost, dear boy," he said as if the possibility afforded him no other emotion than boredom. There was a moment of silence before he spoke again. "Lost in a memory, Guthrie. From a time I was here, not long ago." Despite the tension our dilemma must be causing he smiled wistfully. "At Portobello, that's as we enter Edinburgh, there is a quite significant *S* curve. It suffers, I'm afraid, from the rather insufficient elevation that troubles so many of our main lines here in Britain. Worse yet, this curve ends on a high bridge over a wide road. The event I have been recalling was the last of the great runs in the Race to the North. A chap named Rous-Marten was juggling four watches in order to accurately determine the train's speed. He announced it was eighty-two miles per hour a few miles before we entered the Portabello curve, which is usually taken at less than ten miles per hour. You may imagine the excitement. Everyone appreciated both the speed and his concern. We were all there by invitation, as select a group of rail aficionados as could be found in this island."

"I was returning from the Continent at that time, was I not?" I asked, wanting to fix the time in my thoughts.

"So you were," said Mycroft Holmes. "It was then, as we entered the curve, that Percy Caldecott announced that we had better all brace ourselves or we would be thrown right out of the windows. The two Worsdsells kept running full out and suddenly we were thrown about as if in a Rugby scrum. Most of us ended up on top of Rous-Marten who amazingly held onto all four watches and the left part of a seat. Without his warning I suspect we all might have been thrown through the glass and into the Duddington Road." He chuckled. "When we emerged from the curve we were on mile one, almost into Waverley Station, and after consulting his watches Rous-Marten announced we were still plummeting forward at the rate of sixty-four miles per hour. It was, Guthrie, a good thing that Waverley Station has a long run or we'd have ended that on the stair up to Princes Street." Emerging from his brief reverie, Mycroft Holmes returned abruptly to the very different peril we faced on these same tracks. "So, did you get the replies we desired?" he asked reaching out with an open hand, still smiling faintly.

I took the telegrams from my portfolio and handed them to him. "I came through the baggage compartment," I said as if this were the most usual course available to me.

"Did you? No doubt you will tell me why." He was opening the first of the envelopes but he paused to hear my answer.

"I wanted to see if the door was secured with a chain," I said, steadying myself as the train began to lumber out of the station.

"And is it?" he asked blandly.

"I am not certain. I was distracted by the body I found," I said, doing my best to match his tone.

My employer abandoned his air of unconcern. "Whose body?"

"I rather think it may be Whitfield's," I said apologetically. "I did not see his face, but so near the bar—and Whitfield missing . . ." I made a gesture of resignation.

"So they tell us," he said. "What did you see of him?"

"Not much." I had suddenly to swallow very hard.

"How did he die?" Holmes inquired, his telegram forgotten for the moment.

"I could not tell," I admitted as the train began to make its way out of the Carlisle yard, bound for the tracks leading north. "I saw only the hand protruding from beneath some baggage that appeared to have shifted."

"Then it might be an accident," said Holmes, doubt making this possibility unlikely.

"The man might be someone other than Whitfield," I added, believing it as much as Holmes believed the death was an accident. "It happened not very long ago—the hand was cooling but far from cold."

"Cooling," he said, musing. He went back to opening his telegram, which he read as his frown increased. "Dear me," he said as he folded the first telegram and opened the second. "How very aggravating," he said as he began reading the second; his expression darkened as he scrutinized the message. "The situation is more unsettled than I had hoped it would be. Without doubt I will owe Tyers an apology at the end of all this. He has had more to contend with than even I anticipated."

I could not resist the urge to ask what made him say so, but checked the impulse. "Is Tyers well?"

"Apparently, and Sutton, too. But it would appear these incidents around Prince Oscar have forced the hands of the men within the police who have allied themselves with the Brotherhood. I had thought that they would not act unless I forced them into the open, but they have decided to try to conceal themselves instead. If they assume that hiding makes them inconspicuous, they will learn otherwise before they are much older. I hope this second telegram has no more unwelcome news. How very imprudent of the police to make this an issue of support, as they have done." He looked at the third telegram, which I recognized as coming from the Admiralty. "More posturing," he said as he read it. "Like cocks on a dungheap. This smacks of Cecil, not Scotland Yard. What folly possessed Spencer to throw in his lot with Winslowe, each endorsing the other, and in the most political way. I wish they did not feel the need to—" He broke off. "I shall deal with that later, when our charge is safe."

"Speaking of Herr Schere, how is he?" I thought of him in the next compartment, with my valise stored above him. It struck me as a strange setting for a Scandinavian Prince. I supposed some of my amusement came as a response to the fatigue and cumulative abhorrence the journey had wrought in me. I managed to stop myself smiling, but it was an effort.

"He was embarked on a complicated game of patience when I last looked in on him, while you were fetching the telegrams. I must say that he has weathered this whole—ah, adventure—very well." Holmes was opening the fourth telegram as the train swung onto a connecting rail.

I grabbed the edge of the luggage rack to keep from losing my balance; the train was being shifted over another farther, and the lurch happened again. "Do you think Loki is aboard the train?" I had not wanted to put the question quite so blatantly, but it was out before I could find a less intrusive way to ask.

"I cannot afford to think otherwise," said Holmes remotely as he reviewed the second telegram from Tyers. "Nor can you. This assassin has shown himself—or themselves—to be clever and blood resourceful. If we are not very careful, he may well prevail." He shook his head, "Oh, dear. Well, let us hope that this is nothing more than an unfortunate coincidence," he muttered, then went on in an easier tone, "Loki may not be here, of course; but if we assume he is not, we will make the kind of mistakes that would leave Herr Schere exposed to the assassin's strike. I need not tell you how that would redound." He read the telegram again, taking the time to examine the phrases for the full depth of their meaning. "Somerford has still not been heard from. And the name is troubling. No wonder Tyers is alarmed." He refolded the telegram. "Who knows what the police may have learned from one another? At least Sir Cameron has been inactive. I do not envy his valet, and well you know the reason why."

"I would rather forget that episode in my working with you, sir," I said. "The Brotherhood *and* Sir Cameron provided a most. . . . edifying start to my employment with you. Baptism by ordeal, or so it seemed."

"Still rankles, does it?" He gave a quick, amused look in my direction. "Not that I blame you; it *was* trial by ordeal, I fear," Mycroft Holmes agreed. "Well, back to compartment four. I shall remain at my post here."

But I was not quite ready to be dismissed. "What of the body? Shouldn't we tell someone?"

Mycroft Holmes shook his head. "You are right, of course." He tapped his fingers on the telegrams. "I shall say I need something from my baggage at our next halt. That is Melrose, I believe. At that hour my request will not be remarkable and the staff should be willing to accommodate it." He fingered his watch-fob. "Tell me: if a porter enters the compartment to look at the Edinburgh baggage, is he likely to discover the body?"

"If he notices the over-set trunk, he will; otherwise, I think not. The compartment is quite dark and the body was intended to be hidden; I happened upon it by accident because of the trunk. That is how I came to notice the arm." I did not like the notion of leaving the dead man unattended for so long, so I said, "Shouldn't we do something sooner?"

"What could we do that would not make it plain that one of us had seen the body? Then we would have to explain our delay in reporting, which would complicate the delay we would surely have to contend with. You might have to remain for questioning, for, given the hour, the police are probably unprepared to conduct a formal inquiry so late at night. Not only would that deprive me of your excellent talents, it would throw our mission into the spotlight once again, which is something to be deplored, wouldn't you agree?" He saw me nod and understood my reluctance. "Guthrie, the man is dead. There is nothing more you can do for him, much as you would like to. If you want to help find justice for him, well and good, but understand that you are putting Herr Schere and all that his efforts entail at risk."

I sighed. "Yes, I know," I said. "You have not said anything I haven't thought of myself. But I do not like the necessity—"

"No, no more do I," said Mycroft Holmes. "Do not fret. The train is moving; and if the murderer is aboard, whether it is Loki or some other, the killer is trapped here as much as we are." He nodded to me. "I will let you know when I go to make my request." He held up the last telegram. "One to go. Let me tend to it and then I will deal with the dead man."

"Thank you," I said, gathered up my portfolio and left him in compartment two while I went along to number four. As I closed the door, I wondered if I ought to tap on the wall of compartment five, just to let Miss Gatspy know that I was on duty. Much as I wanted to reassure her, I hesitated, and finally sat on the daybed, my portfolio leaning against the wall. I did not know what more I should do, and so I once again did my best to nap, though I was fully aware that my attempts were futile. I could not allow myself to sleep, not until our journey was finished; and although fatigue weighed on me as heavily as chains, I did not mind them, for I knew my vigilance was required. Should any harm befall Prince Oscar, I would deserve the disgrace that would fall upon me. With this sobering reflection to engage my thoughts, it was hardly surprising that I could not drift off.

As we slowed for Melrose some while later, I heard Mycroft Holmes leave his compartment and go along the passage toward the second-class car, where I recalled a conductor was on duty. I wished I might hear how Holmes would persuade that worthy to venture into the baggage compartment for the purpose of retrieving a nonexistent bag. Knowing how capably he dealt with diplomats, I knew the conductor would be brought to compliance without too much effort. I did not hear him return nor see him pass this compartment, which I found a trifle odd, but not actually occasion for apprehension. I resolved to wait and watch what might transpire, for the body would likely cause more questions to be asked, if not tonight, then tomorrow. I did not look forward to another round of questions by the police which I supposed must follow once the body was found; nor did I think that those passengers who had been willing to provide information to Inspector Carew would be as cooperative now: One murder was exciting, but two became frightening. The only consolation I had was that there would be far fewer passengers to question, for this had clearly happened after Leeds; not only were there fewer passengers aboard, but many of them had not ventured to the lounge car.

Drawing to a stop at the nearly deserted platform at Melrose, which atypically was to the left of the train, not the right, there seemed to be nothing more sinister about the place than a country train station with·four yellow gas lamps burning in the misty night. I opened one of the corridor shades of my compartment enough to allow me to observe what transpired; I did not think I could be seen through two panes of glass—not with the brighter light being outside the car. I noticed two families alighting from the second-class car; sleeping children and drooping adults stopped to wait for their baggage to be brought to them by the single porter still working on the platform. A moment later the baggage compartment door was opened and the porter went inside.

After what seemed an hour or so, but had to have been less than five minutes, the porter emerged, exclaiming in the accents of Belfast that the police must be summoned and a doctor. I saw him cross himself; although I could not see clearly enough to be certain, I supposed he must be pale with shock. Consternation broke out among those few passengers on the platform; I watched, wishing I could hear what was being said. The porter hastened into the station, and shortly thereafter the night Stationmaster emerged, looking like an affronted turkey-cock. He came bustling up to the baggage compartment, a lantern in hand, only to emerge almost at once, deflated and dithering.

The Irish porter came aboard the train to find some help from among the staff; a waiter and a conductor answered the summons, stepping onto the platform with the air of men being led to execution. It took them a short while to ready themselves, during which time the passengers waiting to collect their belongings became restive, a development that finally spurred the porter to encourage the others to go with him. I noticed the passengers began to gather near the baggage compartment door, fascinated and repulsed by what they were watching.

In the midst of this anxious confusion, I saw Mycroft Holmes step onto the platform from what must have been the dining car. I was taken aback to think he would make himself so visible, and at such a time, but I had learned in the last nine years to trust him and all that he did. I saw him speak to the night Stationmaster and receive a kind of abstract nod from that gentleman.

The porter and waiter emerged from the baggage-compartment, supporting the still figure at whose side dangled a clearly broken, discolored arm. As they stepped into the light of the nearest gas lamp, I saw his face, and nearly gasped aloud—for the dead man was not Whitfield, but Quest.

FROM THE PERSONAL JOURNAL OF PHILIP TYERS

Word has come from King's Cross that the Flying Scotsman *has been delayed once again, this time in what was supposed to be a ten-minute halt at Melrose. The train is now scheduled to arrive in Edinburgh as late as two-thirty, making it the slowest run the train has had on the new route that was not brought about by damage to the tracks. The Directors will not be pleased, but the gratitude of the government, private though it may be, will offset the most stringent complaints, or so I suppose it must. I have asked Sid Hastings to remain at King's Cross until we have word from Edinburgh, which he has consented to do.*

Now that Sutton has returned to the flat following his surveillance of the persons implicated by name, he has decided to remain here tonight, waiting to hear that MH and G have arrived safely at Edinburgh, and that HHPO is no longer in immediate danger. I can only express my astonishment at Sutton's loyalty, for he has been as devoted to MH and his work as any man in the Admiralty—perhaps more so in that he is not looking to forward his diplomatic career.

CI Somerford has still not reported to his superiors, and little as any of them wish to suggest it, there is concern about his whereabouts. If Superintendent Spencer would be willing to answer a few questions, it might be a simple matter to set all this to rights, but he has refused to respond to any inquiries, and Commander Winslowe has taken to defending his decision. I am going to prepare a telegram to be sent to Edinburgh before one in the morning so that it will be in MH's hands when he arrives. If we act quickly, we may yet avert a great scandal. . . .

Chapter Twenty-three

I STARED AT the body on the platform, trying to come to terms with what I saw. Quest, not Whitfield, was dead. Therefore Quest was not either of the Lokis. This put Whitfield's disappearance in a new and very sinister light, for it suggested some fell purpose in his absence beyond what we had assumed. From my place in Prince Oscar's compartment, I watched as Mycroft Holmes entered into a discussion with the night Stationmaster, the conductor, and the Irish porter. They stood somewhat apart from the passengers, and although I could watch them,

I could not hear them. This aggravation increased when a young constable arrived and released the passengers. In a short while, Mycroft Holmes arrived at compartment four and tapped. I let him in at once.

"I suppose you saw?" he asked as he came in.

"Yes. Quest, poor chap, is dead. And Whitfield is still unaccounted for." Saying it aloud left me with the uneasy feeling that the trouble we were facing had once again changed its nature and would demand a new approach.

"The constable is of the opinion that Quest was in the baggage-compartment when the load shifted, and he became fatally pinned," said Holmes without any inflection to color his remark.

I knew what he expected me to ask. "And you? What do you think?"

"Why, I think the same thing you do, dear boy; I think Whitfield murdered him and is still on this train, waiting for an opportunity to kill Herr Schere." His grey eyes were as candid as a baby's, and he waited for me to speak.

I coughed in an attempt to conceal my surprise. "Yes, that is foremost in my thoughts," I agreed, wondering as I did what I should prepare to do. "But it is no easy thing to cast Whitfield in the role of a murderer."

"Or an assassin?" The suggestion was made lightly enough but I could see an angle to Mycroft Holmes' square jaw that reminded me of his force of character. On this point he would not readily be challenged.

"You mean Loki?" I asked, startled that the notion, once spoken, was more intriguing than absurd; my own thoughts had tended in just such a direction, and Holmes' observation only served to confirm what I had hoped was a misapprehension.

"Why not?" Holmes said. "What a good job for one of the two to have—a few months running the length of England to get to know the countryside and to make the contacts that might be needed—"

"But he said he had been tending bar for some time—I forget how long," I interjected.

"And no doubt he has. Barkeeps find work throughout the world and may readily move their employment from place to place. As occupations go, this is a very good one for Loki, at least for one of them. Miss Gatspy said the men were convincing in their fallacious identities. Should Whitfield prove to be one of them, I must agree that he has a most persuasive way about him." Mycroft Holmes cocked his head in the direction of the platform. "They will find death to be accidental, or misadventure at the worst, and we will be on our way again at last. But I will lay you five pounds to a farthing that Quest died of a broken neck and was dead before that trunk broke his arm."

"Poor blighter," I said, feeling a bit queasy at my own earlier suspicion that Quest might be the assassin. I still wondered if we had Loki to rights in the person of Whitfield. "What if we are wrong, and Whitfield is as much a victim as Quest? The body could be lying on the tracks or thrown into the verge."

"Yes, true enough. And if we had time enough to examine all the persons on this train with leisure, we could assuage our dubiety without exposing anyone to unjust suspicion. However we will be on our way in half an hour or so, and we will arrive in Edinburgh some time after midnight, so time is a luxury we do not have. In these circumstances, I must choose the most likely person, which is Whitfield. I may be defaming a blameless man with my assumption; I am cognizant of it. But who would you prefer to cast in the role? The maître d'? We have ruled out Sir Cameron's valet, haven't we?" Holmes asked. "Miss Gatspy, perhaps?"

I stood a bit straighter. "You will have your joke, sir," I said.

"She is more than capable of the act if she is convinced of the rightness of her purpose," Mycroft Holmes went on, tweaking me.

"The very reason we have nothing to fear from her. Prince Karl Gustav is the one who is being supported by the Brotherhood, and our friend is therefore under the watchful eye of the Golden Lodge." I did not like dignifying his remarks with any comment, but I could not allow this slight on such a brave woman to go undisputed. "You would not speak this way about her if you had any actual reservations as to her purpose or her character."

"Yes, yes," Mycroft Holmes replied placatingly. "No need to fly into the ropes, Guthrie. I admit I am all admiration for your Miss Gatspy—and since you defend her so eloquently, you will allow me to call her *yours* in this instance." He reached to open the door. "I am going back to the platform for a moment, and then I am returning to my compartment. The body is not likely to be kept here much longer, and once it is gone, the Stationmaster will be allowed to release the train. Continue as you have been, but remain more aware than usual. Loki, no matter whose identity he has taken, must be desperate to complete his work. You will have to maintain fired senses, for this man strikes quickly, relying on confusion, as we have seen." He took a deep breath. "I confess I will be glad to see this journey end."

"And I," I told him.

"Take no chances, my boy. I cannot easily replace you, you know." His smile came and went quickly enough, and then he, too, departed.

I took up my place by the window in my door, looking through the gap in the shade to watch the events on the platform unfold, all the while asking myself if I should have armed myself; the knife in my valise suddenly seemed a most inadequate weapon and hopelessly hard to reach. I wished then I had some free-standing chair to lodge against the door so that it could not be slid open.

A fussy man in a driving coat with a physician's bag arrived on the platform and was hurried over to Quest, ignoring those around him. Mycroft Holmes approached the man only to be rebuffed as the physician set about his work. He seemed offended by the body, for his examination was cursory and his manner disapproving, as if he felt that this presumed misadventure was an unseemly way to die, and his role in it resentful. Finally he issued some orders and the body was carried away, I supposed to a wagon waiting for that purpose. A discussion ensued among the remaining men on the platform. I heard more than saw Mycroft Holmes come back aboard the train as the talking came to an end. Then, as if in a ballet or magical entertainment, the conductor, the porters, the night Stationmaster, and the constables returned from confusion to familiar patterns. The bell sounded its warning, the engine hissed, and the *Flying Scotsman* pulled out of Melrose Station, bound at last for Edinburgh.

I returned to the day-bed and lay down once more, still determined not to sleep and sore enough to be reasonably certain I would not. I did, however, in a while, begin to doze, exhaustion making me light-headed. While I did not entirely lose track of time, it became more malleable, and I paid less attention to our progress and more to the fancies that my mind conjured for me. When I stirred myself to greater wakefulness, I began to long for this journey to end and to hope that we would arrive without further mishap. In this drifting state of mind, I dismissed a whisper in the corridor, for I heard no footsteps, and I thought the train might be passing through woods, where the branches of trees might brush the cars as they passed. The gently waving branches were wonderfully seductive and I let myself be fascinated by them, imagined images that bordered on dreaming.

In the next instant my heart was in my throat and I was full awake as a weight crushed down upon me.

"Guthrie. Don't move," Miss Gatspy breathed as she wriggled atop me. I had never realized how strong she was—not that I thought her a weakling, for our previous experiences together had demonstrated she was not—for I had never had to wrestle with her. "Lie still," she whispered, her lips just below my ear.

"What on earth is—" I began, very quietly, only to have her clap her hand over my mouth. I could not keep from thinking of the one time I had not maintained my composure with her, and the night we had passed together. I was shocked to realize that I was suddenly eager for another such opportunity.

"Hush." The order was so soft that I hardly heard it. She held her head up as much as our position would allow, which pressed her torso more firmly against mine, an action that gave rise to sensations that were utterly inappropriate to our situation. I had to resist the urge to embrace her, to renew my delicious knowledge of the curve of her body . . . I stopped myself from such unworthy ruminations. If she had any awareness of my response, she was too much a lady to mention it as she continued on the qui vive.

I did my best to listen as well, although my pulse was loud in my ears. In a minute or so, I could discern the sound of things being shifted about in compartment five—Miss Gatspy's compartment. The sound was stealthy and so measured that it was most certainly deliberate. I felt a rush of anger that after everything that had happened on this long train ride Miss Gatspy should be subjected to such an invasion of her privacy. Good God, I told myself, she is not some criminal, to be treated without respect; even if the man—for it must be a man—ransacking her things were a criminal himself, he should have confined his searches to Mycroft Holmes and me, never mind that Miss Gatspy was an agent of the Golden Lodge. It galled me that I could do nothing to stop this shameful intrusion.

All these impressions were over-ridden by my renewed and over-whelming awareness that under the bombazine or whatever it is that females make their clothes of, was Miss Gatspy—Miss Gatspy as the living, breathing, captivating creature she had been since we first encountered one another in that train compartment in France, the Miss Gatspy who had spent one terribly wrong, terribly wonderful night with me, the night I had not been able to put out of my mind, strive as I might. I could comprehend now why Mycroft Holmes called her *my* Miss Gatspy, for in this one blissful moment, she was again *my* Miss Gatspy. She was my Penelope. I realized I had been holding her more tightly than was necessary; I willed myself to release her, but for once my body would not obey. I broke the silence in a hushed apology which Miss Gatspy—Penelope—ended by lying full atop me and pressing her lips to mine. I had never experienced the like before but once: all the sensations I had thought were romantic absurdities I now knew were a pale shadow of the reality they sought to describe, and what I had thought was chagrin on her part had been something more intimate. Not in my long engagement to my former fiancée, Miss Elizabeth Roedale of Twyford, had I experienced anything so all-encompassing as this encounter evoked in me. How grateful I was to Miss Roedale for terminating our engagement, for I realized that I would never have felt for her the smallest degree of the passion that filled me now, revived and intensified by the passing of time. I was ruler of the world with Penelope Gatspy in my arms, and nothing would ever be quite the same again, for I knew beyond question that I had not disgusted her during that splendid night, nor would I now. Had the train exploded at that moment, I would not have cared.

How long we remained embraced and kissing, I had no notion, but we were brought back to a sense of ourselves by the sound of Sir Cameron cursing his valet as he made his uncertain way to the lav.

I was immediately aware of how compromised we were, and I started to insist she move when she kissed me a second time. This time I was less shocked and more inspired, as I showed by my enthusiasm. Emboldened by her response, I let my hands wander over her shoulders and back while Sir Cameron continued to careen toward the lav, his unfortunate valet in tow. I would not have been less concerned had he been in the Vale of Kashmir but for my realization that there was someone searching Miss Gatspy's compartment; and with Sir Cameron blundering about, an encounter was not impossible and potentially disastrous.

As Miss Gatspy moved her head enough that our lips were no longer touching, she whispered, "Finally, I was beginning to think you would never do anything again but long." Her hand, an inch from my face, warned me to be quiet and listen.

". . . a whoreson blaggard like you. I don't need you nursemaiding me." His speech was slurred, but not enough to make his insults unintelligible, more was the pity for the valet.

There was a sharp sound from the other side of the wall, from compartment five; I was fairly certain the miscreant had readied his pistol.

"—if you'll allow Sir Cameron," the valet was saying in a tone that cringed.

"I'll see you in Hell, laddie, that I will," Sir Cameron declared with increasing choler.

It was impossible to hear any of the stealthy sounds in the next compartment with Sir Cameron braying in the corridor, and it was hard to concentrate with Miss Gatspy so very near and every one of my nerves attuned to her presence. Still I strove to do what I had sworn to do—act for Mycroft Holmes to protect Prince Oscar. With more difficulty than I would have thought possible, I extricated myself from Miss Gatspy, for I did not want to offend her with any untoward touch or slight her through any inadvertent gesture. At last we moved apart and I began to get to my feet. My hands were steady, which comforted me, for I felt amazingly shaken. I crept to the wall separating compartments four and five and laid my ear against it. Behind me I could hear Miss Gatspy get off the day-bed and begin to set her clothes to order. I heard her skirts rustle more than I heard the culprit in the next compartment.

"We'll be in Edinburgh in a few minutes, Sir Cameron," the valet went on in his attempt to placate the outraged knight. "You'll want to make haste."

"I'll make what I damned well please!" Sir Cameron roared.

It might have been a signal, for the loud report of a pistol punctuated Sir Cameron's outburst, which now became a bellow of rage. I stumbled toward the door, only to find Miss Gatspy a step ahead of me. As she slid the door open, she looked back at me. I noticed she carried something in her hand—I assumed she had brought her pistol in her purse and was planning to use it.

"Well, one of us had to do something, Guthrie," she said before she shoved past Sir Cameron's valet and toward the door to her compartment.

"Penelope!" I cried, just at that instant more apprehensive on her behalf than anyone else on the train. Then I stopped as I saw Sir Cameron sprawled in the narrow confines of the corridor, half-leaning against the wall, cursing steadily and loudly, his hand wrapped around his shoulder which was already wet with blood. I hesitated for a heartbeat only—and I curse myself for doing so—then plunged after Miss

Gatspy, who had placed herself in front of the shattered door to compartment five. I saw Sir Cameron's valet fumble in an attempt to aid his employer, and I had to be agile to avoid either man.

A figure hurtled out of compartment five striking Miss Gatspy a sharp blow on the side of her head, and then firing again in the direction of Sir Cameron. The shot went wild, but in the confusion the man bolted for the lav, got inside and slammed the door.

"We have him!" shouted the valet, abandoning the infuriated Sir Cameron to launch himself at the lav door.

I was about to echo his sentiments when I recalled that broken window and wondered if we had been too quick to assume the criminal was trapped. My worst fears were realized at the sound of splintering glass, and another shot.

"Good Lord, what is he doing?" Miss Gatspy murmured, her hand to her head, her marvelous eyes glazed. Their wavering glance struck me as no bullet could.

I dropped to my knees beside her, pulling her against me. I did not care that the valet stared at me. "Promise me you are not hurt, Miss Gatspy."

"I . . . will be all right. But he is getting away, Paterson; stop him." She had rallied enough to upbraid me, and I was happy to hear it.

"He can only reach the roof of the train from the window," I said. "And he will not be able to go far from there," I soothed her, recalling my own time on the roof of the train.

"If he reaches the engineers, we have trouble," said Sir Cameron's valet, with more purpose than I had seen him display yet.

Mycroft Holmes appeared in the corridor, a pistol in his hand. "Is there anything I can do, Guthrie?" He appeared utterly urbane, but I could discern a note of apprehension in his deep voice.

"Sir Cameron has been shot," said his valet coolly. "I don't think it is serious, but he will need attention." He managed to kick the lav door open. "Leftenant-Commander Thomas Ames, at your service, Mister Holmes," he added with a salute. "I'll be the escort to take your person to his ship."

"I'll need more than a word in the middle of trouble, Ames," said Holmes so brusquely that I knew he was seriously annoyed. "In the meantime, Whitfield is getting away."

"And that could be difficult," said Ames. "I will make my way to the engineers to help them. I have—"

"Am I to bleed to death?" demanded Sir Cameron in stentorian tones.

"The cad shot me!"

"I shall present my credentials when we both have leisure for it," Ames said, and headed for the front of the car. "We are near the station, and time is precious."

"Then hurry. I will see to Sir Cameron," said Mycroft Holmes in a tone of ill-usage. "Guthrie, make sure Miss Gatspy is not seriously injured, then ready yourself for the chase, for it is my belief that Whitfield will try to make his escape as we enter the station at Edinburgh, which is not far ahead.

The view from the train had changed rather abruptly from rough hills to brick-and-shingle buildings growing ever closer together. We were entering the Portabello curve at a much more reasonable speed than when my employer was a passenger during the race. To one side was the wide expanse of the Duddington Road, during the day filled with carts, wagons, and traffic of all sorts, now all but deserted. After crossing a steel bridge over another busy way, the proximity of the station was apparent by the increasing number of tracks visible to both sides of our car. Beyond these iron rails and up a small slope sat a line of tightly packed four-story residences, their walls stained with soot and coal dust. At irregular intervals an even more darkly stained chimney made of the same dark stone as the building's walls shoved into the night sky. I turned away from the window to face Miss Gatsby.

"I am quite able to manage for myself," announced Miss Gatspy, trying to move out of my protective hold. "My head is ringing, but I am not ill."

"Will someone take care of my shoulder?" Sir Cameron held up his blood-stained hand. "Must I—"

Mycroft Holmes came a few steps nearer. "Let me help you up, Sir Cameron." He was able to lever the wounded man to his feet, supporting him with his shoulder.

"Damn, Holmes, what are you doing here?" Sir Cameron said, his voice shaky but much more sober than before he was shot; it was just such outbursts as this one that had caused us to be so careful in regard to the Scot.

"Taking care of you, it would seem," he answered drily. "Guthrie, see to Miss Gatspy, and then be ready."

"Of course," I said, feeling a pang of conscience, for I had been enjoying this opportunity to hold Miss Gatspy. I helped her to stand on her own as Mycroft Holmes took his unwelcome charge to his compartment. "You had best go to my compartment."

"I think rather I should go to . . . Herr Schere," she said to me, as she leaned on my arm. "Someone should be with him."

"Excellent notion," approved Mycroft Holmes just before he shoved Sir Cameron into his compartment. "Tend to it, Guthrie."

I was not entirely pleased with this notion, but I had none better to offer, and there was some urgency. I had an unpleasant moment as I thought that it was very strange that Prince Oscar had not set foot outside his compartment in all this excitement. As I reached for the door, I faltered, afraid that in the turmoil of the last two minutes he might have come to some harm. It was just as well that I hesitated, for Prince Oscar himself pulled the door open, greeting Miss Gatspy and me with a drawn pistol.

"Guthrie!" cried he, lowering his weapon at once. "Miss Gatspy. For goodness sake—" He broke off to say something under his breath in what I supposed must be Swedish, for it sounded something like German. "Hurry."

Miss Gatspy suddenly leaned a bit more heavily against me. "Yes. Do get me in, Guthrie," she said, in a thready voice. "I fear I am . . . somewhat weak after all."

"Oh, Good Lord," I expostulated, and swept her into my arms to carry her into Prince Oscar's compartment; a sweeter burden I had never borne, and I was saddened to put her down on the Prince's daybed.

"Was it Loki?" Prince Oscar asked, sounding very calm for a man who had narrowly escaped assassination.

"It was Whitfield," said Miss Gatspy faintly. "Whether or not he is Loki is uncertain."

"Don't tax yourself, Miss Gatspy," I recommended, holding her hand to assure myself she was not unwell. "I must excuse myself. You will watch after her for me, won't you?" I did not think it inappropriate to entrust the care of Miss Gatspy to the Prince.

"Certainly. Off you go, Guthrie," said Prince Oscar, adding as he gestured toward the window, "We are nearing the station."

Ordinarily I would not like being summarily dismissed in that manner, but I knew Mycroft Holmes was depending upon me. "I will return for her once all is safe."

"Very good," said Prince Oscar as I hastened to the door. The corridor was empty, and I noticed the train was slowing down. The outlines of darkened houses went past, no longer a blur, but distinguishable. I hurried toward the front of the car, unconcerned about attracting the attention of Sir Cameron. I stepped onto the half-platform connecting the first car to the collier just behind the engine. I stood there in the thickening mist, ready to do anything I might to assist Ames in apprehending Whitfield.

The tracks curved, beginning the two-mile-long approach to the station at Edinburgh. I squinted into the darkness and wind, hoping to discover the whereabouts of either Whitfield or the self-announced Leftenant-Commander Ames. I became aware that my hip was aching once again, but it was not sufficient to keep me from my duty. The train slowed still more, to less than ten miles per hour, and I reckoned that if Whitfield were to make a move, he would make it now, when he might have a hope of getting off the train without killing himself.

I heard a shout above me, from the roof of the first-class car. I swung about and looked up and made out the shadowy outline of a man crouched on the lip of the roof, poised as if to climb down the ladder on the outside of the car. I could not see which man it was and so I was not certain what I should do. I tried to move to find a better vantage-point, trying to make the most of the occasional lamp illuminating the tracks leading into the station, which was now less than a mile ahead in the night.

The man on the roof could no longer wait. He dropped onto the ladder and began his descent, moving quickly and in so furtive a manner that I became wary of him. Holding onto the metal railing I leaned out as far as I could to look at the man, and had to draw back as a kick was sharply directed at my head.

I was certain this was Whitfield, and I resolved to capture him. Gathering myself, I launched myself out and around, confining the hips and legs of the man on the ladder. He tried to kick me, but I clung to the ladder rung I had seized, refusing to budge in spite of the blows the fellow directed at my bruised head.

Ahead of us, Edinburgh Station gaped, a dark, open maw. If I could maintain my grip for another minute or so we would be near the station platform, and I would be able to tumble us both onto the boards without much risk of serious injury. But as Whitfield tried to grasp and tear off my ear, and I whipped my head about to prevent him, the station seemed very far off.

FROM THE PERSONAL JOURNAL OF PHILIP TYERS

Sid Hastings has left for King's Cross to send another telegram, with in-structions he is not to return until he has confirmation that the Flying Scotsman *has at last arrived in Edinburgh. It is my hope that the Directors were correct in their estimation and that the* Flying Scotsman *will shortly arrive, thus ending the apprehension that has marked this night.*

Too overwrought to sleep, Sutton is working on Mosca's lines; I shall know that part by heart before the night is over.

Still no word from or regarding CI Somerford, which troubles me a great deal. I cannot rid myself of the conviction that through the investigation I have supervised he has come to grief, but whether through vice or virtue I cannot yet determine. When MH returns in two days, if there has been no contact from the man, we must presume the worst—his death or his flight—and do what we may to repair the damage resulting from it.

Word from the Admiralty has finally identified the agent they have put on the train as Sir Cameron MacMillian's valet, a Leftenant-Commander named Ames. He is the hand-picked aide of Commander Winslowe and comes with encomiums from many high-ranking officers. It would seem that Sir Cameron provided the perfect cover, and so was put aboard the train to account for the Leftenant-Commander's presence. Their information is provided tardily, but I am told that MH will find confirmation of the agent's identity waiting in Edinburgh, to facilitate handing HHPO over to the Navy's care.

On a less reassuring note there has been another message from Yvgeny Tschersky, warning that he has discovered intelligence that suggests an attempt may be made on MH's life in Edinburgh if HHPO is not killed before he is taken into the care of the Royal Navy. I doubt I will have sufficient time to warn MH of this before he is in danger; and since there are so few particulars in Tschersky's information, I do not think my concern would do more than add to the anxiety that MH must deal with. Rumors can be most useful tools; but when they are as insubstantial as this one, I am not easy in my mind about adding to the anxieties of MH and the others, no matter how reliable Tschersky is. Had I specific information, I would make every effort to provide it with all dispatch; but with nothing to offer but a rumor, and a hint of a rumor at that, I am inclined to wait. I trust I have not erred in my judgment in this regard.

Chapter Twenty-four

HANGING ONTO THE side of the first-class car, I struggled with my adversary, my grasp upon him all but failing as the train braked again and again. Finally I took hold of the man himself, anchoring myself as well as I could by hooking my feet under the lowest rung. I felt stretched like a racehorse's girth, but I was able to stop his attempts to poke out my eyes or mutilate me in some other way. I clung to him like grim death as the station grew closer and closer, and the train shuddered from the brakes being applied, causing Whitfield and me to bow outward from the side of the car. I felt my shoulders strain and my thigh quiver with effort.

We were fifty yards or so from the station platform when one lurch proved too much: Whitfield let go and, as I had no purchase but the one upon him, the two of us tumbled back off the train onto the gravel between the various tracks that fed into the station. We hit the ground hard; I knew I was dazed by the spangles before my eyes, though the shock of the fall did not hit me then. For a half-dozen heartbeats I could not move, and then I felt Whitfield try to wrench out of my grip. He managed to get one leg free enough to kick me in the abdomen.

I released him and doubled over, rolling onto my side as he scrambled to his feet and began to race across the tracks, making for the freight warehouse next to the passenger platform, just inside the station. I forced myself onto my knees, and then to my feet, and started after him, wheezing like a grampus as I went. The mist made my footing treacherous, and I took what comfort I could in the realization that my adversary did no better than I in that regard. Behind me, I heard a shout, which I thought must come from Ames, for it seemed to originate high above me. I kept on steadily, taking as much consolation as I could in the observation that Whitfield was limping. Belatedly shock was making me cold, so I strove to keep moving, if only to stay warm. While the *Flying Scotsman* pulled into its Edinburgh platform at last, I continued my pursuit of Whitfield.

As we neared the station itself, I began to see how vast it was; I felt fear welling in me, fear that once Whitfield reached the station, I would have little chance of catching or detaining him, which would crown this long journey of mischances with a disgrace I could not endure. If I failed to apprehend Whitfield, I knew beyond all doubt I would attaint myself in my employer's eyes and dishonor myself in Miss Gatspy's. With these melancholy reflections to goad me on, I redoubled my efforts, ignoring the stitch in my side and the throb in my hip. I was shortly rewarded by visibly closing the gap between me and Whitfield. I summoned up reserves from depths that would have alarmed me had I not been so desperate. With a last effort I plunged ahead, finally reaching the tail of Whitfield's coat. I stopped and pulled on it with all my might and the very last of my flagging strength.

I caught Whitfield on his weak leg and he went down with an oath so vile I was appalled. I landed upon him, pummeling him in the side of the head with all my might; I had never felt rage as I did then, and in truth it frightened me as I became aware that I was trying to beat him to death. Shaken, exhausted, and sore from my head to the soles of my feet, I got to my feet, then dragged him erect, finishing by landing my fist at his waist with all the strength I could summon, in payment for the kick he had delivered me. I was panting as I took hold of his collar and made him straighten up once more. "Come," I ordered him, half-dragging, half-prodding him toward the steps leading up toward the platform where the train had at last come to rest. The stairs proved as difficult to scale as a mountain crag, but I persevered, making Whitfield climb with me, though he cursed and coughed and tried twice to lash out at me. I was very pleased to see Leftenant-Commander Ames waiting, pistol in hand, for us at the head of the porters' stairs.

"Very fine work, Mister Guthrie," said Ames, leveling his pistol at Whitfield.

Looking at Whitfield now I saw almost none of the ingratiating barkeep who had made such an effort to provide good service. There was no trace of that eager good-will that he had shown as he set up drinks for the passengers. His features were harder than I had earlier thought they were, and his demeanor, even beaten and captive, was contemptuous and defiant.

"You'll not keep me. Make the most of your chance, for I will be gone before you are back in London. Mister Vickers protects his own." He spat at me. "Tell Mycroft Holmes he is a fool."

At the mention of Vickers' name, I felt my hands clench at my sides, for I was still somewhat over-wrought. I did not trust myself to speak.

"Come along, you," said Ames, motioning Whitfield to move ahead of him. "You'll lose that sneer soon enough." He looked back in my direction for a moment. "Quite impressive, you were."

"Thanks," I said, certain I deserved no praise. I had done what I had for pride and wrath, which made me feel a sham to accept his compliment. My legs felt watery, and I had to resist the urge to sit down and put my head between my knees and be sick. Now that the immediate danger was over, I felt strangely empty.

"Mister Holmes will tell you the same." He pointed toward the train that was now actually stopped, the conductors letting down the stairs for the passengers.

"Are you so certain of that?" I asked, unwilling to accept him at his word. I had had my fill of people with double and triple purposes about them, and identities that were as fallacious as the claims of horse-dealers.

"Yes. I have proof of identity in my pocket, if you would care to retrieve it." He indicated with his elbow which pocket contained his credentials. Tired though I was, I took it out and examined it, determined not to be deprived of a victory that had cost me so dearly. Finally I nodded. "Leftenant-Commander Ames. Under other circumstances I would say it is a pleasure." I returned his billfold to his pocket while he continued to hold Whitfield with his pistol.

"Quite so, Mister Guthrie. So if you do not mind, I will be about my assignment and deliver this fellow to the proper authorities?" He inclined his head slightly.

This simple reminder gave me the determination to keep to my task. "Be careful with him. He is a very dangerous man, and in the employ of dangerous men," I said, perhaps unnecessarily.

"Do not bother yourself on that account," Ames assured me. "He will rue this night for many long years, unless he is hanged as a murderer." He continued on his way with his prisoner, going off toward a side-door to the station.

I plodded on toward the train, looking at the station as if I had never seen it before. Waverley Station was designed in the still modern and appealing classical style; its light stone walls would have fit well among the ancient buildings of Athens: The train bay was long and deep, with room for over twelve trains to load simultaneously. The ceiling above was partially closed in, protecting the trains and platforms, but not trapping in all the smoke and steam. It was a thoroughly modern design including all of the latest conveniences. A large, glass dome dominated the ceiling over the interior of the station, the light from this being supplemented by a number of flat skylights. This meant that even on a cloudy day, of which there are so many in Scotland, the interior of the station remained well-lit. I wished it were daylight so I could see how pleasant the platform could be.

The walls of the station were of the same golden stone that comprised the walls of so many of the larger buildings in Edinburgh. This stone was accented by areas of eggshell blue and gold with the occasional touch of gilt. From the entrance I could see the shuttered fronts of several restaurants, shops, and pubs that served the hundreds of travelers who passed through the station daily. On the far wall, tall arches marked the location of the brass-and-glass doors. Beyond one door I could just make out the beginning of the famous Waverley steps that lead to the High Street.

There were a few bags already removed from the baggage-compartment, the porters hurrying to do their work; with the hour so late, most of them were tired. I passed them, dragging my feet with every step. I could see most of the train was emptying. The waiters were gone from the dining car, and only the maître d' remained to give his report to the Stationmaster. Finally I climbed aboard at the first-class passenger car and found Mycroft Holmes waiting for me, his pistol at the ready. Behind him, Prince Oscar was lending his arm to Miss Gatspy, who was still a trifle unsteady on her feet. I could see dismay mount in Holmes' deep-grey eyes, and I thought I must truly look a fright now, with new bruises forming on those that were a few hours old.

"Guthrie. What happened?" His simple question nearly unmanned me. "You look a sight, dear boy," he added, giving me time to get a grip on myself.

"Ames has Whitfield in hand," I said. My voice was not as steady as I would have liked. I coughed and tried again. "I kept him from making his getaway."

"I knew you would," Holmes said heartily, belatedly putting his pistol in his pocket. "We will have a short wait for our escort. You can tell me . . . *us* all about it until the Navy comes."

There did not seem to be much for me to say. "Well, Whitfield did his best to vanish before we arrived in the station and I made sure he did not. Leftenant-Commander Ames has him in hand now. I saw his papers. He is who he claims to be." As I spoke my gaze kept drifting from Mycroft Holmes to Miss Gatspy, who was listening with such intent that it seemed almost painful. The soft spill of light from the station platform struck her fair hair, lending it a lunar shine. "Are you going to be all right?"

"Yes," she said calmly. "Are *you?*" The bruise on the side of her head had developed a pronounced lump and I saw that she was still pale.

I nodded heavily. "I must be a dreadful sight."

"Never mind that," Holmes interrupted as a porter came onto the train, going to compartment one, which Sir Cameron MacMillian had occupied.

Knowing Mycroft Holmes intended us to reveal nothing, I obeyed at once. "I trust you will not need me ready at seven in the morning?" I remarked as the porter carried away Sir Cameron's luggage, carefully showing no curiosity at all as he completed his task. "Where is Sir Cameron?"

"He left as soon as we stopped; he demanded the services of a physician on the grounds that he had averted a dangerous criminal from taking over control of the train," said Holmes drily.

"That is a self-serving fabrication," said Prince Oscar indignantly. He had his valise beside him, ready to depart as soon as the Navy officers came. "I shall tell the world how mendacious he is."

Holmes sighed, "I wish you would not, Your Highness, for it would do Britain no service to have the events of this journey known. Let everyone think Sir Cameron routed a bandit—well and good, for it preserves our mission's secrecy." He looked directly at the Prince, his long face remarkably candid.

Miss Gatspy added her support. "He's right, Your Highness. One of the proofs of success for Mister Holmes—and how good it is to use that name again—is that it remains unknown to all but those few for whom it is crucial." She gave me a warm smile. "Think of what Guthrie has been through, and keep your knowledge to yourself."

Prince Oscar thought over what we had said. "All right, I will. But it galls me to think of that sot posturing his way through the world as a hero."

"It does not precisely cause me joy, either," Holmes said, and smiled faintly.

"It is the nature of our work," said Miss Gatspy, a bit more emphatically than before. "If we draw attention to what we do, we can no longer do it well. Keep that in mind when dealing with the Brotherhood—if they are exposed, they lose much of their power."

"True enough," said Mycroft Holmes, and glanced up as four naval officers appeared on the platform. "Ah. Your Highness, your escort has arrived." He bowed slightly. "I will wish you bon voyage, for I doubt we shall meet again before you sail."

"I am grateful to you, Mister Holmes. I have learned much in the last two days that will stand me in good stead in times to come. For all the danger, this was a most enlightening journey, and I thank you for looking after me so well." He removed Miss Gatspy's hand from his arm. "You have been an enchanting nurse. If ever I am truly ill, I will hope for as gracious a woman as you to look after me."

Miss Gatspy flushed a little and bobbed a curtsy. "It was my pleasure," she said, and allowed Prince Oscar to kiss her hand.

A middle-aged man in a Captain's uniform appeared at the end of the corridor. He spoke directly to Prince Oscar. "Captain James

Hollyrood, Your Majesty. At your service." His bow was correct to a fault.

Prince Oscar acknowledged the bow with the automatic hauteur of his position, and I could see he would miss Herr Osrich Schere more than any of the rest of us. "Then let us be gone, Captain." He favored Mycroft Holmes with another nod. "Thank you for all you have done to ensure my safety." With that he handed his valise to Captain Hollyrood and prepared to follow him out of the train. After all we had been through, his departure felt anti-climactic, but that was probably all to the good.

When he was gone, the three of us who remained were silent for a short while. Then Mycroft Holmes stretched. "So, it is time we were gone. The Stationmaster will be wanting us out of his domain, I should think. There are two telegrams yet to send, and we will be on our way." He no longer had the manner of a professional traveler. "Miss Gatspy, is there somewhere we may take you? I do not like the idea of you being abroad at this hour and with so severe a bump on your head."

I waited to hear her speak. "I should not bring you to the place I am going to stay tonight," she said.

"Possibly not," Mycroft Holmes told her, "but if you were in my position, you would insist on seeing you to your door, my dear young woman. You are in no fit state, and this is no sort of hour for you to be out and about without protection."

"You sound like Guthrie," she said, attempting a rallying tone but sounding forlorn to my ears.

"Guthrie would be right in his concern," said Holmes, as smoothly as if he addressed the French Ambassador.

I knew I should return to my cabin to gather my valise and my portfolio, but I could not bring myself to leave her; she might take advantage of my absence to disappear as she had done before. "Your situation does worry me, Miss Gatspy."

"Very well," she said after a moment. "But I rely on your word as gentlemen to forget the address to which you deliver me."

Holmes smiled at her. "My dear Miss Gatspy, surely you would not expect us to take advantage of your indisposition."

"Well, *I* would, were I in your shoes," she said without apology. "I have a few bits of luggage—do you think the porter will fetch them for me?"

"No doubt," Holmes said, and motioned to me to gather up my

belongings. "And then you will walk Miss Gatspy out of the car while I collect my cases."

I ducked into compartment three for my valise, and then into compartment four for my portfolio. The two seemed heavier than when I last carried them, no doubt because of my fatigue and hard use. The way I felt, a serviette would seem as great a burden as a woollen rug. I came to Miss Gatspy's side. "There, I am ready."

"Good," said Holmes. "Then if you will, accompany Miss Gatspy in her hunt for a porter." He went into compartment two for his luggage.

"I truly am grateful to you, Guthrie," she said as we made our way to the platform for the last time.

"After what . . . happened, you will agree that there is no need for gratitude." I would have embraced her then and there had we not been in so public a place. As it was, helping her down the steps to the station platform, I carried her hand to my lips.

"If my head weren't so infernally sore, I would kiss you for that. Did you grow up on tales of chivalry that you have so finely tuned a sense of honor?" She touched my face with her gloved hand. "What *am* I going to do with you?"

"There are a number of possibilities," I said, feeling a trifle breathless as I leaned nearer to her.

"None of which will serve our purposes, you will agree," she said with some of her characteristic firmness of purpose. "Neither of us are in a position to undertake a courtship."

"There must be a way," I said, feeling reckless. I saw a porter approaching and was at once vexed and relieved to have him interrupt our exchange. "You, there. Miss Gatspy's things are in compartment five—fetch them for her, there's a good fellow."

The porter signaled his compliance and made for the first-class car.

"Guthrie," she said very seriously, "you must comprehend that nothing has changed between us."

"Nothing? How can you say that? Why, *everything* has changed," I protested.

She shook her head. "No. You still work for Mycroft Holmes, who is the heart of British diplomacy, and I am an agent of the Golden Lodge. When we had that one night together, it changed nothing but your conviction that you had no right to care for me. That you—

finally—recognize our . . . shared affection makes no difference. Our lives follow different paths."

"Which continue to cross," I said, striving to hold onto a shred of the happiness she had given me. "Do not tell me it—"

Mycroft Holmes came down the steps, his profound gaze lingering on the two of us for a breath or two before he said, "Shall we try to find a cab? There must be something available at this time of night, late though it may be. And where is the telegraph office?"

The porter, emerging with Miss Gatspy's luggage in hand, cocked his jaw in the direction of the long flight of stairs leading from the station platform to the street above. "Just there. You'll have to pay extra; it's past midnight."

"I've no objection to that," said Holmes and set out at a vigorous stride toward the office, leaving Miss Gatspy and me to trail after him, the porter in our wake.

As we went along, Miss Gatspy said, "You'll see I'm right, as soon as you're used to—" She stopped. "I've known how you felt since our second meeting at the Fishing Cat."

"You had a pistol in your hand then," I said, recalling how adorable she had been. I adjusted my hold on my valise so that my portfolio could rest more easily atop it as I kept it tucked under my arm.

"Pay attention," she said as if she read my thoughts. "You have done your utmost to avoid knowing your heart. It's not surprising you would do so. Our dealings are awkward enough without having to add attraction to the lot." She halted. "You don't think Mister Holmes will stop you from working where I might be, do you?"

"I can't think why he should," I lied. I saw Mycroft Holmes enter the telegraph office, and felt, nonsensically, that Miss Gatspy and I were now alone together.

"Don't say so to me, Guthrie," she said, and put her hand through the bend of my arm. "It could be dangerous for both of us."

"It hasn't been thus far," I reminded her.

"Because you have been wearing blinders, Paterson," she said brusquely. "You have made us safe through your obstinacy."

"Then I shall continue to do so," I said, with a lack of conviction that was patently obvious even to me. I abandoned all pretense. "Penelope, I would rather leave my work than lose you."

She smiled up at me. "How very dear of you to say it," she murmured. "And how very untrue." She walked a little faster, making me lengthen my stride to keep up with her. "You could no more leave Mycroft Holmes than I could turn away from the Golden Lodge. You would have no regard for me, and I no respect for you if we could. And well you know it."

"At this moment, all I know is I love you," I said, and all but froze. The enormity of my declaration filled me with the most stringent apprehension, and I struggled to think of some means to mitigate my avowal.

"Yes, Guthrie, I know," said Miss Gatspy prosaically. "And I love you, if it pleases you to hear it."

All the things that had been burgeoning within me, the silly confidences of sweethearts, the endearments that would set the seal upon our mutual tenderness, were routed by her direct articulation of her emotion. I could summon up no phrases more splendid than the one she had just used. "Oh, Penelope."

"Yes, Paterson?" Her playfulness was back, and I did not dare try to reclaim the closeness we had only now found.

I was distantly aware that the porter was following us at a discreet distance.

We had reached the foot of the Waverley Stairs, four long flights made up of blocks cut from the same stone as the station itself. Entrances into the various floors of Waverley Station were to the right as I climbed the steps. Rising a full three tall stories, they marched up the side of the station, affording a view of Edinburgh Castle on the left at the completion of the last flight. I did not look forward to climbing the flight, not only because I was stiff and hurting from all my misadventures, but because I knew it would bring an end to my brief intimacy with Penelope Evangeline Gatspy, which struck me as the greatest cruelty I had suffered in the last two years.

Mycroft Holmes came out of the telegraph office with three sheets of paper clutched in his hand, his face set in hard lines, warning me that not all the news was good. He strode up to us, firm intent in every lineament of his being. "It is no coincidence," he said without explanation. "How could it have slipped by me? I cannot think how I came to overlook anything so questionable."

"What on earth is the matter?" I asked, and saw my concern mirrored in Miss Gatspy's eyes. "Has anything happened in London?"

"Oh, doubtless," said Holmes, dismissing the question without any sign of worry. "But this is quite another . . ." He held out the telegrams. "After Sir Cameron's wife, I should have been more careful.

Superintendent Spencer's wife's maiden name was Vickers."

Miss Gatspy did not appear shocked by this revelation. "Is it the same family?" Her coolness was admirable. "Is the report reliable?"

"Yes, worse luck," said Mycroft Holmes, as we began to make our way up the stairs. "Whoever filed the reports on Spencer will have a question or two to answer in the next few days."

"If a report was filed," said Miss Gatspy significantly. "From what Prince Oscar told me, you may have unreliable men in the police. If such important material goes astray, what else might be missing, as well?" She was not climbing quickly; I could tell that her head was swimming, and I went to lend her my arm.

An instant later the railing of the bannister where I had been standing was shattered as the crack of a rifle echoed in the cavernous station; I dropped my valise as I tried to keep hold of my portfolio. A few inches away from the impact, Mycroft Holmes turned around, murder in his long features as he flung his valise away; he had reached his limit.

"I'll deal with this, Guthrie," he said in so light a tone that I knew he was consumed with fury. With an agility that was rare in large, portly men, Holmes vaulted the bannister and crouched over, rushed down the stairs in the direction the shot had come—toward the storage warehouse at the rear of the platform. He rushed past the porter, who had taken shelter behind Miss Gatspy's luggage, and who cowered lower as a second shot resounded and the stone of the second step cracked, small fragments flying with the ricocheting bullet.

"Can you see where he is?" Miss Gatspy asked from where we huddled together.

"No. In that direction," I said, pointing to where Mycroft Holmes was going, running in a zig-zag pattern to frustrate another clear shot, but ultimately headed toward the warehouse. "I think the man is in the door. It looks ajar."

She turned enough to look once, saying, "I hate this. We should be helping him."

"You would not say so had you seen his face," I said to her, taking her hand. "He has his pistol."

Miss Gatspy took a deep breath. "It is still not—"

There was a third sharp report from the rifle, followed almost at once by two shots from Holmes' pistol. I stood straight at the sounds, confident that the would-be assassin had been felled. That Mycroft Holmes had prevailed there could be no doubt; still I held my breath as I waited for him to make himself known. In a few seconds I saw Holmes come out of the shadows, his head lowered and his pace deliberate. As he reached the stairs once again, he spoke to the porter, who was visibly shaking.

"You had better send for the police. There is a dead man in your storage warehouse." His voice was low, level, and weary beyond anything I had ever felt. He took a little time to pick up his valise, this very mundane action seeming to hold all his concentration. Then, mounting the stairs to where we stood, he said, "I must apologize; we are going to be delayed once more."

The porter hurried off to the Stationmaster's office, the sound of his shoes uncomfortably reminiscent of gunfire.

"Not like Leicester," pleaded Miss Gatspy, "or Sheffield."

"That will depend upon the police," said Holmes, a world of supposition in his remark. "No doubt they will see you to your destination." He sat down on the stairs next to the place on the bannister where the wood was splintered. "It should not be long, Guthrie. Then you may have your well-earned rest at the Royal Scots Club on Abercromby Place. I've been privileged to be asked to become a member. The Royal Scots are, as you must know, the longest-serving regiment in Service to the crown. You'll find the rooms spacious, and the pub room that is on your left as you enter is a convivial place; they have, not surprisingly, one of the best selections of Scotch whiskies in the city."

"Not a minute too soon," I said, trying to match his self-possession. I had secured both my valise and portfolio again.

Mycroft Holmes did not have a rallying answer; instead he contemplated Miss Gatspy. "It might be as well, my dear, if you left now; you do not want to be questioned by the police again tonight, do you?"

The porter returned. "They've been sent for. Be here in five minutes, they say."

"You're most understanding," Miss Gatspy said as if she had not heard the porter, and nodded. "I thank you for your regard for my sensibilities. The porter will know how to find me a cab." Her demeanor softened as she looked at me. "You need not accompany me, Guthrie," she said, forestalling my offer. "The porter will take care of me."

"Based on his heroics?" I could not stop myself from saying.

"That was unkind." She regarded me seriously. "Until we meet again, Paterson." Then she leaned forward and kissed me.

I remained all but transfixed when she broke away and summoned the porter to follow her. Only when she was out of my sight could I speak again.

"It is better that she left," said Holmes. "Safer."

I frowned absently. "No doubt." I had the oddest constriction in my throat which made it hard to speak. "Who was he?" I nodded in the direction of the warehouse door.

"I've no idea. Probably one of Vickers' men. The Brotherhood has been dogging our steps from first until last." He patted the steps beside him on the side away from his luggage. "Sit, sit, dear boy. No need to wear yourself out any longer."

More to accommodate him than from any compulsion on my part, I sank down, putting my valise on the step and moving my port-folio onto my lap. Dumbly I stared at it. There it was, leather, with two buckled straps and the initials PEG in gold. But the letters were in a swashed style, instead of the leaded serif type on my portfolio. For all my efforts to think, I could not comprehend how the portfolio had come to change. "Strange," I muttered.

"What is it, Guthrie?" asked Holmes, who had been watching me.

With a sinking feeling I opened the portfolio, searching for the pencil box and Sutton's sketches, and found instead two files with Golden Lodge seals upon them. I held them as if I expected them to burst into fire. I could not think of what I could say to Sutton to apologize for the loss of his drawings.

Holmes was sitting a bit straighter; he took the files from me and very carefully opened the first, his heavy brows rising sharply. "Dear me. I hope she does not get into trouble for this." He turned apprecia-tively to the second page.

"Who?" I was still holding the portfolio in bewilderment; my thoughts would not budge from the three letters—very nearly correct, but slightly dissimilar from mine.

"Why, your Miss Guthrie. Miss Penelope Evangeline Gatspy," he said, indicating the letters, "Mr. Paterson Erskine Guthrie." He cracked a laugh. "She's very fond of you to do this."

Finally my interest stirred. "What is it?"

"These are copies of the Golden Lodge files of Brotherhood as-sassins, with records of their activities for the last five years." He achieved a tired smile. "I hope she likes the sketches."

The lethargy that had held me finally vanished. "She did this deliberately," I said, intending it as a question, but realizing, as I spoke, that she had switched our portfolios when she had sneaked into my compartment to hide from Loki.

"That she did," Holmes approved as the first shrill whistle announced the arrival of the police. "She's a most capable girl, your Miss Gatspy."

For once I did not protest this designation; I felt my bruised face crease into smiles. "Yes, she is, isn't she?"

FROM THE PERSONAL JOURNAL OF PHILIP TYERS

They are in Edinburgh, safe, and the HHPO is in the care of the Navy. Now Sutton and I can retire for what remains of the night. There is much to do in the morning, and I must make myself ready to finish my tasks.

Epilogue

THE LONG BEAMS of late afternoon sun glowed in the windows in the elegantly rose-and-cream-appointed Day Room near the entrance to the Royal Scots Club, across from the dark wood of the club's pub. To my left, windows opened onto a tree-filled park, and in the distance I could see uphill to the Princes Road, which was becoming a commercial alternative to the shops of the High Street.

We had just been talking with a neatly uniformed Major about the Holybrooke conspiracy, a hidden tunnel, tossing someone off a folly, and meeting with the Queen of Ireland at a mythically named Lyonesse Cottage. From Mycroft Holmes' questions it appeared that this was something that had occurred before my tenure and had happened while some part of the Royal Scots Regiment had been stationed in Ireland for an extended period. It appears that quick action had prevented an insurrection. From the rather ominous end to the conversation, it was apparent that the matter had never been resolved. When I began to ask about the event after the officer had limped painfully across to the pub, my employer changed the subject.

Mycroft Holmes sat in a high-back, overstuffed leather chair with studded arms and back, facing the butler's table where our tea was laid out. A folded newspaper nestled beside the teapot. "You've seen that, I suppose?"

"Swedish Prince Saved by Scottish Knight?" I quoted. "Oh, yes. It was waiting for me after I bathed this morning. Sir Cameron is making all he can of it. Always one to crow on any dungheap he can find." I was unwilling to modify my tone of contempt.

"Let him, dear boy, let him. So long as the world thinks Cameron MacMillian is a hero, they will not bother to inquire into our affairs, which suits my purposes very well—and Miss Gatspy's," he added for emphasis.

"Oh, yes, I understand that. But to have a fool like Sir Cameron feted and praised, I find it hard to bear." I looked down at my skinned knuckles and the rich purple-and-red coloration around the abrasions.

"I do understand your sentiments on this occasion, but I do not share them." He leaned forward and looked speculatively into the pot, replacing the lid with care. "I'll be Mother, if it's all the same to you."

"Just as you please, sir," I said, feeling a bit ashamed that I had been so restful today and he had been active. "I am sorry I haven't put myself at your disposal earlier."

Something of my feelings must have shown themselves on my countenance among the bruises, for Mycroft Holmes said, "So conscience stricken, Guthrie. Why?" He had poured tea into a cup for me.

I shrugged. "I should have been more observant," I said, not wanting to recite the litany of failures I had rehearsed in my thoughts since shortly before sunrise whenever I wakened from my turbulent sleep. "Who knows what we might have been spared had I been more diligent."

"My dear Guthrie, so should I," Holmes said as he poured his own tea. "But consider the whole of our mission and tell me honestly you anticipated half of what we encountered in our efforts to see Prince Oscar to safety. In my nearly fifty-six years I don't think I have seen so many kinds of deceptions packed into a single mission as has been the case with this one." He held out the telegrams he had received that day. "First is the news that Prince Oscar sailed with the morning tide, and no mishaps have overtaken him on the maritime leg of his journey home." He laid that telegram aside. "Well, go on, drink your tea. No sense in letting it get cold."

I looked about, noticing we were alone. "Do none of the other members take their tea here?" I picked up the cup-and-saucer, noticing the tea was Chinese black.

"Of course. But the senior members have very kindly allocated this room for my use while we are here." He looked directly at me. "Most of them do not know the particulars of my work, nor do they wish to."

"No doubt a wise decision," I said, and tasted the tea before deciding to add a little sugar to it.

"I have been reading over the files Miss Gatspy left; most illu-minating, but also profoundly disquieting. I thought we had superior records at the Admiralty, but I discover we are laggards in this arena. You will want to have a look at these when we take the train home tomorrow. They help you while away the hours between Edinburgh and London. For," he went on with an arch smile, "I fear we cannot expect another murder, nor an assassin—let alone two—to liven our journey."

"I shall contrive not to be bored, sir," I responded in the same tone.

Holmes added sugar and milk to his tea, then held up the second telegram. "I fear there is no sign of Chief Inspector Somerford yet. Had I not had confirmation that Missus Spencer was once Miss Vickers, I would not be as concerned as I am, nor would we have been exposed to half the dangers we were. During our journey home, we will have to settle upon some means to root out the corruption that has resulted from that unfortunate liaison. I also have some additional information regarding this lamentable state of affairs provided by Tschersky, which I intend to factor into my deliberations. Do not worry yourself unduly on the matter today."

I drank a little of my tea. "Do you think the Admiralty will want to become entangled with trouble within the police?" It had been both-ering me since I slipped into the bath.

"Once I show them how that corruption has tainted our mission, I think they will understand that they must take action for the sake of their own men in the field." He held up another telegram. "Tyers has done his part, and I must say Sutton has acquitted himself admirably."

"That does not surprise me," I said.

"Nor does it surprise me, but I am still pleased to learn of it," said Holmes, becoming a bit more expansive. "You know, dear boy, I have come to feel very real gratitude toward Inspector Carew, to say nothing of the unfortunate Mister Jardine and the rest of them. I am even, in retrospect, pleased that Mister Burley rode with us as far as he did, hoping to improve the story he would file." He smiled at me, waiting for my response.

I knew he expected me to ask him to explain, and I was curious, so I obliged. "Very well—why this unexpected appreciation for so . . . disruptive an episode?"

Mycroft Holmes fixed his eyes on the far wall, the better to concentrate on what he was about to say. "I spent a good portion of the morning thinking this over. Loki—assuming that Whitfield is half of Loki—had a schedule that the murder disrupted. Loki had been counting on the train being on time. As it was, because of all the delays, he had to hide on the train instead of simply leaving when his shift—and his dirty work—was done."

"He told me he'd worked for the railroad for years," I said, still shamed at how readily I had accepted what he had told me as true. "It was all so plausible."

"And so it should be. Think of it, Guthrie. He is made late by a murder, so he is surrounded by police and passengers who are distressed by the deaths and the delays. He finds himself under scrutiny. He cannot proceed as he intended, and so he is forced to settle for an improvisation that proves to be disastrous for him." His steady gaze returned to me. "Between the delays and Jasper Carew, Whitfield was not able to strike when and how he intended, and for that I will be grateful to Messieurs Jardine, Dunmuir, and Heath. Prince Oscar may owe his life to them. And, of course, to Miss Gatspy."

I felt my pulse jump at her name. "You do not call her mine," I said as lightly as I could.

"I am not one to state the obvious." His austere expression gave way to one less condemning. "You have every reason to be proud of her, Guthrie."

"Yes, sir," I said, nodding once as I drank rather more of my tea than I had intended.

"And," Mycroft Holmes went on in studied casualness, "there was a note sent around about noon. I think you will be glad to have it." He handed a small envelope to me with my name scrawled on it. "A constable brought this; he said it was dropped off at his station by a fair young woman in mourning-clothes."

I took the envelope, staring down at the elegant, curving hand that had written my name, making the initials particularly large. "Do you mind, sir?" I asked, knowing it was rude to read what I assumed was a private note in front of him.

"Of course not. Go on." He leaned back in his chair and gave himself to the perusal of a fresh-baked scone.

The note was on good linen stock but without a trace of an address. It was quite brief.

Dear P. E. G.
I believe each of us has something that belongs to the other. Perhaps we should effect an exchange on some date convenient to us both, what do you think?
Until then, take care of what is mine, as I shall what is yours,
Yr most devoted,
P. E. G.

I read it over several times, though the words remained unchanged, cryptic and liable to many interpretations. "How like her," I said at last, as I refolded the note and put it back in the envelope and placed it in my waistcoat pocket, over my heart, chiding myself for this sentimental gesture even as I made it.

Mycroft Holmes had been watching me from under his heavy brows. "No wish to intrude, dear boy, but it strikes me that Miss Gatspy's not a woman whose affections are given lightly."

"Just as well," I responded. "I am not one to bestow mine lightly."

"I am aware of that," Holmes said, and added, "You and she may not always stand on the same side, as I am sure you are aware." He poured more tea into my cup. "I do not intend to discourage you, but I hope you will not place yourself in an untenable position because your affections are engaged."

"I share that hope," I said with feeling. "And I am certain she does, too."

Holmes leaned back in his chair. "Most assuredly, Guthrie; most assuredly." He glanced at the files she had provided. "We have proof of that in our hands."

Immediately he said this, my heart jumped. "Yes, we do, don't we?" Many of the obstacles I had seen strewn in any path that might bring Miss Gatspy and me together seemed now to be less formidable.

But Mycroft Holmes did not answer my smile. "I think we may also consider ourselves warned that the world has grown more dangerous than ever we thought it was. Our enemies are many and their designs are far more nefarious than we realized. But at least we are no longer ignorant. These files have made it possible for us to buy some time." He lifted his teacup in ironic toast to the files; I mirrored his action, endorsing his conviction. "We have an obligation to make the most of it."